SONG OF SONGS

A Novel of the Queen of Sheba

SONG OF SONGS

A Novel of the Queen of Sheba

Marc Graham

Blank Slate Press | Saint Louis, MO 63116

Blank Slate Press

Saint Louis, MO 63116

Blank Slate Press is an imprint of Amphorae Publishing Group, LLC

a woman- and veteran owned company

www.amphoraepublishing.com

For information, contact:

Blank Slate Press

4168 Hartford Street, Saint Louis, MO 63116

Manufactured in the United States of America

Cover photography and graphics: Shutterstock

Set in Adobe Caslon Pro and Avenir Light

Library of Congress Control Number: 2019934154

ISBN: 9781943075577

For Laura, who makes the journey worth taking

Author's Note

The astute reader will note that I have made the period of transition between Egypt's 18th and 19th Dynasties coincide with the building of the first Temple of Jerusalem, whereas conventional scholarship imposes a span of some three centuries between them. I've based my timing on the New Chronology paradigm, which convincingly applies archaeoastronomy and the latest interpretations from the El Amarna tablets to revise the accepted timeline.

While the academic jury is still out as to who will prove correct, I trust the reader will pardon my little heresy for the purposes of this story. For a detailed and engaging presentation of supporting evidence, I refer you to *From Eden to Exile: The Five-Thousand Year History of the People of the Bible* by David Rohl.

Further, as I note in the Glossary of Principal Names and Places (included at the end of the book), I've tried to use the names of places, people, and gods as they would have been at the turn of the first millennium BCE, prior to being changed by Hellenic, Roman, and Arab conquerors. This was not done simply to make for more challenging reading, but to provide a more authentic feel to the story.

Memory's flame burns low. Fleeting shadows dance before my inner eye, my natural ones having long ago grown dim with time and tears. Distant faces of children and husbands, lovers and tormentors are my sole companions as I await the final journey that all must take.

Fading though they be, these images remain nearer to the truth than what your histories presume to tell. Place-names change as powers rise and fall. People are remembered by titles, if they are remembered at all. And the parts they played, for good or ill, are shaped by the whim of those who weave their tales.

Though my voice be dry and brittle as the dragon tree, yet will I sing for you my story as it was. History calls me Queen of Sheba, though my country was named Saba. We had no kings or queens, only mukarribs who served as judges and priests.

I am Makeda umm-Ayana. Long before I became legend, I was a mere woman. And before that, I was but a child.

And a thief.

A Song of Beginnings

1

Makeda

I sheltered in the vineyard beneath a sky pregnant with doom. In all my seven years, I'd never seen Saba's gods so angry. Elmakah, bringer of rain, rumbled and flashed atop the distant western mountains. The sun goddess Shams hid her face behind Elmakah's cloudy cloak. And Athtar—the most high, whose voice might be heard in the slightest breeze, he of whom all other gods were but dim reflections—held his breath and uttered not a whisper as I huddled among the barren vines.

"I know you're here, Makeda." Bilkis, my half-sister, stalked along the dusty rows. I watched her pacing feet through a cluster of brown leaves. "Give it back, you little demon." She swung a broomstick through the vines, shattering the twigs like desert-parched bones.

I squeezed the stolen treasure in my hand. The silver comb, adorned with a dragonfly of gold and lapis, had been a gift from our father to Bilkis on her reaching womanhood. Since spring, the comb had lain beneath better-favored rings and bracelets and necklaces, ignored until I'd caught the gleam of its wings and, with them, took flight.

Another rattle of branches echoed off the rocky outcroppings of the wadi behind the vineyard. Bilkis screamed a curse and raced toward one end of the field. I shied away from my hiding spot and scuttled in the opposite direction. As I ran, the hem of my robe dropped about my ankles. Before I could slow myself, the stitching broke loose and the generous hem spilled from beneath my robe. Feet tangled in the woolen cloth, I sprawled across the ground.

"If you've broken it, I'll give your hide to the tanner," Bilkis yelled.

I turned to see her sprinting down the length of the vineyard. I groped at the dirt until one hand found the comb. With my other hand I hitched up the oversize robe. Then I ran.

The Wadi Dhanah lay just beyond the edge of the vineyard, a broad, ragged scar on the land's face. If I could reach the dry riverbed before Bilkis caught me, I might escape. Bilkis's legs were longer than mine, but my feet were surer in the rocky wadi. Once there, I could follow it into the hills and lose myself among the outcroppings and caves.

I took a deep breath as I neared the steep bank. My feet left the ground, but instead of leaping forward, I flew back. Bilkis grasped the loose cloth of my robe and flung me to the earth.

Tears clouded my eyes as I looked up at my sister. Her figure was lean and straight, though the curves of womanhood showed where a slight breeze drew her silk robe tight to her body.

Bilkis's cheeks, flushed with anger, matched the hue of her full lips. The rest of her skin, smooth and taut, was the color of polished bronze, while mine was dark, dull, tarnished.

"Give it to me," Bilkis demanded, the broom raised over her head.

"You don't even like it." I surprised myself with the defiance. "You never wear it."

"It matters not. Father gave it to me. Today I wish to wear it. Tomorrow I might bury it or crush it or throw it in the dung pit. What I do with it is none of your concern. Now give it to me."

I cuffed at my nose and thought to run, to roll toward the wadi. I might find shelter among the rocks, but would have to return home eventually. Bilkis would win in the end, and the longer I delayed that fate, the more bitter my defeat. Better to end it now.

Gathering the scraps of my dignity, scattered like the dried grape leaves that danced along the vines under the growing wind, I raised the treasure in defeat, averting my eyes from Bilkis's victorious glare.

Above the mountains, the sun goddess Shams had given herself over to the storm god. Elmakah grew with the influx of her power. He rose dark and menacing, flashing silver streaks of fury.

Still the comb remained in my hand. I chanced a look at my sister. Though the broom still loomed over my head, Bilkis's eyes stared not at me, but at something behind me.

"Give me your hand." Bilkis's voice caught in her throat like stones in the mill. When I was slow to respond, Bilkis took one hand from the broomstick and shook it insistently at me.

"Now," she hissed, and grasped my wrist. She jerked me to my feet so abruptly I lost hold of the comb, and it fell to the ground.

The great god Athtar, roused from his brooding, howled from the mountains. A low moan rose from the wadi's birthplace, and Bilkis pulled me toward the embankment. I chanced a look over my shoulder toward my city to see men, women, and children running from the ravaged fields toward the high mudbrick walls of Maryaba, harried by white-robed horsemen whose bronze blades glinted in the failing sunlight. Three blades flashed brighter than the others, and my heart trembled when the trio of riders urged their mounts toward us.

Bilkis pulled me down the embankment, and we ran along the stone-littered bed of Wadi Dhanah. Rather, I ran while Bilkis stumbled and cursed her way across the uneven ground.

Men's shouts boomed behind us, underscored by the beat of horses' hooves. The very earth seemed to shake with their thundering.

"Shams's teats," Bilkis screamed as she tripped on a rock.

She went down, dragging me with her. Bilkis broke my fall, but a sickening crack echoed through the wadi as her head struck rock.

I clambered to my feet and untangled the folds of my too-long robe.

"Get up, *Dhahbas*," I cried as I tugged on Bilkis's hand, using our father's pet name for the favored daughter.

Bilkis's eyes fluttered open, but her gaze floated about as when she'd drunk too much beer. I helped her to a seated position, and coughed with the dust that rose from the wadi's bed. I marveled as the smaller stones danced upon the ground, but there was no time to think on it.

The raiders appeared at the edge of the wadi, the ends of their headscarves lashing at the wind. The horses shied away from the bank and the men dismounted, shouting all the while.

"You must go," Bilkis said.

3

"Get up," I pleaded. "Come with me."

Bilkis freed herself from my clutch and pushed me away.

"Get to the rocks. Hide." She slurred the words, but her tone was sharp.

The men reached the riverbed and stalked toward us like wolves after a goat's kid. I backed away, took a last look at Bilkis, then turned and ran up the wadi.

Behind me, Bilkis cursed yet again. Her shouts were accompanied by the raiders' laughter. I forced myself to ignore the men's jeers and Bilkis's cries. I pressed ahead, fighting my terror and the wind that screamed from the mountains beyond the wadi. Athtar's breath bellowed through the gorge, violent and cool and—damp?

I slowed, despite the racing footfalls behind me. The earth trembled now, so that the larger rocks danced with the smaller ones as the source of the tremors appeared.

My mother had told me how Elmakah poured out his blessings on the western highlands. His holy waters, preceded by the breath of Athtar, streamed through the gorges to flood the wadi and bring life to the people of Saba for another season. Such a miracle had not occurred during my lifetime, and I wondered how what I now saw could be a blessing.

Sullied with scrub brush and rocks, mud and carcasses, the flood surged toward me as carnage raced along the rocky trace of the wadi. Its edges frothed with foam, this water of the gods carried not life, but destruction.

Fear screamed at me to run for the wadi's bank, but a deeper voice urged me forward. I ran across the lurching earth toward a boulder in the middle of the wadi. Placed there by my distant ancestors, the giant stood sentinel over the dried riverbed. It towered over me, but the wall of water loomed higher still. Even as the flood bore down on me, I threw myself against the boulder. I pulled my knees tight to my chest and looked down the wadi.

The raider who had been chasing me raced back toward his companions who stood beside Bilkis, her arms pinioned between them. Three pairs of eyes traced heavenward toward the wave's crest.

Then they were gone.

Athtar, save me. I'd meant to scream the words, but my breath refused to come. Even so, the god's protective hand enfolded me. The waters swept around the boulder, but I remained untouched within its lee.

For countless heartbeats the storm raged around me. Though the roar dulled my ears and mist stung my eyes, I sat in awe of this display of the gods' power. Until this day, I had only seen tamed water, resting in a bowl or winking from the depths of a well. Never had I seen a flood so angry. Angrier even than Bilkis.

Sorrow swept through my heart. Though Bilkis could be mean as a scorpion tending her brood, she'd never failed to protect me. Whether from our father's wrath or the teasing of other girls who mocked my mixed blood, Bilkis reserved to herself alone the privilege of abusing me, right to the very last.

A cold finger ran down my spine. I spun away from the boulder and looked up to see a stream of water spilling over its edge. The flood slowed and, as it did so, its waters invaded my little haven. At my feet, the trickles grew larger until the earth became as dark as my skin. The rising waters swept me off my feet and washed me along the wadi with the rest of the storm's debris. I beat against the surface of the flood, but I might as well have tried to hold back the wind with a pitchfork. I gagged on dirty water and managed only a feeble gasp before my sodden robe dragged me beneath the surface.

I fought the wool's grip. For once, I blessed the generous cut of the robe. I fumbled with the laces at the collar until its clutch loosened about my throat. I wriggled my shoulders through the neck opening, slithered through the cloth, then thrashed to the surface.

Coughing and sputtering, I slid along with the stream. My ears were numb from the roar of the waters, but I thought I heard a shout and a splash. I again sank under the water before something tugged my hair and dragged me to the surface. A thick arm wrapped about my waist and towed me to the wadi's edge.

"Fear not, little one," said the familiar, gruff voice of Yanuf, the city's gatekeeper.

As we reached the bank, my mother ran to us. She swathed me in the folds of her robe. I wrapped my arms about her neck and sobbed.

When at last I caught my breath, I peeked over her shoulder. My father Karibil, Chieftain of Maryaba and Mukarrib of all Saba, scanned the river with a sharp eye. A dozen warriors formed a screen of spears between the wadi and the city's gate, though the only sign of the raiders now was a cloud of dust on the horizon.

"Where is Bilkis?" my father demanded.

I looked at him, his brow heavy with anger, eyes lined with concern. I shied away from his stern gaze and again buried my face in my mother's robe.

"It's all right, little one," she cajoled me. "Where is your sister? Speak."

I raised my chin, looked first in Mother's eyes, then to my father's. I tried to speak, but the words came out as a mewling sound. Instead, I shifted in my mother's arms, reached out a trembling hand and pointed toward the wadi, whose dark and sullen stream flowed silently toward the desert.

2

Yetzer

Yetzer abi-Huram cursed the burning sky.

He cursed the burning earth.

He cursed his burning hands and shoulders, tongue and eyes. Most of his fourteen summers had been spent in this quarry of Bakhu, amid the wastes of Kemet, land of Pharaoh. In all that time, he could remember no day so hot as this. Oh, there were days when the great river, Iteru, filled the quarry with her stench. Days when the air was as thick as the dung-laden mud that lined the water's edges, and thicker with the flies that feasted on her flanks. This day was all that and more.

The sun blazed overhead in a barren sky. To the quarrymen of Kemet, it was the embodiment of the god Ra. To Yetzer's father, Huram, the orb was Shapash, princess of heaven. But to Yetzer, it was a bane, a curse sent by whatever god ruled over this land of choking dust and fetid water and scorching rock.

"Mind your step, Lord." The voice of Yetzer's father came from behind. Yetzer rested his maul and turned to see Huram's hand outstretched toward the regal figure descending the limestone steps into the quarry. Pharaoh Horemheb, Lord of Upper and Lower Kemet, waved off Huram's help and stepped down from the steep riser.

"How goes the work, Master Huram?" the king asked as he surveyed the laborers with his falcon-sharp eyes.

"Well enough, Lord," came Huram's reply, even as his eyes flicked toward Yetzer. "See to your work!" The lad turned away, heat rising in his cheeks. Yetzer raised his maul and continued to drive a cedar beam into a narrow trench in the limestone.

"The fire?" Pharaoh asked Huram. He gestured toward the flames that engulfed one side of the quarry and added to the swelter.

"Quartz," Huram said.

He explained no further, and the king did not press him. Instead, both men grunted laconically and watched the workers.

The stone pit resounded with the guttural chanting of the quarriers and the chime of copper pickaxes and saws. Yetzer found himself swinging his maul in tempo with his fellows, a measured pace that allowed the men to labor through the long, hot days without exhaustion.

"Water," Yetzer called as he finished wedging the last of his beams into the trench.

A boy came running with a pair of goatskins hung from a rod across his shoulders. Yetzer gazed at the glistening, dripping skins, but they brought no refreshment for him. He and the boy spilled the water over the beams. The dry timber soaked up the moisture, groaning with pleasure as its thirst was slaked. When both skins were empty, Yetzer and the boy hopped down and moved to the side.

"Free stone," Yetzer called, hands cupped around his mouth. "Free stone," he repeated in the other direction, warning all those around of what was about to happen.

"You drove them to full depth?" Huram asked as he led the king to where Yetzer stood.

"Yes, Father."

Huram gave him a hard look.

"Yes, Master," Yetzer corrected himself. Huram might be his father in their home across the Iteru, but once they set foot in the quarry, he was Master of Masons, Overseer of Pharaoh's Works.

"Why do you anoint the stone with water?" Pharaoh asked.

Yetzer looked from his father to the king, Exalted among the Nations, Lord of the Two Lands. Pharaoh Horemheb stood lean and tall. The king had dispensed with his headdress and ceremonial beard, but as the sun cast an aura about his shaved head, there was no question that he was the Beloved of the Gods.

"You see, Lord," Yetzer began, but his voice cracked. "Pardon, Lord. You see, the beams are taken from our cedars of Kenahn. In life, they are full and rich and strong. When they are cut their vigor leaves them. They shrink and become dry as, no doubt, my lord has experienced."

The king raised a shorn and painted brow, while Huram swatted Yetzer's head.

"Go on, young man," Pharaoh said with a tight grin.

"The quarriers cut trenches to outline the rough ashlar," Yetzer explained. "We then wedge the dried beams into the gaps and anoint them with water."

"The beams then drink in life," Pharaoh concluded, "and swell to full potency."

"Even so, Lord."

Yetzer climbed atop the escarpment on which the block stood rooted, then turned to face Pharaoh and his father. He laid his hand on the stone. Though this was Yetzer's first season as a shearer of stone, already he knew the timing and temperament of the rock. As he explained the quarry's workings to the king, he'd noted the pulse of the beams as they grew within their trench. "As the wood reclaims its life, so it imparts life to the stone."

Yetzer slapped his hand on the limestone just as the cedar reached its full potential. A crack echoed across the quarry and the newborn ashlar rocked from its bed.

"Well done, young man," Pharaoh said. "If your stonecraft equals your stagecraft you shall prove a most skilled mason in time."

"Thank you, Lord."

"Assemble your workmen, Master Huram," the king said to Yetzer's father.

"Yes, Lord." Huram climbed beside Yetzer on the escarpment and blew a shrill whistle. Every man paused in his work and looked toward the Master. Huram stood tall, feet together, and stretched his arms out to his sides in the sign of the Ankh, the tree of life. The workmen set down their tools and hurried into formation in the wide, open center of the quarry.

Yetzer, too, moved to his assigned position near the front of the ranks, behind the water-carriers. Toward the rear stood the rows of haulers and hewers, and behind them all were the apprenticed masons who assisted Master Huram in his measurements.

While the laborers settled into place, Yetzer watched in wonder as Pharaoh stepped into line among the apprentices.

If Huram was surprised by this, his face revealed nothing. He simply stepped up to the king, clasped his hand and embraced him in the manner of the more senior masons. Pharaoh returned the embrace and Huram stepped back to the head of the assembly.

"In the name of the Divine Builder," he said, and again formed the Ankh.

The laborers responded, each with the sign of his grade. The boys in front of Yetzer cupped their hands, as though drawing water from a bowl. Along the row of shearers, Yetzer and his companions folded arms across their chests, hands on opposite shoulders. The men behind made signs appropriate to their ranks. Yetzer couldn't see them, and dared not turn his head to look, lest his eyes be put out as punishment. Huram lowered his arms and the assembly did the same.

The Master opened his mouth to continue the invocation but, instead of the expected words, a high-pitched whistle rang throughout the quarry. The workers looked about for the source of the noise. Yetzer's eyes settled on the side of the quarry where the fire blazed before the quartz outcropping. The limestone on the fringe glowed red-orange, while the quartz shimmered behind the veil of heat.

"Water," Huram called, and the neat assembly dissolved as men raced for the great leather bladders that sat on either side of the fire.

Huram had explained to Yetzer how firing the quartz, then rapidly quenching it with water, would make the rock brittle and more easily broken up. That had been his intent. As Yetzer watched, his father's plan rapidly came undone.

Steam hissed from the rock face. The whistle turned into a scream. The very earth seemed to bulge around the outcropping. In a moment, Yetzer foresaw what was to happen and knew he was unable to stop it.

"No," he screamed anyway.

He ran toward his father and Pharaoh, who stood between the water bladders. Each skin held a copper tube, which a pair of workers aimed at the furious rock. Other men lowered cedar beams atop the skins to force the water's flow.

Huram turned toward Yetzer as he cried out, but the men were already pressing down on the bladders. Water streamed toward the outcropping and the scene was lost in a cloud of vapor.

"Yetzer, be silent," Huram ordered, but his shout was overwhelmed as the rock's scream rose in pitch and volume.

Yetzer leapt toward the men. Huram tried to block him, but succeeded only in knocking his son into the king. The boy managed a glance at his father, whose face was masked with fury.

Then the world shattered.

Nature slowed as Yetzer's senses raced ahead of the disaster. A storm of destruction rolled toward him, preceded by the invisible fist of some nameless god who punched him in the chest and drove the air from his lungs. The water bladders ruptured and men were thrown off their feet. They hadn't reached the ground before the next wave struck.

Steam rolled over the men closest to the explosion, cleansed them of the dust that coated their bodies, and turned their skin sun-red. The flood from the bladders outpaced the steam, engulfing Yetzer and protecting him from the searing wave as it passed overhead.

A flurry of dust followed and, behind this, a hail of stone shards. The air hummed with the passage of the missiles. Yetzer lifted a hand in feeble defense, even as Huram clutched his throat. A crimson mist enveloped his father just before Yetzer's upraised hand blossomed with blood.

3

Makeda

I climbed to the roof of the tower house. The height of ten men, the building was the tallest structure in Maryaba. Truly, it was the tallest anything other than the mountains that rose stark and foreboding in the west. From my perch, I would be the first to see Shams rise above the horizon.

The goddess was both mother and destroyer. After nights so cold I could sometimes see my breath, the smile of the sun goddess was a tonic that warmed me to the core. By midday, however, the people of Maryaba would flee to homes or caves or anywhere they might find a scrap of shelter from Shams's wrath.

Even now, that light began to turn night's blackness to crimson. As the first shadows appeared, one caught my eye. A long shadow, a moving shadow chased by a trail of dust that shone as a tiny halo in the diffuse morning light.

I forgot about the sun's awakening. "Umma," I called down the open ladderway. "Riders."

My mother appeared at the foot of the ladder. "Are you sure?"

I nodded.

"Tell the gatekeeper. The army returns."

Two days earlier, my father had led his warriors against the neighboring city of Timnah. No one could have predicted the flood that swept Bilkis away, but he cursed that city's raiders for her loss, and vowed revenge. His sole heir now gone, he'd proclaimed Mother—until then, his slave and bed warmer—as his wife, and declared me his lawful daughter.

While Mother washed and dressed to welcome her returning husband, I scampered down the tower house's ladders and dashed through the marketplace where tradesmen opened their booths. At the foot of the gatehouse, I called up. "Yanuf!"

"I see them, Little One," the gatekeeper answered. "Come up and see."

I climbed the ladder to the platform. Yanuf had long been a favorite of mine. Unlike most people, the old warrior seemed not to care about or even notice my mixed blood, or my eyes of brown so light they were almost yellow. Maybe it was because he was broken, too. I stole a glance at the gatekeeper's empty left sleeve, then turned my attention to the desert.

The plume of dust rose higher. The riders came not in a charge, but at a measured pace. As they drew nearer, instead of the donkeys of my father's warband, I recognized the taller mounts favored by Timnah.

"They're not—" I began, but the gatekeeper had already seen.

Yanuf raised a ram's horn to his lips and sounded a warning trill. Women and children in the fields dropped their tools. Herders drove their flocks toward the gate as Yanuf repeated the alarm twice more. He deftly climbed down the ladder, despite his missing arm. I hurried after him.

"What is it?" Mother called as she approached from the tower house.

"Riders, Lady," Yanuf said.

"Our riders? But why. . .?"

She raised a trembling hand to her mouth. I came to her side and clasped her other hand.

"Not ours, Umma," I told her excitedly. "Horses. From Timnah."

"Can we drive them off?" she asked Yanuf.

"There's only me and a few boys with slings," he told her. "The gates will hold, but our food and water will last not ten days."

"Umma," I complained as Mother squeezed my hand.

She knelt beside me, kissed my forehead, then smoothed my hair.

"We will go speak to them," she said, her voice tremulous.

"Lady, no," Yanuf began, but she cut him off with a look.

"I stand as mukarrib in my husband's absence," she said, her voice stronger. "I will not have our people starve for a hopeless cause. Close the gates behind us. Perhaps we may turn the hearts of Timnah to peace."

"And if you can't?" Yanuf said.

Mother smiled up at him. "Then you and the council will decide the next course."

I gripped her hand as she led me through the gate. Women and children rushed past us in the opposite direction, fleeing for safety behind Maryaba's walls. My feet wanted to turn, to join the townsfolk, but my hand tightened its grip on Mother's.

"Ubasti will protect us," she said.

I nodded and added a silent prayer for good measure. The lion-headed Ubasti was a stranger to Saba, brought to this land when Mother had been captured and sold to my father. The goddess was not from her homeland of Uwene either, but came from yet another country far to the north, a land of red sands, black soil, and a great wadi that flowed year-round.

The sound of trotting horses grew louder. I hoped the foreign goddess was not so far from her home that her powers were lost.

Mother stopped as the gate swung shut. The sound of its closing made me jump. I looked up at my mother and tried to match her expression of calm confidence. That confidence fled her eyes for a moment as the front rank of horsemen arrived and formed a circle about us.

"The gods' blessings on all who come in peace," Mother said.

The lead rider, only his eyes visible behind the scarf wrapped about his head, looked past us to the city walls.

"Who speaks for the people of Maryaba?" he called out in a sonorous voice.

"I speak for Maryaba and for all Saba," Mother said, her voice soft.

The rider squeezed his heels and his mount stepped forward. I flinched, but my mother stood firm. The horse stopped in front of us, close enough that I could feel its breath.

"Who speaks for Maryaba?" the rider called again.

Mother stroked the horse's muzzle, then released my hand and took hold of the bridle. She gently pulled the beast's head down and looked up at the rider.

"I am the mukarrib," she said. "I speak for Saba."

The rider finally looked down at us.

"You?" he said, his eyes sparkling with humor. "You dare to speak for Saba, a slave and a woman? Perhaps Maryaba has fallen so low, but Timnah has not."

"I am no slave," Mother said in a brittle voice.

"You are not of the People," the rider observed. "That dark skin does not lie. You are of the Burned Ones, fit only for washing pots or warming beds."

He pulled his scarf down to reveal a handsome face with a long nose and short beard. "Though as a bed warmer, I daresay you'd serve quite well."

Mother stood taller and took a deep breath. "I am Ayana, wife of Karibil," she said. "I serve as mukarrib in his absence and stand for all the people of Saba."

The man's haughty look faded. He stared at her for a time, then slowly nodded and dismounted. "Then I greet you as your kinsman, for I am Watar of Timnah, your husband's cousin. And this," he added, "belongs to you, I think."

He pulled a sword from beneath his saddle. Yanuf shouted a warning from his post in the gatehouse, but Watar smiled and winked at me. The Lord of Timnah tossed the sword in the air. I squinted as sunlight flashed upon the spinning blade. Watar caught the sword then extended it hilt-first to my mother.

She took the sword. The sun's reflection skittered across the ground as the blade settled into her trembling hands.

"Then my husband is dead?" she whispered.

"Alas, Lady," Watar said, "it is even as you say."

I shivered as coldness emanated from my mother. She made none of the wails of grief so common to the women of Saba. She simply kissed the sweat-stained hilt and pressed her forehead to the flat of the blade.

"He died well," Watar said after a time.

"If by well you mean successfully, of that I have no doubt." Mother's voice bore a keen edge. "And how many of our sons and brothers followed his example?"

"Too many." Sadness softened Watar's words. "A half-dozen, maybe more."

"So few?" Mother said. More than sixty men had followed my father to battle.

"How many would you have had me kill, Lady?" Watar demanded. "They were my brothers, too. Though I am Lord of Timnah, I weep no less for Maryaba. Karibil was headstrong, but his men showed more reason. Once your husband and his escort fell, the others threw down their weapons."

"And what must Maryaba pay to have her sons restored to her?"

"You have but to open your gates," Watar replied. "My son and his men were impetuous in their raid."

Son? Had this man's boy been among those in the wadi?

"The gods have dealt justly with him," Watar continued. "I come to you for peace, not blood."

He turned to the mounted warriors behind him and whistled. The riders nudged their horses aside to make an opening in the circle. Beyond them, flanked by yet more riders from Timnah, stood the defeated army of Maryaba. At its front, four men carried a litter.

"Does my husband finally bring peace to the land?" Mother said, so softly I almost missed the words. In a louder voice, she ordered Yanuf to open the gates.

"Come, Lord Watar," she said as she tucked the sword under her arm and again took my hand. "It appears we have more to discuss."

4

Bilkis

Bilkis awoke.

Maybe.

She had been in utter darkness and now was … not. It wasn't daylight exactly, nor was it night. Instead of blackness or endless blue or heat-shimmering ocher, her vision was a muted field of shapeless shadows.

A stench filled her nose. The air reeked of vomit, unwashed bodies, and—and what? There was something in it of new wool, perhaps rubbed in dung and hung to season above a tanner's pit.

Bilkis's stomach ached. From the pressure in her belly and the throbbing in her head, she reasoned she lay on something broad and coarse. And moving.

She tried to shift her weight, but her wrists and ankles were bound. Fear lurked among the shadows of her heart as the memory of the flood and the raiders clawed its way from the darkness.

A shrill cry pierced the air around her. *Makeda*, Bilkis tried to say, but her throat closed against the words. Much as she despised the little demon, the thought of her being abused at the hands of the filthy horsemen made her stomach revolt.

The cry sounded again, nearer this time. The familiarity of the sound eased her fears.

Donkey. That was it. Foul, stinking, sweat-flanked ass. The beast made an ungainly stride and the lurch sent a jolt through Bilkis's middle. Her head pounded, her mouth filled with saliva, and her stomach heaved.

At least she knew where the vomit smell had come from.

"All praise to Havah. She lives." A man's northern-accented voice came from somewhere—behind? in front? beside her?—and was followed by heavy footfalls on soft earth.

The donkey jerked to a stop with another bray and a swish of its tail. Hands fumbled at Bilkis's wrists and feet, then gripped her under the arms and hauled her roughly over the beast's back.

"Abram, the canopy," the man bellowed. "Rahab, bring water."

Bilkis turned her aching head and strained her eyes against the gloom but could see nothing. Thick arms encircled her. The stench of olibanum and sweat made her long for the donkey's company.

"Why have we stopped?" a woman's voice demanded. "It's early yet. We should press on toward the oasis."

"Our foundling lives, my flower," said the man.

The whisper of feet on sand gave way to a softer tread, and Bilkis was lowered onto a thick rug. Unseen hands pulled a cloth from over her head and the world burst into a blaze of light, albeit one obscured as through layers of veils. Bilkis put her hands to her eyes and found a thick bandage, wet and sticky with ointment.

"Rahab, see to her. Abram, direct the encampment." The man's command was followed by retreating footsteps and the hiss of whispered argument.

A slight figure knelt beside Bilkis and unwound the cloth from her eyes.

"Your face was badly burned when we found you," a girl said in a wispy voice as she finished with the bandage. "The balm should remove the sting and keep your skin from blistering."

"Found me?" Bilkis said, her voice dry and ragged.

She felt a water gourd held to her lips, and she tipped back her head and drank greedily.

"On the desert's edge. What were you doing out there?"

The sound of pouring water was followed by the touch of a damp cloth scented with lavender. A small hand held Bilkis by the chin as the cloth gently stroked her face and wiped the unguent from her eyes.

"There, now. Better?"

Bilkis nodded as a fresh cloth dried her face.

"I'm Rahab," she heard as her vision at last cleared.

The girl was fair-skinned, a few years younger than Bilkis. Her gap-toothed smile seemed genuine, but Bilkis would not be put at ease. She said nothing and glanced about her.

A large man and a larger woman stood several paces away, engaged in a quiet debate punctuated by flailing gestures. A train of donkeys stood in line while a dozen men, women, and children scurried like rats in a storeroom, setting up tents and mangers and picket lines, and building fires despite the late afternoon heat.

Rahab had continued speaking in her outland accent, but Bilkis paid no heed to her words. She pushed the girl aside, scrambled to her feet, and ran.

Rahab's cry was followed by a sharp whistle and the woman's shout.

"Abram!"

Bilkis angled away from the cluster of people, toward the tail of the caravan and the trackless desert beyond. She ran with all her might, though a tender ankle hampered her efforts. A whirring sound chased after her. The sound caught up with her and Bilkis sprawled headlong to the ground. She spat out sand and curses as she clawed at the stones and leather thongs that entangled her ankles.

Heavy footfalls raced toward her. She tried to scuttle away, but the large man and a slender, beardless youth were too fast. Bilkis flung a handful of sand at them and kicked her bound feet.

"That was not very courteous," the man said as the pair took her arms and raised her between them.

"Neither is taking me captive," Bilkis growled.

They carried her back to the canopy and dropped her upon a thick, beautifully embroidered rug.

"Free her legs," the man said as he knelt behind Bilkis and gripped her shoulders.

The lad knelt by Bilkis. His sunburned face grew redder as he raised her gown to her calves and unwound the snare. The woman stalked under the canopy.

"You little fool," she said, and smacked Rahab on the back of the head. "Hold her hands and feet."

The men obeyed, pinning Bilkis to the ground. The woman settled to her knees and lifted Bilkis's skirts. Bilkis screamed and struggled, but her efforts were useless. The woman's head disappeared beneath the silk and surprisingly gentle fingers probed the gates of her womanhood.

"Have you bled yet?" the woman asked as she emerged from beneath the gown and settled it back over Bilkis's legs. "Have you bled?" she repeated when Bilkis was slow to answer. "Your moons, have they come yet?"

Bilkis blinked back tears of humiliation and nodded.

"She is yet virgin." The woman struggled to her feet. "She will do."

"What is the meaning of this?" Bilkis demanded as fury replaced shame. She jerked her arms and legs free and scrambled toward the rug's edge. "Do you know who I am?"

"Of course," the older man answered. "You are Bilkis of Maryaba, daughter of Karibil, King of all Saba."

His thick accent slurred the name of Bilkis's homeland, but the frankness of his admission took the fight from her limbs. "Yes," she said, her defiance gone.

"I am Eliam abi-Terah of Urusalim." The man stood before her and bowed his head. "Your servant."

"Servant?" Bilkis said.

"Of course. What else is a humble merchant to the Daughter of all Saba?"

"Free me then," Bilkis said coolly.

"As you command." Eliam bowed his head. "My lady is free to go."

"She's what?" the woman demanded.

"Quiet, Leah," Eliam said sharply, then smiled at Bilkis and made a sweeping gesture toward the empty sand. "Maryaba lies that way. A mere four days distant."

Bilkis's stomach tightened. "Four days?"

"Perhaps five," Eliam allowed. "No more than six."

"Then give me food, water. Give me a donkey and a servant to guide me."

"It would be my pleasure to provide my lady with all she needs for her journey home." The merchant gave a helpless shrug and sucked air through his teeth. "Alas, my duty prohibits me."

"What duty?"

Eliam nodded toward the west, where the sun sat just above the horizon. "I am, of course, my lady's servant, but I and my household are first servants of Havah, Queen of Heaven. Her holy day approaches, a day of rest when we are forbidden to labor or travel. You are free to do as your gods permit, but I cannot allow those under my care to accompany you."

Frustration rose in Bilkis's throat at the trader's polite stubbornness and his silly rules. "Then give me a donkey and some food and water," she said, her voice tight. "I'll make my own way."

Instead of an answer, Eliam lifted the cowl of his robe over his head and held out his hands toward Rahab.

"Water, my daughter," he said.

Rahab brought the man a copper bowl and waterskin, a small cloth over her shoulder. She poured water over his hands, catching the flow in the bowl. Eliam washed his hands then dried them on the cloth. Rahab repeated the ritual for Abram and her mother. Leah then did the same for her daughter, and the family formed a circle about a pair of candles set in a brass stand.

Leah waved her hands over the candles then covered her eyes. She intoned a prayer of thanksgiving and a plea for protection upon their journey. Bilkis missed most of the words, partly due to the northern accent, partly because of her rumbling stomach.

The prayer finished, Eliam's family sat on small rugs around the candles, and passed around a dish of flatbread and olives.

Bilkis's resolve faded. The terror of the flood, the outrage of her capture, the indignity of Leah's examination—all these washed away as her mouth watered with the scents of the simple meal. Of their own volition, her legs carried her toward an empty rug by the candles.

"Your hands," Rahab whispered to her, indicating the copper bowl.

Bilkis dipped her hands in the bowl then dried them on the small cloth.

"And your hair," Rahab said, and patted the veil covering her head.

Bilkis looked around but found no suitable covering. Desperate to fill her hollow stomach, she placed the damp handcloth over her hair.

Rahab giggled as Bilkis sat beside her, then passed the serving dish to her.

"We rest through the day tomorrow," Eliam said, his voice nearly lost amid the sounds of Bilkis's chewing. "The day after that, you may return home."

Bilkis nodded absently as she took a greedy swallow of watered wine from the cup Rahab offered her.

"However ..."

Bilkis drained the cup and devoured another piece of bread laden with chickpeas before she realized Eliam was looking at her expectantly.

"However?" she said, speaking around her full mouth.

"You are, of course, free to go," Eliam said, "but perhaps you would honor us with your company on our journey. Your gods have dealt harshly with your lands of late, no?"

"So harshly," Leah interjected, "what little we took in trade will not begin to cover the expense of this trip."

"It is true," Eliam said with a heavy sigh. "The journey has been a hardship, though it would be made easier by the richness of your company. The road before us is long, but at its end is Urusalim in Yisrael, a land of gardens and streams of endless water. Come. Abide with us for a time. See how our gods bless us. When we have gathered enough trade goods for another trip, we will return you to your people. It will take some time." The trader rolled a bit of bread between his fingers. "Two years? No more than four."

Bilkis stared into the candlelight. She brushed her fingers across the smooth silk threads of her sitting rug. Her own silk robe was new, but the cloth had been taken in trade years before. It hadn't the sheen of Rahab's or Leah's robes, or the softness of the rug.

She thought of the sands of Saba, the grimy walls of Maryaba. She refilled the wine cup and brought it to her lips. She drank and swallowed.

"Tell me more of Urusalim."

5

Yetzer

"Yetzer." The voice echoed through the abyss. He had been contemplating something. A column? Perhaps a tree. But at the calling of his name his focus shifted and the object of his study disintegrated like charred papyrus on the wind.

Yetzer directed his attention toward the voice. Light wavered in the distance, flickering like lightning upon the plains of Kenahn. He willed himself toward it, crossing immeasurable distance in moments. As he drew near, the light took shape. What had first seemed a streak of lightning took the form of a cobra dancing before him.

"Yetzer," the serpent repeated with a hiss.

"I am here," he replied.

The cobra flared its hood, the inner surface patterned with twin *Udjatu*, eyes of the god Haru, one white, the other red.

"Yetzer," the snake said yet again, and teased the air with its forked tongue.

"It is I," Yetzer said.

The serpent arced its sinewy form and loomed over him. Its natural eyes glinted black and sinister, while the painted ones studied him with cool indifference. As the cobra swayed from side to side, Yetzer's focus faltered, as from too much wine.

A flick of the snake's tongue rallied his attention. The reptilian mouth opened to reveal a pair of fangs. Yetzer tried to back away, but the cobra's tail encircled him in a crushing embrace.

"He who passes through the darkness shall see great light." As the cobra spoke, twin beads of milky venom formed at the tips of the fangs. "He shall face the sun and not be blinded. He shall walk through fire and not be burned."

The beads of venom grew to the size of pomegranates, shining with ethereal light.

"He shall feel the bite of the serpent and not be poisoned."

The venom dripped from the fangs and fell toward Yetzer, who raised a hand to protect his face. One of the drops landed on his belly, seeped through his skin and penetrated his liver before surging throughout his body like liquid fire. Yetzer might have screamed with agony, but his breath turned to water in his lungs.

The second drop fell on his upraised hand. The flesh turned white as a leper's, then flaked away. Skin gave way to muscle and sinew until these too dissolved, leaving only bone. The venom dripped through the skeletal frame of Yetzer's hand and plunged toward him. For an instant, he saw his horrified face reflected in the shimmering surface of the deadly orb.

The venom struck his eye with the force of a sandstorm. Thousands of needles stabbed into him through the socket of his eye and the base of his skull.

"Behold," the cobra said, its voice nearly lost in the flood of pain, "he shall taste the bitterness of death, yet shall he live."

Through his remaining eye, Yetzer caught the motion of the giant snake. Its cavernous maw stretched wide as it swooped toward him. Yetzer's heart seized as the fangs scraped down his back, and he was surrounded by darkness.

❁

Yetzer bolted upright.

"Steady," a deep voice cautioned.

Yetzer looked toward the speaker. His vision slowly cleared and the image of the cobra faded to reveal the grim smile of Pharaoh Horemheb.

"My father?" Yetzer said, his voice ragged.

Pharaoh's expression darkened. "Huram of Tsur has joined the Ageless Ones."

It took a moment for the meaning to seep through Yetzer's understanding.

"He's dead?" he finally whispered.

"His shell is no longer animated," Pharaoh said, "but his essence is now free to walk the fields of eternity."

Tears blurred Yetzer's vision and he moved to brush them away. He stopped as his linen-wrapped hand came into view, a red stain in the center of the white bandage. With cruel clarity, truth rushed into the void of his memory.

The explosion of rock. His father's torn throat. The stone shard that pierced his own hand and … Yetzer put his fingertips to his face. They disappeared from view as they neared his left eye. Instead of flesh he found more linen. His breath caught in his chest as he ran his fingers up and down. Bandages covered one side of his head from temple to jaw.

"What happened?"

"The outcropping apparently held a reservoir of water," Pharaoh said as he filled a silver bowl and held it to Yetzer's lips. "The fire made the rock brittle, as intended, but it also heated the water to boiling. As the heat increased, so did the pressure within the formation until …"

Yetzer swallowed, the water at once soothing and grating. "How many?" he asked.

Pharaoh nodded with solemn approval. "A true leader puts the welfare of his people before all else. Seven men accompanied your father to the West. I fear another two or three may join them before long."

"Lime?" Yetzer said after a moment's consideration.

"Even so," Pharaoh affirmed. "The steam mixed with limestone dust. Those closest to the blast have severe burns. Most will recover, though some may wish they hadn't."

"And me?"

Pharaoh's expression was flat as polished stone. "Your eye was ruptured and could not be restored. Lime burned your face and arm," Pharaoh continued. "The rock, of course, pierced your hand. My physicians believe you will regain its use, and they continue to do all they can for the son of Pharaoh."

Yetzer raised his left hand. The fingertips that peeked out from the bandage were pink and healthy. He tried to move them and pain shot from his palm to his shoulder. His head fell back onto the wooden headrest, but he clenched his teeth and tried again. His breath went ragged as he fought for control over his body. Fire stretched from his shoulder into his chest until, through watery eyes—eye, he reminded himself—he saw the twitch of his forefinger.

"Very good," the king said as Yetzer dropped his hand to the bed.

Sweat mixed with the tears that ran down Yetzer's cheek. He filled his lungs with a shuddering breath, then emptied them with a harsh cough as Horemheb's words sank in.

"Son of Pharaoh?"

The king gave a thin smile. "You saved my life and lost your own father in doing so. The highest duty—after service to the gods—is to care for widows and orphans. How much more so for those created in service to Pharaoh?"

"Widow," Yetzer repeated, his heart caught in a whirlwind. "What of my mother?"

"I have taken her into the royal harem," Pharaoh said, then raised a hand to silence Yetzer's protest. "As my guest only. When the days of mourning are past, she will be free to return to her people in Kenahn. Or she may remain in Kemet, as my guest or my wife, whichever she wishes."

"She is but a common woman," Yetzer said, "and I am only the son of a mason, not even apprenticed in my own right. I thank you for your kindness, Lord, but we have no more place at court than—"

"Than a rough soldier?" Pharaoh interrupted, a sly grin creasing his lips. "I was but a commoner, a simple spearman, until the gods used me to serve Pharaoh Tutankhamun, peace be upon him." He traced an ankh across his forehead. "Men may put stock in bloodlines, but it is service to the gods, to Kemet, and to our fellows that defines nobility." He patted Yetzer's hand. "Now is the time of preparation and mourning. Politics may come later. Ameniye."

A light tread sounded behind Yetzer's cot, revealing for the first time that he and Pharaoh were not alone. Shame inflamed his face at the thought that he'd displayed tears of weakness not only to Pharaoh, but to … A beautiful young woman, with olive skin and flowing black hair, stepped to Horemheb's side. Yetzer's lungs seized at the sight of her.

"Yes, Father?"

The air filled with her lotus-sweet breath. Yetzer's heart faltered at the music of her voice, and he wondered how he had missed her presence before.

"Ameniye, this is Yetzer, your brother. I charge you to care for him as Auset tended Osaure. I place his well-being in your hands."

Ameniye's large eyes sparkled and her lips turned upward. She placed a henna-stained hand upon her breast, against the diaphanous gown that did little to hide her feminine virtues.

"As Pharaoh wills, so shall it be done."

Horemheb nodded and turned back to Yetzer. "I will look in on you as I am able."

Even as Pharaoh turned away, Ameniye's hand stroked Yetzer's cheek. The cool touch of her fingers revealed the fire that burned beneath his flesh.

"You have fever," she said. She turned to a small table and sorted through a collection of jars and bowls. With a wooden spoon she measured portions from three of the containers and mixed these with water in a silver cup.

"The medicines are powerful." She held the cup to Yetzer's lips and he swallowed the bitter potion without complaint. "They are made stronger still by rest. Sleep now and let the healing energies do their work."

Yetzer wanted to argue, to say her company would bring more healing than sleep, but his tongue grew heavy. He fought to keep his eyes—eye—open, but the medicines were as swift as they were strong. Ameniye's image shifted between princess and flower as Yetzer blinked and strained to keep her in focus. Yetzer's mouth twisted into a grin as the lotus won.

6

Makeda

"Seventy *korim*," Lord Watar said from his seat in the council chamber. "Seventy?" Yanuf repeated in disgust. "That's enough grain to feed two armies for a year."

"I have many men," Watar said calmly, "and they have much strength to support."

For the fifth time—sixth? I'd lost count—the meeting room erupted in discord. I sat by the ladderway on the floor above and did my best to stay silent and out of sight, while still keeping eyes and ears on the happenings below. Watar and three other men from Timnah sat on one side of the room opposite my mother, Yanuf, and a pair of Maryaba's elders. The remembrancer sat between the two sides, stroking his head as though trying to massage the heated words into his memory.

"If we give you seventy *korim* of grain each year—"

"Each harvest," Watar interjected, and chaos burst forth yet again.

The argument centered around Maryaba's place as principal city of Saba. The Mukarrib of all Saba, going back to my father's great-grandfather, was headman of the cities, towns, and villages from the great sea of the west, to the impassable desert of the east, and down to the limitless waters of the south.

The most fertile of all the cities of Saba, Maryaba traded her harvests for the aromatic myrrh and olibanum resin harvested by the rest of the people and, more importantly, for their loyalty. In recent years, Maryaba's surplus of food had diminished while the demand for olibanum increased.

A betrothal between Watar's son and Bilkis had been intended to ease tensions between our two great cities. The young man had been one of those in the wadi when the flood struck. His impatience to claim his bride had not only taken his and Bilkis's lives, but the fires he'd started had ruined the few remaining fields that could still bear fruit.

"If Maryaba can no longer meet her obligations," Watar said when the furor again subsided, "perhaps it is time for a new arrangement."

"What sort of arrangement?" my mother asked warily.

"The line of our fathers is diminished. Maryaba is ruled by a woman, a foreigner. The weapons the city once possessed now lie scattered before the walls of Timnah."

"Weapons are easily made," Yanuf said.

"But suitable leaders are not," Watar countered. "A mukarrib should have a cock between the legs." He leered at my mother. "And perhaps that could be remedied—"

Yanuf lurched toward Watar, but Mother grasped his arm and bade him sit. "Our guest's words are bitter as early grapes, but they cannot be ignored."

"I don't intend to ignore them," the gatekeeper growled. "I intend to stuff them back down his gullet."

Mother did not respond. Instead, she turned back to the Lord of Timnah and repeated, "What sort of arrangement?"

Watar scraped his fingers through his beard. "It may be time for Timnah to take its rightful place as head of Saba."

Once more, the room filled with shouts. I clapped my hands to my ears and shook my head, but could not hold back the clamor.

"Why won't you just share?" I cried, my voice cutting through the din.

All eyes bored into me. I shied back from the ladderway, but Mother gestured for me to come down. I obeyed and sat beside her.

"What do you suggest?" Mother asked me in the tongue of her native Uwene, the language in which we shared our secrets.

Too abashed to look at any of the others, I locked my eyes onto hers and explained. When I finished, Mother smiled, pulled me into an embrace, then faced the men around us. She broke off a piece of flatbread from the central platter and dipped it in a bowl of olive oil.

"Brother Watar's words are not without merit," she said, and took a bite. "Maryaba has, indeed, fallen short of her duties as caretaker of Saba. But tell me, Lord, how does Timnah intend to feed her subjects?"

"We will take what we need," Watar replied.

"From whom?" she asked. "No other town produces as much as Maryaba. With our men tasked to defend against your raids, we have scarcely enough workers to feed ourselves, let alone Timnah and the rest of Saba."

Watar leaned back and folded his arms across his chest. The men on either side of him whispered their counsel, gesturing toward Mother and me as they did so.

At length, the Lord of Timnah sat forward, spread his hands and smiled. "What do you suggest?"

Mother, too, leaned forward and pushed the platter of bread toward Watar.

"Like a good mother, Maryaba will continue to guide and nourish her children of Saba."

Watar's men started to protest, but he silenced them with an upraised hand. "Go on."

"Like a good father, Timnah shall protect and provide for his family, sacrificing his wants for their needs."

Watar's eyes narrowed as he looked from Mother to me.

"And what else do father and mother do?"

Mother's cheeks darkened, but she kept her gaze steady. "Brother Watar, I am a new widow. When my days of mourning are past, I will dedicate myself to the gods that I may serve the people of Saba without distraction."

Disappointment clouded Watar's eyes.

"However," Mother continued, "I have a daughter."

I shot a look toward her. I hadn't meant to be part of the plan.

"She is Karibil's acknowledged daughter," she went on, "descended from your own ancestors. I believe you have another son?"

Watar nodded. "Dhamar. He has just passed his trials of manhood."

"Makeda will be a woman in seven years," Ayana said, "perhaps sooner. In that time, let our cities rebuild what envy and sloth have torn down. Let us restore all of Saba to prosperity and greatness. And then— " She placed her hand atop my head. I realized I hadn't breathed for some time. I took a ragged breath and my heart resumed its beat. "And then," Mother continued with a smile at me, "when their time has come, mother and father shall be made one."

A fly's buzzing was the only sound in the room. For a span of thirty heartbeats or more, the councillors held their tongues. At length, Watar smiled, leaned forward and broke off a piece of bread.

7

Bilkis

Sand was everywhere. Not only upon the ground and in the air, but in sandals and robes and undergarments. In food, wine, and water. And hair. Bilkis's chief vanity—she had many, she was learning—was her hair. With it she had drawn the attention of many suitors. As the caravan crossed the desert, she had been forced to adopt Leah and Rahab's traditional dress, covering herself from head to foot, concealing her wondrous hair to keep it free of the blowing sand.

The moon turned ten times while the caravan followed some unseen path. The wind aided in keeping the trail a secret as it erased all signs of their passage with each step. Day followed tedious day as the caravan's guide, a Bedou slave boy, led them from one stone-walled well to the next.

Each evening, the travelers set their tents and made their fires. Each morning, they again loaded their animals in a cycle Bilkis began to fear had no end.

"How much longer?" she asked Rahab.

The pair secured their rolled sleeping mats upon their donkeys under the assault of sun and sand and wind.

"Soon," the Habiru girl replied, as she did each time Bilkis asked the question.

Thunder rumbled in the distance. It wasn't uncommon for clouds to gather in the evenings, massive and ominous and rippling with lightning. Bilkis couldn't recall such a display in the morning hours, and the skies appeared empty.

The thunder grew louder. Bilkis realized it came from behind her. Ululating cries joined the rumble and Bilkis's breath seized. She and her friends in Maryaba used to make up stories of Bedou raiders, wild horsemen that prowled the desert wastes. Their tales had been romantic and wondrous and exciting, but it was fear that now grasped Bilkis in its thrall.

Before her lips could form a warning, dozens of black-robed horsemen burst from the blinding disk of the rising sun. Sword blades flashed in the morning light as they slashed at tent ropes and fleeing servants.

"Get to the stores!" Eliam shouted.

He pushed Rahab and Bilkis toward the center of the camp. Bilkis took the girl's hand and pulled her toward the baskets and bales of supplies. After ten months of travel, the pile of goods was much smaller than when Bilkis had joined the caravan. Still, she hoped they might find some shelter there. She pulled Rahab over a palisade of stacked fleece and sank into a shadowed corner.

The camp rang with men's shouts and the clatter of weapons. The merchants carried staves and clubs, but how would they stand against bronze swords? A rattle of jars sounded from outside the hiding place. Bilkis feared they had been discovered but, when the intruder's head appeared, she breathed once more.

"Umma," Rahab cried.

The girl scrambled into Leah's arms and the two sank to the ground in the first show of affection Bilkis had witnessed between them.

"Peace, daughter," Leah said, her voice muffled by the girl's tangled hair. "Be still."

She stretched a hand toward Bilkis, who crawled into the big woman's embrace. Leah and Rahab whispered prayers of deliverance to the goddess Havah and Yah, her consort, while Bilkis sheltered beneath the peace of their words.

"Leah!" Eliam's shout pierced the mystical veil, and heavy steps raced toward the shelter.

"Husband," Leah said. She freed herself from the girls' arms and struggled to her feet. "I knew all would be well."

Her words ended abruptly and Bilkis looked up. Leah's eyes met hers before drifting downward to where a javelin sprouted from her bosom. A stain of crimson spread across her blue silk robe. The woman staggered back a step then fell heavily onto her backside.

"Umma!" Rahab screamed, and rushed to her mother's side.

Bilkis turned away as the girl eased Leah onto her back. She peered over the makeshift rampart and came face-to-face with dark-eyed terror. The man's face was covered with a black cloth, only his eyes and scarred nose visible. The eyes blazed with bloodlust that turned to something else when they fell on Bilkis.

She had seen looks of desire from the men of Saba, but the raw hunger in the eyes of the man before her stole her breath. The Bedou pulled down his scarf to reveal the full length of the scar. It ran from the bridge of his nose, down his right cheek to the corner of his mouth, which twisted into an evil sneer. The sneer widened into a smile of rotted teeth, and the man gave a throaty laugh. Laughter turned to a choking gasp as a shadow swooped over him. A flash of sunlight blinded Bilkis for a moment. When her vision returned, she thought she must have the desert madness for the Bedou lay on the ground, blood spilling from his throat. Over him stood a bronze-clad warrior who shone like gold with the light of the gods. Brown eyes sparked with passion while his dark hair flashed with streaks of fire.

A pair of Bedou rushed the warrior. He turned toward them on sleek, muscled legs, bare from the top of his bronze greaves to the hem of the tunic that scarcely covered his loincloth. Twin swords spun in his long-fingered hands and whistled with blood thirst.

The warrior sidestepped one of his attackers, who tripped over the dead Bedou in his headlong rush. The golden one then ducked beneath the sword stroke of the other man and plunged one of his blades into the man's groin. The raider shrieked and fell to the ground. The warrior turned toward the remaining man who scrambled back toward Bilkis in her refuge.

Without a thought, Bilkis yanked the javelin from the wound in Leah's breast. Ignoring Rahab's cries, she leapt atop the bales of fleece against which the Bedou cowered. He looked up at Bilkis to reveal a boy's tear-streaked face. He muttered what Bilkis assumed were prayers to the gods of the desert.

"There's no need to pray," Bilkis said in a soft, soothing voice.

The boy wiped his eyes and cracked a wary smile.

"You may speak to the gods directly," Bilkis added, and plunged the javelin downward.

The boy raised a hand in feeble defense, but the blade pierced him under the arm, slid through his chest, and emerged low on his other side to sink into the sand. The depth of the blow took Bilkis by surprise and threw her off balance. She teetered off her perch, but the shining one caught her in his arms.

"The honeybee stings," he said, his voice like a song and his breath sweet in Bilkis's nostrils.

Before she could respond, the warrior set her on her feet and rushed to where a dozen more bronze-clad warriors exchanged blows with the Bedou. There seemed to be three times as many of the desert raiders, each with a horse, but the sure-footed warriors stood strong against them.

Bilkis cried out as a Bedou on a large, black horse bore down on her golden savior. The warrior turned, dove under the galloping hooves, then raised his twin swords into the beast's belly. Rider and mount tumbled in a dusty cloud. The warrior sprang to his feet, raced toward the stunned raider and, with a single stroke, separated head from shoulders.

At that, the surviving Bedou lost heart. Fewer than a dozen remained, and these pulled hard on their horses' reins and fled to the desert from which they had come. The warriors cheered them on their way, but there was no rejoicing among the members of the caravan.

Rahab's wails echoed through the camp, closely matched by cries of the few men and fewer women who remained. Eliam, his head bleeding and eyes unfocused, staggered toward the makeshift barricade. Abram came close behind him. He and Bilkis helped the merchant over the stacked goods. The abbreviated family fell into one another's arms.

Bilkis turned away to let them grieve in peace. She managed three steps before the world spun, her knees buckled, and she fell to the ground. It was only a few moments before strong hands took her by the shoulders and sat her upright.

"Here, now, my honey. Be at peace." The warrior held a flask to Bilkis's lips and she eagerly drank. Fire coursed over her tongue and down her throat. She coughed and spat up the foul brew.

"What is that?" she demanded as her eyes flooded with tears.

"Nectar for the bee," the man said, his eyes full of humor.

He took a pull from the flask, shook his head like a shying horse, and gave a lion's roar. Despite the horror strewn around them, Bilkis couldn't help but laugh. The warrior raised an eyebrow and tipped the flask toward Bilkis. She nodded and took a cautious sip. The drink warmed her to her belly and calmed what fright her warrior's touch had not yet eased.

"Does the bee have a name?" he asked.

"Bilkis, daughter of Karibil, Mukarrib of all Saba."

The warrior frowned as he repeated her words, his northern tongue stumbling over them.

"Daughter of Saba," he at last dubbed her. "I am Auriyah, son of King Tadua of Yisrael, and commander of the Hatti guard. And I think you, Bilkis bat-Saba, shall be my bride."

8

Yetzer

"This one shows the savior-god Haru in his struggle against Sutah, the destroyer."

Ameniye led Yetzer through the gallery of Pharaoh's palace. As she had for months, she pointed out the murals depicting scenes from the lore of Kemet. The daughter of Pharaoh—"Sister," she often chided Yetzer, "you must call me Sister"—had nursed him back to health, keeping him company as he lay on his sickbed, and filling the long days with tales of the gods and the foundations of the world.

"And what does it mean?" Yetzer asked, as he did after every tale she wove.

Ameniye smiled prettily, as she ever did. "It means, sweet Brother, that through Sutah's darkest storms, the brilliant eye of Haru will pierce the clouds even as—"

"Even as ...?" Yetzer prompted her, noting how her eyes flitted away.

Her voice was soft as she added, "Even as the lance of Sutah pierced Haru's other eye."

Yetzer raised his fingers to the bandage that covered his empty left eye socket. The pain of the injury had long since passed, and Ameniye's salves had healed most of his burned and torn flesh. The wound to his heart was not so easily mended.

In his dreams, Yetzer was still haunted by the shades of his father and the others killed in the quarry. They demanded to know why he hadn't saved them. They offered mocking hopes that he slept warm in Pharaoh's house while they slept in the cold earth. Yetzer would awaken from these visitations in a sweat, the pain of his wounds as fresh as the scourge in his heart.

On those nights, Ameniye would come to him and wipe his brow. She would sing to him of Osaure and Auset, of their love that kept harmony in the land. She would hold him until he fell asleep and, in the dreams of early morning, he was Osaure and she Auset.

He loved her in those moments, when she was the goddess made flesh, beautiful and regal. In day's light she was no less beautiful, and she moved with fluid steps that made him envy the ground beneath her feet. But the girl lacked the depth of the dream. Auset was wisdom embodied, attuned to the mysteries of creation, while Ameniye cared more for court gossip than the hidden truth behind Kemet's myths.

"What is it, Brother?" Ameniye took his hand and stirred him from his thoughts. "Oh, do not be angry with me. I could not bear it. I only meant to point out how like the god you are."

Yetzer forced a smile and squeezed her hand.

"It's not that. It's good I have only one eye to look upon you. Had I both to take in your beauty, I fear I should go mad."

Ameniye's expression brightened with the flattery. She threw her arms about Yetzer's neck and kissed him on the mouth. Her lips were soft and warm, her body firm as she pressed against him.

Yetzer allowed that wisdom might not be the only quality worth embracing.

❈

"Yetzer abi-Huram begs Pharaoh's attention," the fat eunuch announced at the doorway to Horemheb's audience hall.

Men's grunts and the clash of weapons found their way through the door. The sword song intensified and the men's voices grew louder until the hiss of sliding blades was followed by a victorious shout and the clatter of metal on wood.

"Show him in, Mika," Pharaoh's voice called. "Show him in."

"At your command, Great Kemet." The steward bowed, and the thin fabric of his robe revealed more of his backside than Yetzer cared to see.

Yetzer stepped around the eunuch and entered the chamber. Granite columns rose the height of six men. Alabaster sconces and bronze chandeliers shone upon plastered walls whose murals portrayed Pharaoh's victories. The floor was lined with planks of polished cedar from Yetzer's homeland, but Horemheb had pulled up most of these to make a fighting pit.

In the middle of the pit stood Pharaoh, an unarmed man kneeling before him.

"You fought well, Meren," Horemheb said, and patted the man on the shoulder. "Take up your sword and see to your wounds."

The young soldier touched his forehead to the ground, crawled back from Pharaoh, collected his sword and left.

"Friend of Pharaoh." Horemheb turned toward Yetzer and spread his arms. "Come, Yetzer. Greet me as a father."

Despite the warm welcome, Yetzer was suddenly aware of his place as a foreigner and an orphan in Kemet. He fell to his knees and groveled forward.

"Great is Pharaoh, Mighty One of Kemet, Brother to the Gods. May all the gods preserve him and—"

"Nonsense," Horemheb said. He stepped toward Yetzer, raised him by the shoulders and embraced him. "I may be Pharaoh, whether by the will of the gods or of man. But you, Yetzer, are the savior and friend of Pharaoh. As such, you are the savior and friend of all Kemet. Come. Sit and eat."

Horemheb led Yetzer around the sand pit to the far corner of the hall where a low table sat surrounded by thick cushions. Ameniye and Pharaoh's principal wife, Mutnedjmet, shared one side of the table. The princess looked at Yetzer through her eyelashes and smiled. Opposite the women sat a withered man with a long robe draped over his bony frame. Pharaoh made the introductions.

"Yetzer, greet Huy, High Priest and Servant of Amun." In a louder voice he said, "Master Huy, your servant presents—"

"No need to shout, Ouros," the priest said, calling Pharaoh by his birth name. "These old ears can still hear a dragonfly's whisper. And no need to introduce the hero of Bakhu."

"Please, don't get up," Yetzer said as the priest pushed away from the table.

Huy brushed off Pharaoh's offer of help. Ancient bones and parched sinews creaked as they straightened beneath the priest. When he had finished his noisy unfolding, he stood a head taller than Pharaoh, despite the stoop that bent the priest's spine.

"You are Yetzer abi-Huram, eh?"

Cold hands clamped onto Yetzer's face, turning his head side to side, contorting his features as though to reshape his image.

"Ah, there he is," Huy said at last. "The father rests in the son." He released his hold and tapped Yetzer's nose. "Something of the Habiru, too, hmm? Of what tribe is your mother, boy?"

"Naftali," Yetzer said.

The priest squeezed his eyes shut and furrowed his brow, then snapped his fingers. "'Naftali is a fleeting deer who gives good instruction.' Are you a fleeting deer, young Yetzer?"

"I don't—" Yetzer stammered for an answer, but Pharaoh interceded.

"Sit, Master. Eat," he said, and led the priest back to his seat. "The duck will not stay warm forever."

"The student becomes the teacher," Huy said, and patted Horemheb's hand.

Pharaoh gestured Yetzer to a cushion at one end of the table, between Ameniye and the High Priest, then sat opposite him.

"Would you sanctify the food, Master Huy?" he said to the priest.

The old man spread out his hands. "As it was before the beginning," Huy intoned in a reedy chant, "may it be soon and forever. As it is in the heavens, let it be upon the earth."

He took up some bread, raised his eyes toward the ceiling and broke the loaf in two. "As the body of Osaure has gone to the earth, so does the earth return his body in the grain of the field, to nourish and sanctify us to the service of the gods and one another."

The priest took a portion of the bread then handed the remaining parts to Horemheb and Yetzer. Each in turn broke his portion in two and handed a part to the woman beside him.

Huy then raised a silver chalice filled with wine from the oasis of Faiyum. "The blood of Osaure, spilled upon the earth and enlivened in the grape to revive the spirit of man." He dipped his bread into the wine, ate his portion, then handed the cup to Horemheb. Pharaoh repeated the motions, and the ceremony continued around the table until Ameniye handed the cup to Yetzer.

Her fingers burned under his as she passed the wine to him, her eyes alight. Yetzer took the chalice, dipped in his bread …

And was dumbfounded.

He had dined in Pharaoh's house many times, had drunk from the best of the royal vineyards, but those feasts had never affected him like this simple meal.

Light shone around those seated at the table, like the halo about the moon on a fog-shrouded night. Yetzer blinked to clear his vision, but the auras only glowed stronger when he saw them through his missing eye. Pharaoh blazed with an orange light, Mutnedjmet the color of amethyst, while Ameniye glowed an ardent red. About Huy shone a pure white that returned to his features a youthfulness time had stolen.

Yetzer opened his eye. In his natural vision, the halos faded.

"Let sight be granted to him with an eye to see," said the priest. He winked at Yetzer and nudged Horemheb with his elbow.

Pharaoh offered a grim smile and the slightest of nods, then carved the roasted duck.

"Ameniye tells me you have become quite the scholar," Mutnedjmet said to Yetzer.

"She is an excellent tutor," Yetzer replied.

"And what subjects has our princess taught?" asked the priest.

Ameniye almost spilled the vegetables into Yetzer's lap.

"Pharaoh's daughter is well versed in the legends of Kemet," Yetzer said. "By her very voice she gives breath to the tales of the ancients."

Huy accepted the platter and Yetzer's answer with a curt grunt, and Pharaoh redirected the conversation to talk of court, the latest inundation, rumors from neighboring lands.

"Will you and your mother be returning to your father's country?" Mutnedjmet asked Yetzer as the servants cleared the table and refilled the cups.

Ameniye looked with wide, eager eyes at Yetzer who took a long drink of wine.

"Kemet is the very heart of wisdom and learning," he said after wiping his chin. "As long as Pharaoh and the gods will it, I shall be content to live and learn beside the Iteru."

Horemheb set down his cup and fixed his eyes on Yetzer.

"And what, exactly, would you learn beside the river, Friend of Pharaoh?"

Yetzer's mouth went dry. His thoughts raced, but no answer came to his aid.

"As you bear the mark of the savior Haru," Pharaoh continued, and tapped beside his own left eye, "you have but to ask and all shall be given to you. Knock on any door, and it will open before you."

Ameniye clasped her hand over Yetzer's and gave a hopeful smile.

"Pharaoh has been too generous already," Yetzer demurred. "Your servant can ask nothing more."

Ameniye's grip tightened and she cleared her throat. The old priest covered a cough with his hand.

"If you will not ask, then I will offer." Pharaoh spread his hands, palms down, over the table then turned up his right. "With this hand I offer you all the riches and treasures of the world. I have called you Son. If you wish, you shall be my son before the gods and men, as husband to my daughter."

Ameniye shook Yetzer's fingers.

"With the other hand," Horemheb continued before Yetzer could reply, turning up his left palm, "I offer you the light of the heavens. As I called your father Huram my brother before the gods, so would I call you, and stand for you before the celestial throne."

Yetzer's mouth fell open as the import of Pharaoh's words rolled over him. Ameniye's eyes shone in the lamplight, full of ardor and joy. The queen absently sifted through a bunch of grapes. Only a few years older than her step-daughter, Mutnedjmet had been near to Ameniye's age when her father, Pharaoh Aya, married her to his strongest rival, Horemheb. She was still beautiful, but her eyes were as vacant as Ameniye's became when Yetzer tried to discuss the meanings behind the murals.

"Yetzer abi-Huram," Pharaoh intoned, "this day I set before you life and light. Choose life and become master of this world. Or choose light, die to the desires of the flesh, and become master of the world beyond the veil." Horemheb clasped his hands together, set them on the table, and held Yetzer's gaze. "What say you?"

Yetzer thought to ask for time, but something told him Pharaoh's offer held as much demand as promise. Hesitate, and all could be lost. He squeezed Ameniye's fingers, gave her a soft smile, then pulled his hand from hers.

"Give me light."

9
Makeda

My belly rumbled its discontent. For months we'd survived on hard bread, bitter nuts, and salted fish. I might have complained, but my mother—indeed, all the souls throughout Saba—fared no better. Across the land, people sacrificed the better part of their rations to feed the men and women who worked on Mother's grand project.

At the mouth of the Wadi Dhanah, where the mountains met the desert, laborers went about their grueling tasks. Women trudged in mud troughs, blending dirt and straw and precious water. After they formed the putty into bricks and baked them beneath the burning sun, the men hauled and stacked these in a great wall that spanned the width of the wadi.

Centered on the boulder that had once sheltered me from the flood, the dam stretched from bank to bank and stood the height of three men. From either end, canals ran into the fields, each branching into a network of smaller channels that spread throughout the onetime oasis.

Generations of neglect had left the irrigation channels blocked with silt and debris, and my mother's goal was to clear the channels and revitalize our fields. While women and men formed and stacked the bricks of the dam, the children and elders dredged out the waterways. I was no exception.

"You will lead these people one day," my mother had told me. "If a ruler expects to share her people's bounty, she must also share their trials."

From the city walls, the fields stretched into the distance, and I chose the channel branches that took me farthest from the city. A wooden stake marked my progress from the day before, and I pulled it up and hummed a little tune as I set to work.

It wasn't that I relished the work, nor that I wanted to set an example or earn my mother's approval. What drove me early to the fields and late to the gates was this, silence and solitude. A respite from the other children.

If I happened to draw near to where they worked, there would be joking and laughter and jeers of *Mud-skin* and *Brush-head*. I'd inherited the complexion and hair of my mother's people across the Western Sea in Uwene, and my springy locks refused to be tamed.

"Good morning, Piss-eye."

I turned at the fresh insult. Mother called my eyes honey or amber or gold. Yanuf said they were the shade of harvest beer, which was more valuable than any of these. Leave it to Dhamar to turn my most favored attribute into a source of derision. The son of Watar of Timnah—and my betrothed, I tried to forget—Dhamar had spent the past year in Maryaba as a surety of peace between our two cities.

"The sun has only just risen," I said, ignoring the taunt. "Shouldn't you still be abed?"

"It was cold and I had no company."

I looked away as he parted his robes and passed water on the sunbaked field.

"Tell me that isn't your color exactly," he added, raising his voice over the splattering stream.

I edged away and drove my dredging stick once more into the earth. I tensed as Dhamar crouched behind me and placed his hands on my shoulders.

"And when will the mukarrib's daughter join me on my sleeping mat?"

A shiver ran down my spine, but I forced calm into my voice. "As soon as Shams awakens from there," I said, nodding toward the cloud bedecked western mountains. "What of Aisha and Tahira and Magda? Have they so quickly tired of you that you must seek out a child not yet in her moons?"

Dhamar's relations with the daughters of Maryaba's wealthiest tradesmen were an open secret. What would otherwise have been a cause for stoning of the young women and a heavy fine for Dhamar was overlooked for the cause of peace and the hoped-for prosperity of all involved.

"Tahira's pleasure slit is too loose since she gave birth," he said. "Aisha's is tight enough, but she stinks of goat sweat. Magda at least smells of incense, but she constantly chatters like a locust." He reached an arm around my waist and pulled me against him. "And none of them is daughter of the mukarrib." He slipped his other hand beneath my robe.

I blinked and found myself standing, both hands tight about the dredging stick, and a war cry fading from my ears. Dhamar sprawled on the ground, blood streaming from his temple. He raised a hand to the wound, studied the blood on his fingers then licked them clean.

"You've brought forth my blood," he said, his eyes piercing me. "Now I shall do the same for you."

"Is this the pride of Timnah?" Yanuf said as he walked up behind the young lord, spear in hand. "Whelping bastards and threatening children?"

"This isn't your concern, cripple," Dhamar snapped.

"Your mother summons you," the old warrior told me, ignoring the insult. "It is time."

"Time?" I asked.

Yanuf pointed his spear toward the mountains. A year had passed since the flood of the Wadi Dhanah. As the dam's completion neared, Mother had dispatched messengers throughout Saba to summon the people to the dedication. She'd even sent word across the Western Sea to Uwene, where her brother sat upon the throne of our ancestors. For weeks visitors had streamed to Maryaba, in anticipation of the gods' renewed blessings. As black clouds flashed with light above the distant peaks, it appeared that time had come.

❀

Thunder echoed off the walls of the Wadi Dhanah. Not the thunder of the gods, but of new goatskins stretched over willow frames. The freshly skinned carcasses lay at the foot of the dam, sunlight gleaming upon raw flesh. People trampled the freshly cleared fields, crowded the banks of the wadi, and drained the overtaxed wells. From atop the dam I studied the sky to find some omen of the gods' intent.

Elmakah's clouds streaked with glory far away on the western horizon. Would this day bring the flood so desperately needed? Might life return to the desert and bring peace and prosperity once more to Maryaba, to all Saba? The skies gave no answer I could discern so I turned my attention back to the ceremony.

Yatha, priest of the great god Athtar, stood with bloody hands raised to the sky. His voice weakened by the daylong ceremony, still he cried for the gods' attention. He lowered his hands when Ismail the tanner stepped forward with the final sacrifice, the joint offering of Timnah and Maryaba.

Ismail's daughter Tahira wailed as the priest took the offering, her newborn bastard. A pang of sympathy tugged at my heart for the girl who'd fought for Dhamar's attention, a battle I'd been happy to surrender.

Dhamar stood with his father and the elders from Timnah. I looked for any sign of regret at the imminent sacrifice of his daughter but saw none. Had Tahira produced a son, Dhamar might have protested. As the child was but a girl, he seemed content to let the ceremony proceed. His virility, in any case, had been proven.

"Accept, mighty Athtar," Yatha intoned, "the return of this child, exchanged for your watchfulness and protection."

The child made no sound as the priest dangled her by the feet over the edge of the dam. She simply gummed on her tiny fist.

My breath came faster. I fought the urge to seize the child from the priest's gnarled hand and give her into the safety of Tahira's arms, but my mother had explained the need to sacrifice a blameless one for the salvation of all. I clenched my fists and invoked a silent prayer.

Return to the gods, Little One. Bid them send us life.

As though taking his cue from my unspoken words, Yatha drew his blood-stained flint across the infant's throat. Tahira screamed and lurched forward but her father caught her about the waist and dragged her away as the crimson font streamed onto the pile of offerings. When the child's twitching ended, the priest dropped her lifeless husk onto the sacrificial heap.

Tahira's cries were overwhelmed by the shouts of adulation from the assembly. Urged on by the priest, the people called for the gods' mercy. The thunder of the drums grew louder and pulsed through my chest.

As one, the crowd swayed back and forth, arms raised toward the distant, flashing clouds. The very foundations of the dam seemed to tremble in sympathy. I lost my balance and fell to my knees. Yanuf, ever present, helped me to my feet. He set me beside my mother on the shivering bricks of the dam.

The rhythm of the earth grew stronger, outpacing that of the drums. Pebbles danced in the wadi just as they had on that fateful day a year earlier. The day Bilkis had been lost. The day Mother and I had been granted our freedom. The strange stillness in the air was not unlike the emptiness that had preceded—

"Athtar's breath." My words came so softly I wondered if I'd spoken them aloud.

Mother took me by the shoulders. "What did you say?"

"It's Athtar's breath," I repeated. "The god speaks."

She cocked an ear toward the mouth of the wadi. After a moment, she flashed a hopeful glance at Yanuf. She stood and placed me in front of her as she faced the people. She raised her arms and the drums and voices gradually fell silent.

"The prayers of the people have been heard," she proclaimed. "Our sacrifices have been accepted. Witness now the answer, the blessing of the gods."

Mother turned back toward the mountains, with me between her and Yanuf. On either side of us, the priest and elders and visiting chieftains gathered in a line that stretched the width of the dam.

The world fell silent save for the rattle of the dancing pebbles. Countless heartbeats pulsed in my ears before the slightest zephyr brushed my cheek. The breezy sigh grew to a whisper, then a whine. The earth trembled more violently, and a cry of fear rose from the crowd.

Makeda, run!

There was no mistaking Bilkis's voice. I spun around. Thousands of faces looked toward me, toward the wadi, but none belonged to Bilkis. The memory's echo faded.

"What is it?" Mother asked.

I shook my head and turned back. Athtar's breath was now a scream, cold and dank as it howled down from the mountains. With his breath came the terror of Elmakah. Fear shook me as a dark wall of water appeared in the canyon. The flood snarled and foamed like some horrid fiend as it stooped down to devour the people of Saba.

Screams pierced the air. The men on the dam jostled and trampled one another as they raced toward the banks of the wadi. Even Yanuf took a step back from the dam's face.

But I stepped forward. "We're safe," I told my mother, even as she grabbed my hand to pull me back. "Umma, we're safe," I insisted.

She glanced toward Yanuf.

"She has the vision of the gods," he said. "If she says they will protect us, that is what they will do. Or we shall all be very wet."

Yanuf let out a hearty laugh and again faced the flood. He gave a shout of defiance to which Mother added her voice. I joined in, though my cry was less of defiance than terror.

The sound had scarcely reached my ears before the flood was upon us. Yanuf swept around to put his bulk between me and the surge. He could not, however, shield me from the noise, from the tremors that shook the dam, or from the waves that turned the air around us to mist. I closed my eyes against the stinging droplets, clapped my hands to my ears. How long Yanuf sheltered me, I could not be sure. Yet after what seemed an age, the gods' fury eased, and I looked up.

The dam stood.

A roiling pool of water rose almost to the wall's full height and stretched away toward the mouth of the wadi. Already the irrigation channels directed their life-giving streams to the fields of Maryaba where the people danced and laughed and splashed one another.

I turned to hug my mother, but she wasn't there. I looked along the dam and scanned the crowds upon the banks to no avail. I turned back to find Yanuf standing at the downstream edge of the dam. My belly twisted as my feet carried me to the gatekeeper's side.

Ayana, Mukarrib of all Saba, daughter of the kings of Uwene, lay at the foot of the dam. Water puddled around her as her unblinking eyes stared toward the heavens where the gods had claimed a final sacrifice.

10

Yetzer

"The hierophant summons Yetzer abi-Huram."

Yetzer's heart recognized the words and floated to a shallower state of meditation.

"Yetzer of Tsur, you are called forth."

His *ka*, the intangible part of himself, twitched. The clarity of the inner world dissolved into a fine mist.

"Yetzer, Friend of Pharaoh, arise."

Like an air-filled bladder released from the bottom of a pond, Yetzer's awareness escaped its anchor and leapt to the surface. His eye sprang open and his lungs drew a sharp breath. His vision spun, and it was only by force of will that he restored focus.

The painted image before him resolved into the Wanderer, shoulders stooped by his pack as he leaned on his walking staff. A dog nipped at the traveler's heels while a crocodile lay beside the path, jaws open, awaiting a misstep.

For months Yetzer had sat before this painting and its twenty-one companions gracing the walls of the Chamber of the Postulants. Scattered about the hypostyle hall, Yetzer and his fellow students sat upon the marble floor, meditating on the various images of the sacred trinity. Osaure and Auset and Haru—father, mother, and son—posed in their various guises. The priest-instructors bade them not to think about the images, but simply to open their hearts and allow the message of each to speak for itself.

Yetzer was a craftsman, the son of a mason. Reality was what his hands made of it, yet his heart whispered there was more to existence than simply manifest creation. Until arriving at the temple of Amun, he had only glimpsed that other world in his dreams. That world now called to him, and he longed for it more than he longed for Pharaoh's daughter.

He'd followed the priests' instructions. He'd fought boredom and fatigue. He'd sat before each of the twenty-two images numerous times with no results. With each failed session, he fought the desire to give up, to return to Pharaoh's house and Ameniye's embrace.

Hope finally came with his seventh round as he again sat before the Wanderer. For an instant, Yetzer was unaware of the marble beneath him. He was oblivious to the weight of his hands upon his knees, of the breath in his lungs or the rhythm of his heart. Even the Wanderer disappeared from before his eye as he found himself enveloped in a sheath of white light. The sensation fled from him as soon as he became aware of it, but he knew he had glimpsed *Aaru*, the realm of the gods.

Another round of study had passed before the vision repeated. Yetzer managed to sustain it for perhaps the span of two heartbeats. As a hunter stills his movements when a deer approaches the brook, Yetzer stilled his thoughts. The sensation lingered, then fled as Yetzer's thoughts moved in its direction.

Now, at the end of his twelfth round of the murals, Yetzer was able to separate *ka* from body at will, to travel in the celestial plane while the sacred images communicated with his innermost being.

A hand on his shoulder drew him fully from his reverie. Yetzer knocked three times on the marble floor. The sound and sensation grounded his *ka* within his body.

"The hierophant beckons," the priest told him.

Yetzer nodded and rose, mindful of the vow of silence he'd observed since entering the temple. His guide led him to the rear of the chamber, to a narrow doorway hidden among the shadows of the great columns.

"You have passed the first threshold," the priest said in a grave voice. "The profane may enter the Chamber of the Postulants and leave of their own volition."

Yetzer nodded, having received similar instruction upon his arrival.

"You now stand at the second threshold, the Gate of the Initiates. Only those marked by the gods may enter, and only those fully admitted to the priesthood may leave. Pass the ordeals set before you, and you shall join the ranks of the brothers of light. Fail, and you shall ever remain behind these walls." The priest's expression turned grim. "As a slave or as a corpse."

Yetzer might have laughed, but the priest's humorless eyes told him this was no jest. He put on an expression he hoped would match his guide's solemnity and nodded.

The priest placed his fingers on Yetzer's lips. "As you have successfully passed the tests of a postulant, your vow of silence is lifted. You may speak, but only if directly addressed. The path ahead holds many dangers and even more curiosities. Trust that those who have gone before you have anticipated every need and every question. All will be provided to the one who is worthy. Are you ready to proceed?"

Yetzer nodded again, caught the hint of his guide's raised eyebrow, then spoke. "I am ready."

His voice sounded foreign, and the priest gave a sympathetic smile. He placed his right hand on Yetzer's forehead and raised his other toward the heavens. The priest's palm was hot against Yetzer's skin and combined with a pressure beneath the scalp. It seemed an opening formed there, an eye in the center of his forehead. Yetzer took a steadying breath to set aside the strange sensation.

"Yetzer abi-Huram," the priest intoned, "you arrived at this hall in search of light. Have you found what you sought?"

"I have," Yetzer replied, and the pressure behind his brow increased.

"Having attained the object of your quest, what do you seek as you pass the second threshold?"

Answers flooded Yetzer's heart. Wealth. Security. Ameniye. These and countless others vied to be his response, but as he took a breath to form the seed of his answer, the would-be desires were extinguished until only one remained.

"I seek more light."

The priest lowered his hands and smiled. "Your desire being noble, may the gods smile upon your journey."

The guide ushered him through the doorway. Yetzer stepped into a courtyard of whitewashed stone. The midday sun reflected from every surface, and Yetzer raised a hand to shield his eyes. A metallic coldness settled against his breast. As his sight adjusted to the savage rays, it revealed two men wearing the blue-striped headscarves of Pharaoh's royal guard. One soldier held the blade of his sword against Yetzer's chest. The other stood to the side, his sword raised overhead, poised to cleave through Yetzer's skull.

Yetzer drew a sharp breath. He might have cried out, but he remembered his guide's instructions. Instead, he clamped his teeth together, raised his chin, and swallowed his fear.

The guard before him waited through nine of Yetzer's rapid heartbeats, then spoke.

"Who are you, and what do you seek here?"

"I was told—" Yetzer began, then took a breath and started again. "I am Yetzer abi-Huram. I come in search of more light."

The pressure of the blade eased slightly.

"By what right do you enter the Court of the Initiates?" the guard demanded.

"By having entered the Postulants' Chamber and been led to the second threshold."

"Show me the stance of the Postulant."

The first guard took a step back and drew the sword above his shoulder, poised to plunge it into Yetzer's heart, while the other stood unmoving. Unease turned to bowel-melting panic as Yetzer struggled to interpret the demand.

From the day of his arrival he had learned the proper forms of prayer, the foods most beneficial to body and soul, and the patterns of the heavenly lights. He'd studied the natures of form and number, which brought harmony and which discord. Above all, he had learned the secret of entering and moving through the inner world. But he had never been taught a stance of any kind.

The guard drew back his sword for the fatal strike. Yetzer raised a hand against the blow, and the image of the Hermit, ninth among the mystical figures, leapt to his memory's aid. Though his left hand was empty, it mimicked the Hermit's raised lantern that illumined the path before him.

Hesitantly, Yetzer stretched forward his right hand in imitation of the Hermit's staff that steadied his pace. He searched the guard's face, but the man's expression remained inscrutable. As a final, hesitant measure, Yetzer stretched his left foot forward to complete the sign.

Both guards immediately lowered their weapons and stepped to the side.

"Follow the path," the lead guard told Yetzer. "When you reach the gate at its end, knock three times and you will be admitted. Give the sign and the word, *hreri*."

Yetzer nodded and followed the path through an alabaster gateway. Where the Postulants' Chamber was a wonder of construction and artistry, the Courtyard of the Initiates was a tribute to nature. Trees and plants of every description stretched heavenward in praise to Amun, the eternal shining one.

Yetzer traced the meandering pathway, intoxicated by the scent of the flowers, and lulled by the drone of bees. He sobered as the path ended at a high, vine-covered wall. He looked about, but the promised gate was nowhere to be seen. He was about to follow the trail back when his eye settled on a small flower, its pink petals nearly lost among the green tangle of the vines.

The lily—*hreri* in the language of Kemet—beckoned to Yetzer. He scanned the area around the flower and, seeing nothing amiss, gently pulled on the bud. When it remained firmly planted amongst the vines, Yetzer stretched a hand into the green. Thorns raked his skin. His elbow had just disappeared amid the vines when his fingers brushed hard stone.

He groped about the hidden surface, heedless of the ravaging thorns. He touched metal and a jolt of excitement ran up his arm. Yetzer traced the outline of a metal boss then found a handle in its center. He wrapped his fingers about the handle and pulled.

Nothing happened.

He tightened his grip, settled back on his heels and tugged again. Still nothing. He was about to tear leaf from vine when Pharaoh's words rose in his memory.

Knock on any door, and it will open before you.

The king had spoken the words during dinner at the palace, the night Yetzer chose the temple over Ameniye. Yetzer set aside his longing for the princess, his thoughts of comfort and riches. It was for light he had chosen, and for light he was here. Following Pharaoh's advice, he adjusted his grip on the handle and knocked three times.

Silence filled the span of five heartbeats. Relief came with the soft rasp of metal upon stone. The grinding stopped and the throwing of a latch was followed by Yetzer's scream.

The paving stones dropped away, and Yetzer fell into the earth. His cries echoed within a shaft little more than an arm's span across. He had no time to examine the walls or to silence his shouts before he plunged into water. The impact jolted up his legs and spine. His scream turned to a gasp that sucked in water and choked his lungs.

Yetzer beat and kicked against death's fist that closed around him. He struggled to right himself, then burst through the surface. Still thrashing, he fought to keep his head within the life-giving air. He forced a calm he did not feel, commanded his breathing to slow and his flailing to cease.

"Help me," he shouted up the shaft.

Water choked his voice, so he coughed and called again. When the response came it was not the hoped-for assistance, but the grating of stone as the trapdoor rose back into position.

"No," Yetzer cried. "Don't leave me here."

The door slid inexorably shut. As daylight retreated, Yetzer frantically looked about for some means of escape, but between the water's surface and his freedom there was only the blank wall. The shaft went dark as the stones locked in place with a heartbreaking rumble that resounded through the well.

"Don't leave me." Yetzer's voice was scarcely above a whisper, but the shaft mocked him with the echoes of his plaintive sigh.

Panic nipped at his heart, and he fought to keep fear at bay. With clumsy strokes he pushed through the water until he found the wall. He felt along the stone above and below the surface, revealing only slime-slick rock. He treaded water and felt the walls all around the pool but found no handhold to aid his escape.

"Amun, strengthen me. Haru, give me light," he prayed to the gods of Kemet. As an afterthought, in case his father's gods might hear from Kenahn, he added, "Yah and Hadad, deliver me."

The gods remained distant, and Yetzer continued his futile circuit about the walls, the better to keep his thoughts occupied. As his muscles started burning, fear renewed its attack. His breath came faster, his panting amplified as the echoes built on one another. The sound added to his desperation and he felt reason slip. In the half-light, the faces of demons peered out from the rock walls, slavering with hunger and ready to devour …

Half-light? A glow that hadn't been there before now rose from the bottom of the pool. Yetzer tried to gauge the depth, but the weakness of the light and the featureless walls made the task impossible. Grasping at hope, he filled his lungs and ducked beneath the surface. He kicked and clawed at the water, but the light drew no closer. With the first spark of fire in his lungs, he turned upright and reached for the surface.

His gasps filled the well as he broached. Haunting laughter sounded in the echoes and he flailed his arms against whatever demons might have joined him in the pool. His eye and his thoughts cleared, and Yetzer found himself still alone. Still trapped.

With effort, he set reason above panic. He could struggle at the water's surface until his muscles gave out, or he could use what strength remained to him and again try to reach the source of the light. He might drown in the attempt, but that chance was better than the certainty of his fate if he did nothing.

"Ameniye, pray for me," he whispered into the void, then drew what might be his last breath, and dove beneath the surface.

11

Makeda

Red-tipped mountain peaks bathed in the sun goddess's glory, while the flat desert stagnated in gloom. I edged closer to the brooding embers of the campfire that Yanuf poked and coaxed and breathed back to life.

"That's the way," the old warrior said as a flame leapt from the slumbering coals. Yanuf encouraged the spark with bits of straw and, when those took up the fiery dance, added a small brick of dried goat's dung.

"The gods' best gift to man, fire." Yanuf stretched his hand over the growing flames. "It lights the dark, warms the cold, heats our food ... " He flexed his fingers and breathed a sigh. "And loosens old joints."

Yanuf cast a smile my way. I wanted to smile back, but between my heart and lips the expression lost its way. My gaze held Yanuf's for the briefest of moments before falling again to the dancing flames.

"Aye, a fire's just the thing ... " Yanuf continued, but his voice faded to a drone as sorrow wrapped its heavy cloak about me.

My eyes drifted toward the camp's edge where Yanuf had tethered our donkeys and where, gleaming white in the predawn murk, my mother's shrouded body lay. Despite her being downwind of the fire, and despite the thick unguents that perfumed the death-wrappings, I couldn't miss the taint of death that hung on the air. My mother who, even when a slave, had ever smelled of olibanum and honey, now stank of rot and decay.

"But come now." Yanuf's words filtered through the folds of grief's mantle. "Shams awakens. We must greet her."

The warrior's knees creaked as he rose. He extended his hand toward me. His fingers were thick, the joints swollen, the nails caked with grime. But his was the only hand of kindness left in all the world. I grasped it with both of mine and pressed it to my forehead.

Yanuf gently squeezed my fingers, then cleared his throat. "Come," he said. "Mustn't keep the goddess waiting."

I nodded and followed him to the edge of the camp.

"Will you say the words, or should I?" Yanuf asked when we knelt before the brightening horizon.

With another squeeze of his fingers and a nod of my head, I silently urged him to say the prayer.

"Right, then."

Yanuf settled onto his haunches. He awkwardly prostrated himself, the stump of his missing arm twitching within its flaccid sleeve. I shuddered but lay prone beside him.

"Hail, the East," Yanuf said as he pushed himself back onto his knees.

I matched his movements, resting briefly on my heels before again stretching out upon the sand.

"Hail, the morning," Yanuf continued, and we again rose to our knees, paused, then prostrated once more.

"Hail, the dawn."

The old warrior hefted his bulk from the dirt a third time, then stretched his hand toward Shams's rising. He pointed his crossed index and middle fingers at the horizon, the other fingers and thumb tucked against his palm.

"Rise, O Shams, Queen of Heaven, Mother of Light. Cast off darkness, put away coldness, and of night make an ending."

His gruff voice faltered.

I glanced up to discover a sheen in his eyes. My throat tightened as Yanuf pressed on. I wished I could cry, that tears might cleanse my heart of grief, of guilt. Of anger.

"Bathe your children in warmth," Yanuf prayed. "Press us to your radiant bosom so that, when we cross over the mountains and pass beyond the sea, your glory may sustain us through the long sleeping, 'til we awaken with you in the new dawn."

The words squeezed my heart, but my eyes remained as dry as the bleak desertscape.

The first curve of the sun edged above the horizon. At the sight of the radiant goddess, fury welled in my breast. I glared at Shams who, with her heavenly companions, had taken away my mother and father and sister, as though their lives meant nothing. As though the gods had greater need of them than I.

I did not speak.

I refused to give voice to sadness, so held my tongue as I had since Mother had gone to the West. I simply stared into the rising disk in a test of will. Shams might blind me, might take my sight as she'd taken all else, but I refused to turn away or lower my eyes.

Where sorrow had been impotent, the brilliant light at last brought tears to my eyes. They blurred my sight even as they intensified the sun's wrath. Still I fixed my gaze, pitting my will against that of the goddess.

As though sensing my resolve, Shams at last relented. Her heat fell away from my face, and her burning glory began to fade.

With this small victory, I allowed my eyes to close, though the sun's image still shone behind my eyelids. I blinked several times until the rest of the world slowly came into view at the edges of my vision. When at last I could focus, it was to see Yanuf standing before me, his hand outstretched.

"Come, Shara," he said, calling me by the title of a princess of Saba. "We have far yet to go."

❈

Twilight again cloaked the land when Yanuf clucked his tongue and brought our small caravan to a halt. Lulled by the hot, still air and the rocking of my donkey's gait, I'd dozed fitfully through the day, but now came fully awake.

Shams had disappeared behind the mountains, but the rocky walls still radiated her warmth in contrast with the coolness that drifted off the eastern sands. The desert stretched toward the horizon in red and orange and purple dunes, littered with mounds of heaped stone and drifting sand.

The Place of the Dead.

A chill raced down my spine as I took in countless tombs filled with the bones of my father and his people, dating back untold generations. The tombs that would soon hold the bones and the flesh of my mother.

I slid off the donkey's back and patted its neck as I studied Yanuf. The guardian surveyed the field of tombs, combing his fingers through his beard and mumbling to himself as he looked from one featureless mound to another.

"Ah," he said at length, "that's the one."

He took the donkey's lead, and the animal followed Yanuf down the slope toward one of the tombs. I fell in alongside. "It's not much." He gestured toward the scattered tombs. "I don't even know if it's the way of her people, but she'll be with your father. I reckon that'll do."

His words struck a sour note with me. It hadn't occurred to me that the gods of Saba might gather their dead differently than the gods of Uwene. Mother had reigned as Mukarrib of all Saba, but when she'd sung it had been with the words and tunes of Uwene. When she'd prayed she called upon Ubasti, not Shams.

My heart trembled with the sudden thought that she might be lost among the sands of her adopted land, unable to return to the mountains and forests and rivers of the Song Land. For the first time since Mother died, I started to speak, to voice my fears. Before the words formed, Yanuf stopped the donkeys near one of the tombs.

"Come, my lady." His voice was soft as he lifted Mother from the donkey's back. "Your husband's bed awaits." He brought his lips close to her shrouded head to whisper something, then laid her before the tomb.

"I'll clear her place," he said, then climbed though a waist-high opening in the dry-stone wall of the tomb.

I rubbed my arms to smooth the bumps that sprang up on being left alone among the burial mounds. The breeze off the desert carried with it the songs of the dead. Their soft moans made me shiver. I hugged myself tighter against the chill and moved closer to the snorting donkeys.

A rattle punctuated the death-song. It took a moment for me to realize it came from my father's tomb. I stepped toward the opening, then reeled back as Yanuf suddenly appeared.

"There's a flask of oil and a flint in the pack, Shara," he said. "Would you fetch them for me?"

I nodded, my cheeks warm from being so easily startled. I found the items and passed them up to Yanuf.

A few moments later he reappeared, handed me the flask, then reached down and awkwardly lifted my mother through the tomb's mouth. After a short time he squeezed through the opening and rejoined me in the living world.

"I need you to light the lamp for her," Yanuf said with a nod toward his empty sleeve.

I glanced toward the tomb's mouth, black against a darkening landscape.

"Take your time," he added. "Tell her whatever you need. Athtar willing, we'll not be back this way for some years, so make your peace. I'll set up camp there." He gestured toward the higher ground at the foot of the mountains. "Follow the fire's light when you're through."

Yanuf turned and shambled through the sand with the donkeys, his shoulders a stooped silhouette against the waxing night.

The desert wind blew stronger, picking at the hem and sleeves of my robe. The dead raised their voices in weird harmony, and I scrambled through the opening into the solitary blackness of the tomb. I groped about until I found Yanuf's flint, then felt for the wick and struck a spark.

Mother's body appeared in the brief flash of light, long and slender beneath the linen. Her shrouded form stretched toward the far side of the tomb. I struck again. Another spark. A second glimpse of my mother. Had she moved?

The wick drew in the fire-seed and gave birth to a warm yellow flame. The lamp rinsed darkness from the stone walls, and created an oasis of life, a place for me to rest amid this desert of death. A desert whose occupants dwelt all about me.

From every side of the tomb, skulls gazed at me and my mother, the newcomer to this place of long sleeping. To one side of the low stone slab where Mother lay, a heap of remains sat apart from the others. Bits of cloth and flesh and hair clung to bones not yet yellowed with age or blackened by smoke. I made an obeisance to what had once been my father, and tried to fit the memory of his face around the gleaming skull.

Failing this, I took a deep breath of stale air then set about my final duty to my mother. Beginning at her feet, where the ends of the shroud came together, I untied the linen bindings and rolled back the upper cloth.

Mother's dark skin, damp with the unguent of oil and resin, glistened in the lamplight. Eyelids slightly parted and lips pursed, she looked as she had when taking in the sun on the roof of our tower house.

With trembling fingers I stroked Mother's cheek. Instead of soft, warm flesh I found the skin cold, hardened by the myrrh resin. A shell lay before me, as lovely and bereft of life as those brought from the desert by pilgrims, shells the elders claimed had once contained magnificent sea creatures.

My mother was gone. Perhaps she was with Ubasti, or in Shams's bright garden. Maybe she had altogether ceased to be, an echo that rang within the Wadi Dhanah for a time, then faded, never to return.

I shook away such gloomy musings and stood up straight. I was the shara, daughter of the Mukarribs of all Saba, and of untold generations before them. War had taken my father. Floodwaters had taken my mother and my sister. Peace had taken my very freedom. Only duty was left to me, and in that moment I embraced duty as tightly as ever I'd clung to my mother.

Following instructions given me by the old women of Maryaba, I placed my mother's left hand modestly over the base of her belly. I folded her right arm to place a hand over her left breast. All the while, I silently recited the sacred words.

Athtar, Father of Life, who from the earth's womb fashioned our bones and clothed them with flesh, whose breath enlivens the soul. Now draw back that breath and, with it, receive to your bosom your daughter Ayana, Shara of Uwene, Mukarrib of all Saba.

As I mouthed the final words, the lamp sputtered. I took a backward step to brace myself against a gust of wind that rushed from the tomb. The faltering light illumined Mother's face amid dancing shadows, her lips parted and quirked in the slightest of grins.

I looked from my mother to the tomb's black opening through which Athtar had drawn his breath, then back to Mother's husk.

"Goodbye, Umma." The words scratched my dry throat and tumbled from my lips. As they bounced off the stone walls, I heard in them the echo of my mother's song.

With the lamp still burning to keep vigil, I climbed out of the tomb and followed the glow of Yanuf's fire back to the realm of the living.

12

Yetzer

Fire raged in Yetzer's chest. Blackness nipped at the edges of his vision. He managed to reach the bottom of the well only to find the light emanating from a side tunnel that stretched away from the main shaft.

He clawed at the smooth walls of the tunnel barely wide enough to accommodate his shoulders. The tight confines made forward progress nearly impossible, but he kept his focus on the circle of light that shone before him. To turn back would mean failure and a slow, shameful death in the well. Assuming his breath would sustain him to the water's surface.

With his palms and heels he forced himself an ant's pace closer to the light. The light that shrank as his vision narrowed. The light that was now interspersed with shooting stars that streaked before Yetzer's sight.

The tunnel filled with the sound of escaping bubbles. Yetzer clamped his lips together, fighting the impulse of his lungs to expel spent air in exchange for fresh. He redoubled his efforts but managed only two more lurches forward before his lungs again rebelled. More bubbles fled, rushing along the tunnel's roof toward the light, as though unwilling to remain trapped with Yetzer in death. He fought the urge to inhale. His lungs demanded it, burned with the craving for life.

The ache in Yetzer's chest increased. It seemed as though Ammut, devourer of the dead, closed her crocodile jaws about him. Unwilling yet to be dragged to the underworld, Yetzer edged forward once more, again, and yet again. His lungs contracted a third time and the pearls of life danced away into the light. Yetzer felt his lips part, inviting the water to end his suffering. He closed his eye and the inner darkness blazed with streams of light and with the haloed figures of what must be custodians of the dead, come to escort him to the West.

As Yetzer gave his lungs leave to drink, his fingers brushed the tunnel wall. Rather than featureless stone, they reported a sharp corner. Yetzer's eye snapped open. He fought to hold back the fatal breath as his hands groped about the edge. With his last measure of strength, he pulled himself through the tunnel's opening.

Free of the stone cocoon, he took only a moment to right himself within this second pool. The light glowed strongly above him, and he pushed off the bottom, following his last bubbles upward until he burst through the surface. The sound of his hungry gasps resounded off the stone walls. His lungs drew breath after ravenous breath, devouring the air as a starving man might gorge himself on bread. When he'd given them their fill and his breathing slowed, Yetzer examined his surroundings.

The pool sat in a low-ceilinged chamber of rough-hewn stone. Candles of purest wax burned brightly from sconces, illuminating lifelike statues of animal-headed gods set in niches along the walls. Stone-carved steps led from the pool to a broad landing where a brazier sent trails of perfumed smoke toward a small hole in the ceiling. Yetzer swam to the stairway and dragged himself from the water. He crawled naked from the pool, his kilt and loincloth somehow lost.

Come to the tomb where lies the beloved of Amun.

Come to the place where the body lies without its ka.

The sound of men's voices echoed through the chamber. Their harmony resonated within Yetzer's breast and raised gooseflesh on his arms.

In the midst of the garden, in the rock-cut tomb

We seek him who was too soon taken from our midst.

The first singer emerged from a cleft in the rock. Yetzer tried to cover himself as best he could when he recognized Imtef, one of his priest-tutors. The man's nasally voice never failed to grate in Yetzer's ears as he delivered endless lectures on the goddess of justice and right-doing. But within this sacred space, his voice rose in harmony with those of his brother priests to celebrate Yetzer's return from death. Imtef's lessons stirred in Yetzer's heart and gave life to Mayat, the personification of balance.

Behind Imtef came eight more priests, including Huy, the hierophant and high priest of Amun. A leopard pelt hung loosely from his bony frame, but his voice rang clear and bright.

Why is his tomb disturbed, his sarcophagus laid open?
The winding cloths lie tangled, still damp with myrrh and olibanum.

The priests formed a semi-circle about the brazier, Huy in the middle.

Speak, O Djehuti, giver of words. Where is our brother gone?
Speak, Khnum and Khonsu. Speak, Mihos of Per-Bast.
You gods who stand beside the open tomb, say what has become of him we seek.

At the invocation of the gods' names, the hierophant gestured toward the statues in their niches. Yetzer's heart beat faster as, one by one, the statues came to life and stepped forward.

Djehuti, the ibis-headed god of writing and wisdom, gazed with black eyes past his long, curved beak. Ram-headed Khnum, potter of men's bodies, stood regal and stoic beside Khonsu, keeper of the night hours, whose youthful features bore the green pallor of death. Last came Mihos, lion-headed god of war, whose amber eyes glared hungrily at Yetzer.

Say the gods, the guardians of all man's ways,
He is not here. The one you seek has left this place.
Like Father Osaure, he has overcome the body's death.
How lovely to see, how pleasing to behold is the resurrected one.

The priests concluded their song, hands lifted in praise to Amun, the infinite All. The gods stood regal and unmoving. All eyes rested on Yetzer in silent expectation. He remembered the guard's instructions and slowly stood.

Yetzer hesitated to expose himself to the priests, let alone the gods, but the requisite gestures gave him little choice. He raised his left hand in pantomime of the Hermit's lantern. His right he stretched forward, as if holding a walking staff. He slid his left foot forward then spoke the password.

"*Hreri.*"

Gods and priests alike matched Yetzer's stance and spoke the word in reply.

The hierophant stepped forward and the others lowered their arms. Huy gestured for Yetzer to do the same. "Yetzer abi-Huram," the high priest intoned, "you have passed the tests of the postulant. You have crossed the threshold of the initiates, and you have withstood the trial of the Well of Souls."

Huy reached under the altar and withdrew a bundle. He stepped toward Yetzer and unfolded an apron made of lambskin.

"In water and blood were you born into the world of flesh. So have you been cleansed and reborn of water into the world of light. Your first birth came through the desire of your father and the labor of your mother. This rebirth is the result of your own desire for knowledge and the labors of your body and will."

The hierophant tied the apron around Yetzer's waist.

"You stand self-created within the shrine of Amun, who founded his own existence out of chaos." Huy stepped back to his place behind the altar. "The path of creation, of reintegration with the All, is fraught with danger, to your body and to your *ka*. You have tasted this danger. Your fortitude and endurance have preserved you where many have failed. Few survive the Well of Souls. Fewer still pass the challenges that lie before you."

"Quit now," one of the priests hissed. Ptah-Hor was a fat man who instructed the postulants in the nature and order of the stars. Yetzer wondered how the rotund priest had ever passed through the narrow tunnel beneath the well. "Be a slave," the man continued, "but live."

"He has no business here to begin with." Merisutah, a rat-faced priest who taught numbers, glared at Yetzer and pointed to his own left eye. "Only those whole in body may attain the priesthood."

The other priests joined in the debate. Some urged Yetzer to spare himself further danger. Others argued against his right even to have joined the postulants, let alone the initiates. Huy and the gods stood silent and expressionless throughout. When the priests had finished their litany and Yetzer felt himself wilting under their judgments, the hierophant spoke.

"You have heard the concerns of the brethren," he said. "How do you respond?"

Yetzer chased after thoughts that darted like rabbits.

"I am only a poor widow's son," he said as he snared a line of reasoning. "What little I had and the much I might have gained, I gave up to enter these halls in search of light. You yourself summoned me here," he told Huy, "you who stand before the All. If the high priest of Amun deems me worthy, I stand under his judgment."

Yetzer fixed his gaze on Merisutah. "I have but one eye, it is true," he said, "but the eye is merely a window through which to view the world. It is the heart that sees, and study and meditation perfect that vision. In truth," he added, "does not the great god Haru have but one eye? Yet none contests his right to stand among the gods and the holy ones."

Merisutah grunted.

"As to the dangers that lie in wait," Yetzer continued, "to quit now is to become a slave. I have sacrificed much—have nearly sacrificed all—to stand before you, to pursue that light which illumines the heart. I will continue that pursuit, whether the journey be completed in this life or carry me into the next. In that light is freedom, and I would rather die in the finding of it than live a slave for its abandonment."

The priests stared in silence at Yetzer. Afraid he'd spoken too boldly, he opened his mouth to emend his reply, then closed it again. If he was to be enslaved, it would be for speaking truth, not for equivocating.

"Brethren," the high priest said, "you have heard the reply of the candidate. What say you? Shall he be admitted to the trials?"

"Yes," said Imtef, a slight curl at the corner of his mouth.

"Yes," said another, and another, until seven of the priests had given their blessings.

"Brother Merisutah?" the hierophant prompted.

The priest twitched his nose and studied Yetzer through sharp black eyes. "If he wishes to chase after light in the afterlife, so be it. I daresay he'll be dead or in shackles ere he leaves this place. Yes."

"And I say yes," Huy said before Yetzer could interject. "The candidate has passed the first trial and has gained the approval of the brethren, yet even greater tests lie ahead. In the trials, as in life, one is never truly alone. Others have gone before and share your journey, in spirit if not in body." The hierophant gestured toward the priests on either side of him. "All who stand here have completed the journey you now undertake. You may choose one to serve as guide and companion. Yetzer abi-Huram, in whom do you trust?"

The question startled Yetzer. He hadn't anticipated help on his quest. The priests were all able instructors but, given the nature of the Well of Souls, he questioned how much aid fat Ptah-Hor or feeble Huy would be.

The hierophant raised a painted eyebrow, urging a response.

"I choose Djehuti," Yetzer blurted his half-considered response.

Huy's eyes narrowed, but his lips pressed into a slight grin.

"Your trust being in the god, your faith is well founded." He gestured toward the niche where the ibis-headed god had first stood. "Follow your conductor and fear no evil. But be forewarned."

Yetzer paused midstride and looked back at the high priest.

"The gods do not speak directly to man. They may whisper to the heart, but each of us must infer for ourselves what it is they say."

Yetzer nodded, took a deep breath, then followed the god into darkness.

13

Bilkis

Bilkis cradled a weeping Rahab, while Auriyah and his men collected the remaining Bedou, or Nabati, as they called these northern tribesmen. Dead or soon to be, the men were stripped, staked alongside the caravan trail, and castrated. When the vultures came to peck at their eyes and the bloody roots of their manhood, a clear message would be sent to Nabati and trader alike.

This road was under Auriyah's protection.

The caravanners gathered up the bodies of Leah and the servants who had fallen. They wrapped them in shrouds, gently loaded them upon the donkeys, and set out with the warriors along the northward road. Bilkis rode alongside her warrior-prince, and soon the caravan reached a land called Edom, where the yellow desert gave way to red mountains. Allied to Yisrael's King Tadua, the country's roads were patrolled and guarded by Auriyah's band of Hatti fighters.

Though the caravan had traded mercantile garb for funereal, Bilkis was unable to truly share their grief. Certainly, she was sorry for Rahab and Abram and Eliam. Leah had been nothing but an old she-wolf, but the others had been kind and merited her sympathy.

But she had no space in her heart for the sadness of others, and often had to hide her face so her laughter, brought on by Auriyah's jests or tales of adventure, might be perceived as cries of mourning.

While Bilkis sat with the prince that first evening, he confessed to being an exile, banished from Yisrael. Bilkis was appalled that Auriyah had been accused of murdering his half-brother, their father's heir. She was still more shocked when he admitted to the crime.

"He was a pig," Auriyah told her, adding, "Yah's peace be upon him. He defiled my sister, the daughter of his father. The swine then refused to marry her when she came with child. I delivered the justice my father would not, the justice demanded by Yah's law."

"And what of your sister?" Bilkis had asked.

"Tamar?" Auriyah shrugged. "Her bastard, the spawn of perversion, could not be allowed to draw breath. I cut the abomination from her womb, even as I cut out the branch of its father by the root. Tamar did not survive the purification."

A shiver raced down Bilkis's spine. Despite her misgivings, Auriyah soon again had her enthralled with his humor and charm. As she rode beside him and the plain gave way to deep canyons that gouged the earth, Bilkis forgot her qualms. By the time the war band led the caravan into Sela, Edom's capital city, Bilkis was sure her rightful place was by the side of the golden prince.

Seven days after arriving at the capital—a city of red stone dwellings cut from the living rock—Bilkis took that place. Beneath a canopy of blue and white—the colors of Auriyah's tribe—she became the Princess of all Yisrael.

Immediately following the ceremony, a bevy of old women escorted Bilkis to the bridal chamber. They bathed her, spread a new, white fleece upon a bed of goatskins, and left her to await her bridegroom. Excitement and dread were her only companions. Each in its turn whispered to her heart, her blood running hot then cold, then hot again. The turns of mood soon had her exhausted, as impatience and irritation joined her bridal party.

The oil lamps had nearly burned dry by the time a staggering, foul-smelling Auriyah burst into the chamber. So violent was his entry, the wooden door tore from its leather hinges. Bilkis screamed and tried to cover herself when the Hatti warriors stumbled in after their captain.

Auriyah made no effort to send his men away or to replace the door. He stalked toward the bed and tore away the covers, leaving Bilkis with only her hands to cover her shame.

"Do not hide yourself from me, woman," Auriyah snarled, then struck her across the face with the back of his hand.

Bilkis was too stunned to resist as he grasped her hips and spun her facedown. Her cries of protest were drowned out by the laughter of the warriors, then silenced by a bolt of pain as Auriyah entered her. As quick as he was violent, the prince made two sharp thrusts. With the third, he pulled Bilkis's hair so hard her head snapped back. She feared her scalp would rend as he held her tight to him. Auriyah shuddered, loosed his grip, and fell atop Bilkis before she could wrest herself away.

Still laughing, a pair of Auriyah's men peeled their captain from his bride. Another tugged the fleece from underneath Bilkis, spinning her hard against the rock wall as he did so. Without a glance at the humiliated bride, the Hatti warriors ushered the prince from the chamber.

A cheer rose from outside as the last man raised the banner of Auriyah's virility, stained with the mingling of royal seed and virgin blood. Inside, Bilkis's heart raced with terror and shame. Back against the wall, she hugged her knees to her chest. Her ruptured maidenhead shed tears of blood that seeped warm from her hidden place. She trembled while the gleeful shouts of men and women spilled through the open doorway, accompanied by a high-pitched keen. Distorted shadows danced upon her walls, seeming demons from the Pit come to claim her soul as Auriyah had claimed her purity.

She shut her eyes against the wretched figures, but her heart fed her inner vision with images even more fearsome. What if Auriyah returned? What if he sent his men to take their pleasure with her as well?

A hand touched her on the shoulder. Heedless of her nakedness, Bilkis screamed and struck at her assailant, a slight figure draped in black robe and veil. The black-clad arms first crossed in defense, then stretched out, hands grasping her flailing wrists.

"Bilkis, stop." A reedy voice filtered through the din in her ears. "My sister, it is only Rahab. Stop this."

Though Bilkis continued to struggle, her resistance waned as recognition dawned. With gentle strength, Rahab wrapped an arm about Bilkis's shoulders.

"You're shaking," Rahab observed, and pulled a goatskin around Bilkis. "Have you caught a fever just after your wedding night?"

Rahab pressed her hands against Bilkis's forehead and cheek. She swept back the new bride's hair from her eyes.

"What has happened to you, Sister?" she said, her voice muffled by her hands over her mouth.

"My husband." Bilkis spat the word out and pulled the goatskin more tightly about her. "This is how a prince of the Habiru welcomes his bride on their wedding night."

The younger girl placed a hand on the tender cheek, her cool skin drawing out the heat.

"Did he ..." Rahab began, then lowered her eyes. "Did he hurt you?"

"Of course he hurt me," Bilkis snapped back. "He struck me, then took me like a whore in front of his men."

Rahab's eyes widened and glistened with tears. "Oh, Bilkis—" She did not finish the thought. Whatever she might have said was lost amid her sobs. Bilkis's pain fell away like a veil, and she reached out to Rahab and drew her into an embrace.

"Hush, little sister," she said when Rahab's outburst lessened enough that she might hear. "It is not so bad as that. I'm sure all wives must endure such treatment from time to time."

"Why would he treat you so?"

Bilkis shrugged. "He is a man. Men take what they need with little thought of the cost to others."

"But he is a prince," Rahab protested.

"Yes, and perhaps a king one day. He is not bound to take only what he needs, but whatsoever he desires. Such is the way of nobility."

"Might he take it of me?" Rahab's voice was little more than a whisper.

Bilkis took Rahab by the shoulders and held her at arm's length. She ignored the goatskin that slid down about her waist.

"Why do you say such a thing? What has he done?"

"He—he bought me from Abba," Rahab stammered. "He paid your bride price, then offered half as much again to take me as your handmaid."

"And your father agreed to this?" Bilkis's cheeks grew warm.

"He did not want to, but Auriyah is a prince of Yisrael. My bond price would make up Abba's loss from this journey. Besides, I—"

"You what?" Bilkis demanded. She despised Auriyah for his treatment of her yet felt jealousy's claws scratching at her heart.

"I do not wish to be separated from you," Rahab said, surprising Bilkis as the girl's eyes filled with new tears. "I have only just lost my mother. I could not bear so soon to lose my sister as well."

Bilkis blinked dry eyes then clutched Rahab to her bosom. "You are truly a flower among brambles," she whispered in Rahab's ear. "You honor me with your devotion, but will your father not need you?"

"He has Abram and his servants to manage affairs. When he looks at me, it is only with sadness. If he has need of a woman in his tent, it is as a wife, not a daughter." Rahab sat up straight, wiped her eyes on her mourning veil and shook her head. "The best service I can provide as a daughter is to be bonded to Auriyah. To you."

"You show Havah's own wisdom," Bilkis said with a smile. "It shall be as you say. But you come into my household as my sister, not as a servant."

14

Yetzer

Hot air engulfed him. Through the tunnels Yetzer followed his guide as each step took them deeper into the earth, into searing heat that scorched his lungs. The pair walked in silence, but Yetzer's heart thrummed with questions and misgivings.

Yetzer had first assumed this manifestation of Djehuti to be a priest with an elaborate headdress. The ibis mask must make breathing difficult, yet his guide moved with even steps and apparent ease. Yetzer wondered if his companion was something more than a man. Perhaps he was truly the god incarnate.

He gritted his teeth and tried to mute his fears. As the heat increased and each breath became a greater struggle, his duty to silent obedience grew more challenging. Was he being punished for his impertinence? Had he failed some secret test and was now being led to his doom?

Still they forged ahead until they reached a chamber bright with flames. Yetzer's pace faltered at the inferno's threshold. Djehuti walked through, unfazed by the molten sea beneath his feet or the flames dancing about his head. In fewer than a dozen strides, he passed the fiery vault and disappeared through a doorway at the far end.

Yetzer struggled to reason. If his guide were only a man, Yetzer should be able to follow in his footsteps. If, however, it truly was the god, there was no certainty of surviving the test. As in the pool, the choice was between likely death by going on and certain death by staying. He stepped forward.

The flames did not consume him. The air was hotter than a noonday quarry, but that was all. He took another step and realized the chamber was filled with mirrors, all reflecting the light of a small fire that burned strongly but safely in one corner of the room.

Yetzer laughed. His voice echoed off walls shaped to magnify every sound, such that the crackle of the modest flame became a roar. He paced to the end of the chamber, stepped through the doorway then reeled back.

The path ended at a black abyss. No ledge ringed the pit, no trail by which he might skirt around it. Only a sheer drop into nothingness. Yetzer looked for some hidden rope or handhold by which he might continue. Finding none, he stretched his sight into the darkness. The black walls absorbed all light, their secrets hidden.

A small explosion made Yetzer spin around. Oil streamed from an opening near the fire, catching flame as it passed. The fiery stream caught hold of the wicker frames of the mirrors, and soon the entire room was ablaze. The inferno flowed toward Yetzer. He turned back to the pit, and the fire's light revealed hope within the blackness. As the approaching wave singed his heels, Yetzer leapt into the void.

Pain seared his hands as he slid down a rope suspended within the pit. He jarred against a knot and dangled in the void as flames spilled over the edge where he had stood only moments before. Liquid fire plunged into the depths but spent its fuel before reaching the bottom of the shaft.

With nowhere to go but down, Yetzer wrapped his feet about the rope and found it knotted at regular intervals. He lowered himself into the depths, scanning the walls and seeking some hint of the way his guide might have gone. He passed the limits of the falling oil, but no escape revealed itself. The rope slipped between his feet, and his hands bit into the last knot, but still no hope appeared.

Even as he dangled on the end of the line, the light from the fire dimmed. The flow of oil ceased, leaving only the glow from the chamber's doorway. Even that began to fade, and darkness tightened its grip on Yetzer.

A hint of myrrh on the air caught his attention. Yetzer frantically searched the walls in the last vestiges of light.

There. Perhaps eight cubits below him—more than twice his height—the black wall showed an even blacker opening. Yetzer swung his feet in that direction, then toward the opposite side until he had enough momentum to reach the opening.

The fire breathed its last, and darkness flooded the shaft.

Yetzer screamed as he let go of the rope and flew into oblivion. He fell for eons, but his blood pulsed only twice before he skidded along a rough surface. His head struck rock. Pain flashed through his vision, the only light in the space.

He eased himself into a sitting position, fighting dizziness. Stretching out his arms, he found he could reach both sides of the tunnel. He shifted onto his knees and slowly stood. The tunnel's ceiling brushed his head, but he needed only a slight stoop to keep clear. He took a deep breath. Reassured by the stronger scent of myrrh and spices, he moved into the darkness, tracing his hands along the walls then sweeping a foot in front of him, ensuring there was solid floor ahead.

After fifteen paces, the path turned left and angled upward. Another fifteen strides, and the path veered right. Yetzer's heart leapt as the tunnel's end shone in twilight. He increased his pace, still taking care lest the floor drop away beneath him.

The incense grew stronger as Yetzer reached the illuminated wall and found a doorway behind a thick scarlet veil. He pushed aside the curtain and stepped through.

He hadn't known what to expect. He might have anticipated a shrine like the first, with altar and candles, incense and priests, but he was not prepared for this.

Carpets lined a small room as richly appointed as any in Pharaoh's palace. Soft light filled the space from golden lamps. Along one wall, an ebony bed frame supported a thick mattress. In front of this, a low table held bowls of fruit, platters of meat, and pitchers of wine.

Yetzer's eye caught movement across the room. He stepped back at the sight of two men standing beside a large copper basin. The men sported the shaved heads and simple linen kilts common to all who lived within the temple precinct. The bronze bands at ankle and wrist and neck proclaimed them slaves.

Recognition was slow to come, but when it did Yetzer's jaw went slack. The pair had been fellow postulants, chosen within the past month to undergo their own trials of initiation. Each had shown promise, yet their presence here suggested they had somehow failed the tests.

The slaves gestured toward the basin filled with steaming water. A side table held salts and soap, along with thick towels. One of the men took Yetzer's soot-stained apron, and the slaves departed.

Yetzer sprinkled in a handful of salts, then slipped into the basin. The hot water steeped into his muscles and soothed his weary heart. The bath had grown tepid by the time Yetzer's rumbling stomach roused him. He scrubbed himself clean, then stepped out of the tub.

Wrapping one of the towels about his waist, he moved to the table of food. Judging by his stomach's protests, it had been days since he'd last eaten, and he helped himself accordingly. When he'd had his fill of duck and melon and wine, exhaustion settled over him and he stretched out on the bed.

"Yetzer?"

The voice stirred him and his eye floated open.

"Yetzer," he again heard, this time accompanied by a stroke on his cheek. He turned toward the voice and his heart seized.

Ameniye.

Pharaoh's daughter smiled as their eyes met. She stepped back from him and Yetzer's eye drank in the view.

Framed by lustrous black hair, Ameniye's face had been expertly painted to accentuate her doe eyes, high cheeks, and full lips. Yetzer's gaze descended past slender shoulders to where the straps of her gown crossed between her small, flawless breasts. Below her waist, the thin linen did little to conceal the dark pattern of womanhood at the base of her flat belly.

Yetzer forgot his weariness and rose from the bed. He took Ameniye in his arms and pressed her to his chest. His lips found hers, their passion as water for one who had been too long in the desert.

"How are you here?" he said, the words muffled by kisses.

Ameniye giggled and pulled away from him. "You have passed your trials," she said, her eyes alight, "and I am your reward."

Yetzer squeezed her hands between his. "Your father knows of this? He has approved?"

Ameniye's eyes darted away for an instant. "He will. All has been arranged.

But is it Father you've been thinking of all these months? I've thought only of this."

She removed the clasp that fastened the straps of her gown to the bodice. The sheer dress slid down her body, and Ameniye unhitched the towel from Yetzer's waist. As his linen joined hers, she pushed him back onto the bed and lay atop him. "Now, sage," she said in a low, throaty voice, "take your reward."

Yetzer wrapped his arms about her, but Ameniye spun away when three sharp raps sounded from the doorway. A pair of guards entered the chamber followed by the line of priests. Ameniye pulled up the bedclothes while Yetzer tried to cover his arousal.

Huy stepped forward. His eyes turned to Ameniye, and his expression flashed from confusion to recognition to rage. With visible effort, he restored his neutral mask.

"Yetzer abi-Huram," he said, "you have passed the threshold of the initiates and have completed the trials of the four base elements, of water and fire, air and earth."

Yetzer nodded but wondered—with no little annoyance—why the acclamation couldn't have waited until after he'd claimed his reward.

"You have failed, however, the trial of the fifth element, of your own nature."

"But I passed all the tests," Yetzer objected. "My reward was—"

"The candidate will remain silent," Merisutah snapped. The rat-faced priest could scarcely contain his mirth as he added, "I beg the hierophant's pardon. Continue, Master Huy."

The high priest did not acknowledge Merisutah, but kept his sad eyes focused on Yetzer. "You came to these chambers in search of what?"

"More light," Yetzer answered, defiance draining from his voice and from his heart.

"And you were instructed to remain steadfast in your quest until you had attained that goal," Huy reminded him. "Have you attained it?"

Yetzer's eye misted as he recognized his failure.

"Answer the hierophant," Merisutah commanded him.

"No," Yetzer said, his voice tight.

"No." Huy's voice was tinged with regret. "No, you have not. And you have been well apprised of the cost of failure."

Yetzer looked to Ameniye, her face as lovely and expressionless as a statue. He turned back to Huy and nodded his acknowledgment.

Merisutah gestured to the guards. They hauled Yetzer off the bed and pinioned him between them. Five of the priests stepped forward, each with a bronze band. Yetzer offered no resistance as they fastened them around his ankles, wrists, and neck.

Bile rose in Yetzer's throat as Merisutah revealed a mallet and a handful of pins, knelt before Yetzer, and hammered the pins into the hasps of the shackles. Yetzer clenched his teeth against the pain, resolved to accept his fate—his failure—without complaint.

"You are now counted among the nameless ones," Huy intoned as Merisutah attacked Yetzer's wrist bands. "For you there is no longer name nor remembrance, none to remind you to the gods when you stand before the scales of judgment."

The metal collar struck Yetzer's chin as Merisutah drove in the final pin. Blood trickled along Yetzer's jaw and neck, but he made no sound, took no effort to wipe it away.

"So shall it be unto all who vainly seek to climb the mountain of the gods," the hierophant continued as the last stroke of the mallet sealed Yetzer's fate.

Huy stepped aside and the priests formed lines on either side of the passageway. One of the guards prodded Yetzer with the butt of his spear. As Yetzer moved to go, he caught the unmistakable gleam of triumph in Merisutah's eyes as he cast a wink toward Ameniye.

Yetzer's stomach churned as he finally understood. He wanted to turn back, to see the truth in her eyes, to curse her. But what right had a slave to look upon a princess? Instead, he lowered his gaze, passed the gauntlet of priests, and stepped into deepest darkness.

15

Bilkis

At Auriyah's command, his men and the remnants of Eliam's party left rock-hewn Sela. The warrior rode beside Bilkis as he had along the desert trail. Before Sela. Before he'd shown her what marriage truly was. If he noticed her unease, he showed no sign of it. The prince joked and laughed and regaled his bride with stories, as though nothing amiss had passed between them.

"My father charged me to bring him the foreskins of a hundred raiders," Auriyah told her, "as the blood-price for my brother." The exiled prince spat, then patted the reeking, blood-soaked bags tied behind him. "I bring him two hundred phalluses," he gravely pronounced. "Let us see what that buys me."

Auriyah kept apart from her during the nights, standing watch with his men. Still, Bilkis slept poorly, afraid that any little sound might signal her husband's approach.

Each morning she mounted her donkey. Each evening, the caravan made a new camp, its ranks increased by the Habiru who flocked to Auriyah's banner. Fewer than a score had left Sela. More than a hundred now rode in celebration toward another great city.

"Ebiren," Auriyah said as they approached the stone walls. "Where our ancestors are buried, and where our kings are made."

That news meant little to Bilkis, but she rejoiced when the prince told her they would tarry there a fortnight, until the new moon. Her backside would not miss the donkey.

Over the next several days Auriyah met with Yisrael's priests and tribal elders. By night the people reveled at their prince's return. After one such night of feasting and drinking, Auriyah again forced himself on his bride, though without his men present.

The next morning, as the slender crescent of the new moon faded, Auriyah knelt with one hand on an altar of stone, the other on the head of a calf. The senior priest—a lean, bent-framed man called Abdi-Havah, with one eye milky white, the other black as onyx—slaughtered the calf, mixed its blood with olive oil and spices, and anointed Auriyah's head and the stone. The cloying scent of olibanum from Saba fouled Bilkis's nostrils even as it tugged at her heart and memories.

She had little time for homesickness, however. With the sounding of rams' horns and shouts of acclamation, Auriyah was proclaimed king over Yisrael. Bilkis, as his first wife—*Of how many to come?* she distantly wondered—was named Queen, and the pair were paraded around the tomb of the patriarchs in a canopied litter.

Auriyah came to her bed again that night, this time sober. Though Bilkis at first resisted, Auriyah cajoled her as a rider with a skittish horse. She discovered that her husband, when not corrupted with wine or beer, could be a generous lover. Throughout the long night they explored and pleasured one another, and Bilkis at last learned the bliss that every bride should know.

❁

Bilkis shifted uncomfortably. The fibers of the donkey's blanket stabbed through her silk robe, pricking her backside. The lumbering gait made matters worse, adding new stings and jarring her bladder with each step.

But she could only smile and nod. Hundreds, thousands of peasants lined the road, cheering and waving palm fronds. Auriyah's men separated the caravan from the crowd on either side of the road, but they couldn't shield Bilkis from the noise or the stench.

Auriyah's father had captured the city and made it his capital more than twenty years before. He'd invited settlers from all the Habiru tribes and the neighboring peoples, and now their crumbling hovels lined the hillside of Urusalim, outside the walls of Tsion, the king's city.

King Tadua. Bilkis looked toward the north, the horizon marred by the dust raised by the king and his court as they fled the city. The cheers of the people and Auriyah's laughter took Bilkis's attention from the cowardly Tadua. "What is it they're shouting?" she asked Auriyah, who again rode beside her. "What does it mean?"

The new king's grin widened. "*Hoshiahna*," he repeated. "Literally, it is a prayer for deliverance, but here—" he gestured toward the crowd.

"It means their savior has come," Bilkis finished the sentence.

Auriyah nodded. "Their excitement will fade in a few days' time, when the fields must again be tended. But while the people celebrate, they are full of love for their king and queen."

"As they loved their old king and his queens?" Bilkis asked with a smile.

Auriyah's face darkened at the jest. Bilkis laughed and placed a hand against his cheek.

"A jest, Husband," she said. "I'm certain your people will love you until the sun no longer graces the noonday sky."

Fury bled from the king's cheeks, and his good humor returned. Auriyah took Bilkis's hand and squeezed it. "I have indeed chosen well in my queen. Who else could learn my humors so quickly, or so easily tame them?"

He leaned over to kiss Bilkis. The cheers of the crowd redoubled in approval. Auriyah raised Bilkis's hand in his and waved with his other.

"They do love us," the young king said, so softly the words might have been only for himself. "And they will continue to love us. We will give them feasts. We will fill their shrines with olibanum. The fragrance will perfume the highest heavens. Yah will draw near to his people, and they will bless the king who restored their god's favor."

He released Bilkis's hand, spread his arms and leaned back, his face toward the sky. The crowd's voices grew louder still at their king's display. As the sun brightened his features and his oiled skin shone with the radiance of red gold, even Bilkis felt a reverent awe.

Yes, Auriyah was a man, and a flawed one. But were not all men flawed? And did not the gods still choose flawed men to enact their will?

The procession rounded the last turn before the city's gate. The entrance to Urusalim was wide enough only for two donkeys abreast. Auriyah's Hatti guards slowed to scan the walls before hurrying the king and his queen through the gates.

The hovels of wood and mudbrick gave way to stone houses. The crowd, too, transformed from malnourished peasants in rough woolens to well-fed gentry wrapped in dyed linens and silks. The reception from this new crowd struck Bilkis with its politeness, formality and—fear?

Unlike the rabble outside the gates, the people who lined the streets of the upper city must have fared well under Tadua. Not so well to have felt the need to flee with their old king, but well enough to worry how the new one might affect their comfortable lives.

Bilkis smiled. The peasants would love their new queen, of that she was certain. The poor were ever satisfied with beauty and novelty and little more, so long as that little was enough to fend off starvation. Yes, the poor of Urusalim would cherish their handsome new king and his beautiful queen. They would bless them before their gods for the gift of scraps from the royal table.

But Bilkis's smile was not for the adoration of the poor. It was the uncertainty of the wealthy that brought the curve to her mouth. These—the merchants and landholders, priests and scholars—these were the ones whose fortunes relied on stability, and they would give much to retain enough.

Bilkis nodded reassuringly to the plump, half-hearted celebrants. These were the hearts and the purses she would win. While Auriyah secured his kingdom, Bilkis would secure stability for these, her people. In return, they would keep food on her table, roses in her bathwater, and silk in her wardrobe. She would be their queen, and they would learn to love her.

As if sensing her benevolence, the crowd cheered more heartily. Soaking in their adoration, Bilkis spread her arms and, in imitation of Auriyah's display before the peasants, raised her face to the heavens.

A cloud passed before the sun, shielding Bilkis from the harsh glare. Her throat tightened and her heart filled with gratitude at the omen. She had never given much credence to the tales of the gods. Nevertheless, here in a strange city of the far-distant north, the sun goddess Shams showed her blessing to the daughter of Saba. The young queen sat up straighter as her donkey passed through a second gate into the palace of Tadua. Now Auriyah's palace.

Soon to be the palace of Bilkis bat-Saba.

A SONG OF BECOMING

16
Yetzer

Stinging flies darted about the quarry. Their drone underscored men's grunts, accompanied by slaps and curses as the pests alighted on exposed flesh. Yetzer swung his pick with the other men, but there was no common rhythm among them. Two years had passed since he'd last seen a quarry, but his muscles retained the memory of his father's steady pace.

Upon the snow-capped Leban mountains, he sang, then drove his pick into the rock. *Where earth-mother meets sky-father.* Swing.

The impact of copper on limestone coursed up Yetzer's arms and into his chest but could not dislodge the shame from his heart.

Even where heaven stoops to the ground. Swing.

Ameniye's betrayal. His inability to resist her, to stay his path. Merisutah's glee at Yetzer's failure. These and a hundred other evils pulsed through his blood like venom.

I met my love among the cedars. Swing.

"Faster!"

The incongruously high voice of the overseer was followed by the toneless whistle of his flail. Slave-laborers moved just fast enough to avoid earning the lash. Yetzer thought to look for whoever had fallen short but had only enough strength to focus on the stone beneath his pick.

Knotted lashes tore into his shoulders. Claws of white heat raked down his spine as a cry escaped his lips. The pick fell from his hands. Another whistle announced a lancing pain across his lower back.

"Take up that pick," the overseer shouted. "Work, dog. Keep up the pace."

Yetzer's temper flared, but he forced himself to remain calm, to remember his place. This was no lodging of free masons like his father had led. He was a slave, a nameless one, no longer a man but an animal to be treated as his masters saw fit. If he chanced to forget, his chafing, burning skin beneath the sun-heated manacles was a steady reminder.

He stooped to retrieve his pick. Bright spots shot through his vision as he swung the tool. The overseer's curse and another stroke of the lashes across his thighs made it clear that Yetzer must endure the pain or be slowly flayed, strip by bloody strip. He clenched his jaw, squeezed his eye shut to clear his vision, then heaved his pick.

Again and again, he swung the blade through its arc toward the rock. Sweat streamed down his back, seeped into his wounds, but Yetzer ignored the salt-sting. He ignored the flies that lapped at his blood, ignored the spittle from the overseer's curses. There was only copper and stone, with Yetzer in between. His failure had shaped his destiny. His fate was to shape this rock.

And so he raised the pick and swung again.

❖

Respite came as the sun settled on the horizon. With the sounding of a ram's horn, the picks fell silent, and Yetzer joined the stream of nameless ones as they spilled out of the quarry. He left his pick along with the others in the closely guarded racks, then trudged along to a field of dirt encircled by sheaves of thorns and straw. At the entrance of the enclosure sat a small cart loaded with the slaves' dinner.

Yetzer ignored the ache in his muscles and the fire of his wounds as he awaited his reward, a shallow clay bowl containing a gruel of chickpeas and a piece of coarse bread with bits of grinding stone among the weevils.

The meal seemed scarcely enough to feed a scribe, let alone a laborer. Yetzer took the food without complaint, stepped into the holding pen, and found a clear patch of ground upwind of the latrine scratched into the earth at one end of the corral.

"The singing quarryman," a thin voice said.

Yetzer looked up to see a wraith, as grey and bony as the skeleton in the temple's Hall of the Body. He blinked, but the apparition refused to fade as any well-behaved specter should. It simply stood there, a chipped-tooth smile beaming from a wizened face wreathed by wispy white hair. Its eyes were sunken almost as deeply as the hollow cheeks, but shone with curiosity and compassion that told Yetzer this was no phantom.

"Fresh from the temple, are you?" the old man said.

Yetzer hesitated before nodding.

"Reckoned as much. Too well fed to be a debtor. And you don't have the look of a criminal about you. That leaves the temple or Pharaoh's court. Don't mind if I sit."

The old man settled to the ground with surprising grace.

"How do you know I'm not from court?" Yetzer said. He took a bite of bread and carefully chewed around the stones.

"I suppose it's possible," the old man said with a shrug. "We'll get them from time to time. A baker who cooks like this." He rattled his bread against his bowl. "A wine steward who spills in some noble's lap. A courtier who stares too long at the wazir's lady, hmm?" He waggled his hairless brows. "But, no, you're not pretty enough for court, and you know how to work. That leaves the temple."

Yetzer couldn't fault the man's reasoning. He grunted and sipped at his gruel. The talk of court sent his memories chasing after Ameniye. He could almost hear her laughter, smell her perfume, taste her lips. See the knowing smirk on her face as he was shackled and led away.

"How far did you get?" The reedy voice ruptured Yetzer's memory, and he nearly spat out his gruel.

"What?" he demanded.

"In the temple. How far?" The old man wrapped his arms around his legs and rested his chin upon knobby knees. "I've heard of men stuck in that cave for days. Seen them scarred from the fire chamber. Me? They'd probably have had to fish my body out of the water tunnel. How far?"

"I'm not permitted to speak of it," Yetzer said. "I took a vow."

The old man scoffed. "A vow? Much good that did you. What of their vows? Put a man through unspeakable tortures, and for what? To become a slave? To be beaten by a creature not fit to lace your sandals? What obligation can you still have to men like that?"

Yetzer considered that. It had been a cruel test. But for a few slim chances, he might have left the temple a corpse rather than a slave. To use Ameniye to snare him, however—that had been cruelest of all. Still, hadn't Huy warned him of the trials? Hadn't he said Yetzer would leave enlightened, enslaved, or embalmed? Fair or not, Yetzer had failed the greatest trial and received his due. The priest had kept his word, and Yetzer would do no less. He shrugged.

"As you will," the old man said. "It's not my concern. Never let it be said that Sinuhe pried where he wasn't welcome. That's me, by the way. Sinuhe the wise. Sinuhe the physician."

"Sinuhe the old woman."

Yetzer turned toward the deep voice that sounded behind him. His back screamed in protest as the movement tore at wounds that had begun to close, and a whimper escaped his lips.

"Yamu the ox," Sinuhe said, by way of introduction.

The epithet fit. The newcomer stood half a cubit taller than Yetzer, with shoulders twice as broad as most men's. Yetzer wondered how such a stature could be sustained on so meager a diet as dinner had proven to be.

"Your bread is cold," Yamu observed, and took Sinuhe's last scrap. "Can't abide to see food gone to waste," he said around the mouthful.

Yetzer drained his cup of gruel and shoved the remainder of his bread in his mouth, lest the giant offer to keep his meal from spoiling, too.

"Since you're finished," the big man said to Sinuhe, "why don't you see if you can find something for our friend's wounds? Let's see if you can heal as well as you meddle."

The old man said nothing, but rose with a scowl.

"And see if there's any more bread," Yamu added as he settled to the ground, still chewing. A cracking sound split the air and interrupted the movement of the ox's jaws. Yetzer winced as the big man probed with his tongue and spat. In the waning light, Yetzer couldn't say whether the debris was limestone or tooth, but he redoubled his caution and slowly chewed the wad of bread in his mouth.

"Old man will talk you deaf," Yamu said, "but he's right good to have around. Keep those little scratches of yours from festering."

"He's a real physician?" Yetzer asked after swallowing the last of his bread—stones, weevils, and all.

"Near enough," Yamu grunted. He slowly looked around, then leaned toward Yetzer, and spoke more softly. "They say he was the one to tend young Pharaoh Tutankhamun, that it was him let the boy die. Oh, old Aya didn't mind so much when he took up the crook and flail. Never mind he was the only one with the king when he fell. Never mind Horemheb was the boy's acknowledged heir. No, first thing Pharaoh Aya does is clap the boy's doctor in bronze and send him to the priests of Amun. Get rid of him that really knows what happened, see?"

"Why didn't Horemheb free Sinuhe when he took back the throne?" Yetzer said. "Tutankhamun was like a son to him. Surely he'd want to reward the man who tried to save him."

Yamu fixed him with a patronizing stare and shook his head. "Sutah's bollocks," he swore. "You're Pharaoh of Kemet, Brother of the Gods, Master of the Two Lands. Are you going to give a thought to a mere slave rotting in your quarries?"

The words hit Yetzer like a cudgel. Part of him had hoped for salvation, hoped that after a few days Horemheb might proclaim his freedom. But Yamu's words rang true. Yetzer had earned his fate. He was a slave, a nameless one, blotted from the remembrance of man or god. He shook his head.

"No," Yamu said. "So here he sits. Here we all sit, 'til Ammut has mercy and drags us down to Duat." He picked up Sinuhe's bowl and dipped the last bit of stolen bread into stolen gruel. "From Retenu?" he asked, lips smacking around the moistened bread.

It took Yetzer a moment to realize the man was asking about him. "From Kenahn, yes."

"Retenu, Kenahn—it's all the same."

"My parents called their land Kenahn, so will I." Yetzer shrugged. "Not that it matters to me. I was born there, but almost all my memories are of Kemet."

"A man should know where he's from," Sinuhe said behind them, his reedy voice like lute-song on the cooling night air. "Even if his path ahead is less certain."

Yamu looked up at him expectantly.

"No more bread," the old man told him. "But I did manage some ointment, if you'd like to help me tend our singing friend."

"I wouldn't want to be in your way." Yamu rose to his feet and dusted his hands against the seat of his loincloth. "I'll just see if any of the others need looking after."

The big man stalked away. Yetzer watched men shove bread into their mouths or tuck it into the folds of their breechcloths as Yamu neared them.

"On your stomach, then," Sinuhe ordered.

Yetzer looked up at the old man, who presented a clay jar and a bundle of linen.

"'Easier to apply if the patient is prone.' Added that bit to the physicians' scrolls myself. Insightful lot, from Immutef right down, but sometimes lacking in common sense. On your belly, now."

Yetzer did as instructed. The dirt was warm from the day, and reasonably clear of stones. Heat seeped into weary muscles, and Yetzer sank quickly into somnolence until lightning strikes of pain shot through his stupor.

"This might sting a bit," Sinuhe belatedly warned him.

"What is that?" Yetzer asked through gritted teeth, his fingers clawing into the baked earth.

"A bit of beer," Sinuhe said as he daubed at Yetzer's wounds. "Some willow bark. Oh, and cow's urine. Lie still."

Yetzer fought the urge to roll away from the mad physician and his filthy ointment. He called to memory a lesson from one of the priests of Hawt-Hor. Often portrayed with a cow's head, the goddess had imbued that animal with a host of attributes for the benefit of its human masters. Who was to say the goddess hadn't blessed the beast's urine as much as its milk? Yetzer kept his peace, braced himself against the sting, breathed through his mouth.

"These aren't so bad," Sinuhe said as he scrubbed away dried blood and reopened the wounds. "Inteb must be losing his skill."

"Inteb," Yetzer wheezed through the pain. "The overseer?"

Sinuhe grunted.

"Seemed to do just fine from where I was standing."

"And just how many lashings have you seen or received before today?"

"None," Yetzer said after a pause.

"No? Ah, yes, because your father practiced free masonry, none of this slavery business."

Yetzer looked over his shoulder. "How do you know of my father?"

"What's that?" Sinuhe asked, his eyes fixed on Yetzer's wounds. "Oh, you told Yamu your father was from Tsur. Seeing the way you handled yourself in the quarry, I assumed he was a mason."

"He was," Yetzer said, trying to remember if he'd mentioned his father's home city.

"There you are, then," Sinuhe said, moving to the stripes on Yetzer's thighs. "You'll find the slavers' quarries not so welcoming as the free. No songs, no ranks, no pay. Just dust and sweat and men with flails."

Yetzer shook his head.

"Men work better when they're treated with dignity, when they're justly compensated, when they believe they're part of something greater than themselves."

He hadn't meant to sound like his father. Huram had once made that same argument before Pharaoh, when competing against the priests of Amun for work on Horemheb's House of Eternity. He'd made his case well. He won the work and lost his life.

Sinuhe's cackling laughter pulled Yetzer from his gloomy thoughts.

"You think the priests care how well a man works? Whether he's satisfied with his labor? Men are cattle, boy, to be herded and harnessed and bred as their masters see fit. Give them enough food and water and leather, and they'll work 'til you're done with them—or until they can't work anymore, which amounts to the same thing."

"I'm no beast for the drover." Yetzer's voice cut with a ragged edge.

"Nor I," Sinuhe admitted. "There are a great few who raise their heads, who can see beyond the next scrap of pasturage. Gods have mercy on us. Better we were cast into Duat than suffer a common man's lot. But look at Yamu."

Yetzer glanced to where the big man scavenged bread and gruel from a group of old men.

"There is mankind writ small," Sinuhe continued. "He'll rut and root 'til he can't do either anymore. Then it's back to the bosom of the earth whence he came, where not god nor man nor beast remembers he was here."

Yetzer bristled at the words, unwilling to believe them. "When they're led well, they can become more. Better."

The words fell lame even as Yetzer spoke them. The old man laughed again. "Are you such a one to lead them, Yetzer abi-Huram?"

Yetzer held his tongue as he looked around the slaves' paddock, at the ill-fed rabble. Criminals, debtors, oath-breakers. Not even Yetzer's father had dared such a challenge, limiting his crew to freemen of good character. Then again, Yetzer reminded himself, his father had never been a nameless one.

"I am," Yetzer said, almost to himself.

"Hmm?" the old man said. "What's that?"

"We may be forgotten," Yetzer said, "forsaken by men, unnamed before the gods. But if only we know, if only we remember we are more than beasts, we will truly have been men and our *ka* will speak for us before the scales of Mayat."

Sinuhe laughed again and slapped Yetzer on the buttocks—the only part of his backside not scarred and drenched in the foul-smelling ointment.

"If you truly intend to lead this rabble," he said, his voice light with mirth, "you may want to choose a different song."

17

Bilkis

The palace of Tsion was a sandstorm of activity. Servants scrambled to restore some order from the chaos left by the fleeing court. Rahab screamed at the serving women such that Bilkis could not understand her. Despite the similarities between the Sabaean and Habiru tongues, the flurry of the girl's words was impossible to follow.

"Just have them bring water," Bilkis told Rahab. "I don't care about the mess. I only want a bath."

The servants had led them to the set of rooms formerly occupied by Tadua's chief wife Mikhel. Linens sprawled like sand dunes across the floor. Pots and bowls lay in pieces, their contents spilled and scattered.

None of it mattered. For a year Bilkis had lived with blowing grit. She had slapped at flies and fleas, scratched at their bites until her skin was raw. She was now a queen in her own palace, in her own rooms. She had windows covered with waxed linen that kept out the dirt and flies, but admitted light and breeze. Should the natural breeze fail, fans of palm leaves stood ready. Thick rugs covered the polished wood floors. The monstrous frame of Bilkis's bed held a thick, soft mattress. She had Rahab to tend her, plus a dozen servants to tidy the rooms, fluff the pillows, wave the fans and fill her cup, but all she wanted was a Shams-forsaken bath.

The room fell silent. Judging from the quiver in Rahab's chin and the wide-eyed expressions of the serving women, not all of her thoughts had been confined within her heart. She dowsed the fire in her eyes and forced a sweet smile. "Please?"

"You heard the queen," Rahab said, first to recover her wits. "Go. Draw water."

Bilkis made a satisfied purr. "And I will bathe on the roof."

❖

Refreshed and dressed in a silken robe, Bilkis descended to Auriyah's audience hall. She kept a neutral expression on her face, but her heart raced as she passed through the corridors.

Her own rooms were larger than Maryaba's tower house. The palace dwarfed her chambers, the whole constructed of dressed stone and lined with more timber than had ever been seen in all of Saba. Though the sun baked the earth outside, within the thick walls the air was cool and invigorating. Her husband had brought her to a true land of marvels.

The sound of men's arguments reached Bilkis as she neared the audience hall. A pair of guards bowed their heads and pulled open heavy wooden doors. Voices faded as Bilkis crossed the threshold, and the men who flanked the throne turned to follow Auriyah's gaze.

"My wife." The king stood and gestured to a small chair beside him. "Come, sit."

Auriyah's throne was of heavy timber carved with lions and rams and harps, inlaid with gold. The seat was covered with animal skins, suggesting this was the throne of a warrior. The queen's, by contrast, was a thing of sublime grace, fashioned of lighter wood with silver rosettes, six-pointed stars, and trimmed in pure white fleece. Bilkis climbed the dais steps amid the bows and greetings of the king's council. Most were among those who had accompanied Auriyah to Urusalim. Two of the men, however, were strangers.

One had a warrior's ruddy complexion and sharp features. The other was a pallid, narrow-eyed creature in bejewelled robes, leaning upon a gilt staff. Auriyah kissed Bilkis's hand as she sat, but dispensed with introductions.

"You were saying, venerable priest?" The king motioned to Abdi-Havah, who had anointed him at Ebiren.

"My Lord, Lady," he began. "You sit upon the throne of Urusalim as *moshiach*, the anointed one of Yisrael. Your father lost favor with Yah and Havah. It is fitting he should have fled from their wrath." The priest gestured with a mangled, age-spotted hand although his voice was that of a much younger man, clear and strong. "Only let my king remember the precepts of the gods," he continued. "That is, to do justice, love mercy, and walk humbly before them. As it is written, be generous to the widow and drive her not from your land."

"Bah!"

All eyes turned toward the squint-eyed priest.

"You disagree, Abiattar?" Auriyah said with thinly veiled humor.

"May Yah preserve the king," the man said in a voice as bitter as sulfur water. "Abdi-Havah is as shrewd as he is aged, but he speaks with two mouths. Even as he anointed the new king, he seeks favor with the old. By urging you to show mercy to the wives of Tadua, he ingratiates himself with your father."

Bilkis looked to where the man gestured. To one side of the hall, nearly lost in shadows, huddled a group of women clinging to one another. They ranged from young women of Bilkis's age to wrinkled crones.

"The goddess has withdrawn her blessing from Tadua," Abdi-Havah insisted. "In the eyes of Havah he is as one already dead. Let his wives be counted among the widows of Yisrael. Let them be treated with due consideration."

"Or let them be free to wed," Abiattar sneered, "that Abdi-Havah might take them into his own household and claim the alliances forged by Tadua. Hatti, Alassiya, and Edom. The rulers of those lands care not who sits upon the throne of Yisrael, but in whose bed their daughters and sisters lie. Free these women and it will not be long before Abdi-Havah seeks to reclaim what once he lost."

Auriyah made a fist. His veins stood out as color rose in his cheeks.

"This is madness," Abdi-Havah protested. "It is true your father took this city from me."

Bilkis's eyes shot to the old man. He had been king in Urusalim before Tadua?

"I was foolish then," he went on, "full of pride, and it was Havah's will that I be brought low. Yet she saw fit to spare my daughter, to send her into the victor's house and, through her, to give Yisrael her new king. If I was old when I lost this city, I am ancient now. I have no desire for the throne. I am content that my seed sits upon the throne of my fathers and seek only to see the king established in peace."

Some of the fury drained from Auriyah's face as the old man spoke. "My grandfather offers words of silk," the king allowed. "How does Abiattar say?"

"May the king live forever," the other man said. "If the priest of Havah speaks with silk, then let the voice of Yah speak with sackcloth. Peace is a luxury, but it is the child of strength. Let the king first secure his throne, then he may be gracious."

"And what you suggest—"

"Is the surest way," Abiattar boldly interrupted Auriyah. "You must take to bed the wives of your father."

Claws scratched at Bilkis's heart with those words. She clenched her teeth to hold back a cry of fury. Auriyah had only just become a husband of worth. Must she now share him with these huddled geese?

"Not in secret, as a lover in the night," the priest continued, "but as a conqueror. Erect a pavilion atop the palace and there show your kingdom and all the world that the time of Tadua is past, that the son has possessed all the father acquired."

"It is an abomination," Abdi-Havah cried.

The council erupted into shouting but Bilkis heard only a low drone beneath the pounding in her ears. Her gaze drifted again to the cluster of women. One with silver-streaked hair locked eyes with her. The new queen shifted on the throne that must once have belonged to the elder.

Was that Mikhel? And which was Auriyah's mother, Maacah, daughter of Abdi-Havah? Would he take her, too, or spare her and allow her to take her own life? And what of the younger ones, princesses of the most powerful nations on earth, girls with red- and gold- and wheat-colored hair, with painted eyes and painted lips? How could she compete with their foreign manners and courtly airs?

"And what of Tadua's army?"

A bellicose voice cut through Bilkis's clouded thoughts. She tore her eyes from her rivals and focused on the other stranger amid Auriyah's councillors. His burnished skin told of one who spent his time out-of-doors. The pale scar along his jaw and the fresh red one across his shoulder proclaimed him a man accustomed to violence.

"What of it, Cousin?" Auriyah asked bitterly.

Cousin? Bilkis mused. *Has all of Tadua's family turned against him?*

"Your father has run," the warrior said, "but it is only a question of time before he assembles enough men to threaten Urusalim. And your throne."

Auriyah laughed loudly and a handful of sycophants joined in with him. "What have I to fear from an old man and an army of shepherds?"

"I have fought by the side of that old man since before you were a tickle in his loincloth. He has seen trials far more desperate than this and has overcome them all."

"Yes, yes, Ayub, I know," Auriyah groaned. "I have heard the stories. How he slew the lion with his bare hands. How he killed giant Gulatu with a mere pebble. How he crawled through a newly fertilized field and came out smelling of olibanum."

Ayub's eyes came alight as Auriyah summarized his father's legendary feats. This warrior might serve a new king, but the flames of love and respect for the old still burned.

"What would you have me do?" Auriyah continued. "Rally my Hatti? Raise the host of Yisrael?"

"If need be, yes," Ayub insisted. "If you value your throne, you will do all that and more."

"Perhaps we should call upon the priests of Yah," Abiattar suggested. "Let them blast their rams' horns and summon the Host of Heaven to fight for us." He paused to let the laughter subside. "The lion has been declawed, defanged, and gelded. Raising an army against him would only bolster his reputation and demean your own, my lord."

Auriyah weighed Abiattar's words, and the sly one pressed on before anyone else could speak.

"Besides, our law prohibits a man from taking up arms within the year of his marriage. The king has only just brought his bride under his roof." Abiattar made a sweeping gesture toward Bilkis. "And I suspect he will have his fill of brides within the week."

Some of the men made crude gestures. Bilkis felt her insides twist as Tadua's wives whimpered and consoled one another.

Auriyah tugged at his short beard, his brow wrinkled. His gaze settled on the women at the far end of the hall, and hunger replaced ambivalence. He reached for Bilkis's hand, and she managed not to pull away in disgust.

"What say you, my queen? What course do you advise?"

Bilkis could not meet his eyes and would not look at the other women. She surveyed the eyes of the councilors, from Abdi-Havah's righteous fire to Ayub's martial zeal to Abiattar's—what? The man's expression was inscrutable, but Bilkis sensed whatever lay behind it might be turned to her favor.

She vowed to discover what it was.

"Do as seems right to my lord," she at last said to Auriyah. "The king must see to his throne."

While I see to mine.

18

Yetzer

Yetzer pushed himself to his knees, muscles protesting the previous day's abuse and the night spent upon hard ground. He turned toward the rising sun and spread his arms. "Blessed Shapash," he prayed, "Queen of Heaven. As you mount the heavens upon the wings of dawn, may your hand direct my path. So even may your right hand hold me fast."

Yamu barked with derisive laughter and slapped a broad hand on Yetzer's scarred shoulders.

"A singer and a priest," he said. "Save your prayers, boy. Didn't they tell you? The gods can't hear us nameless ones."

Yetzer ignored him and his ceaseless prattle as they filed through the gateway to receive a breakfast of stale bread. The picks remained dull from countless days of use. Yetzer kept his eyes down as he passed Inteb the overseer and found his place along the narrow trench gouged into the limestone.

He gripped the handle of his pick and began to sing. *My heart rejoiced when they called unto me.* Swing.

The tune was a common one, sung at festivals throughout Kemet, from the southern cataracts to the northern marshlands.

Come, now, to the temple of Amun. Swing.

Yetzer felt the other men's stares, heard their pitiless laughter.

Let your feet stand in Uaset's gate. Swing.

Footfalls rapidly drew near, gravel crunching beneath leather sandals. "I told you not to sing, slave."

Yetzer fought to keep a straight face at the child's voice issuing from the giant's body. "With respect," he said, keeping the tempo of his swings, "you told me to go faster." Swing. "Not to stop singing."

"Then go faster, dog."

Inteb swung back the flail then lashed forward. The knotted cords bit into Yetzer's back, tearing open day-old wounds and carving out new ones. Yetzer braced against the pain. He edged one foot forward to keep his balance and managed to hold his tempo.

"I think you'll find," he said through clenched teeth, "that this really"— Swing— "Is the best pace, and singing helps keep the pace."

"Foreign pig." The overseer's voice climbed nearly an octave. "You will work faster."

From the corner of his eye Yetzer watched Inteb's shadow reel back the flail.

In the walls of Uaset, built by gods.

CRACK.

Swing.

Teeth clenched, Yetzer managed not to scream as pain mounted upon pain.

There gather the faithful of Kemet.

CRACK.

Swing.

Sinuhe's voice, wavering with age, joined Yetzer's.

There Pharaoh sits in righteous judgment.

CRACK.

Swing.

A handful of others added to the harmony, softly lest they draw Inteb's attention away from the mad singer from Kenahn.

Whence peace flows throughout the lands.

The last word hung on Yetzer's lips when the overseer unleashed his fury. He struck the backs of Yetzer's legs so hard they buckled. Yetzer fell to his knees. The impact snapped his teeth together upon his tongue. Blood filled his mouth even as more lashes fell across his back, his shoulders, his chest, his head.

Yetzer rolled onto his side. He pulled his knees to his chest just in time to block a kick to his belly. There was little he could do but smile as the big man raised a foot and drove it toward his head.

❀

A cool cloth soothed Yetzer's forehead. He kept his eye closed as he assessed his injuries.

Toes wiggled. Shins were bruised, knees battered. Along the length of his body he found more of the same, pain but no severe injury. That pattern changed when he reached his head.

His jaw ached when he tested it. His tongue lay swollen against loosened teeth. From temple to crown, his skull felt as though squeezed in a carpenter's vise. He willed his eye open. After several attempts he managed to peer through a blurry slit. A figure moved over him against a sky fired by evening's last light. Yetzer fleetingly hoped it was Ameniye. Hoped the past few days, the years, had been but a bad dream. Hoped he would wake upon his cot in Pharaoh's palace.

When his eye focused, it revealed withered brown skin and a gap-toothed grin. Sinuhe's lips moved, but no words sounded. It was then Yetzer noticed the ringing in his ears.

"A damned fool, I tell you." Sinuhe's voice sifted through the din, and Yetzer recognized more humor than recrimination. "I'm running out of favors," the old man continued, "and you're beginning to smell like a tavern's alley."

Yetzer smiled. The effort sent boulders crashing through his skull.

"How many?" he asked when the rockslide stopped.

The physician smeared salve across Yetzer's tattered chest.

"Twelve."

Twelve. Out of fifty men. Nearly one man in four had followed Yetzer's lead.

"Of course, they fell into their own rhythms once Inteb finished with you," Sinuhe added.

"Then we start again in the morning," Yetzer said.

The old man gave a short laugh and shook his head. "It's morning now."

Yetzer lurched onto his elbows to scan the sky, then fell back as dizziness overwhelmed him. Sinuhe had spoken true. The sun lay behind the quarry, not the western mountains.

"I slept through a day and a night?"

"It would seem you needed the rest," Sinuhe said. "A good knock on the head can be a fine thing from time to time."

"I have to get to the quarry." Yetzer pushed himself up again, and managed to remain sitting.

"Steady, boy." Sinuhe placed a hand on Yetzer's shoulder. "You'll do no work today."

"But the others." Yetzer slurred as pain and nausea wrapped around him. "I can't let them see Inteb win."

"They saw it well enough yesterday," Yamu said with a coarse laugh as he approached behind the old physician. "If you need me to piss on him, Sinuhe, I'm happy to help."

"Osaure turns water to wine." The old man winked at Yetzer. "All this one's good for is turning cold water to warm urine. But there will be no work for you today, nor anyone else. Today is tenth-day."

Yetzer blinked at that. He'd lost track of time since entering the quarry. Throughout the land of Kemet, each tenth day was dedicated to the gods, free of secular pursuits and labor.

"Your only duty today is rest." Sinuhe reached into his cloth bundle and held out a piece of bread.

"It's only half of yesterday's," Yetzer observed.

"No work, not as much needed," Yamu said as he eyed Yetzer's meager share. Yetzer took the bread. "It will do."

❖

With dawn's light, Yetzer rose, welcomed the sun, and filed out with the other men. His muscles more stiff than sore, Yetzer swung his arms to loosen them. The picks, he saw, had been hammered down to tolerably sharp points. The handle fit his hand so well, it seemed a part of himself. An otherworldly peace settled over him. A slave he might be, forgotten by Kemet's gods. But he knew himself, and with his pick in his hands, he was master over his lot.

All praise to Amun who lifts me up, he sang, unable to contain the incongruous joy of the morning.

To Osaure, who plucked my ka *from Duat.* Some of the other men sang in response to the familiar verse.

Sing praises to Amun and all the gods.

Give thanks for all their goodness. More men joined in the response, smiles spreading from face to face.

Though their anger be fierce, like darkest storms.

Still, life abounds 'neath their mercy.

Though night brings fear and tears of grief.

In the dawn come laughter and singing.

The overseers waited at the entrance to the quarry. Inteb held his arms folded across his chest. His flail tapped against his shoulder in time with the men's song, and he sneered as Yetzer passed by.

"I hope you're well rested, slave," he said, and Yetzer grinned back at him.

"I was going to say the same to you."

Inteb's sneer turned to a scowl, the muscles of his jaws tensed, and veins stood out on his neck. Yetzer laughed. He was the one in bonds, yet he had the power to dictate this freeman's actions.

He followed the others into the quarry. During the two days he'd been there, not one block of stone had been freed from the rocky bed. A properly run crew of this size should have been able to turn out five rough ashlars in a day. He resolved to see what he could make of these men.

Yamu and a few others set immediately to work, their picks beating out disparate tempos that filled the quarry with dissonance. Yetzer spit in his palms then looked at the two-score men who eyed him expectantly. He set his stance and drew back his pick.

How mighty are your works, great Amun.

Swing.

The sound of the men's grunts, followed by the ringing of the copper blades, made the very stones sing in harmony.

Each one formed and filled with wisdom.

Swing.

Yetzer's heart soared as dozens of voices joined in the song.

Ageless Geb is full with your creation.

Swing.

"Faster!"

Yetzer braced himself for the blow, but kept his eyes fixed on the trench in front of him.

Yam's waves teem with your creatures.

Swing.

CRACK.

The whistle and snap of the lashes echoed from the rock walls, but it was not Yetzer's voice that cried out with pain.

"Work, dog," the overseer screamed at Yamu, and delivered another set of stripes to the big man's back. "All of you, set to."

Every pick had fallen silent as men stood bemused by the turn of events. Not wishing Inteb's wrath to fall on any of the men who had cast their lots with his, Yetzer quickly resumed the rhythm.

It is Amun who causes Iteru to flow.

Swing.

From the cataracts its waters feed the land.

Swing.

Causing grain to grow from the earth, for bread.

Swing.

And wine to enliven man's heart.

Swing.

19
Bilkis

"**M**ore milk?"
Bilkis and Rahab looked up toward their host. Abdi-Havah stooped across a low table.

"No, Grandfather," Bilkis replied, and clasped his cold, gnarled hand. "I need only your company and your wisdom."

The old priest smiled and patted her hand as a servant eased him to his chair. "I am old enough to know flattery when I hear it," Abdi-Havah said, then leaned toward Rahab as toward a conspirator. "And vain enough not to mind."

Priest, queen, and handmaid sat in silence for a time, looking out over the Kederon Valley. Not eight days earlier Bilkis had watched the dust rise in the valley from Tadua's retreat. Instead of dust, there now rose smoke from hundreds of campfires as the host of Yisrael gathered in support of the new king to hunt down the old.

For his part, King Auriyah remained in Tsion. To Bilkis's revulsion, if not her surprise, her husband had followed Abiattar's advice. Beneath a pavilion erected on the roof of the palace, Auriyah took his father's wives into his own bed. First and, mercifully, the quickest had been his mother Maacah, followed by Mikhel, and Ahinoam. The king had taken considerably more time with the latter two, drawing out the humiliation for Tadua's principal wife and the mother of Amun-On, the prince who had despoiled Auriyah's sister.

"You really should eat something more." Rahab broke the silence and gestured toward the table. "You've hardly taken any food or wine these last few days."

Abdi-Havah had invited the queen to his hilltop villa outside the walls of Urusalim, but it was not so far from the palace that Bilkis could not see the shameful display atop her own roof. The planted rows of olive trees, however, screened the view, and the distance removed Bilkis from the jeers of the crowd gathered to watch the spectacle.

"Eat," Rahab insisted, and slid a platter toward her.

Bilkis tore off a bit of bread and dipped it in olive oil. She ate the morsel and followed it with a deep draft of wine.

Rahab turned to the old priest. "What will happen when the army catches up with the king?" She looked sheepishly at Bilkis. "I mean, when they catch up with Tadua."

Abdi-Havah fumbled on the table for a knife, which the servant snatched up to carve off a piece of cheese for him. "I'm not yet an invalid," the old man snapped even as he accepted the food. Speaking between bites he said, "That depends on where they find him. If they meet on the open plain, Auriyah's Hatti cavalry will sweep Tadua's troops straight to Sheol."

"And if they don't?" Bilkis asked, unable to refrain from the conversation.

"The Vale of Yarden is a wild land, riddled with caves and narrow passes. Tadua fought and thrived in such terrain for years, first as a war chief, then as a renegade, and finally as a king."

The old man accepted a goblet of wine from his servant. "Thank you, Gad. Yes, Tadua is clever as a hyrax and fearsome as an adder. If Ayub leads the host into those defiles, Auriyah's whole army will be lost."

Bilkis gaped at the great assembly spread across the valley floor. "There must be five thousand warriors. How could Tadua possibly defeat them with a band of only a few hundred?"

"Five thousand men," Abdi-Havah allowed, "but likely not more than one in ten is a seasoned fighter. The rest are farmers or shepherds called from their fields. All of Tadua's men are warriors trained to the bow or spear from the time they left their nursemaids' breasts."

"But how could so few kill so many?" Rahab asked.

"They needn't kill them all," the priest explained. "It will start with a foraging party. Little by little, men will vanish and uncertainty will rise among the ranks. When the hands or heads of the missing reappear, panic will spread through the army, and the conscripts will flee to their homes." Abdi-Havah gave a mirthless laugh and shook his head. "Tadua is a master of terror. By such methods he won his kingdom and captured the most impregnable fortress in all Kenahn."

"Urusalim?" Bilkis guessed.

The onetime king nodded. "Men of my line have served in Urusalim as *Melchi-tzedekim*, as priest-kings, from time immemorial. When Abram, patriarch of the Habiru, paid tribute to my ancestor, we had already reigned here for a thousand years. Ever since man has looked to the heavens and seen the great works of Yah and looked about the earth to witness the marvels of great mother Havah, for as long as we have called upon the gods, a *Melchi-tzedek* has served here."

The old man's hands trembled as he reached for his wine. He drank, and a trickle of red stained his white beard. "And in one day," he continued, "it all ended. Because of my folly, because of my trust in man rather than the gods, the legacy of a hundred generations of priest-kings has come to an end." The old man sat back on his couch, his good eye taking on a far-away look.

"When Tadua approached my city, I mocked him. I boasted even the blind and lame could guard these walls from the likes of him." The old man raised a crooked hand and gestured toward his milky eye. "Such was the cost of my pride."

"You are still high priest," Rahab said. "Surely the gods still smile upon you."

"We will see whether my position is blessing or curse as the cult of Yah grows stronger. The gods desire service, not sacrifice. They require justice and right-doing toward one another, not the blood of animals and blind obedience to law."

"But it is the law that tells us how to treat one another," Rahab objected.

"Do you need the law to tell you to respect your elders?" the priest demanded, his voice sharp. "To honor the marriage bed? Is it the law that keeps a man from killing another or from taking his property?"

Gad placed a hand on the old man's shoulder. Abdi-Havah smiled sheepishly and waved his hand before his face, as though to dispel the air of contention.

"Forgive me, child. You gave no cause for me to speak so harshly. Quite simply, the gods have written the true law upon the hearts of man. They whisper it in the ear of all who would listen. The more laws we make, the greater the clamor and confusion. It will not be long before the din is so great that divine law will be drowned out and only the laws of man will remain."

"But if just and holy men make the laws ... "

The priest smiled, though sadness clouded his eyes. "Should such a wonder ever occur, I am sure the gods will be happy to rest their voices."

Silence settled atop Mount Morhavah. A slight breeze whispered through the leaves of the olive trees. Bilkis cocked her head as she tried to pick out Havah's voice, but the goddess seemed to have nothing to say.

"If Tadua is so strong," she finally asked the old man, "why did he flee? Why not stay in the city, fight from behind its walls?"

Abdi-Havah flashed a look toward Gad, shrugged, and offered a small grin, his good eye sparkling.

Bilkis clasped her hands and leaned forward.

"What did you do?"

"Tadua is a brigand and a war-chief, as well as a charmer and schemer. For more than thirty years he has coerced, cajoled, and extorted his way to power undreamed of. But with that power comes guilt. He is forever seeking the pardon and the will of the gods. Whosoever might give voice to the Old Ones will find a ready ear with Tadua."

Bilkis studied the servant Gad, unremarkable save for a striking plainness. "He speaks for the gods?" she asked.

"He is their most favored vessel," Abdi-Havah said with a grin. "Should he tell Tadua to fight, the king would scarcely take time to arm himself. Should he advise him to flee— "

"He would quit his city without so much as taking his wives," Bilkis finished.

A shrug.

Bilkis smiled at the wily old priest and accepted a cup from Gad. She raised the wine to her lips, but her hand faltered as her stomach turned sour. She pressed her free hand against her belly and swallowed back the saliva that flooded her mouth.

"Are you unwell, my lady?" Gad asked as Rahab knelt by Bilkis.

"Sister, what is it?"

Abdi-Havah locked his black, all-seeing eye on Bilkis and she shrank back. The old man's gaze softened and he gave an almost imperceptible nod.

"Gad," he said, his voice soft, "go to my storeroom and prepare a bit of ginger root for the queen. You know the recipe?" The young man nodded. "Take Lady Rahab with you. It may take two pairs of eyes to find all the ingredients."

"I know where—"

Abdi-Havah cut off the objection with a sharp flash of his eyes.

"Yes, Lord. My lady?"

"Go on, child," the priest said gently. "Gad will show you how to prepare the tonic. Your mistress may have need of it in the future."

Rahab looked at Bilkis, her eyes wide with concern. Bilkis smiled and nodded.

Abdi-Havah waited until the pair disappeared through a curtained doorway. "How long?" he demanded as he moved to sit beside her.

Bilkis's eyes burned as her vision blurred with tears. She tried to speak but a sob clutched at her throat.

"Hush, child." The old man gently squeezed her hands. "How long?"

The Queen of Yisrael drew a pair of stuttering breaths and blinked away her tears.

"My moon flow should have begun ten days ago."

"Has it ever been delayed before?"

"Yes, but … This is no delay. I carry Auriyah's seed."

The priest's expression darkened. "I miscalculated my grandson. I had hoped he would serve the gods, serve the people, but he has proven himself a slave to his passions and a tool of his councillors. He has turned the nuptial couch into an abomination. Forgive me, my dear," he added with a pat of Bilkis's hands. "I do not mean to offend. He is still your husband."

"What you say is true. He can be noble and generous." Her thoughts flew to the night following their acclamation, and her cheeks grew warm. "But a king ought first to govern himself. Whether by cup or cock or council, Auriyah will ever be ruled from without. But what can be done? He is king."

Abdi-Havah shrugged. "As was Tadua. As was Labaya before him. As was I in this city before either of them."

"You would choose another?" Bilkis said, and her heart turned as sour as her stomach. She had been queen not yet a fortnight and was unwilling to relinquish her throne.

The priest rose and strode to the parapet overlooking the valley. "Tadua has many sons, born to the daughters of all the tribes of Yisrael, not to mention the neighboring kingdoms. Sadly, Auriyah was the best among them. It is a cruel trick of the gods that a nation's finest example should be so sorry a man. There will be no new king, but neither must Auriyah continue to reign." He spun back toward Bilkis and pointed a long, gnarled finger at her. "And neither must his heir be permitted to draw breath."

Bilkis's gut tightened and her hands moved to her belly. The thought of some crone's stick rooting out her husband's seed made her stomach churn again.

Abdi-Havah sat beside her and took her hands. "Fear not. There is a way to rid Urusalim of this king and for you and your child to be safe. Now, here is what you will do."

20

Bilkis

Bilkis stood on the roof of her chambers. The servants had long since removed the pavilion and cleansed the defilement Auriyah had wrought here with his father's wives. They could not, however, remove the humiliation with which he'd stained her, the new queen supplanted by her husband's stepmothers.

She crossed her arms and clenched her teeth against the nausea that squeezed her belly. Abdi-Havah had laid out her course of action, but as the time neared, doubt muddled her reason. With a deep breath, she forced calm upon her heart, then followed the cedar-lined corridors to Auriyah's chambers.

"Stand aside," Bilkis ordered the Hatti guards who stood outside the doors.

"The king is not to be disturbed," one of them said.

"A rider approaches from the east," Bilkis said, "bearing the standard of Ayub. You will meet him at the gate and bring him to the king."

She ignored the guards' protests and pushed through the wooden doors. Thus far, Abdi-Havah's scheme had worked. In private meetings with Abiattar and Ayub, priest and warrior had each confessed a lingering affection for old King Tadua and dissatisfaction with Auriyah.

"If Tadua could sire a proper whelp," Ayub had declared, "he'd have my love and my sword. But his lawful sons are greater bastards than his bastards. And Auriyah is the greatest bastard of all."

"What if Tadua had another son?" Abdi-Havah said. "A lawful son, one who could be raised and trained to become the king that Tadua should have been?"

When the old priest had finished laying out his plan, the three conspirators exchanged sandals, and all was done. Abiattar returned to the king's council hall, and the next day Ayub had led the host of Yisrael to find the exiled king.

Now it was time for Bilkis to play her part. As the thick wooden doors swung open, feminine laughter pricked at her ears. When the doors banged against their stops, giggles turned to squeals. Auriyah's youngest brides—a red-headed beauty from Hattusa and a yellow-haired goddess from the island empire of Alassiya—scrambled to cover themselves.

"Get out," Bilkis commanded in a calm voice.

"Ah, my queen," Auriyah said, looking up from between the legs of the Alassiyan. "Have you come to join us?"

"Your queen does not wallow in filth. I have come to remind you that you are the King of Yisrael, not a whoremonger. A rider comes under Ayub's banner. If you would remain King, I suggest you greet him."

"Nonsense." Auriyah reached one hand toward a jar of wine while the other remained busy beneath the sheets. "Abiattar can deal with any dispatches. If my judgment is required, the Council will summon me."

"The Council has fled the palace."

Bilkis's words fell hard upon the cedar floor. Auriyah over-tipped the jar and spilled the wine on himself.

"What are you saying?" he demanded, ignoring the blood-red stain on his chest.

"I mean the king has no adviser but his queen," Bilkis said coolly. "Unless you count these children."

The young queens were of an age with Bilkis, and probably knew more of palace life and court intrigue than she, but those points did not merit mentioning. Nor did anyone seem willing to contradict her.

"Go," Auriyah said to his bedmates. "Get out," he shouted when they were slow to move.

He shoved the Hatti away and kicked the Alassiyan onto the floor. The girls tugged at sheets to cover themselves then ran from the chamber, simpering and huddling together as they went.

Auriyah rose from the bed, wrapped a woolen kilt about his waist and strapped on his sword belt.

"A messenger of General Ayub, my king," one of the guards announced.

"Send him in," Bilkis said before Auriyah could respond.

The rider entered, road-worn and breathless. His tunic was soaked with sweat and clotted with dust. He dropped to his knees then stretched out on the floor toward Auriyah.

"May the king live forever," he rasped.

"Rise," Auriyah said, his voice tremulous. "Speak."

"The word of Ayub, servant of the king, Prince of Yehuda, Captain of the Host—"

"I know who he is," Auriyah shouted. "What is his message?"

The rider shuddered as he took a deep breath and swallowed. "The army is lost. The forces of Tadua have taken the field at Machneh and crossed the fords of the Yarden. Even now they march on Urus—"

He almost finished the last word.

At mention of the defeat, Auriyah stalked toward the man, drawing his sword as he went. The messenger hastened his words when the king's blade hissed from its scabbard. His voice rose in pitch as Auriyah raised the sword over his head. The final words were a scream as the blade sliced through the man's neck and across his chest.

Bilkis ignored the blood that fountained from the man's wounds as Auriyah continued to hack at the corpse. She laid a hand on her husband's shoulder.

"Come. We must leave the palace."

With a feral cry, Auriyah plunged his sword into the man's chest. The blade sank into the wooden floor and the enraged king had to use both hands to pry it free.

"Find Manapa," he shouted at the guards, referring to the chief of his Hatti warriors. "Tell him to secure the palace gate."

"My lord sent Manapa to lead his warriors against my lord's father," one of the guards replied.

"Then you do it," Auriyah screamed, and flung his sword at the man. It bounced off the doorpost and clattered to the floor. "Bring what food and wine you can from the upper city, then seal the gates. No one enters the palace."

"Yes, Lord," the men said, already backing out of the king's presence.

"We cannot stay here," Bilkis said, her voice calm.

"We have food and wine and water." Auriyah paced as he spoke, his words soft as though he spoke to himself. "The gate. The gate is the only way in. Protect the gate, keep the palace."

"My lord. Husband." Bilkis stepped in front of Auriyah and placed her hands on his cheeks. "You heard the message of your war chief. The army is lost. Tadua comes."

"We are safe in the palace," Auriyah protested, his voice like a child's.

"Tadua took this city, took this palace once before," Bilkis reminded him. "And with fewer men than he now commands. We must flee while we can. Come."

She held out her hand to the king, but he shook his head.

"Come," she repeated, her voice firmer.

Auriyah's eyes were pleading now, but his shoulders drooped and he took Bilkis's hand. She led him to the door, stooping to take up his sword as they passed. The corridor lay empty, though panicked shouts sounded from deeper in the palace.

"Where are we going?" Auriyah asked when Bilkis led him into her quarters. "There is not time for this."

Bilkis said nothing, but led him to one corner of the room. With her toe she pressed against a section of wooden trim Abdi-Havah had revealed to her.

"What is this?" the King demanded as a hidden door sprang open. "How do you know of this?"

"I caught one of my serving girls returning from a tryst with her lover." Bilkis took a lamp from beside her bed and entered the passageway. "The tunnel leads beyond the wall, to the slope above the Gihon Spring."

She took a few steps into the tunnel then turned around when Auriyah held back.

"Brave husband," she said, and offered Auriyah a sad smile. "Will you stay to defend your crown? Then I will stay as well. Let it not be said that Auriyah and his queen fled like mice into the walls. Rather, let songs be sung of how we chose death over shame."

Auriyah's wine-blotched cheeks went pale. "Let them sing what they want," he said, and grabbed the lamp from Bilkis. He pushed past her and led the way through the tunnel.

Bilkis closed the hidden door and followed him.

The lamplight reached a few paces ahead of Auriyah's long stride. Bilkis had traversed the tunnel twice before, led by Gad to the exit and back. She'd been safe in his company and hadn't noticed the spiders and bats and droppings that fouled her path as she followed Auriyah's shadow.

"Which way?" Auriyah asked when they reached a fork in the path. His voice echoed from the rough stone walls and surrounded Bilkis, crushing her with the pressure of his demand as his body had so often done before.

Bilkis clenched her hand about the hilt of the sword. Her heart settled its rhythm. She took a deep breath and found her voice. "That way," she said, and pointed along the left-hand path.

The sword's hilt pulsed in her hand, as with a heartbeat all its own. It seemed to Bilkis the blade shone with inner light as Auriyah raised his lamp and continued upon the path.

Before long the darkness within the tunnel began to fade. The walls and floor became visible outside the lamp's glow. The king hurried his pace, and when daylight finally burst upon the cave, he ran toward the opening in the hillside.

Bilkis raced after him. She did not stop when he reached the tunnel's mouth. She did not stop when he braced himself against the cave wall and peered down what she knew was a sheer drop. Only when she was three paces behind him did she slow. Only when the sword's tip met the small of his back did she stop.

"What are you doing, woman?" Auriyah said, a growl in his throat.

"You will shame me no more," Bilkis vowed. "You will—"

Auriyah spun about with the speed of a serpent. He grasped the blade, wrenching it in Bilkis's hand. She wrapped the other about the pommel to secure her hold. Blood pooled between Auriyah's fingers as he tightened his grip and pulled Bilkis off balance. Instinct told her to pull back lest they both go over the edge. Instead, she ran forward. The king's eyes flashed with rage as, with a cry of fury, Bilkis drove him back. When his body teetered over the precipice, she released her grip and Auriyah plunged from view.

With the sword went her strength. She fell to her knees beside a pile of stones that, until two days earlier, had blocked the cave's mouth. Her stomach heaved, but the bitterness could not overcome the sweet taste of victory.

"You faithless bitch."

The words rose feebly to her ears, and the bile grew stronger on her tongue. Bilkis crawled to the cave's mouth and peered over the edge. The hillside dropped sharply away but grew shallower as it neared the valley floor where thickets huddled around Tsion's base.

Auriyah sprawled amid the bramble. Blood streaked his chest and legs from the slash of thorns. Twigs snagged his unkempt hair, but he seemed otherwise unharmed.

"When I get my hands on you," he hissed, his voice filled with venom, "I'll run my sword from your cunny to your gullet." He fought against the bramble's grasp, his thrashing slowed by the clutch upon his hair. Bilkis tried to stand, but her strength betrayed her. She rose only to fall again, her hand landing hard upon the pile of stone. Of its own volition, her fist closed about a small rock. Her other hand pulled her to the tunnel's mouth. Before she could form a thought, she watched the rock fall toward her husband. It plunged through the brush two hand-breadths from Auriyah's head.

A smile spread across the king's lips.

"I shall plow your every furrow," he called up to her. "You will know my wrath throughout your entire body. When I've finished with you, I'll give you to my men for a whore. And when you beg me to let you die—"

Another stone fell through the air and crushed the words from Auriyah's chest. Bilkis's scream flooded her ears as she cast down a third. That one missed, but a fourth struck the king in the middle of his kilt. The fifth, a rock about the size of a bread loaf, took him full in the face.

Auriyah's struggles stopped then, but Bilkis continued to hurl stone after stone until her attack reduced the bed of thickets to stubble. The king's battered body fell through the hole in the bramble, but his flowing locks remained caught in their snare. Like a rabbit from a hunter's staff, the King of Yisrael hung suspended over the Valley of Kederon.

Bilkis's throat burned from her screams. Her tongue cleaved to the roof of her mouth, and her fingers bled from the sharp edges of the stones. But her heart sang. Auriyah—husband, lover, tormentor—was dead. It remained only to greet the once and future king, and to secure the crown for herself and for the child that grew in her womb.

21

Bilkis

For the second time in as many months, the people of Urusalim turned out for the triumphal entry of their king. As before, palm branches and shouts of *Hoshiahna* filled the air. As before, eager peasants lined the slope while nervous elites milled about the upper city.

And Bilkis watched.

In Auriyah's name she had ordered the palace gate barred, ordered the twice-made widows shut in the harem. While the Hatti guard kept an uneasy watch atop the palace wall, Bilkis surveyed all from the roof of her apartments. She had washed away the filth and blood, anointed herself with myrrh-scented oil, and put on a gown of sheer linen.

When Tadua, mounted on his white donkey, reached the upper city, Bilkis climbed down the stairs to her room. With measured steps she moved through the empty corridors of the palace and crossed the courtyard. A pair of Hatti swordsmen murmured between themselves, casting glances from the gate to the walls.

"Open the gate," Bilkis commanded. The men looked blankly at her. "In the name of the king, open the gate."

"In the king's name we sealed the gate," one of the men replied.

"Different king," Bilkis said, a grin tugging at the corner of her mouth. "Your commander has fled. The true king arrives even now."

As though on command, a boom echoed through the gatehouse.

"Open in the name of the king." General Ayub's voice was unmistakable.

"The king commands," Bilkis said, her tone calm as she stepped toward the men. "Open the gate."

"Auriyah is gone?" the first man said, fear creeping into his eyes. "We must flee."

He hadn't finished the words before Bilkis swept his sword from its scabbard. Bronze scraped on bronze as she shoved the blade up beneath his breastplate. Surprise replaced fear on both men's faces. Bilkis's victim opened his mouth, but instead of words a gout of blood poured forth. His legs buckled and the sword escaped the queen's hands as he fell.

"The gate," Bilkis ordered the other man.

The Hatti warrior who had fought beside Auriyah for years, who had slain armed enemies by the dozen, now backed away from the young queen. His hands trembled as he waved them before him, as though to ward her off. When a few paces separated them, he turned and ran back into the palace.

The guards atop the wall gaped at the scene below, then dropped their weapons and followed their comrade's example.

"Fearless warriors." Bilkis spat, then wrenched the sword from the dead man's belly.

The palace gate was sealed by timbers propped against the cedar panels. Bilkis couldn't quite reach the cradles that held the beams against the gate. Instead, she used the sword to pry one of the timbers from its socket in the pavement. The heavy walnut crashed to the ground, overwhelming Ayub's shouts.

Bilkis rolled the beam out of the way then tugged on one great bronze handle. The gate slowly swung open to reveal Tadua's general.

Ayub's eyes widened and his mouth fell open as he stared at Bilkis. The queen followed his gaze and found her new gown stained in fresh blood.

"Havah's tits," she cursed under her breath, then looked up at Ayub. "Five Hatti are left. They may have fled, but your men should clear the palace before the king goes in."

"Auriyah?" the general asked.

A cold smile settled on Bilkis's lips. "Look for him by the spring of Gihon." Ayub nodded gravely.

"Tsion belongs to King Tadua," Bilkis said, her voice loud enough to carry beyond the gate, "and Bilkis bat-Saba is his handmaid."

She stepped back then prostrated herself upon the ground. Ayub summoned a few of his warriors to clear the other bar and swing the gate wide. Hooves echoed through the gatehouse and drew near, but Bilkis kept her face to the ground. Sandals scraped along the pavement and a touch fell lightly upon her head.

"Arise, child."

The voice was tight with age, but even those two words sounded like music. Bilkis stood but kept her gaze lowered. A cold finger hooked under her chin and raised her head.

Tadua, King of Yisrael, stood before her, tall and lean. Ropy muscles stood out on sun-kissed arms and legs. His short beard glistened red and gold in the sunlight, while his long hair, encircled by a thin silver band, retained only a hint of color. Sharp eyes, the shade of a midsummer's sky, gazed into Bilkis's. The young queen's cheeks grew warm.

"Six-score chosen warriors, and it is this tender rose who returns my palace to me."

Tadua turned Bilkis's head from side to side and looked slowly along her blood-soaked gown, then at the dead Hatti behind her.

"Though the rose appears to have thorns."

"Havah has blessed me to be of service to my lord," Bilkis replied.

"Perhaps you may be of greater service still," the king said.

The hungry look in his eyes was not unlike what Bilkis had seen in Auriyah's.

"I am my lord's to command. Only … " She allowed her words to trail off and looked away.

"What is it, child?" Tadua asked with a stroke of her cheek.

"The time of my uncleanness approaches," she said, and the king jerked his hand away as though he'd been struck. "I would not defile my lord or his laws. Allow me to go into seclusion. When I have been purified, if my lord still wishes, I shall come to him then."

Disappointment clouded those sky-blue eyes, though it was tempered by something that looked like relief.

"It shall be even as you say," Tadua replied. "You will remain in the royal harem until then."

"If it please my lord," Bilkis hastily added, "I would go to the house of Eliam abi-Terah. His daughter is as a sister to me, and will be a greater help than—"

"Than the women of my own household?" Tadua completed the thought, his expression turning grave.

"Even so, my lord."

"Benyahu will escort you wherever you please," the king said, and gestured toward a warrior.

"My lord?" the man said, his eyes wide as he took in Bilkis's bloody attire.

"Take our redeemer to the house of Eliam the merchant. And be careful to mark the way. I shall have need of her in a few days' time."

"Yes, Lord."

Benyahu motioned for Bilkis to lead the way. The young queen bowed her head to Tadua then walked regally toward the gate. She fought to keep her gait steady and her expression neutral when the king next spoke.

"Ayub, go find my son."

22

Bilkis

Eliam's house lay in the upper city, only two streets from the palace. Bilkis remained there during the week of her supposed impurity. She knew no blood would come, but she must feign the uncleanness if Abdi-Havah's plan was to succeed. Rahab went daily to the priest's home where the old man met with Ayub and Abiattar to further their plans.

"It is good you are not in the palace," Rahab told Bilkis the day after Tadua's return. "Soldiers found Auriyah's body and brought him to the king."

"How did he reward them?" Bilkis asked. Might she have strengthened her position by telling Tadua how she had restored his throne?

"He hacked off one man's head," Rahab said. "The other lost a hand before Ayub managed to take the king's sword. They say the king mourns as a mother over her lost child."

Bilkis leaned back against her cushion and mused on what kind of man this King Tadua was. "He whelps a brute and a traitor," she observed, "a son who conspires against his own father, then grieves when justice is done?"

Rahab shrugged. "Ayub says it has always been so. Tadua is a lion to his enemies, but a lamb when it comes to his children. Or to women."

"What of his queens? How does the lamb treat his defiled wives?"

Rahab sat beside Bilkis and started brushing out her hair. "They are still shut away in the harem. He summoned Maacah to the audience hall to tell her their son is dead. Ayub says the king did not touch her, scarcely looked upon her. He sent her back to the harem to mourn."

The next day, Rahab told how the remaining Hatti had been found. How the king had castrated them with his own sword. How he stuffed their manhood in their mouths then had them hanged from the palace walls.

The day after that, Bilkis learned that Tadua had acknowledged Auriyah's claim to the royal wives. They were to be kept in the palace as widows. By the seventh day, Tadua had accepted the pledges of the priests and tribal elders, most of whom had, not a month earlier, given their oaths to his son.

"King Tadua says the gods love nothing more than to show mercy to one's enemies," Rahab explained.

"And what does Ayub say?" Bilkis prompted her, knowing what the general's response would be.

"He said the king should sow the fields with his enemies' bones, fertilize them with their blood, and see if the gods didn't increase the harvest."

Bilkis laughed. "And Abdi-Havah?"

Rahab's fair skin paled, and the girl took Bilkis's hands in hers.

"He says it is time."

※

Bilkis awakened the next morning and crossed the courtyard. Eliam's household shrine lay near the gate, where the gods could more easily keep watch over the comings and goings. The young queen knelt upon silk cushions before the altar. Effigies of Yisrael's gods sat within a small temple of alabaster lit by a continually burning lamp.

Yah, Ancient of Days, sat upon his throne. Havah, Queen of Heaven, stood with hands supporting her full breasts over a very pregnant belly. Hadad, Rider on the Clouds, posed within his chariot while Ashtart, She of the Javelin, crouched in her leonine form.

Though Bilkis rarely addressed the gods, this day was different. All she had endured—the humiliation, the brutality—all could be made right this day. Today she would welcome any divine assistance she might receive. She anointed the gods with oil, then lit a candle, set it before Havah, and sprinkled incense over its flame. "Queen of Heaven, hear my prayer," she murmured, "and give me success."

Rahab had just awakened when Bilkis returned to the living area. The pair broke their fast with dates, bread, and curds.

"You should start a fire and draw the water for my bath," Bilkis suggested when she'd had her fill. "Ayub plans to have the king in place before noon."

Rahab glanced at her half-full plate.

"Must I start now?"

"The water must be warm, and it will take many buckets to fill the basin. There are also the trellises to set up and the carpets to hang."

Rahab stuffed a date and some bread into her mouth. "It will go more quickly if you help," she suggested, the food muffling her words.

"My sister," Bilkis said, smiling as she rested her hands upon her still-flat belly, "I would gladly help, but it would not do for me to be seen at such chores if I am to be Queen."

"You are already Queen," Rahab insisted.

"And I must be seen as such. Oh, do not pout. Here, I will make the fire," Bilkis offered. "But, you must stack the wood. I mustn't risk a splinter."

Another piece of bread went into Rahab's mouth before she shoved her plate aside and went about her chores.

"At least the cistern is full," Bilkis called after her. "Be happy you don't have to go down to the spring."

A short time later, Rahab had the fire going with pots hung about the hearth to heat the water. "I really shouldn't risk a burn," Bilkis had demurred as Rahab worked.

While Rahab shuttled steaming water to the roof, Bilkis went into her bedchamber to ensure her gown and jewelry were prepared. "The water mustn't be too hot," she called up through the roof opening. "I can't simply stand there waiting for it to cool. And not too cold. It makes my skin shrivel."

After another armload of wood on the fire and an untold number of buckets ferried up the ladder, Rahab at last had the basin filled. The sun was not quite at noon when she called down.

"He's there."

Bilkis's stomach tightened. Her breath stuttered and a sudden dryness scratched her throat. She offered up another quick plea for Havah's blessing, then climbed the stairs to the roof.

Rahab had everything arranged. Willow frames hung with carpets provided seclusion from the neighboring houses but left a clear view to the palace. Veils of blue silk spanned the tops of the screens to cast the bathing area in a soft glow.

"Don't stare," Bilkis hissed to Rahab, then cast her own furtive glance toward the royal compound.

Across the distance—more than a stone's flight but close enough to make out details—Tadua walked atop the roof of the palace. Ayub accompanied the king, who held his nephew's arm and seemed to lean upon him. The general led Tadua to the parapet, where the two looked out over Urusalim. Bilkis imagined that Ayub cast her the slightest of nods. She moved to the basin, stripped off her linen shift, and allowed Rahab to help her into the water.

Bilkis went about the routine of brushes and sponges and soaps. She fought the urge to watch Tadua and Ayub. After a time, the water's embrace and Rahab's brushstrokes through the queen's hair eased her anxiety and lulled her close to sleep.

"They've gone," Rahab whispered.

Bilkis blinked heavy eyelids open and looked toward the palace, its roof now empty. Rahab helped her out of the bath and gave her a towel. Bilkis dried herself then went down to her dressing room.

The gown she'd chosen was finest silk, dyed in the rare purple available only from the merchants of Tsur. Its cut was modest, though crafted to display her figure to advantage. Bilkis adorned her ears and neck and wrists with gold.

Rahab coiled the queen's hair atop her head and secured it with ivory combs, then applied paints and powders to accentuate Bilkis's eyes and to highlight the shape of her lips and cheeks. When she'd finished, the girl held up a polished silver mirror.

"You could rival Ashtart herself," Rahab said.

Bilkis gazed at her reflection and smiled. She was beautiful, and soon that beauty would win her yet another king's favor.

A knock sounded at the gate. Bilkis looked at Rahab and took a deep breath. They crossed the courtyard, where Rahab opened the gate to reveal Benyahu.

The war-captain was old, perhaps thirty, but he gawped at Bilkis like an unblooded youth. His mouth fell open, his eyes devouring her. Throat bobbed, lips twitched as though to form words, but no sound came out.

Bilkis grinned and stood a little taller. She pulled back her shoulders, and Benyahu's neck and cheeks flushed red. He tore his eyes away and cleared his throat. "If the time of your seclusion is complete," he said, "King Tadua summons you for an audience."

❧

Tadua, as it turned out, was a more gentle lover than his son. Whether owing to temperament or age—he'd seen nearly seventy summers—the king brought a patient and giving spirit to the conjugal couch. So much so that Bilkis fairly had to wrest his seed from him.

After she rolled off him, Tadua pulled on his robe, kissed Bilkis lightly on the forehead, then left her chamber without a word. Rahab came in a short time later, and the two moved to the roof to enjoy the late afternoon breeze.

"Three weeks more," Bilkis mused aloud. "I must share my couch with the king another time or two, and then I will tell him of the gods' blessing."

On the appointed day, Bilkis dressed simply in a robe of pale blue, the king's favorite color. She found Tadua in his audience hall, surrounded by his council. Ayub, Abiattar, and the other councillors bowed their heads when Bilkis entered. Tadua leaned forward on his throne and stretched a hand toward her.

"Most joyous of days," Bilkis said after she'd taken the king's hand and kissed it. "Havah has answered my prayer. The gods have given me a child. Your seed grows in my womb."

Tadua's pale eyes grew rheumy with tears. A smile spread behind his thin beard. "All praise to Yah," he said. "Can it be? Shall my last years be spent in joy and not grieving?"

Tadua had a tendency toward the poetic, Bilkis had learned, an endearing affectation that raised the spirits of those around him.

For the most part.

As Bilkis stepped onto the dais and took her seat beside Tadua's throne, she noticed the distinct lack of joy on the face of Prince Baaliyah. The king's eldest son looked as though he'd tasted an unripe persimmon. Born before Tadua had taken Urusalim from Abdi-Havah, Baaliyah had endured his father's wars and the rebellions of two of his younger brothers. All the while, the prince remained steadfast by his father.

Baaliyah now glared at Bilkis, a brutish mix of disdain and hunger on his broad features. The queen smiled at her brother-in-law-made-stepson, then turned her attention to the other members of the court. Ayub nodded with grim approval. Abiattar cast the thinnest of veils over his pride, while the other members of the council seemed to share the king's joy. As Bilkis made her survey of the faces, she noted whose eyes matched their expressions, and she tucked the information safely in her heart.

23

Bilkis

When the days of Bilkis's counting were complete, she sent Rahab for the midwife and for Abdi-Havah.

"You would bring my enemy into my very house?" Tadua demanded when he learned of her request.

Bilkis blinked in surprise. The king had never before raised his voice to her. Not only that, but he put aside his usual poetic ramblings and cut to the very heart of the matter.

"My love," she said, "my morning and evening star." Tadua cocked his head at the pretty speech. His countenance brightened. "Abdi-Havah is not your enemy," Bilkis continued. "He has been a friend to me and was of great comfort during your absence, when your son kept the throne. It was in part Abdi-Havah's good counsel that opened the gates for your return."

"Which is why he yet lives." The king's voice came as cold as the wind that beat upon Bilkis's shuttered windows.

"He is now no king, but a priest. As he is high priest of the mother goddess, I have especial need of his prayers this day." She took the king's hand and placed it atop her swollen belly. "Surely, goodness and mercy are stronger in your heart than base rivalry."

Tadua's expression softened.

"Never," he said in a low voice.

Bilkis started to renew her argument, but the king laughed and stroked her cheek.

"Never shall Abdi-Havah come into my house, but that I will prepare a table before him."

"Thank you, my lord," Bilkis said, and brought his hand to her lips.

A sudden pain squeezed Bilkis's womb. Her grip tightened about Tadua's fingers, and he gave a gasp of his own.

For the span of some twenty rapid heartbeats there was no air. There was no light. There was only the demon's spawn within her that slashed long claws inside her belly. Could she have breathed she would have cursed Auriyah, cursed all men, all the gods for creating so vile a means of populating the earth.

The pain faded and Bilkis managed a few breaths before realizing she still clutched Tadua's fingers. She released her grip, and the king withdrew his hand, flexing and massaging the joints.

"My lord, forgive me," Bilkis said. "I didn't mean—"

"Hush, child," Tadua said in his kind voice. "These hands have torn apart lions and bears. I think they will survive this." He shook his fingers, safely out of Bilkis's reach. "Though I fear I may never again play the harp."

Bilkis laughed with the king and fell back onto her pillows.

"Would you mock the gods?" a stern voice said from the doorway.

Bilkis looked up to see a small woman, no taller than Rahab and thin as a spear. A black veil covered her hair, and a robe of the same color stretched from her narrow shoulders to the floor.

"A birthing chamber is no place for laughter," the woman said in a voice as soothing as a crow's. "Nor for men. Your part in this was done with the sowing, my lord. Now begone."

The woman approached Tadua and had the audacity to grasp his elbow and pull him up from his stool. Bilkis opened her mouth to chastise this peasant, but Tadua soothed her temper with a wink and a smile.

"As you say, Keren." He offered the woman a slight bow. "You have birthed enough of my children for me to know there is but one sovereign within these walls. I leave you to your labors."

Tadua swept a lock of hair from Bilkis's brow and kissed her forehead.

"I shall add my prayers to those of Abdi-Havah, child, that all may be well."

"Thank you, my lord," Bilkis said, true affection in her words.

The king nodded to Rahab, who struggled with a cumbersome box, and he left the room.

"Set the chest over there, girl," Keren ordered Rahab, and pointed to the corner of the room nearest the bed. "Open those shutters and sweep out the hearth."

"It's too cold out," Bilkis said. "Rahab, keep the shutters closed."

"Do as I say," Keren snapped. She turned to Bilkis and, with slightly more civility, said, "You'll be plenty warm by the time your work's done here. I'll not have foul spirits bound up in this place. You may have your fire—"

Rahab let out a frustrated groan, as she had just shoveled the ash and embers into a copper pail.

"You may have a fire," the midwife continued, "but it must be of cedar, not of dung. And it must be kindled from a sanctified flame."

"Rahab, go find wood," Bilkis pleaded, the chill air already raising gooseflesh on her sweat-dampened skin. "It's so cold. Try the kitchen. The king always prefers his venison roasted over a wood fire."

"And take that filth away with you." Keren indicated the pail, now filled with ash and smoldering dung.

The girl's face contorted, her lips twisted. She said nothing but left with the bucket.

Keren offered a satisfied grunt then turned her attention to the crate. She unstopped a pair of oil-filled jars and set them on the windowsill. The breeze took up their scents and carried them to Bilkis. Her nostrils flared and fire coursed deep into her skull and down her throat, carrying the spirits into her lungs. She coughed, and the midwife turned to her.

"Purifying oils," Keren said, "to drive any unclean spirits from this place, and to keep any others at bay."

The midwife then drew out a fleece and spread it on the floor. On this she set a silver basin, along with a second pair of jars and a spice box. She sprinkled spices into the basin, followed by oil from one of the jars. She opened the second jar and poured what appeared to be plain water.

"From the mountains of Hermon," she explained, a reverent tone to her voice. "Taken from virgin snow."

"Snow?" Bilkis hadn't heard the word before.

"Snow, my lady. Frozen water that falls from the heavens like manna."

"Frozen?"

"Mind you not," the woman replied with a shake of her head. "Know only that it is the purest water in all the nations."

Keren stirred the concoction with a silver stick, then took a sprig of hyssop, dipped it in the basin, and proceeded to sprinkle the mix about the room, all the while muttering to herself. When she'd completed her circuit, Keren wiped the hyssop over the seat of the bedside stool. Some scarlet silken threads went into the basin, then the midwife unrolled a set of bronze instruments whose use Bilkis did not want to imagine.

The clatter of falling logs announced Rahab's return.

"They only had kindling of cedar," she told the old woman. "The logs are oak."

"It will serve," Keren said, her tone almost gentle.

Rahab stacked the logs and set the kindling underneath, then looked helplessly about the room.

"What do I do for fire?"

Some flame was always kept burning in the palace, whether candle or lamp or hearth. Bilkis glanced around the room and realized that Keren had extinguished the few burning tapers during her round with the dripping hyssop.

"I told you," the old woman said. "Fire kindled from a sanctified flame. Made by a virgin, at the new moon following the new spring sun, the sign of rebirth. Our queen, of course, cannot fulfill the role, but you, my child ... "

Keren held out a bow drill.

"Me?" Rahab said, her face drained of color. "I am to make the holy fire?"

"Even so," the midwife said.

Bilkis was about to ask the significance of this holy fire when the unholy pain again grasped her womb. She had strength enough to scream this time as her fingers dug into the mattress.

Rahab rushed toward her, but Keren intercepted the girl and sent her back to the hearth. The old woman supported Bilkis at her lower back with surprising strength. She breathed in Bilkis's ear, and the queen found herself following that rhythm, taking in rich, cleansing air and exhaling the pain.

By the time Bilkis could again breathe normally, Rahab had kindled the fire and the hearth's warmth began to chase back the cold. Keren took a chalkstone from her seemingly bottomless box. The midwife traced out a circle upon the floor then drew a five-pointed star within it. She placed the stool in its center, and the basin and her set of tools on either side of one point.

"Help your lady undress," she told Rahab, "then bring her to the stool."

While Rahab attended Bilkis, Keren set five small lamps outside the circle, one near each point of the star. She sprinkled the purifying water over the queen's belly and between her legs. The midwife looked expectantly at Bilkis and smiled.

"You may begin."

※

Untold hours, days, weeks passed. Weeks filled with agony like no other. Weeks during which the fire burned down but little, during which the lamps never went dry. Weeks upon which the sun never rose to mark the days. By what magic the witch Keren conjured to slow the natural passage of time, Bilkis knew not. She knew only that the vile wretch must have been in league with all the demons of the Pit who feed upon human misery and suffering. When the foul viperess spoke, her voice was disguised in tones of joy and encouragement.

"A hand," Keren said as Bilkis felt a queer sensation between her legs. "The time is near."

The midwife drew a scarlet thread from the basin. Deftly and quickly, she looped the string about a tiny wrist and knotted it before the hand withdrew into Bilkis's womb. Keren pressed her hands against Bilkis's swollen belly, prodding and manipulating the creature that writhed within.

The queen leaned back against Rahab, who wiped Bilkis's brow and held a cool sponge to her lips.

"Brave sister," the girl cooed in her ear. "You are doing well."

Bilkis wanted to tell the little bitch just how well she was doing, when pain beyond measure once more wracked her womb. She grasped Rahab's hands and screamed, though it came out as little more than a sigh.

"This is it, my lady," Keren said. "Do not fight it. Let the spirit of the goddess flow through you."

Too exhausted to struggle any longer, Bilkis relented. She relaxed the muscles that held her body together. If her belly burst with the lapse, then so be it.

Something shifted within her, a sensation at once unnatural and perfectly right.

"There you are, Lady," the midwife encouraged her. "Almost ready. Wait. Now, push."

"I cannot," Bilkis whispered. "I dare not."

Rahab leaned close, slid her arms about Bilkis and interlaced their fingers.

"Would you make all this effort for naught, Sister?" she said. "Your labors are almost finished. Now breathe with me and do as Keren says."

Bilkis nodded and forced back tears. She drew a pair of tentative breaths, then filled her lungs and bore down. The movement resumed, slowly at first and then with unsettling speed.

"Well done, my lady. Well done," Keren said.

The pain subsided, followed by some tugging sensations. A light smack produced a feeble cough that turned into a wail.

"You have a son, my queen," the midwife said. She placed the naked, squirming, squalling thing in Bilkis's arms. A look of concern flashed across Keren's eyes.

"What is it?" Bilkis asked as the baby latched onto a teat.

Keren smiled and shook her head. She took up the infant, who screamed in protest at being taken from his first meal.

"How would you call him, Lady?" the old woman asked.

"Yahtadua," Bilkis said. "After his father and his god."

The midwife nodded and swaddled the boy in a blue-and-white cloth. She held the child out to Rahab, who tentatively took him in her arms.

"Present him to the king," Keren told her. "Announce the arrival of Prince Yahtadua."

Rahab gave a silly grin and held out a finger for the prince to suckle. She kissed Bilkis on the cheek then left to find the king.

Keren sighed and settled to her knees before Bilkis.

"What is it?" Bilkis insisted. "What's wrong?"

"All is well, Lady," Keren said, and offered an encouraging smile. "It is simply time to bring forth the next one."

24

Bilkis

"Next one?" Bilkis placed her hands on her stomach. "How many are there?"

"Only the one more," Keren said hopefully. "Yahtadua did not wear the scarlet thread. His brother or sister tried first to break through, but he somehow gained the advantage."

"Perhaps it simply came loose."

The midwife offered a patient smile as she pressed and felt about Bilkis's belly.

"Only if it grew a head and legs," she said.

A fresh surge of pain rolled through Bilkis, though it paled against the earlier agony.

"That's the way," Keren said as she manipulated the latecomer. In only a short time, and with far greater ease than Yahtadua had offered, another boy—scarlet thread securely about his wrist—came forth. The midwife set the child upon the fleece, cut the cord, then helped Bilkis into her bed.

"Is he breathing?" the queen asked as Keren simply stood over the flailing infant, his face turning a sickly blue. "Do something."

The old woman sighed, picked up the child by his legs and smacked him firmly on the backside. The boy gave a startled cough, then made smacking noises with his lips.

"Give him to me," Bilkis insisted, then repeated herself when the midwife hesitated.

"You should not nurse him, my lady," the midwife advised as she put the child in Bilkis's arms. "And you would be wise not to give him a name. It would have been better for me to have strangled him on his cord."

Bilkis stretched out her hand to slap the old fool but managed only to clip the top of her head.

"Mind your tongue, witch. You speak of the king's son, a prince of Yisrael. If one heir is good, then two make the throne doubly safe."

"In all our people's history," Keren said with a shake of her head, "it has never gone well with twins."

"What do you mean?" Bilkis asked as she stroked the boy's pale cheek and looked into soft blue eyes that gazed deeply into hers.

"I mean that two backsides cannot fill the same throne, nor two heads share but one crown. Heartbreak, strife, and war spring from the seed of twins opposed."

"But why must they be opposed?" Bilkis pressed. "Yahtadua is firstborn, and will have primacy. His younger brother will love and support him."

"This child has King Tadua's temperament," Keren observed. "Already, he is fair and of an easy disposition. He will have clear thoughts and draw all people to him."

The old woman stretched out a slender finger, which the young prince promptly grasped.

"Yahtadua," she continued, her countenance darkening, "bears more a likeness unto Prince Auriyah."

Bilkis recoiled at the mention of her dead husband's name, but Keren's face gave no sign that she noticed or suspected the boys' parentage.

"That one was as a firebrand in a granary, quick to temper and slow to reason. Beg pardon, Lady," she added, "I do not intend to speak ill of the dead, only to tell you what I know. Yahtadua will win the loyalty of his people, but this one would win their hearts. Should he ever get the notion to supplant his brother, what do you suppose would happen?"

Bilkis considered the woman's words. Before she could frame a response, Rahab returned bearing a fussy Yahtadua.

"Oh, Sister, King Tadua is fairly alight with joy. Abdi-Havah was— " She stopped mid-stride when her eyes settled on Bilkis and the nursing infant. "What child is this?" she exclaimed.

Bilkis glanced at the midwife, whose eyes blazed with dread. A sharp pain in Bilkis's heart told her the old woman was right. Bilkis had risked all on this scheme, for Tadua to believe Auriyah's child was his own.

If the plan was to succeed, if Yahtadua was to usurp the position of his uncles—his elder brothers, if the lie were true—Bilkis could ill afford to split Tadua's affection betw en two sons. A piece of her heart fell silent and still as her will asserted itself.

"This is a child of Havah," she told Rahab.

The queen plucked her breast from the infant's grasp. He protested briefly then contented himself with gnawing on his fist. Bilkis handed the child to Keren, then reached out to take Yahtadua from Rahab. With the young prince hungrily suckling, Bilkis turned to Rahab.

"You will take that child and go by the secret way to the high place, to the shrine of Havah. When Abdi-Havah returns, you will give the boy into his keeping, to be raised as a servant of the goddess."

"I don't understand," Rahab said as Keren placed the boy in her arms. "Who—"

"Do as I say," Bilkis snapped.

Both infants looked up at her. The prince cast a scolding look while the priest-to-be fixed her eyes with a placid gaze. Bilkis turned her head away.

"Go," she said, the strength sapped from her voice. "Speak to no one of this but Abdi-Havah. Do you understand?"

"Yes," Rahab answered.

The girl moved to the corner of the room and released the hidden latch. Bilkis longed to call after her, to hold and kiss her son once more, but she stoppered her heart. Keren sealed the door behind Rahab, then looked at Bilkis and shook her head gravely.

"What, crone?" Bilkis demanded. "Speak."

The woman bowed low then looked up and smiled.

"In all my years, I have never beheld so natural-born a queen."

25

Bilkis

Not a month passed before Keren was called back to the palace, then again a few days later. Auriyah's young widows—the red-haired Pudu-Estan, and the flaxen-headed Taniri—had both become pregnant during the rebel's short-lived reign.

"Strange." Haggit, Prince Baaliyah's mother, looked up from her spindle when Bilkis came to look in on them. "Tadua got a child on you a month after Auriyah planted his seed in these two, yet your son came a month sooner."

Bilkis kept her expression neutral, save for one eyebrow that pricked up.

"My southern womb is much warmer than yours of the north. Does not bread rise faster in a hotter oven?"

A few of the other women laughed, but Haggit sneered at Bilkis and turned back to her spinning.

The queen went to where the young mothers lay nursing their children. Taniri, the princess of Alassiya, bore a golden-haired infant of fair skin. The Hatti princess, Pudu-Estan, held a child of ruddy features with a mat of dark hair. The pair of young women looked up as Bilkis approached, their expressions shifting from the bliss of mothers giving suck to the anxiety of interlopers in the palace.

"Both boys?" the queen asked, and the women's eyes narrowed.

"Yes, Lady," Taniri replied.

"I'm sure Prince Auriyah would have been pleased. They are healthy? Feeding well?"

"Yes, Lady."

"Good. If you need anything of me, you have but to ask."

"Thank you, Lady," both women muttered.

They shied away as Bilkis approached, but relaxed when she laid her hands upon the tiny heads.

"Havah's blessings upon you both. May your sons find worth in her service."

The harem fell silent as Bilkis intoned her blessing. She turned away from the young women, nodded to the elders, and left the room.

❖

"Your son's children thrive," Bilkis told Tadua later that evening.

The king bounced a gurgling Yahtadua on his knee, supporting the fragile head with one hand. At her words, he ceased the motion.

"They were to have been my sons," he said glumly, "to cheer me in my waning years. Instead, the gods have heaped ashes upon my head. A man's sons should lay his bones in the earth. As it is, I have buried half of my boys."

Yahtadua wrapped a pudgy hand in the king's beard and tugged the wispy hairs.

"Your son corrects you," Bilkis said. She went to her knees before the king, laid a hand upon his thigh and stroked his cheek with the other.

"My lord, this is the gods' blessing. Here is their reward. The son of your dotage rests upon your knee. Your loyal queen kneels before you. It is you and I who will raise him up in the way he should go, to be true and wise, faithful to you and to the gods."

Tadua smiled, but his soft eyes belied the expression.

"If the king's other sons are wildlings," Bilkis added, "if they strike out against your will, you must not think it a failing of yours. You must not fear for their love. As a warrior you built your kingdom, with the sword you founded it. Your sons were raised to the bow and the spear. Their natural inclination is to violence, which is a blessing when violence is needful, but a curse in time of peace."

Yahtadua reached for his mother, and Bilkis lifted him from the king's lap.

"You now reign in peace," she continued, "but your other sons know only how to rule with sharpened bronze. If you would preserve what you have built, if you would have your name and your deeds live forever, let Yahtadua be your heir. Let him be trained in the ways of peace, that your greatness may be known among all the nations."

"Make Yahtadua my heir?" the king said, his brows knitted together. "But he is only an infant, the youngest of all my sons."

"Was not my lord the youngest of Yishai's sons?" Bilkis said, delivering Abdi-Havah's prepared response for this objection. "And have you not surpassed all your brothers? Should not the seventh son of a seventh son follow in his father's steps?"

The king leaned back and combed trembling fingers through his beard. His eyes shifted downward as Yahtadua caught hold of Bilkis's gown and tugged away the silk to reveal a plump breast. The queen cooed at her son but made no attempt to cover herself.

"My lady's lips are sweetened by her words of wisdom," Tadua said, then wiped a hand across his mouth. "I would taste more."

Bilkis allowed a slight smile.

"Rahab," she called, her eyes never leaving the king's.

The girl had sat silently near the hearth, spinning out wool. She set down her spindle and came to Bilkis's side.

"Take Yahtadua to his nurse, then put him down for the night," Bilkis told her. "The king and I have much to discuss."

Rahab took the boy, who fussed and reached for his mother.

"Yes, Sister," she replied, then bowed to the king. "My lord."

Tadua made some gesture of dismissal, and Rahab carried the prince from the chamber. Even before the door closed behind them, Bilkis slipped the gown from her shoulders and let it fall about her waist. She stooped to kiss the king's feet, then looked up at him from between his knees. Tadua's breathing grew heavy as Bilkis eased her hands beneath his robes and slid them up his legs and along his thighs.

"What more would my lord discuss?"

26
Bilkis

Wails sliced through the curtain of Bilkis's dreams. She opened her eyes upon the half-light of dawn. Her first thought was to have Yahtadua's nurse beaten and cast out of the palace for allowing the prince to cry so. As sleep's veil parted, she recognized not an infant's petulance, but the grief of grown women.

Tadua stirred and made a guttural sound.

"Rest, Husband," Bilkis said. "I will see what disturbs your peace."

She disentangled herself from the sheets, slipped into her gown, and stuffed her feet into sheepskin slippers. The palace stewards had yet to kindle the hearth, so she threw the king's heavy scarlet mantle over her shoulders. She opened the door to find Rahab in muted argument with the guard posted outside Tadua's chamber.

"What is happening?" Bilkis demanded after she pulled the door closed.

"There is trouble in the harem," Rahab said.

"Do not let anyone disturb the king," Bilkis ordered the guard. "He needs his rest. What trouble?" she asked as she led Rahab along the corridor.

Rahab shook her head. "I only heard the screams from the women, then came to find you."

When they reached the harem, the guard bowed low before Bilkis. She pushed past him and flung open the door to the women's quarters.

"What is the meaning of this?" she demanded. "You'll disturb the king and wake the dead with your noise."

All the women had gathered at one end of the chamber, where space had been set aside for the nursing mothers. Taniri held a child protectively in her arms while she cursed and screamed at Pudu-Estan. The Hatti princess's face was streaked with tears, but she returned insults and had to be restrained by the other women who added their shouts to the fray.

Mikhel sat quietly apart from the others. The erstwhile great royal wife of Tadua nestled the other infant in her arms and rocked to and fro. The former queen, alone among the widows, had borne no children, but she cuddled and kissed the fair-cheeked babe as if it were her own.

A cold voice whispered in Bilkis's ear that all was not right. She stepped toward Mikhel, whose tears anointed the boy's face. The baby did not fuss. He simply lay still, pale, unmoving. A shudder rippled along Bilkis's spine when she saw the blue tinge around the tiny, pursed lips.

"What happened?" she asked. Mikhel did not respond, and it took a moment for Bilkis to realize she couldn't be heard over the bickering women. "Quiet, you bleating goats," she shouted. The women fell silent, save for the stifled sobs of Pudu-Estan and Haggit's whispers of comfort.

"What is the meaning of this?" Bilkis demanded once more. The older women held their tongues and looked away. Pudu-Estan's words remained choked with tears. Only Taniri found voice to answer the queen.

"This cow," she said, balancing her squirming child in one arm and pointing to the Hatti, "rolled onto her son as she slept. Now she tries to claim mine for herself."

"Not so," Pudu-Estan objected. Between her accent and sobs, Bilkis struggled to understand her. "The demon Lilit came for her son in the night. As I slept she exchanged her dead boy for my living one. See his ruddy skin? His dark hair? Surely I know my own child."

"Yours was the fair one," the yellow-haired Taniri claimed. "You speak with a serpent's twisted tongue."

Pudu-Estan might have gouged out the other's eyes had the older women not caught her about the waist and restrained her. "You are a murderer of children and a slayer of truth," she spat.

The room erupted into chaos once more, and Bilkis rubbed her fingers against the ache that crept from her temple to her forehead.

"Quiet," she shouted again, but the women were beyond hearing her.

Clearly, one of the women was lying. The dead child's hair did resemble Taniri's, but did that make certainty? Another whisper sounded in Bilkis's ear, and she cocked her head. The message—what could only be the voice of the goddess—repeated.

Bilkis stalked to the door and jerked it open. She yanked the sword from the scabbard of the startled guard, then slammed the door closed. When she swung the heavy bronze blade through a water jar, the women gave her their attention. Even Mikhel, whose focus had been entirely on the dead child, looked up.

A tightness gripped Bilkis's stomach, clawed along her throat, and squeezed her heart and lungs. The sound of a hundred mosquitoes filled her ears as she looked from one woman to the next.

Protect your throne, the goddess whispered, her voice alone rising above the din.

"Rahab, bring me the child," Bilkis ordered.

The girl nodded and stepped toward Mikhel.

"Not him." Bilkis pointed the sword toward Taniri with her mewling infant. "That one."

"Sister—"

"Do it," Bilkis snapped.

Rahab looked from Bilkis to the women, then slowly obeyed. She lifted the child from Taniri's arms. Pudu-Estan began to protest, but the other women hushed her.

"Put him there." Bilkis indicated a low brass table, wet and littered with fragments of the water jar.

The girl did as she was told, then stepped away. The infant squalled in protest at being left alone on the cold, wet metal.

"Does anyone speak for one of these women?" Bilkis asked, her words slow and measured. "Does anyone call the other a speaker of falsehood?"

"She lies," Pudu-Estan declared. "Please, let me have my son."

"The child is mine," Taniri countered. "That Hatti whore is the one who lies."

Bilkis raised her empty hand. "Enough." The young women glared at one another, but said no more.

"No one else speaks?" Bilkis prompted, and received only silence. "Very well. As we have but these two competing claims, it is left to us to decide."

The queen stood over the child and gripped the sword's hilt with both hands. She raised the blade over her head, the scarlet mantle falling to the floor as she did so.

"As both of you claim this child, you each shall have a share of him."

"No," Pudu-Estan cried. "It was me. I lied. The child belongs to Taniri. Let her have him. Only let him live."

"The queen has spoken justly," Taniri countered. "Let her do as she deems best."

Bilkis paused. Her eyes flicked from one woman to the other, the truth made clear by word and deed.

Another truth stood plainly before her. One potential rival to Yahtadua's future—to Bilkis's own future—lay dead in Mikhel's arms. Another lay squirming upon the table.

Protect your throne, the goddess again advised her. Bilkis had given up a child of her own, given a son to the goddess so that her other son could gain that throne. But could she ask another woman to make a similar sacrifice? The sword wavered and grew heavier in her hands.

"Do it," Taniri shouted.

The room again burst into a storm of voices, Taniri's calling for blood, the others pleading for mercy.

"Sister, please." Rahab's voice slashed through the cacophony like lightning through a storm cloud, but another voice flashed even brighter.

Protect your son.

Bilkis swung the sword.

A SONG OF GATHERING

27

Makeda

Seasons passed. Stars, moon, and sun tracked their courses. Three times the Wadi Dhanah flooded. Three times devastation transformed to life as the floodwaters fed the fields of Maryaba.

The Council of Elders, bolstered now by emissaries from Timnah and Qani and Nahran—even a pair of Bedou from the desert tribes—formed the Grand Council of Saba. In the absence of a Mukarrib, the old men sat and argued, chewed their bunn berries and drank their beer, while all of Saba shared in the labor and the bounty of Maryaba's oasis.

And I thrived. Not yet a woman, I was still too young to marry Dhamar of Timnah and take my place as Mukarrib. I spent my days among the crops, studying the plants and the creatures—animal and human—that tended them. By night I tracked the moon and stars until I knew their cycles, their risings and their settings.

Shayma, an old widow who'd moved into the tower house to look after me, told me the names of the Star Dwellers and the stories of their origins. I'd listened dutifully, more interested in their importance to my people than in the myths. When the stars of the Maiden appeared in the evening sky, Elmakah's storm clouds would soon form in the west, presage of the flooding of Wadi Dhanah. With the arrival of the Archer came the time for the first harvest.

"You should be resting," Shayma chided me, as she did most mornings, "not spending your night in the cold, looking at nothing."

"How can you say that?" I asked as I sat at the table. "You taught me about the Star Dwellers. Am I now to ignore them?"

"I taught you those stories so you could tell them yourself one day." Shayma sat down and wrapped thick, callused fingers around mine. "The tales are meant to be shared around the hearth with children. Or on a lover's pillow." She waggled one hairless eyebrow and gave a toothless grin. "Don't forget your pomegranate."

I eyed the pomegranate, could almost taste its juice, feel its pulp burst on my tongue. I craved it, but, since learning Shayma's purpose in serving it to me, refused to indulge myself.

"Lord Dhamar arrives today, yes?" Shayma asked, as though sensing my thoughts.

The sowing equinox was in three days' time and was one of four yearly festivals when the lords of Saba convened at Maryaba. Here they would worship the gods, make new laws, and pledge fidelity to one another. Their real intent, I knew, was to inspect the dam and the fields, and to ensure each received a proper share of the harvest.

For Watar of Timnah, there was another reason. Along with the dam and the crops he would also inspect me, to determine whether I was ready to marry and produce his grandchild who would become Mukarrib of all Saba.

"I'm going to the vineyards," I said, ignoring Shayma's question.

"Don't forget your pomegranate."

I started to protest but checked myself and picked up the fruit. Easier simply to take it and placate the old woman. I could always give it to a beggar.

I climbed down from the tower house—the old wooden ladder having been replaced with a mud-brick stairway—and wandered toward the city's gate. Crowds swarmed the streets of Maryaba. The city's population had nearly tripled since the dam's completion. Scores of children had been born and more than half survived, thanks to the increased food stores. The majority of the influx, however, were immigrants from across Saba, from the desert tribes, even from Uwene beyond the sea. All were drawn by the prosperity wrought by the dam and fields, and by the peace that reigned throughout the land.

In the marketplace, carts and stalls held all manner of foodstuffs, crafts, and wares. It had been more than four years since a trade caravan had come to Maryaba, so there were no exotic silks or gems or spices. A few luxuries arrived from Uwene, but those ivories and pelts were quickly snatched up by the wealthier elders.

I ignored the merchants and passed on to the great wooden gate. Yanuf sat behind a table, a brightly dyed awning stretched over him while he collected tolls on the goods that entered the city.

"The shara's husband arrives today." Yanuf spoke to the merchant who stood before his table, but his voice was raised so I knew the words were for me. "An ugly toad of a man. All warts and pocks, but at least he's a weakling."

I stopped and glared at Yanuf.

"Oh, of course he has good qualities." The old warrior scratched under his beard as he tried to think of some. "He's old," he finally offered. "Must be nigh on twenty years, so he shouldn't vex his wife for too long."

I hurled the pomegranate at Yanuf. The waiting merchant chose a poor time to shift his position, and the juice-laden fruit took him full in the back. Yanuf's laughter echoed through the marketplace, while I slunk behind a donkey and sidled out the gate.

Yanuf's jests burrowed into my heart as I followed the pathway that led to the dam. I despised Dhamar, dreaded the very notion of becoming his wife, but saw no alternative. The great dam had been built and the crops secured by the peace between Maryaba and Timnah. A peace brokered between Mother and Watar as the dowry for their heirs.

I'd discussed the matter with Yanuf, who had become a father to me. The old warrior could see no other way—none that kept the peace—than for me to fulfill my mother's bargain. He'd consoled me, then set about a series of jests and teasing that appeared to have no end.

The strategy had worked, I admitted. My irritation with Yanuf's continual jibes kept my thoughts from the dread that soured my stomach, a dread that Shayma dismissed.

"Any woman should be fortunate to win such a man as Dhamar," the old woman repeatedly told me. "Spun on the wheel of the gods, that one."

She made a point. Dhamar was the very image of manhood. His limbs lean and muscled, he moved with a lion's grace. He could outrun, outfight, and outshoot any other man. More than a few girls of Maryaba claimed the lord's attentions. I drew their looks in the market as Bilkis had so long ago. Looks of awe and envy from the young women who craved my fate.

They could have it. For all his manly grace, Dhamar of Timnah was an ill-formed wretch. A black emptiness sat in him where in other men dwelt honor, duty, gentleness. Without these, he was nothing more than an eye-pleasing beast. Men might admire him, women desire him, but he would never win the hearts of his people—or the love of his bride.

A pang of anxiety twisted deep within me, and I gasped with the suddenness of it. I pressed a hand to my belly as I continued up the path to the vineyards, then turned off the path when I reached the rows of grapevines.

Their shade formed a refuge from the heat. I ran a hand along the leaves, noting clusters of tiny green berries that, by harvest time, would be bursting with sweet red juice.

Claws of pain sliced through my abdomen. I clutched a branch to keep from falling as my knees buckled. Something skittered down my leg, and I lurched back. I searched the ground for whatever it was, but spied only a drop of red, bright against the black earth. The pain receded, giving way to a sandstorm of fear that swept through my heart. Hesitantly, I raised the skirts of my robe.

A rivulet of blood stretched from my ankle to my inner thigh. My heart cried out in denial, but there was no escaping the truth.

I was a woman.

Shayma's tricks had worked. The pomegranate had quickened my womb, and I must soon become a wife. Wife to Dhamar.

I dropped to my knees. I grabbed handfuls of dirt and scrubbed my legs to remove the stain of womanhood. When I'd replaced the red streak with smears of mud I tore at the soil that had been spotted with my blood. I took another fistful of earth, then pulled back when something bit into my flesh.

Fearing a snake, I scanned the ground but saw only a glint of metal where I'd disturbed the earth. I brushed away the soil to reveal a silver dragonfly, its wings studded with dirt-encrusted jewels.

Bilkis's comb.

I plucked the trinket from the earth. A chill coursed down my spine, and emotions flooded through me. Guilt. Loneliness. Gratitude, that the gods had spared me from the flood. A scornful laugh burst through my lips. The gods had saved me only to condemn me to a living death as Dhamar's wife. Were they truly so cruel?

Sunlight caressed my cheek as Shams rose in the sky. Warmth seeped through my skin, eased my suffering womb, stilled my harried thoughts. Yes, the gods had saved me. Perhaps they would save me again.

The seed of an idea took root in my heart. There was a way. A precarious way, but there nonetheless. Hope smoldering in my breast, I headed back toward the gate. I needed to speak with Yanuf, to work out this mad plan.

Succeed, and I would win my place as Mukarrib and my freedom from Dhamar.

Fail and, whether to my body or to my spirit, the cost would be death.

28

Makeda

I stood rigid, doing my best not to shrink under the weight of thousands of stares. From the hillock where I stood, I looked over the heads of the crowd. The walls of Maryaba glowed orange in the light of the rising sun, dulled by the red veil that covered my head. To the south, distant but fast drawing near, a cloud of dust rose above the fields.

Surrounded by the elders and people of Saba, I waited atop the hill. Waited for my groom. Shayma fluttered beside me like a mother duck. Her pride was evident, at having fostered the next mukarrib from hatchling to hen.

"Stop your pecking, old woman," Yanuf growled under his breath.

I tried and failed to suppress a grin. Yanuf stood behind me and to one side, ever the faithful guardian, and my partner in the day's mischief. My grin faded, though, as the dust cloud loomed nearer. A dry breeze washed over me, sweeping the veil from my face. I swallowed against my suddenly parched throat as Athtar's breath caressed my cheek. Shayma fixed the veil in its place, then continued to pluck at my green silk robe.

A shout rose from the edge of the crowd where the dust plume hung. The lake of people made way, and through them rode Dhamar and his groomsmen. Armed for battle, they charged toward the hillock, heedless of any in their path.

Holding to tradition, the elders linked arms in a feeble blockade at the foot of the hill. Their line wavered as Dhamar charged them unchecked. Just as I thought he would trample the elders, Dhamar yanked back on his horse's reins. The stallion screamed in protest and slewed away from the line, showering the fuming old men with dust.

Dhamar drove the beast in a tight circle before the elders. The stallion's mane was dull with dust, but its dark flanks gleamed in the morning sun. The animal shook dirt from its mane, its head erect as it pranced its circle.

Its rider was no less haughty. Dhamar had replaced his usual robe with a short kilt and tunic of leather. The warrior's garb accentuated muscled arms and legs. His wavy black hair hung loose, almost to his shoulders, and framed his face.

Despite myself, I was drawn to this lord, this warrior, this man after the gods' own mold. Until I met his gaze. His cold, black eyes had none of Yanuf's good humor or the wisdom of Watar, Dhamar's father. Instead, the young man's eyes bore a dull, lifeless look that bespoke only raw, bestial hunger.

"I have come for the woman Makeda," Dhamar shouted. "I have come for the daughter of Karibil, for the daughter of Ayana."

He raised a leather flail toward me, and the first spark of life illumined his features. I cringed inwardly at the cruelty in his eyes.

"Does any elder dispute my claim?"

Dhamar paced his horse along the row of tribal leaders and priests, fixing his gaze on each man as if daring him to object. A grin twisted Dhamar's mouth when the elders remained silent.

"Does any man contest my will?"

Dhamar looked past me to where Yanuf stood. The old warrior growled but my bridegroom appeared not to notice. Dhamar reined his horse around to face the crowd.

"Does anyone oppose my right?" The question met silence, save for the snorts and pawing of restless horses. And the crashing of my heartbeat in my ears.

I took a tremulous breath, then stepped forward as Dhamar turned to claim his prize.

"I." My voice rang clear and bright. "I speak in opposition."

Another silence greeted my pronouncement, this one broken only by the shuffling of sandals as the crowd edged closer to the hillock.

"You?" Dhamar demanded. "You are party to the betrothal. To break your oath—"

155

"I speak on behalf of the god Athtar, before whom the oath was made, by whose blessing the oath was sealed."

The crowd broke its silence at that.

"By what reason—" Dhamar began, then spun toward the assembly. "Silence, dogs," he shouted, spittle leaping from his lips.

His demand went unheeded, the outcry becoming even greater when Dhamar signaled his men and they began harrying the foremost rows of onlookers.

Yanuf took two steps forward and raised his spear horizontally over his head.

"Silence!"

The voice that had once rung in battle now echoed across the plain. The people ceased their clamor. The warriors stopped their jostling. Even Dhamar backed his horse a step, its ears flattened.

"The shara speaks." Yanuf lowered his spear, winked at me, then stepped back to his place.

I scanned the crowd, licked my lips, and rubbed damp palms against my robe. "Athtar has claimed me as his bride. He has set aside my betrothal to Dhamar of Timnah."

"You break your oath." Dhamar pointed his flail at me. "You break our peace."

"Athtar annuls the oath," I said. "If you deny his right to do so, then what good is a vow sworn before him?"

Dhamar looked as though I'd struck him, and I pressed on before he found his tongue. I sought out Watar and stepped toward the Lord of Timnah.

"You and my mother made peace before Athtar. My betrothal to your son was but the surety of that peace, not its cause. This … " I spread my arms, gesturing toward the verdant fields and the well-fed masses from throughout Saba. "This was the cause of our peace. And the gods have blessed that peace. Saba thrives. Timnah, Maryaba, all the people thrive. Should not Athtar receive his thank-offering in return?"

"She speaks with the tongue of a serpent," Dhamar cried, his voice rising in pitch. "She belongs to me." He nudged his horse forward, but Watar grabbed the bridle and stopped him.

"Silence, boy," he hissed. "Do not dishonor yourself any further." To the elders he said, "My brothers, we invoke your judgment. Many of you bore witness to the oath between Ayana and me. Can it be set aside?"

All eyes turned toward the remembrancer. Frail and withered, the old man blinked his sunken black eyes. He combed the gnarled fingers of one hand through his straggly beard. With the others he tapped his forehead, as though to aid his recollection.

I bit my lip. Yanuf had already prompted the old man's memory, after I'd proposed this mad scheme. Whether the remembrancer had forgotten or was playing to the crowd, I couldn't say. Every face stared with rapt attention, awaiting the man's announcement. Every mouth fell open when his eyes went wide and he waggled an index finger.

"Ah, yes. 'In the name of Athtar, by Shams's light and under the blessing of Elmakah, Ayana, Mukarrib of all Saba, resolves to rebuild the dam at Wadi Dhanah. Watar, Lord of Timnah, pledges to protect Maryaba and its holdings from any attack, for a time not less than three years after the dam's completion. In exchange for which, Timnah shall receive a half-tithe of each harvest, during such time as this treaty stands between Ayana and her successors, and Watar and his heirs. In token of this, Ayana offers in betrothal her daughter Makeda to Dhamar of Timnah, son of Watar, their union to be celebrated upon her coming of age. To all this, Ayana and Watar make their oath before Athtar, and before the Council of Elders, in the first year of Ayana, Mukarrib of all Saba.'"

"You see?" Dhamar said when the man finished. "She breaks her mother's oath. She breaks our peace."

"Peace remains," Yanuf declared, stepping once more beside me, "as long as Timnah wishes to be fed. The shara is correct. The harvest-share is the peace bounty. The betrothal is but a token, a symbol of that peace."

Dhamar persisted. "If the symbol is broken, then the peace is broken."

A handful of elders muttered agreement.

"Not so." Walid, a merchant from Qani on the southern coast, stepped forward and gestured to the others. "A token may be traded or exchanged, but its value remains. The token is a sign of intent before the gods. If Athtar chooses to claim the bride for himself, he makes the token his."

More men nodded, including a few who had sided with Dhamar. I cast a sideways glance at Yanuf, whose quiet calm gave me confidence. I was about to speak when Watar raised his voice again.

"I thank my brothers for their words of wisdom. I declare to you that as long as I live, peace shall stand among our cities."

"And how long will that be, old man?"

All eyes turned toward Dhamar. From the look on his face, it was clear he hadn't intended to speak the words so loudly. Watar glared at his son, who slowly bowed his head.

"The gods have shown us," Watar continued, "that all Saba prospers when her people work together, rather than each for his own gain."

A rumble of approval greeted the words. Anxiety loosened its clutch on my heart.

"As for the token, however," Watar added, and my heart tightened again, "can we be sure of Athtar's claim? Has any priest received a vision? Have any auguries confirmed it?"

"The mukarrib is high priestess of all the gods," Yanuf said. "She speaks for the people and for the gods."

Watar nodded. "Granted. However, the shara is but a girl who—"

"A woman," Shayma squawked. "She is a woman now."

"A noble woman," Watar agreed, "but also a young woman. One who faces the great responsibilities of leading her people and of becoming a bride. It would be natural for her to have doubts, or to confuse a mere dream for the word of the gods."

Silence again hugged the plain. Watar presented an escape from the impasse. I could end the dispute now. I could admit confusing a dream with a vision, go through with the wedding, and preserve both my and Dhamar's dignities.

And be wife to a half-man. No. I would not, could not accept that.

Peace was secure. Watar had declared it. My future was less certain. I might become Mukarrib. I might have my inheritance stripped away for defying the gods. I might even be killed for daring to speak falsely in Athtar's name. Any of these possibilities was preferable to the certain misery of being wed to Dhamar.

"Athtar has claimed me," I said, my voice soft but clear.

Pity darkened Watar's face. He was a pragmatic man, if not visionary. He seemed to read the future now, however, and my heart almost broke for the sadness it brought to his eyes.

"A challenge," Walid suggested.

"What do you mean?" Yatha, the priest of Athtar, asked.

"The shara claims Athtar spoke to her," the merchant explained. "Dhamar says she lies."

"He says no such thing," Watar interjected, despite Dhamar's vigorous nod.

"Of course," Walid said. "That she is mistaken, then. In any case, the god's will is disputed. Unless his priest has any guidance to offer?"

The holy man said nothing.

"Tradition requires a challenge," Walid said. "A trial to determine what the gods desire."

"A test of arms," Yanuf declared. "And I will stand for the shara."

"A test of arms?" Dhamar's voice was thick with scorn. "I have two. I win."

The young lord and his comrades barked with laughter. Yanuf's ruddy face flushed as his empty sleeve wafted on the light wind.

I laid a hand atop Yanuf's. "A trial by combat is fitting," I said, "when the claim to a bride is contested."

"That is true," Yatha said, "but that is in a dispute between the combatants. Does Yanuf claim the shara's hand, or does Athtar? No, if it is to be a test of arms then I fear the god must fight for himself. Is that your wish?"

A breeze washed through the silence and tugged at my veil. Despite all the pins Shayma had used to fasten it in place, the wind plucked the red silk from my head. Shayma grasped for the veil, but it floated high on Athtar's breath and drifted toward the desert. I fixed my gaze on the veil, a red scratch upon the eastern sky. "The wilderness." I spoke the words the breeze whispered in my ear.

"Shara, no," Yanuf said in a low voice.

"What was that?" Watar asked.

I turned back to the elders. "I accept the Trial of the Wilderness."

Shayma wailed when I delivered the words. Few had ever undertaken the challenge to journey to Eram, a legendary city lost in the desert wastes far toward the sunrise. None in my lifetime had ever returned.

"Shara, what are you saying?" Yanuf's voice cracked.

I looked into the old warrior's eyes, filled with worry. "I am saying what I must, for myself and for my people." I turned toward the elders and the assembly.

"People of Saba," I began, my voice stoked with more conviction than I felt. "Even now the great god Athtar has claimed me, for who but a husband may unveil his bride?"

"And if you fail?" Yanuf prompted, his voice deep with emotion.

I stood up straighter. "If Athtar releases me from his claim," I said in a determined voice, "I shall return, humbled and subject to Dhamar as wife." I managed to smile at my would-be bridegroom. "If, however, Athtar sustains and guides me across the desert and back, I shall return beholden to no mortal man, reserved to the god and ordained as inheritor of the line of Karibil, Mukarrib of all Saba."

"And in the third case?" Dhamar's voice rang cold through the morning air.

"After the prescribed forty days, if I do not return," I said, "then I will have failed as Shara of Maryaba. I will be proven to have misread the god's intentions and shown myself unworthy to lead our great people. The Council of Elders will then select your next leader."

"Agreed," Dhamar shouted, then seemed to become aware of the eyes upon him. "If Athtar should prove true in his desire for my betrothed, I will bow before him. If, however, our shara returns from the wilderness unfulfilled ... " He fixed me with a hungry gaze that chilled my spine. "Then shall I welcome her with a loving husband's embrace."

I returned Dhamar's stare, my eyes hardened as a shield before my heart.

"So may it be done," I said.

"So may it be done," the elders agreed.

"So shall it be remembered." The old remembrancer tapped his temple in a familiar cadence.

"Shara."

I turned to Yanuf, his face engraved with worry.

"All will be well," I assured the old warrior, my guardian and friend.

Yanuf nodded, though his eyes betrayed his doubts. He pulled his sheathed janbiya, the curved dagger favored by the men of Saba, from its place at the front of his waist sash and offered it to me.

"She cannot receive help from any human hand." Dhamar's voice rose with petulance.

The elders turned toward Yatha. The old man shrank under their gaze. I thought I saw the slightest of nods from Lord Watar.

"It is permitted," Athtar's priest declared.

I took the dagger and smiled up at Yanuf. "Forty days," I said, struggling to keep my voice even. "It's not so very long."

Yanuf squeezed my shoulder, then turned away.

Shayma started an ululating cry, which was taken up by the assembly as I turned toward the rising sun. My ears ringing with the mourners' voices, I climbed down the hillock and set out toward the endless wasteland.

29

Makeda

What have I done?

I huddled in the shallow, sandy burrow I'd hollowed out of the wadi. It offered some protection from Shams's midday fury, but did little to ease my fear of being stranded in this desert waste.

Trust the gods, I reminded myself.

But Athtar offered no cooling breeze. Elmakah made no clouds to temper Shams's flame. The goddess raged in naked wrath upon this small, impudent child who'd had the audacity to invade her sandy fastness. I wished for tears, but none came. Perhaps it was just as well. I would need all the moisture my body could retain for the journey ahead. I pulled my veil close about me and hugged my knees to my chest.

The veil. That swath of silk, red as the blood that marked the death of the child and the birth of the woman. The token claimed by Athtar to lure me into the desert, where I'd recovered it from the sands. The cloth that might well become my burial shroud. I'd been a fool, I knew. A fool to challenge Dhamar's claim upon me. A fool to presume to speak for the gods. Yet the omens had seemed so clear. With a resigned sigh I committed myself to the gods' care.

The Trial of the Wilderness required the pilgrim to pass through the desert to the long-dead city of Eram. The ruins lay some fifteen days to the east. According to the elders, Eram once prospered where the Wadi Dhanah flowed into a great inland sea. In that long-ago time, the wadi ran year-round, fed by frequent rains and mountain run-off.

The Eramites had thrived on agriculture and fishing and trade with distant lands. When they grew prideful and stopped giving the gods their due, the rains stopped, the wadi dried up, and the sea disappeared beneath the desert. The people fled and the mighty walls crumbled. So complete was the destruction, legend said, that only by the gods' mercy might a pilgrim find his way to the lost ruins, gather a shell from the dry lake bed, and return once more across the sands.

I only half-believed the stories. There must be some truth to them, or Yanuf would never have let me pursue this mad quest. I feared, though, that I might survive the journey into the wilderness, might reach the shores of the lost sea only to mistake the wondrous city of the ancients for a jumble of rocks.

Yanuf's dagger—its blade buried in the sand of the wadi—stretched its shadow farther toward the east. Shams's fury would soon ease, and I knew I must make use of the remaining daylight hours rather than risk losing my way in the cold, moonless night.

I took another breath of the relatively cool air, then retrieved the janbiya and again stepped into the furnace.

❖

A shadow stretched before me, sprawled across the heat-shimmering earth. The figure seemed more beast than human, cast upon all fours as it scrabbled through the sand. The creature's mane stood out in tangled locks, its hide gaunt and limp where it hung from a skeletal frame. Each faltering step looked as though it must be its last, yet still the stubborn wretch trudged forward across the rocky ground.

"Stop," I pleaded, my voice a ragged hiss that twisted past my parched throat and cracked lips. "Quit."

The wraith ignored me and continued its shambling stride. For three days the shadow had been my desert companion. At times lagging behind, sometimes beside me, and other times racing ahead, my dark self mimicked every move in weirdly exaggerated form. Only at night, when all the world's shadows melded into an earth-blanketing whole—only then did I feel alone. Abandoned.

Now I craved that abandon. I longed to cut the threads that bound me to the fiend that mercilessly dragged me on when a sane person would long ago have quit. But the shadow persisted in its hold on me, forcing my arms and legs to carry me forward.

No matter. It would soon be night. The shadow would leave, only to return with dawn's light to find its host gone.

The wraith lurched to one side. I felt myself drawn toward the edge of the sand-choked wadi. A pile of stones cast their own shadows far to the east, having basked in Shams's glory throughout the long day. Properly arranged, they would emit enough heat to warm me—or my corpse, if the gods were merciful—throughout the bitter night.

I arrived at the stones just as the shadow did, and reached out to move the rocks into better position. The shadow's hand jerked back even as heat stung my fingers. The stones yet burned from Shams's touch. I hissed a curse that lingered on the still air. It took a few moments to realize the sound came not from the echo of my curse, but from the rocks themselves.

Panic flooded my veins, restoring the strength sapped by the sun. I reared onto my haunches as the susurrus from the rocks rose in pitch. I groped among the folds of my veil for Yanuf's dagger. Even as my fingers wrapped about the ivory hilt, a scaly snout emerged from amid the stones. The viper's jaws gaped. Quicker than a thought, it sprang from its hiding place. I fell onto my backside and the dagger came free. The blade whistled through the air and caught the viper just behind its head.

The momentum of the fall carried me onto my back, the snake's body close behind. The heavy, leathery coils muffled my cries. Scales scratched my face and neck. I dropped the dagger and clawed at the viper with both hands. I flung the serpent away, my screams spiced with the tang of its blood.

I swallowed, the blood soothing as it crept down my throat. I swept my tongue over my lips, then wiped my hands over my face and licked my fingers clean. Strength flowed into my limbs as the blood reached my stomach.

The snake had not flown far. I scrambled over the rocky earth to where it lay. Without reasoning, I grasped it by the tail, opened my mouth to its headless neck and ran my free hand along its body. Blood coursed over my teeth and tongue, spilled onto my lips when I closed them to swallow, then cascaded into my mouth again. I milked the blood from the viper until it had no more to give.

With renewed vigor, I arose—still clutching the snake's tail—and strode to where the dagger lay. My shadow stretched long and sinewy before me. I picked up the janbiya and wiped it clean with my robe.

I sheathed the dagger and stooped to retrieve the snake's head. Careful of the fangs, I set it atop the piled rocks.

Ears alert for the sound of rustling scales, I knelt before the makeshift altar, stretched the viper's body before me, and bowed my head to the ground.

My heart swelled with gratitude for the snake's demonstration of the gods' protection. For in the serpent I'd found salvation.

With Yanuf's dagger, I butchered the snake, separating skin and meat, fat and entrails. After setting the meat and skin to cure on the warm rocks, I rubbed the fat into my bridal veil until it glistened like oiled canvas.

I then dug a pit in the bed of the dry wadi, reaching deeper than my elbows before the soil appeared dark with moisture. I urinated into the pit and threw in the viper's entrails, then set in the center half the husk of a melon I'd taken from Maryaba's fields. With rocks to secure the veil across the mouth of the pit, I placed a smaller stone in the middle, above the melon.

Then I waited.

I waited through the night and the waxing morning, through the heat of Shams's zenith and into her descent. When the sun eased more than halfway toward the western horizon, I finally crept from my den to see what magic my labors had wrought.

I removed the stones and lifted the veil from above the pit. The stench of urine and offal bludgeoned my senses, but my heart soared when I saw water droplets on the underside of the veil. Holding my breath, I reached into the hole, took hold of the melon husk, and lifted it from the pit.

Yanuf's miracle had worked.

Throughout the long, scorching day, Shams's heat had filled the pit, evaporating any moisture within. Unable to pass the fat-coated silk, the vapor collected there until it formed droplets that fell into the husk. The process had created enough water to fill a third of the melon.

I sniffed at the cup, wary of any rot that may have tainted the water. I smelled only melon, so tentatively brought the makeshift bowl to my mouth. Pure water—warm, but refreshing—tickled my lips and tongue, and slid down my throat. Greedily, I tipped the melon and drank. Not enough to fill my mouth, still the water invigorated me and lifted my spirits.

Hope swelled in my breast. No, more than hope. Promise.

I could create water. I had food—perhaps only enough for a few days, but I possessed the tools to find more. With the moon's waxing, I could see to travel at night, then rest and distill water during the heat of the day.

If legends were true, Eram lay not twelve days farther along the wadi. An inner voice objected that I might simply be drifting deeper into the land of death, but I quashed the thought.

I would hope. I would live. And, gods willing, I would fulfill my quest and win control over my destiny.

30

Makeda

Ten more days came and went. Then another day, and another.
Each morning I made my obeisance to Shams, dug a water pit, and burrowed into whatever shade I could find. Twice more, snakes disputed my resting place and became my food. Each evening I drank my water, surveyed my path by the long shadows cast by the setting sun, and set out once more.

On the twelfth day, I began watching for stacked rocks or some other landmark that might have given rise to the legend of Eram. By the fifteenth day, fear edged into the recesses of my heart, displacing the hope and promise that had sustained me. As the sky lightened with the dawning of the eighteenth day, promise fled and hope was all but gone. Not for the first time, I looked toward the west, my footprints faint smudges in the sand of the long-dried wadi, the slenderest of ribbons connecting me to home.

I summoned Dhamar's image, and the thought of his gloating over my failure strengthened my resolve. I turned once more to greet the rising sun. "Hail the East," I intoned after making my first prostration. "Hail the morning." I bowed and rose again. "Hail the—"

Sham's first rays stretched along the wadi, casting the long shadows that had helped me track the dry riverbed's course. Accustomed to the gentle swells that defined the wadi's banks, I gaped at the angular shadows cast by the morning light and marveled at a trio of slender black fingers that beckoned me toward the horizon.

I moved eastward, my tentative pace becoming more deliberate with each stride. The shadows retreated step by step, and I still couldn't see what cast them. I willed my feet through their motions, but when a long swath of green sprouted from the horizon, I no longer needed to force them. Of their own volition, my feet brought me into a run.

I ran without trying. I ran without thinking. I ran without breathing until my burning lungs demanded to be quenched. Shams consumed the horizon as she burst into view in all her blinding glory.

And still I ran.

My eyes cast on the ground only a few paces ahead, I took an occasional glance toward the sun. Little by little, silhouettes began to mar Shams's perfect countenance. The lines stretched and deepened until there was more dark than light. By the time Shams cleared the horizon, I found myself within a tangle of shadows.

I came to a stop, resting my hands on my knees as my lungs labored to keep pace with my pounding heart. Breath by breath, I drew in air, cool and dank. As I looked around, my heart began to race again, not from exertion but in awe of the sight.

Date palms—taller than I'd ever before seen—stretched toward the sky. Their broad, tattered leaves cast mottled shadows over the grove that spread as far as I could see. In the shade grew vines and shrubs, studded with fruit and flower. More than this natural bounty, the artificial wonders sapped my breath. At regular intervals throughout the grove stood great stone pillars, high as the tallest trees. I reached out to touch one, the stone cool and smooth beneath my hands. Great blocks—nearly as tall as me, and twice the width of my arm span—fit together so tightly I could barely make out the joints.

I fell to my knees, bowed my face to the ground, and covered my head with my hands.

"Athtar, forgive me."

Surely I'd passed Eram's ruins and intruded into Athtar's garden, ringed by boundary markers raised by his own hand, for no mortal could have placed such great stones in perfect harmony.

A trace of wind stroked my cheek. I lifted my eyes, half-expecting to see the god standing before me. But my bridegroom remained invisible.

Bridegroom.

I smiled at the thought. Perhaps Athtar really had chosen me. My scheme had been a simple enough means of keeping myself free of Dhamar's bed, and I fully intended to keep my vows to the great god. I would take no other husband, bear no children. I would live as a widow, my life dedicated in service to the god and to my people.

That had been my plan, the fruit of my own heart. But as I knelt beneath the green canopy, before this stone monument, amid this garden hidden half a moon's journey into the desert, I wondered if Athtar had, indeed, claimed me as his own.

The breeze cooled my cheeks, Athtar's breath sweet with the scent of flowers and honey. And something more.

I breathed deeply, unable to identify the scent. I stood, turned my face into the wind, and followed my nose deeper into the grove.

My ears were next to inform me with the sounds of gentle lapping from somewhere ahead, where my eyes could not yet penetrate. I increased my pace and followed a trail only my nose and ears could discern.

Something flashed among the trees ahead of me. The canopy grew brighter, shimmering as though lit from below by great, flickering candles. I now ran, dodging branches and vines and roots until I burst into a clearing. My heart thrummed, my breath faltered. I was only dimly aware of my actions as I kicked off my sandals, and stripped off my robe. I raced forward, stretched my arms over my head and dove through the air.

With a splash, I landed in the pool of the oasis, its clear waters drawing me into their embrace. I opened my mouth, and the liquid—sweet as honey—washed over my tongue. I swallowed, tried to breathe in the life-giving water, to imbibe it with my whole being, but my burning nose and lungs forced me to stroke for the surface.

Choking, sputtering, laughing, I paddled and splashed my way to the pool's edge. I dragged myself onto the sandy bank where I sprawled on my back and closed my eyes. Shifting patterns of light and shadow played across my eyelids as the palm leaves danced and swayed in Shams's glory. A rather large shadow blotted out the sun completely. When it failed to give way to the light, I cracked one eye open.

A pair of broad, hairy nostrils loomed less than a hand's breadth from my face. My mouth fell open, and the nostrils flared and disgorged a thick, fetid cloud of mucus. Gagging, I rolled to my side and scrambled for the safety of the pool. I plunged under the water, rinsing my mouth and scrubbing my face as I went. I broke the surface, squeezed the water from my eyes, and rose only far enough to breathe through my nose while I surveyed the shore.

A camel calf stood by the water's edge, its forelegs spread wide and neck stretched low as it slupped at the pool. Its eyes settled on me. The calf raised its head and took a backward step. It pulled back its lips in a hideous grin, thick streams of water dripping from its muzzle.

"It's all right," I said as I rose from the water and edged toward the shore, one hand stretched out.

The camel brayed, turned, and dashed into the cover of the trees.

"Wait," I called after it. I slogged through the shallows, raced up the beach and into the verge.

Only twice before had I seen camels. Bedou tribesmen drove their herds into Maryaba to trade milk and meat, hides and dung for fruits and vegetables, wheat and beer. Shayma had been quick to buy as much dung as she could, trading five jars of beer and a bolt of silk cloth.

"Best dung there is," she'd explained. "Burns cleaner than goat or donkey."

I smiled at the memory, thankful for the secret the old woman had taught me about making the best fire. Much as curiosity urged me to follow the young camel, reason told me I would find what I needed near the pool.

It took only a brief search for me to collect a few lumps of precious, seasoned dung. I then reclaimed my belongings. After washing the worst of the stains from my robe, I hunted for a place to make my camp.

No more than a dozen paces from the pool, blocks of stone formed part of what seemed a giant staircase. I climbed one high step after another, marveling at what sort of men could have built, let alone used such a stairway. I left my belongings on the third riser, then continued to scale the stones. As I crested the fifteenth and final step, I knew this was no simple set of stairs, not even for a race of giants. Surely, this was the stairway of the gods.

My tower house was the loftiest dwelling place in all of Saba. Yet here I stood on a platform twice as high as my home. Tall as it was, the top step barely cleared the treetops. In three other places stone pillars thrust above the foliage to an even greater height. Their shadows spread across the canopy of leaves, and I realized they were the three fingers that had beckoned me to Eram's oasis.

Amid the shadows I noticed a pattern. Though only these few structures reached above the treetops, between them ran a string of gaps in the foliage. With only a little imagination, I envisioned the walls and towers, temples and homes that once decorated the plain. The walls ended abruptly at the edge of the oasis, where the desert sands held back the verdant growth.

Unlike the desert I'd traversed these many days, the terrain at the eastern end of the oasis was perfectly flat, a dusty white expanse that stretched to the horizon. I realized this was the lake of legend, the great Eramite sea that sank into the sands. If I was to find a shell, the token of my pilgrimage, it would be along that ancient shore.

I climbed down the great stones and, taking my bearing from the pool, set out to claim my prize.

Athtar's hand set my path straight as an arrow's flight. I pressed through the undergrowth of Eram's oasis, using Yanuf's janbiya to clear the way. Shams hadn't yet climbed to noon when I reached the vast white plain.

I needed only a short time of searching before I found the object of my pilgrimage. The shell fit neatly in my palm, its smooth inner surface seeming to ripple in pale yellows and pinks as it caught the sunlight. I pressed the shell to my lips, whispered a prayer of thanks to my husband-god, and turned back toward the lost city.

I was only a few steps past the verge when the ground began to tremble. The crackle of fallen leaves and a rumble like distant thunder were accompanied by something akin to the chortle of demons. I dropped to my knees and crawled to shelter behind a wall of toppled stones. I clutched the shell to my breast and breathed a plea for protection to Ubasti. The goddess must have heard, for the demons transformed into a mere herd of camels.

The beasts tramped among the palm trees, pausing occasionally to snatch up dates fallen on the ground. I thought I recognized the calf from the pool. Large as it had seemed then, the creature was dwarfed by the camel it followed. The honey-colored cow strode gracefully at the front of the herd, snuffling at the air and keeping a careful watch. I ducked lower as the animal looked in my direction and bellowed something between a bray and a belch. Seeming to sense no threat, the camel moved on into the brush, followed by its herd.

My heart felt a whisper, a soft voice that was now becoming familiar. The voice that had led me to defy Dhamar, the voice that had led me into the trackless desert. The same voice that had reminded me how to make pure water, had urged me onward until I reached Eram's shelter.

I rose and followed the herd.

The camels made a circuit around the edge of the oasis before they led me to a broad clearing among the trees. Nestled within the grove lay a low stone enclosure, the interior flat and closely grazed. I was drawn toward one end of the corral, where one wall stood slightly higher than the rest.

The stones of the little stable failed to impress with their size, each a mere pebble beside the mighty works scattered around the oasis. The carvings that decorated the faces of the stones, however, stopped my breath.

Carved images showed human and camel figures in various poses. Camels being fed. Camels being made to kneel. Camels bearing packs and riders. Strange groupings of shapes accompanied each figure. I could make no sense of these, but the carvings and their meanings stood clearly enough.

The whisper spoke again, and the revelation of yet another mad scheme burst fully formed from my heart. I smiled despite the gravity of the choice before me. The gods had blessed my journey with success thus far. How could I do other than entrust them once more with my fate, and with that of my people?

Following the example of the images on the wall, I cut and stripped a palm frond, and gathered a handful of dates. Goad and reward in hand, I stepped into the camels' enclosure.

The large cow was the first to notice me. While the others huddled along a far wall, the herd's leader flattened her ears and raced toward me. My heart pounded, but I stood my ground. The beast thundered by, the breeze of her passing almost blowing me off my feet. Twice more the camel charged, but I remained still. Curiosity replaced alarm as the cow approached the fourth time, slowly now. I held out the dates, and the camel tentatively nibbled at the sweet fruit.

"Very good, Dhahbas," I said softly.

Dhahbas—Honey—was the pet name my father had used for my half-sister Bilkis. The name suited the shade of the animal's coat and, from what I remembered, sister and camel had similar personalities. Bitterness, spite, stubbornness, tempered by a protective nature.

"Now, let us begin."

31

Makeda

The walls of Maryaba glowed red above the fields. My heart quickened, and I squeezed the camel's neck with my knees. "Hurry, Dhahbas," I squealed, and tapped the cow's flank with the palm frond.

The camel brayed and shook her head in protest, but hurried her pace nonetheless.

It had taken days for me to win the animal's trust, days of wandering among the herd to show them I meant no harm. Whether from instinct or bribes of dates, finally the herd accepted my presence.

Armed with the palm frond, I'd mimicked the poses of the drover from the rock carvings. After much frustration and several douses of camel spit, I at last succeeded. I had Dhahbas kneel, allow me upon her shoulders, and move under my command.

The thrill of that first ride dwindled to naught, replaced by the exhilaration of returning to Maryaba, to my home. I had tested the gods, had been tested by them, and now returned from my pilgrimage.

My caravan hadn't reached the outermost fields when I heard the echo of drums from the city. Dhahbas checked her stride and flattened her ears, but I urged her on. As we followed the path through the fields and toward Maryaba, farmers peered out from the crops. Shouts of surprise and prayers of thanksgiving flew from their lips when they recognized me.

Brays of protest rose from the cows and bull that had followed Dhahbas from Eram's oasis. The calves tucked in close to their mothers as the crowd grew thick on the narrow trail to the city. I patted Dhahbas's neck and drove her onward, the camel's gait made awkward as she stepped over the offerings of leaves and flowers strewn across the way.

The drums grew louder as we neared the walls, but they were drowned out by the songs of the people.

Honored is she who comes in the glory of the gods.

The harmony rose from a thousand voices, loud enough to reach the very dwelling place of Athtar. The sound thrummed against my chest, but my heart beat with even greater vigor when I saw the line of elders outside the gate.

"*Atsar*, Dhahbas," I said. "*Karah.*"

The camel stopped and knelt at my commands. I swung down from the beast's neck and gestured toward a drover who tended the donkeys and horses of visiting nobles.

"See to these animals," I said to him.

"Yes, Shara," he replied, his eyes cast upon his toes. "For slaughter?"

My throat tightened at the thought of Dhahbas and her calf turning on spits, but I kept my voice even. "For safekeeping. Feed them. Water them."

"Yes, Shara," the man replied, then signaled a pair of boys to help him.

"They like dates," I whispered when the trio of drovers seemed at a loss for getting the beasts to move.

"Thank you, Shara." The man sent one of the boys to fetch some fruit, while he and the other used water skins to coax the herd to follow them.

A shrill cry rose from the direction of the gates. A black-robed wraith flew from the city and charged toward me. The creature was nearly upon me before I recognized Shayma.

The old woman's face was gaunt and deeply scratched. Her hair—where it wasn't torn out—hung in matted, grey tangles. Shayma fell to the ground and clutched my ankles.

"My child, my child," she cried, "returned from the Pit."

My heart twisted at the woman's torment, though her love and devotion brought a smile. I knelt and took her hands in mine.

"Rise," I said. Her sobs continued, so in a softer voice I added, "Stand, old mother."

Shayma looked up through sunken, tear-filled eyes.

"I am well," I assured her. "Your prayers and the gods' blessings have sustained me through my ordeal. Now rise, bathe, eat. Mourn no more."

Shayma nodded, and I helped her stand. She wrapped me in a frail embrace before turning back toward the gates and shouting at the other servants who waited behind the walls.

"Sammara, Fazia, bring water. Latif, a fire. We've a feast to prepare."

My eyes followed the old woman then drifted upward to the gate tower. There at his post, spear in hand, Yanuf stood tall and stoic. I flashed him a smile, and the slightest hint of a grin creased his lips.

"Hail the shara," one of the elders exclaimed. "Hail the gods who have returned her to her people."

"And hail the Bedou swine who aided her." Dhamar staggered out from the crowd. He looked as disheveled as Shayma, his robes in disarray, his hair tangled, though I doubted these were from mourning.

I ignored him and stepped forward. He circled and sniffed at me as a dog around a dining table. "Revered elders," I said. "In keeping with tradition, I have completed the Trial of the Wilderness. Athtar's will has been tested and confirmed. The god has chosen me for his bride."

"What did you trade the Bedou dogs for their camels?" Dhamar stopped in front of me, stooped until our noses were a mere finger's breadth apart, and fixed his red-rimmed eyes on mine. His breath stank of stale beer and vomit. "I hope the god hasn't lost the bounty of your maidenhead."

My hand curled into a fist and struck out. Pain flowed up my arm as my knuckles connected with Dhamar's throat.

His eyes went wide. He wheezed and clutched at his throat. With my other hand, I grasped him by the hair then swung my knee into his belly. Wheezes turned to heaves, and the contents of Dhamar's stomach spilled onto the dirt. I swept my leg across his shins, and he collapsed facedown in his vomit.

Gasps issued from the crowd, and no little laughter. I shook out my throbbing fingers, then turned back to the slack-jawed elders.

"Athtar provided these camels from the oasis of Eram, as my dowry. I also offer this token as witness of my sojourn to the City of the Pillars." I snapped the braided palm fronds that held the shell around my neck and offered the delicate trinket to Yatha, priest of Athtar, who stared dumbly at it.

"It is the token of Eram," declared Walid the merchant. "She has fulfilled the challenge."

"Athtar has fulfilled the challenge," I corrected him. "It was his word that was disputed. It is his word that is confirmed. Does any yet deny it?"

The elders remained silent, though those closest to Watar sidled away from him. The Lord of Timnah looked sullenly from his son—still wallowing in his own filth and struggling to breathe—to me. Slowly, he stepped forward.

"I am sorry, Shara." His voice thrummed with emotion. "I am sorry I did not make a better son for your husband. I am sorry I will not have the privilege to call you my daughter."

My breath stuttered as Watar came forward, prostrated himself before me, then rose to his knees.

"But I have the joy to call you the wife of my god." Watar's proclamation was greeted with cheers from the elders and the people. "And I have the honor to kneel before you, Mukarrib of all Saba."

32

Yetzer

They came for him in the night. Unseen hands bagged Yetzer's head, chained his manacles, and carried him from the slaves' pen. Heavy feet trod the slope from the quarry down to the bank of the Iteru, Yetzer dangling from the chains at ankle and wrist. His captors paused, swung him from his chains and sent him soaring through the air.

Yetzer sucked in a breath, for all the good it would do. If he landed in the Iteru, his bonds would carry him to the silty riverbed, fertilizer for next season's crops. If a crocodile awaited him, his passage to Duat would be much swifter, and he would become much more refined fertilizer for next season's crops.

The air fled his lungs as he landed on a pile of coarse sacks. The grain-stuffed bags were more welcome than river water or crocodile teeth, but still, it took several moments for his body to respond to his command to breathe.

"What is this? Where are you taking me?" His words came out in gasps, his breath ragged.

The only answer was a rocking of the sacks beneath him as they shifted to one side. A series of slaps sounded on the water, and the world lurched into motion. Yetzer tried to sit up, but a sharp jab to his ribs stopped him. Blinded and bound, there was nothing to do but lie back and settle in for the journey.

Days passed as the ship, under the power of sail and oar, made its way along the river. After Yetzer's first taste of fish in more than a year, his captors left his hood off. The muddy shores drifted by them, a nearly endless ribbon of black silt and green wheat.

When at last the helmsman angled his steering oar toward shore, the guards again hooded Yetzer. The ship jolted to a stop with the muted thud of hull against pier and the groan of timbers. Strong hands grasped him under each arm and hefted him to his feet. Left to move under his own power, Yetzer took a step.

The chain at his ankles checked his stride, and Yetzer pitched forward. The thick fingers loosened their grips, freeing him to crash to the planks. Amid a string of curses—Yetzer's—and laughter—theirs—the guards yanked him to his feet again and half-carried him across the deck. They lifted him over the rail and onto a walkway, then supported him as he learned to walk within the bounds of the chain's reach.

Yetzer shuffled under the guards' direction up a long slope then through a series of turns. The sounds of splashing water and clanging tools filled his ears, accompanied by grunts and curses and laughter. Yetzer's nostrils twitched under the assault of lye baths, charcoal smoke, cesspits and other stenches of civilization.

From the clang of metal and the wheeze of a bellows, Yetzer knew he passed a forge. His escorts steered him around a corner, then another, and finally jerked him to a halt. They unchained his wrists and pulled the hood from his head. Yetzer blinked against daylight's attack as the guards turned and walked silently away.

He thought to call after them, but knew he would get no answers. As the world came into focus, he found himself in a shaded courtyard. A single, narrow alley stretched back the way the guards had left, while bare walls faced him on four sides. The mudbrick beneath high, curtained windows was stained with night soil. Puddles of filth surrounded the courtyard and filled the air with a thick stench and the noise of flies.

Blocks of stone lay scattered amid the puddles, all roughly the same size. To one side lay a perfect ashlar, its faces smooth and square. The tools to turn the rough ashlars into copies of the finished one lay upon a reed mat beneath a tattered linen canopy.

Yetzer wandered about the yard as he considered his situation. Work the stones and fail, and he'd likely be sent back to the quarry. Work them and succeed? At the very least, he would have staved off boredom and learned a new skill. Might he even win his freedom?

Careful to avoid the fetid puddles, he shuffled to the canopy and examined the tools. Maul and chisel, to smooth the stones' faces. Mason's square to true the corners. Ruled staff to ensure uniformity. With no other option before him, he picked up chisel and maul and set to work.

❖

The Iteru swelled and receded while Yetzer worked his stones. Once each week, a priest wearing the leather apron of a master mason came to inspect Yetzer's work. A gang of slaves carried away baskets of rubble and the accepted stones, and delivered rough ashlars in their place.

It took time, but Yetzer learned the best angle of the chisel and force behind the maul. He learned to read the stones, which could be shaped and which would fracture under the slightest stress. By closing his eye and opening his inner sight to the cloudy images behind his empty left socket, he learned to see with his fingers. Over time, he could discern by touch the shape and irregularities of the stone in far greater detail than he could with his natural vision.

For each ashlar perfected, Yetzer received a day's supply of beer, bread, and olive oil. For each flawed stone, a day's allowance was taken away. He might have starved in his first month if not for the metalworker at the head of the alley.

The gruff old man had brought a basket of bread and roasted pork at sunset on the day of Yetzer's arrival. It was the first meat Yetzer had tasted in two years.

He'd eaten greedily as the smith talked of bronze and gold and silver, as other men might speak of their families.

Each evening, the two shared bread and oil and beer. At the end of the week, if Yetzer had completed his stonework, he shuffled in his chains to the forge, where he learned the smith's art. How much heat to work each type of metal. The proper mix of tin to make the best bronze. Even how to shape and cast a mold. Yetzer's first execution—a bronze bull to honor Hapi-Ankh—had been a poor, misshapen thing, but his skill steadily grew.

"Have to talk to the priests about buying you," the smith told Yetzer. "Make the price back in a month, I would. Free you after that, of course. Of course I would."

Yetzer lay on his mat that night, musing on life as a freeman, an artisan no less. He might take a wife, have children. His dreams of Ameniye had been buried among the stones in the quarry. Here he might build a life from the rubble of his youthful hubris, and die young and unknown, common and complete.

And then they came again.

Black hood, strong hands, lumpy grain sacks, and a trip to another port. Each year they came to take Yetzer from his work just as he mastered it, just as he stood to make a place for himself. Just as he began to hope.

At Iunu he learned to shape round column stones and devised a means to raise them into place with half the effort and time as before. At Hut-Uaret he scraped the earth to lay the foundation for a temple to Sutah. At Sena, where the Iteru's lowlands met the Great Green Sea, he worked the rough cedar timbers from his homeland of Kenahn, floated by sea to Kemet's shores.

They came the last time early in Yetzer's twenty-first year, five years into his enslavement. His captors spared him the hood, as the river journey took several days. They rowed past Iunu with its soaring columns, past Men-Nefer with its majestic pyramids, past the quarry at Zauty and the work-town of Iunet.

Upon reaching the southern capital of Uaset, the helmsman deftly brought the ship to rest at the pier belonging to the Temple of Amun. Yetzer's heart raced, his breath came shallow as the guards led him through the bronze gates, past the Hall of the Postulants, and into the hierophant's audience room.

Yetzer's wait was short, as a jangle of bells announced the high priest's approach. The cedar doors of the inner chamber swung open. The guards knelt, gesturing for Yetzer to do the same. His ankle chain made the motion difficult. Yetzer fell the last half-cubit onto his knees and bowed his head.

Incense cushioned under Yetzer's nose, and the sound of shuffling sandals swept across the limestone floor. The sandals stopped directly in front of Yetzer.

"Rise, slave."

The voice was harsh, cold, commanding. Yetzer stood and looked into the flat, grey eyes of Merisutah. Yetzer's blood turned cold as the priest's thin lips stretched into a hideous grin.

"Welcome back."

33

Bilkis

Seven winters came and went, and Bilkis waited. Twice more, Keren delivered the queen's sons, but neither survived to leave the birthing chamber. Twice more, Tadua mourned his children before the altar and tent of the gods upon the high place. Twice more, Bilkis bade the king to take comfort in his living son who had grown into a hale, round little prince, affectionate to his mother, obedient to the king.

In that same year, when the sun rose high enough to thaw the frozen waters of the northern countries, Eliam and Abram led a donkey train from the far-distant east. Rahab clung to her father and brother. She wept over them as they spread their finest merchandise before the king, who lay on a cot in the throne room. Bolts of silk in yellow and red and green. Baskets of spices, the scent of which made Bilkis's eyes water. Bags of jewels and uncut gemstones.

"We welcome you home," Tadua told the merchants after they'd presented the king's share. "Your gifts are well received, though your greatest two gifts are those you entrusted to us before your departure." The king gestured toward Bilkis and Rahab. The queen had commanded the younger woman to Tadua's bed to warm the king after a violent chill had seized him. Surprise flashed across Eliam's face, but he replaced it with the merchant's neutral joviality. Before he could speak, the seer, Gad, pushed through the doors of the audience chamber.

"Tadua abi-Yishai," the young prophet said, his voice deep and resonant, "as Yah reigns over the gods, as Havah sits upon her heavenly throne, you will answer for what you have done."

All eyes turned upon the righteous intruder, and Bilkis noticed a hint of color in Rahab's cheeks. The king's face, on the other hand, turned ashen. His lips trembled, his eyes flitted about as though searching his memory for whatever transgression he'd been caught at.

"How dare you speak unbidden to your lord?" Captain Benyahu demanded from his post at the foot of the dais.

Tadua gestured for him to be silent. "Upon my beard, Prophet," the king said, "I know not of what you speak. Tell me my sin that I may atone before the gods."

Gad looked uncertain and shot a questioning glance toward Bilkis.

"Did the king not proclaim his son Baaliyah as his heir?" he said. "Did he not raise a king over Yisrael without seeking the gods' will?"

Rage and no little fear squeezed the breath from Bilkis's throat. She clasped a hand over Tadua's.

"Is this true?" Her words came in a whisper. "Did you place Baaliyah over Yahtadua? Did you break your promise to me?"

"Promise?" the king slurred, his eyes still vacant.

"By Yah and by Havah, you swore to me that our son would follow you on the throne, to rule in peace over what you have won by the sword."

That Tadua had never actually made that promise was of little matter. Bilkis had made the bargain with her body and her affection, as the price of her son's crown.

Tadua's head shook, his hands trembled. "I may have promised you," he admitted, his speech halting, "but I made no proclamation regarding Baaliyah. If you have aught to say, Prophet, speak plain."

Gad's lips parted, but he closed them again. Confusion clouded his eyes as he looked to Rahab and Bilkis, then back to the king. "The king's son," he said finally, "Prince Baaliyah, hosts a feast at the Fuller's Spring. General Ayub led the prince's donkey. The priest Abiattar anointed Baaliyah's head with oil and spoke the blessing of Yah over him."

"They make him a king," Benyahu said.

The tremors spread from Tadua's hands to the whole of his upper body. He clutched the blanket that lay atop him, whether to restrain himself or to pull himself upright Bilkis wasn't sure. Blood filled his cheeks and ugly veins stood out at neck and temple.

"Cursed, cursed is my seed," he cried, spittle flecking his lips. "Is this the reward for my folly? Have I not built a kingdom to Yah and Havah's glory? And do they repay me only with sons who claim it for themselves?"

The chamber fell silent, Tadua's question was answered only by his sobs. Even Bilkis found no words, no means to turn this to her favor.

"Abba?" a small voice said.

Bilkis looked down to find Yahtadua standing before the king. The boy rarely spoke, certainly never before the king. Yet he stood now with hands folded, back straight, eyes fixed on Tadua's.

"Abba," the boy said again, "don't cry. I'll be good."

Tadua's sobbing stopped with the prince's words. Tears yet streamed down his cheeks, but a sad smile curved his lips.

"Will you?" the king said, his voice pleading. "Will you make my name live? Will you honor me before the gods, and preserve what I have made?"

Yahtadua nodded solemnly.

"Swear it, boy," Tadua insisted. "Swear it by the gods."

The prince glanced at Bilkis, who smiled and nodded. "By Yah and by Havah," Yahtadua said, his thin voice full of conviction. "I swear to keep your kingdom." He paused and pursed his lips. After a moment, he looked back to the king and completed his oath. "Upon my beard."

Phlegm choked Tadua's laughter, but his delight was unfettered. The king laid his trembling hands atop Yahtadua's head.

"I'll take that in surety," he said. "You have spoken well, my son. All praise to the gods who have heard my prayers." Tadua looked to Gad and added, "But we must make certain. Have you the seer stones?"

The prophet bowed his head. He drew a pouch from within his robe, hung about his neck by a leather thong. He shook the pouch, and it made a small rattling sound.

"Then inquire of the gods for me," Tadua ordered him.

Gad pulled a pair of gloves from the belt at his waist and tugged them over his hands. The seer closed his eyes, mumbled a few words, then drew a deep breath. Bilkis jerked back in her throne when Gad opened his eyes, only the whites showing.

"Ask of the gods what you will," he said in a raspy voice.

Tadua supported himself upon his elbows and rose to a half-sitting position. Rahab stuffed pillows behind him to support his back. The king took Yahtadua's hand and turned the boy to face Gad.

"Shall I name a son to succeed me?" Tadua asked.

Gad reached into the pouch, drew out his fist, and opened it to reveal a small white stone.

"Yes," Benyahu said, a tone of awe in his voice.

Gad placed the stone back in the pouch and shook it again.

"Shall it be Baaliyah?" Tadua asked.

Again Gad drew from the pouch, this time revealing a black stone of the same size and shape.

"No," Rahab whispered, her hands over her mouth.

Bilkis looked around the chamber and found every eye turned toward the young prophet, the voice of the gods.

"Shall it be Shepatiyah?" the king asked, referring to one of Baaliyah's younger brothers.

Black.

"Shall it be Itream?"

Black.

Tadua whispered in Yahtadua's ear, and the boy nodded.

"Shall it be me?" the boy asked quietly. Then he cleared his throat. "Shall it be Yahtadua?"

The very world seemed to still as Gad again reached into the pouch and withdrew his hand. Bilkis found herself leaning forward, elbows upon her knees, breath stopped in her lungs.

White.

A sigh filled the chamber as breaths released.

"So shall it be," Tadua declared. "Summon Abdi-Havah. Have him bring the stone of Yaakob from the Sanctuary. Benyahu, you shall set Yahtadua upon my own donkey and with my personal guard lead him down to the Gihon Spring. There have Abdi-Havah anoint him with oil and with water. Sound the rams' horns and thrice proclaim him King of Yisrael, before the gods, before the people, and before the very land."

"You will not proclaim him yourself?" Bilkis asked.

"I have done so," Tadua said. "The people should see their king hale and young, not as a dotard confined to his couch. Go now."

"Of course," Bilkis said, and kissed the king's hand. "Rahab will stay to wait upon you."

The girl began to protest, but Bilkis silenced her with a stern look.

"I am at my lord's service," Rahab said.

The king smiled, and the assembly bowed then set about obeying his commands. "Send a runner to the Fuller's Spring," Tadua said as they were leaving the chamber. "I'm sure Baaliyah and his party will want to pay their respects."

34

Yetzer

Yetzer set down his stylus and flexed cramped fingers. Pressing his hands against his lower back, he stretched muscles made stiff from hours at his post. The reed mat and wooden writing surface were positioned to capture light from the clerestory windows, the pots of red and black ink in easy reach, but the arrangement did little to aid Yetzer's comfort. Or his conscience.

Since his return to the temple, Yetzer had been assigned to the docks, the gardens, the scullery—every menial task his masters could find. Merisutah must eventually have decided there was more benefit to be had in making use of Yetzer's skills than in tormenting him. The hierophant set him among the temple's archives, to record sales of land and livestock, the intake of crops, and the distribution of food among the temple's holdings.

It hadn't taken Yetzer long to recognize the discrepancies. Shipping statements did not match the Temple's receipts. The goods delivered to the Temple did not square with those sent to the kitchens and storehouses, or to the labor camps.

Three times Yetzer pointed out the disparity to the hierophant. Three times Merisutah cursed whatever thief might dare to steal from the gods. Yetzer had never cared for the new high priest, selected to fill the post following old Huy's death. Still, he'd wanted to believe the man sincere in his service to Amun, even if that service did not entail kindness to mere humanity.

As Yetzer finished this day's tally, however, his faith in the hierophant vanished. Despite Merisutah's vows to investigate the matter, the theft continued. Yetzer's only conclusion was that the high priest himself was taking from the Temple, defying Mayat's divine order by stealing from Amun, from his brother priests, from the very land and people of Kemet.

Yetzer closed and massaged his weary eye. He had accepted enslavement and humiliation, endured scourges and hunger and want, because he deserved no better. He'd failed his initiation, the same initiation that Merisutah had passed. To suborn himself to better men was no failing, it was just. But to bow before one who breached his sacred trust, who mocked the god he purported to serve—that was intolerable.

Yetzer rose and left the archives. Though his ankle chain had been removed upon returning to the temple, he often slipped into the shuffling gait to which he'd become accustomed over the years. He willed strength into his steps as he stalked toward the Adepts' Gate. The guards noticed his approach and moved to block his way.

"Be about your work, slave," the older of the two men said. "None pass this way but the Masters."

Yetzer pressed on, and the guard put a hand on the hilt of his sword.

"Come no farther," the guard ordered.

Yetzer ignored him, his stride sure and bold. The guard's blade gave a musical hiss as it slid from its scabbard. Still Yetzer moved forward. The blade whistled through the air, and Yetzer stopped only when the sword's tip pressed against his chest.

"Stand aside for an adept of the mysteries of Amun," Yetzer commanded, his voice sending deep echoes through the courtyard.

The younger guard fumbled with his sword, pointing it alternately at Yetzer's chest and at the ground.

"Maybe we should let him pass," he said in a raspy voice.

"Bah," the older man spat. "He's no adept. He's but a slave with grand ideas. Go back to your ink pots, boy," he said to Yetzer. "I'd rather not bloody my sword."

"Summon a Master, then," Yetzer said. "Summon the hierophant. Yetzer abi-Huram would pass these gates."

Sandals slapped against the paving stones behind him. Yetzer released his gaze from the guard and looked about. Priests and servants gathered around the yard. A few shared whispers, but most stared at the upstart slave. The older guard gave a gravelly chuckle and nodded.

"As you wish. Summon Hierophant Merisutah," he told the younger man. "This thing wants to pass the gate? Not my worry. We'll let the high priest decide whether it's on foot or in a pickling jar."

The younger guard nodded and started away but stopped short as the hierophant himself approached.

"What goes on here?" Merisutah inquired, his voice placid.

"This slave—" the older guard began, but Yetzer cut him off.

"Yetzer abi-Huram demands to pass."

Merisutah barked out a laugh.

"Of course you may pass. Give me the Masters' word and the gates will open before you. Give me a false word, however, and your throat will be ripped out before you draw another breath." The hierophant's eyes glinted and a grin twisted his lips. "Or simply spare us the bother and return to your scripts."

Yetzer wavered.

Had he been too proud? All the gods knew his pride was as thick and high as a cedar. Pride lay at the feet of every ill that had befallen him and might now be his undoing. But pride's twin, dignity, also urged him on. Better to die trying to be free than to live as corruption's slave.

Merisutah stood within a small alcove set in the wall beside the gate. Yetzer stepped toward him while his heart chased after the Masters' word. Since entering Pharaoh's care he'd known starvation and gluttony, exhaustion and ease, privation and plenty. The gods had placed the world at his feet, then taken all away.

Through the trials, through the years, one thread remained constant. Its name might not be the Masters' word, but if it was the last to fall from his lips, perhaps the gods would again hear him, remember his name, and save him from death's oblivion.

Yetzer leaned close to Merisutah and whispered in his ear.

The hierophant shuddered and took a step back against the wall. He fixed Yetzer's eye with his gaze, then glanced about at the gaping priests and guards. Merisutah drew a deep breath and released it with a sigh.

"Strike off his ..."

Yetzer sucked air into his lungs and stood tall as he savored the aromas of incense, water lilies, and the earthy fullness of Iteru's waters.

" ... bonds," Merisutah finished.

Silence cloaked the courtyard. Even the Iteru seemed to check its flow as the breeze held its breath. Only Yetzer's heartbeat gave evidence that the world still moved.

Shuffling feet broke the stillness as a priest came alongside him. With a pair of tongs he drew the pins from Yetzer's bonds and dropped the bronze shackles to the ground.

"Yetzer abi-Huram," Merisutah intoned in a deep voice, "I call you by name before great Amun and before all the gods. Having completed the ordeals of an initiate, having discovered the sacred word of the hidden Masters, you now stand as a brother among the priests of Amun, an adept of the mysteries of Light."

35

Bilkis

Prince Baaliyah, as it turned out, was not anxious to pay his respects. General Ayub and the priest Abiattar, however, hastened to the palace and crawled to the throne to kiss Yahtadua's feet, their robes torn, ashes in their hair.

"Baaliyah deceived us," Abiattar cried. "He claimed our lord the king had named him his heir."

The old priest's tears wet Yahtadua's sandals. Ayub neither affirmed nor refuted Abiattar's claim. He simply drew his sword and, under Benyahu's watchful eye, placed the blade beneath Yahtadua's feet.

"My sword and all the tribe of Yehuda are at the command of the king," the old general said.

Tadua nodded from his couch as Yahtadua accepted priest and warrior into his grace. After the rest of the princes and tribal elders made their professions of loyalty, the young king sent Benyahu to fetch Baaliyah from the altar of the Sanctuary, where the prince had taken refuge.

"Be gentle with him," Yahtadua told his new general. "If he won't come, assure him of my good will. So long as he behaves, he needn't fear."

Benyahu grumbled but gave his assent. Bilkis watched with awe as her son transformed from pampered child to regal king.

Tadua, however, hadn't long to enjoy his heir's reign. Rahab warmed his bed through the remainder of the summer and autumn. The king's chills returned with the winter's rains. On the first new moon following the birth of spring, eight years after Bilkis had chosen between Auriyah's sons, Rahab dashed into Bilkis's chamber.

"It is time," she said, then hastily retreated.

Yahtadua had been asleep, but Bilkis sat upon his bed and stroked his cheek. "Awake, my darling king," she said. "Your father calls us."

The boy blinked his eyes open, stretched, then took his mother's hand and followed her from the room.

"Summon General Benyahu," Bilkis told the guard at her door. "The king will have need of him this night."

She led a yawning Yahtadua to the king's chamber. The guard at Tadua's door tugged on the bronze ring and drew it open. Heat poured from the room, and Bilkis first thought the palace had been set ablaze. All the braziers burned safely upon their hearthstones, the smoke swept through openings cut high in the chamber's walls. Bilkis crossed the threshold then turned back to the guard before he closed the door.

"Send word to the widow Mikhel. She may wish to know of the king's condition."

The man nodded and closed the door.

Rahab sat on a stool beside Tadua's bed. The king lay on his back, hands folded across his chest, atop the thick covers. His tremors had stilled. By the fixed gaze of his eyes upon the smoke-obscured ceiling, Bilkis feared they had come too late, but a short, quick movement of the hands upon his chest bore witness that the king yet drew breath.

Bilkis ushered Yahtadua forward, boosted the lad onto the bed, then crossed around and sat at Tadua's other side. The king turned his head to her, and a smile broke the crusted saliva at the corner of his mouth.

"So ends the glory of the House of Yisrael." Tadua's voice cracked like parched goatskin.

"So it continues," Bilkis corrected him. "For you have established a throne to span a hundred generations."

"Labaya established it," Tadua said, referring to his predecessor, Mikhel's father. "I simply gathered the scraps from his table."

"Then truly you are favored of the gods, for from a few crumbs of bread and bits of fish you have set a great feast." Bilkis laid a hand atop the king's.

"You are the *moshiach*, the anointed one of Yah and Havah. Your seed shall continue what you have begun, even as you built upon Labaya's foundation. Instruct your son now in the way you would have him go."

Tadua rolled his grey head toward the boy. Yahtadua's eyes were wide and gleamed in the firelight.

"My son," the king said, "I have drawn the sword for more years than most men draw breath. In my heart, however, I have always yearned for peace. Now I go to it. Your boundary stones are secure, your fields and pasturelands made safe. Yisrael is a friend to those on its north and its south, its east and its west. Your marriage bed will one day fortify those friendships and add to the peace and prosperity of the land."

The king's voice flagged, and Rahab stepped forward with a bowl of watered wine. Tadua drank, spluttered a little, then looked upon the young woman with gratitude.

"Be gracious with your neighbors," he went on, "but also be wary. Hatti and Kemet are as two great millstones that might feed or destroy. The Pelesti are wanderers but their loyalty cannot be surpassed, so long as there is gold in their purses and wine in their cups. Tsur is an especial friend, for I helped abi-Milku to the throne, and his daughter Remeg remembers that debt."

Tadua gestured to Rahab, and she offered him another sip of wine.

"As to your court," he continued, "surround yourself with wise men, and trustworthy. Your mother will be your truest guide, for in your wellbeing is her own. Benyahu has never failed me, and you may rely upon him also. For the rest, trust in the gods with all your heart and they will make your way clear."

The king leaned back on his pillows. Rahab again held up the bowl, but Tadua shook his head. His gaze drifted toward the smoke that clung to the ceiling. A shudder seized his body, his hands tightened about the bedclothes, and a tear dampened the corner of one eye.

"I once dreamed of raising a temple unto Yah and Havah," he said at length. His words came ragged and strained. "When we were like the Nabati, wandering from well to well, pasture to pasture, it was meet that our gods should dwell in a tent as we did. But a settled people, a true kingdom should have a proper home for its gods. I would like to have seen such a temple."

A startled expression creased Tadua's face. His gaze darted to Rahab then Yahtadua. When he settled his eyes on Bilkis, he smiled and gave a deep sigh. Bilkis returned the smile. The tear rolled down Tadua's cheek, and Bilkis held his stare for several long moments before she realized his chest no longer rose and fell beneath his hands.

❊

Benyahu arrived a short time later. He fell to his knees before Tadua's bed, clutched the feet of his king, and wept as only a warrior can. When he'd made his peace, he wiped his eyes, crawled to Yahtadua and placed his head beneath the boy's foot.

"Arise, General," Bilkis told him.

The warrior obeyed and bowed his head to the queen.

"My husband's final words were that we may trust you." Bilkis held the man's eyes with a soft gaze. "Is this so?"

"As I live, my lady, it is," Benyahu said. "My sword belongs to you and to the king."

Bilkis considered this for a moment, then said, "No."

The general's mouth opened in protest, but Bilkis gestured him to silence. "Your faithfulness is not in question," she assured him, "but it is our sword that belongs to you."

She reached above the king's bed where hung Tadua's great sword with its gilded hilt and blade of rare iron. Bilkis pulled the sword down, surprised by its lightness compared to bronze. Bearing the sword upon her hands, she stepped close to Benyahu. The warrior placed his hands beside hers to receive the sword, and Bilkis allowed their fingers to touch a moment longer than needed. She smiled, withdrew her hands, but did not step back.

"The Pelesti are loyal to you?" she asked him.

"They will heed my commands," Benyahu affirmed with a nod.

"And the army?" she pressed. "What of the Host of Yisrael?"

The warrior grimaced. "As chief elder of Yehuda, Ayub commands his tribe's loyalty. The other tribes follow Yehuda."

"And if Ayub were removed from command?" she asked.

"The host would follow his successor," Benyahu said.

"And his successor would have the queen's gratitude," Bilkis said, and leaned toward Benyahu. "Find Ayub. Bring him to the king's presence to be reconciled at last."

"What if he will not come?" Benyahu asked.

A shrug. "His head will suffice."

Benyahu's shoulders twitched, but he smiled. "It shall be even as my lady commands." He rested the sword against his shoulder, bowed to Yahtadua, then left the chamber.

"Summon the serving women," Bilkis told Rahab when Benyahu was gone. "Then look in upon the royal widows."

Rahab looked up from where she still knelt by Tadua's side and blinked tear-filled eyes.

"What?" she asked in little more than a whisper.

"Women, to wash and dress the king's body," Bilkis said. "His people will want to pay their respects, to see his heir seated upon the throne. And for the affection Tadua once showed them, the usurper's widows should be invited to see their king upon his journey to Sheol."

Rahab snuffled and wiped her cheeks.

"But shouldn't we take a moment—"

"For what?" Bilkis snapped. "Tadua is gone and his remains already begin to reek. I will not have this palace fouled. Do as I've said, then you can mourn to your heart's fullness."

Rahab buried her face among the bedclothes again, her shoulders shaking. Bilkis stalked toward her, grabbed her by the hair and jerked her to her feet.

"Do as I say, you sniveling brat," Bilkis snarled, then swung Rahab toward the open door. "Go!"

Rahab covered her face with her hands as she left. Bilkis took a deep breath, composed her expression, then knelt before Yahtadua. The boy seemed not to have noticed the rancor. He simply sat with one of Tadua's hands in his, wide eyes fixed on the unmoving face.

"My lamb." Bilkis placed a hand on the boy's cheek and turned his head to face her. "We must get dressed. You sit upon the throne in your own name today."

"Does that mean I finally get to do what I want?" Yahtadua asked.

"It means you are the one true King of Yisrael. Your council and I will still help you make decisions. One day, when you have grown into a shrewd and wise man, your choices will be your own."

Yahtadua considered that for a time, then nodded his assent. Bilkis smiled, took him by the hand, and led him back to their chambers.

"They're dead," Rahab cried as she burst into the room a short time later.

Bilkis finished pulling a fresh linen tunic over Yahtadua. She pointed to her couch, and the boy lay down and closed his eyes.

"Who's dead?" she asked, using the same tone in which she might inquire about dinner.

"Auriyah's widows. They're all dead."

"Slain?" Bilkis mused, wondering if Benyahu had anticipated her wishes.

Rahab shook her head. "No, they don't appear to have been harmed. I first thought them asleep, but they weren't breathing. There were spilled wine cups beside each of them. And I found this." She held out a small alabaster jar. "It was in Mikhel's hand."

Bilkis took the vial, brought it to her nose, and carefully sniffed. She quickly pulled the jar away, but the scent lingered—earthy mushroom smells accompanied by bitter plantlike notes. The queen smiled in admiration. Rather than await whatever doom Bilkis might have planned, Mikhel chose to craft her own destiny, a final queenly act for the daughter and bride of Yisrael's first kings.

"It is fitting they should greet the king in Sheol," Bilkis said.

She sealed the jar and placed it in a small chest beside her bed. Rahab's mouth hung open, her red-rimmed eyes unblinking.

"Why do you look at me so?" Bilkis demanded. "If they chose to follow Tadua to the Pit, it's none of my doing. Had they done this when the king fled his son, they might have saved themselves the humiliation."

"Is there no kindness in your heart?" Rahab said in a pleading voice. "No sympathy?"

"Life is too full of pain to feel all things for all people." Bilkis stepped toward Rahab and took her by the shoulders. "What I allow myself to feel I reserve for my family. For you, my sister. For your father, for Abdi-Havah. For my son."

"Your sons," Rahab corrected her. "Natan is also your son, or have you closed your heart to him as well?"

A stinging sensation burned Bilkis's hand. She glanced down to see her palm glowing an angry red. When she looked back to Rahab, the younger woman had one hand cupped against her left cheek, the other covering her mouth as tears spilled from her eyes.

Bilkis squeezed her eyes shut and slowed her breathing. She glanced at Yahtadua and found the young king still curled upon the couch, his chest rising and falling gently in the sleep of innocence.

"I have no other son, but Havah has a fine young priest to attend her shrine." Bilkis's voice was sharp as a warrior's blade. "If you would have him remain well and in Havah's service, you will never speak those words again."

A knock sounded upon the chamber's door. Bilkis forced a neutral expression. "Yes?" she said.

The door swung upon its bronze hinges to reveal Benyahu, crimson-streaked sword in one hand, a red-stained sack in the other. A feral look shone in the warrior's eyes, but the expression faded when he saw Rahab and the sleeping king.

"Ah, General," Bilkis said in her warmest voice. "Your task is complete?"

"Yes, Lady," he replied, the words scarcely more than grunts.

"Sister, I have matters to discuss with General Benyahu," Bilkis told Rahab. "Look after Yahtadua. See that he is properly dressed by dawn. He must receive his court while the day is yet young."

She glided toward the door without waiting for a response. Benyahu stalked along in her wake. Bilkis led him to the private audience chamber behind the great hall. Securely behind the doors, she settled onto the little couch and pulled the skirts of her gown above her hips. The soft lamplight of the wall sconce cast Benyahu in silhouette. Bilkis could not see his expression, but the warrior's every motion shouted his desire.

The general dropped his sword and blood-stained sack. He fumbled beneath his kilt until he loosened his breechcloth, then fell upon the queen.

Bilkis winced when the general entered her. He grasped her hair with one hand and squeezed a breast with the other. Benyahu grunted as he moved his hips against hers. It took only a few rough thrusts before the warrior shuddered with ecstasy. Bilkis gritted her teeth to keep from crying out as Benyahu pulled hard against her hair. After he'd spent his seed, the warrior rested his full weight upon Bilkis, threatening to crush her with each rapid breath.

When the man's breathing slowed, Bilkis pushed against one of his shoulders and levered him off her. She reached for his fallen breechcloth and wiped between her legs.

"Your service is rewarded, General," she said. "Now, there are a few more things we would ask of you."

36
Yetzer

Yetzer walked toward Pharaoh's palace along an avenue of polished limestone. Had the street been made of gold, it could not have stirred more wonder in his heart.

From the port, the main thoroughfare of the northern capital, Men-Nefer, ran straight as a plumb line toward the walls of the royal compound. Temples lined the way, along with monuments honoring the pharaohs back to Narmer, who first unified the Upper and Lower Kingdoms of Kemet.

Yetzer ignored the beggars, the vendors, the prostitutes who promised visions of paradise. He paused only when he reached Pharaoh's palace. His youth had been spent in the southern court at Uaset. As Horemheb had restored order to the land after years of neglect, he established his court at Men-Nefer, the ancient capital in the very heart of Kemet.

Sandstone pylons stretched high above the palace's wall. A pair of soldiers stood before the open bronze gates. Each man bore a copper lance and wore the blue-and-white headdress of Pharaoh's personal guard. Their weapons and scowls barred the entrance as Yetzer approached. He straightened his shoulder cloth, the gold fabric that now proclaimed him a member of Amun's priesthood. The lances separated and the men bowed low, arms stretched out at knee level.

Yetzer had received the priestly courtesy several times during his journey downriver, but hadn't expected such a reception at Pharaoh's very doorstep. He stood tall, lengthened his stride, and stepped through the outer gate. Inside the courtyard, a rotund, bald man sat behind a table. He flipped a horsehair switch over one shoulder then the other, and fanned himself with an ostrich plume.

"State your business in Pharaoh's court," he said in the honeyed sibilance of a eunuch.

"Amun's blessing upon Great Pharaoh and all in his house," Yetzer said. The gate steward stared at him blankly. "I am Yetzer abi-Huram, from the temple of—"

"Yetzer?" The eunuch sat up straight.

"From the temple of Amun at Uaset," Yetzer continued, his voice faltering. "I beg audience—"

"Wait here." The man heaved himself onto his feet. He sidled out from behind the table, eyes fixed on Yetzer all the while. "Wait," he repeated, his voice several tones higher. He hitched his robe above his knees and fast-waddled to the end of the courtyard and through the inner gate.

Yetzer stared after the eunuch. He turned toward the guards, but their attention remained focused outside the gates. The eunuch had abandoned a bowl of fruit, so Yetzer leaned against the table and helped himself to a cluster of grapes.

His wait was short. Before he plucked the last grape from its stem, the eunuch returned with a taller, broader man in tow. It took a moment for Yetzer to recognize Mika, keeper of Pharaoh's throne room. The man gave a short scream when he saw Yetzer, and raised his hands to his cheeks.

"What are you doing here?" the chief eunuch demanded.

"I came for my mother," Yetzer said, struggling to keep his voice level. "To speak with Pharaoh, if he will see me. And, perhaps, to see—"

"Not here," Mika said, waving his hands in Yetzer's face. He looked about before adding in a low voice, "Come with me."

Yetzer checked his objections and followed the man through the peristyle court, a forest of giant stone columns as dense as the forests of Kenahn. When they reached the outer wall of the palace, decorated with murals, the eunuch pressed a hidden switch beneath the images of a pair of young princes hunting with throwing sticks. Mika pushed open a concealed door and led Yetzer inside.

Yetzer blinked in the dimness of the space as the door slid shut behind him. After several moments he was able to make out a small room appointed in purple silks and furniture of ebony and cedar. Mika gestured him toward a cushioned stool while he settled his bulk upon a wide, throne-like couch.

"My mother," Yetzer said, still standing, arms across his chest.

"She's not here, boy," Mika said, and flapped his hand at the stool. "Sit, sit."

The steward took a jar from a table beside his throne, broke the seal, and filled two silver chalices with gold-colored wine. He handed one to Yetzer, then leaned back on his throne.

"Where is she?" Yetzer said, rolling the chalice between his palms. "Still in Uaset?" He'd sought his mother there after leaving the temple, but had been told none of the royal household was still in the old capital.

"Mm-mm," the eunuch grunted behind a mouthful of wine, shaking his head. "She returned to Retenu after your disgrace."

The news was delivered in an even tone, but sent fire up Yetzer's neck.

"Pharaoh said he would keep her in his household," Yetzer said through gritted teeth.

"And he would have. But he would not keep her against her will, and she would not stay under the … " He paused and stroked his chin as he seemed to search the rafters for the right words. "Under the same roof as the pagan whore who sold her son into slavery. The Habiru have such a way with words. Pharaoh granted her safe conduct and passage aboard a merchant ship bound for Tsur. Must have been five, six inundations ago. Oh, Pharaoh and Lady Mutnedjmet tried to convince her to stay, but her will was fixed. Can't blame her, I must say. If it was a slave girl in that chamber as it was supposed to be, I daresay you'd have completed your initiation that very night. But Ameniye?" The eunuch clucked his tongue. "Not even the most enlightened of men could have resisted her."

Yetzer's fingers tightened around his cup. "Slave girl?" The question scraped against his throat.

"Of course," Mika said after another quaff of wine. "Always a slave girl, and always the most beautiful. From Uwene or Napata, sometimes even from Retenu or Hatti. But never from Kemet, and certainly never from Pharaoh's own household. It's one thing to deflower a slave, but a daughter of Kemet?" He shook his head and grimaced.

"A frightened girl would have been easier to turn away," Yetzer said, his voice sounding distant in his ears.

"Not so easy as you think," Mika countered. "And not so frightened. If she succeeds in luring the initiate to her couch, she wins her freedom. You can see how she might be motivated to give up her lotus flower."

The eunuch took another drink as Yetzer took his first sip.

"And the Temple benefits either way. They gain a truly worthy adept, or they sift out the chaff—no offense—and exchange a lovely little bird for a man strong and smart enough to endure the other ordeals." He shrugged. "Come to think of it, she'll likely end up in one of the Temple's brothels, so they really do benefit all around."

"And a princess?" Yetzer spoke the words mainly to himself.

"There is the mystery," Mika said with a thoughtful nod. "Nothing there for her but love."

Yetzer scoffed. "Or hate."

"Two words for the same thing." Mika waved his hand dismissively.

"I chose the temple over her," Yetzer went on, "so she made certain I'd have neither."

"Yet here you sit, an Adept of Amun, Master of the Seven Arts." Mika saluted Yetzer with his cup.

Yetzer took another sip from his own chalice. He mused on the path that had led him from a slave's rags to the adept's robe. The scourges and starvation had played no small roles, the echoes of their pain frequently rippling through Yetzer's back and belly.

The subtler disciplines—the arts of shaping men, of molding them into a unified band—he might never have learned as a master over them, as an initiate of the House of Life. But as one of them, as a slave himself, he'd found the thread of shared humanity that bound one man to another.

"What I wouldn't give," Mika said, dispelling Yetzer's thoughts, "to have seen Merisutah's face when you spoke the word to him."

"He was … " Yetzer thought back to the moment, to the tensing in the hierophant's body, the lion's grip on Yetzer's hand as he whispered the adept's word into Merisutah's ear. "He was gracious."

Mika almost choked on his wine. "Gracious? Bah!"

"He freed me," Yetzer continued. "No one else heard me. He could have denied I'd given him the true word, could have had me slain right there."

"He could have," Mika agreed, and splashed more wine into the cups. "He could have rid himself of a half-blind foreigner who had no place entering the Temple to begin with." The eunuch gave a crooked grin, raised his cup and drank deeply. Mika's humor overcame Yetzer's defenses, and he smiled for the first time in he knew not how long. He lifted his own cup and took a long drink.

"Merisutah may be many things," Mika said, "some of them not entirely evil. For all his faults, not even he would stand against Pharaoh or Amun. What is whispered between men does not escape the gods' ears."

"Or those of Pharaoh's steward?" Yetzer ventured.

Mika gave a shrug. "I have many little bees who buzz about through all of Kemet. Such pollen as they gather becomes honey that I might pour in Pharaoh's ear. Had Merisutah denied you, he would have been cast among the nameless ones. Pharaoh would have seen to it."

Yetzer sipped again at his wine while he recalled the courtyard of Amun's temple. The corbeled vault with its rounded back, where he'd stood with Merisutah. The matching alcove on the other side of the yard. The priest who'd stood within the second vault.

"The whispering arch," Yetzer said.

Mika nodded. "A lovely little feature. And a most valuable tool for the builder who knows how to make use of it."

"It was Pharaoh," Yetzer said. "The reason I was moved from place to place. Pharaoh was behind it."

"He let it be known that he wished you to be looked after," Mika allowed. "He was not pleased with Merisutah and Ameniye's deception, and he wanted you yet to have the opportunity to prove yourself."

Yetzer sat in silence beneath the weight of Mika's words. Pharaoh Horemheb—Master of the Two Lands, brother of the gods—had remembered his friendship with Huram, had remained Yetzer's guardian.

"May I see him?" Yetzer asked.

Mika shook his head. "Pharaoh is traveling to inspect all the districts. It will be some time before he returns."

"When did he leave?" Yetzer asked.

"Last new moon," Mika said. "He should have reached Yebu by now, but ... "

Yetzer grimaced. The forty-two administrative districts spanned Kemet from the Great Green Sea in the north to the wild waters of the Iteru's first cataract, well south of Uaset. If it took a month to reach the first *sepat* of Upper Kemet, it could well take twice as long to make a proper inspection of all the southern districts.

"And Ameniye?"

Mika drained his cup and set it on the serving table. With a somber look, he laced his fingers together and leaned his elbows upon his knees.

"She is here," he said with a heavy sigh. "She is well. And she is betrothed."

Pain lanced through Yetzer's heart, fixing him upon his stool as though impaled. He could not breathe, could not think. There was only a searing heat, a flood of emotions, and in their wake, a cold void.

"Betrothed." The word squeezed from his throat with all the strength of a mewling infant.

"To Ramessu."

It took a few moments for Yetzer to place the name of the wazir, second in power only to Pharaoh. The old man had more years than Horemheb. Though he'd never led men in battle, the wazir commanded Pharaoh's trust and the respect of a nation.

And now Ameniye.

"She is destined to be queen one day," Mika said, his voice grave. "And woe to the king who attaches her to his throne."

"You speak of Pharaoh's daughter," Yetzer snapped. "She is a princess of Kemet, descended from the gods."

"She is a spoiled child who breaks whatever toy she tires of, then demands another." The eunuch fixed Yetzer with a patient look. "You know this better than most."

Yetzer tried to meet the gaze, but tears flooded his vision. His chalice fell to the floor, spilling its contents upon the rug.

Yetzer covered his face with his hands as grief folded about him like a burial shroud. His body shook with sobs as the pain of his losses crashed down upon him. His father, taken by the quarry. His mother, gone to her distant homeland. His dignity, stolen by the overseer's whip. And his love lost to a ruler's scepter and a woman's restless heart.

"What do I do?" he said when at last he could speak.

"Leave Kemet," came Mika's immediate reply. "Go to Retenu—to Kenahn." Yetzer looked up at that. For a Kemeti to use the indigenous name of a land, rather than the conqueror's epithet, was a feat of great compassion. The eunuch smiled at him.

"Go to the land of your ancestors. Take your father's body and let him rest among his people, guarded by his own gods. Return to your mother."

He picked up Yetzer's chalice. After recharging both cups with wine, he handed back Yetzer's and half-drained his before speaking again.

"Kemet is changing. We once welcomed foreigners, enriched ourselves with their goods, with their ideas." He drank yet again. "There are many loud voices now that claim the recent unpleasantness was due to foreign influence that must be rooted out."

More than twenty years had passed since the end of Akhenaten's heretical and tyrannical rule, but to the people of Kemet it was still that recent unpleasantness. When they referred to the disgraced pharaoh it was only by hint or innuendo, never by name lest merely speaking the word should wake him from his slumber and cast the Two Lands once more into ruin.

"Pharaoh travels not merely to inspect each district," Mika continued, his words misshapen by the wine. "He goes to erase the very being of the ill-favored one and those of his household, to strike their names and effigies from every monument, every scroll. Between Yebu and the Great Green Sea, not one memory of the heresy will remain."

Mika set his empty cup on the floor and stretched out on his couch. His great belly, swollen with wine, gleamed in the lamplight.

"And you're next." The words staggered from his tongue as he waggled a finger at Yetzer. "You Kenahni, the Hatti, Habiru, Keftiu—all those of foreign lands, with strange gods and strange dress will soon find no place in Kemet. Go home, boy. There's nothing here for you anymore."

The eunuch dropped one hand to the floor, the other splayed across his chest. His wine-thickened breathing quickly turned to snores. Yetzer stared dumbly at Pharaoh's steward. Emotions spent, will crushed, only reason stood to counsel him. Mika had spoken true, whether from wisdom or wine. Yetzer rose to go.

Mika mumbled something. Yetzer assumed it to be drunken rambling and continued toward the door.

"The dispensation," the eunuch said more forcefully, and gestured toward a small scroll on the table.

A golden cobra, its body about as thick as Yetzer's little finger, coiled around the lambskin parchment. The snake's metal scales and carnelian eyes shimmered in the dancing light of the oil lamps as Yetzer slid the scroll from the serpentine embrace and squeezed the coils over his wrist.

In the name of Amun-Ra, the dispensation began, its message inked in the glyphs and script of Kemet, as well as the broad, arrowhead strokes of Akkadian, used from Kemet to distant Subartu, the land between the two great rivers of the east.

He who bears this is the friend of Pharaoh Horemheb-Djeserkheperure, Chosen of Ra. Into his hands shall be given whatsoever he desires, even should he ask for half my kingdom. The blessings of Amun be upon all who come to his aid, for such a one shall have aided Pharaoh himself. But woe betide any who turns his back, for Pharaoh shall surely turn his back upon such a one, who shall be made nameless, forgotten among gods and men.

"Your father is in Pharaoh's House of Eternity, in Anpu's Quarter," Mika mumbled from his couch. "All you need is there."

The steward's head rolled back on the pillows and fell back into snoring before Yetzer could question him. Scroll in hand, Yetzer crossed to the door and slid back into the sunlight.

37

Bilkis

Bilkis suffered through the endless procession of Urusalim's nobles, who offered obeisance and blessing to her son. She occasionally had to pinch the boy's arm to keep his attention on the proceedings. Yahtadua came fully awake, though, when the priests arrived.

Abiattar strode into the audience chamber, his footsteps punctuated by the tap of his staff on the flagstones. The priest of Yah bowed grandly. Upon rising, he extended the head of his staff toward the king, and Yahtadua eagerly plucked an almond from among the golden branches.

Abdi-Havah followed. The ancient priest leaned upon the arm of the prophet Gad. Behind them, struggling with the burden of Abdi-Havah's great oak staff with its bronze serpent, came young Natan. Abdi-Havah stooped over the bier to kiss Tadua's hand and cheek, then priest, seer, and acolyte bowed before Yahtadua. Before they could rise, Abiattar let out a piercing wail and flung himself across Tadua's body.

"Oh, that I had gone early to Sheol, there to greet my king, my lord. Sorry is the day I first drew breath, that I should bear the loss of one so noble."

Bilkis made a swatting gesture toward Benyahu who stepped around the bier, dragged the simpering priest off the corpse, and hauled him before the throne.

"Take your hands off me, swine," Abiattar protested.

"Your tears do you credit, priest," Bilkis said, ignoring the man's struggles to break free of Benyahu's grip. "I wonder, did you mourn the king when you sought to usurp his throne for Baaliyah?"

The color drained from the old man's features. "I never—"

"You never thought to consult your king before you proclaimed his successor?" Bilkis demanded. "You never thought to inquire of your god before choosing his anointed one?"

Abiattar opened his mouth to protest, but Bilkis interrupted him again.

"Stay your tongue or I'll have it ripped from your mouth. Seer," she said to Gad, "come forth and inquire of the gods for me."

The young man did as commanded. Yahtadua's face lit up and he leaned forward on his throne.

"Ask what you will, my lady," Gad said as he pulled on his gloves.

"Has Abiattar acted in the right toward the throne of Yisrael?"

Gad muttered under his breath and rocked back and forth. His eyes rolled back and he reached into his pouch.

"Black," Yahtadua said when Gad revealed the seer stone. The king pointed at Abiattar. "You have not acted in the right."

Bilkis placed her hand over her son's, but the boy pressed on with royal zeal.

"What shall be his punishment?" the boy asked. "Shall I have him executed?"

"My lord—" Abiattar began, but Benyahu choked off the protest with a sharp tug on the neck of his robe.

"No," Yahtadua said, crestfallen when Gad again revealed the black stone.

"Shall he be removed from his office?" Bilkis asked before Yahtadua could interject another question.

White.

"Shall his lands be forfeit to the crown?" the queen continued and fought to keep her anger in check when Gad revealed the black stone.

"Who will replace him?" Yahtadua asked while Bilkis gritted her teeth. "Is he in the hall?"

White.

"Is he to my right?" the king asked from the very edge of his throne.

Black.

Yahtadua scanned the left side of the audience hall where Eliam, Abram, Abdi-Havah, and a dozen others stood in perplexed silence.

"Ask," the king commanded them. "Ask him."

The men all shared looks, then Eliam cleared his throat and stepped forward. "Is it I?" the merchant asked.

Gad, still facing the king with eyes rolled back, reached into his pouch and revealed the black stone. Abram asked next, and along the line until all the men had inquired and all received a negative response.

Yahtadua sat back in his throne and rubbed his chin thoughtfully.

"What does it mean?" he wondered aloud.

In reply, Abdi-Havah stooped down and whispered in the ear of his acolyte. Young Natan looked at the withered old man and whispered something back. The priest simply smiled and patted the boy on the shoulder.

"Is it I?" Natan asked in a soft voice.

The seer again reached into his pouch and withdrew his gloved hand to reveal the white stone.

"It's him! It's Natan!" Yahtadua cried, and clapped his hands together.

"This is an outrage," Abiattar exclaimed. "To be usurped by a child?"

"I was younger still when my father named me his heir," Yahtadua said, his voice matter-of-fact. "Think you the gods make use only of bearded men? Or do you doubt the very seer stones that affirmed your calling upon a time?"

The old man stammered a reply, but Yahtadua waved him to silence. "As the gods have spared you and preserved your inheritance," the king said, "you will go to your lands, never again to leave them. Should you venture away from that place of sanctuary, your blood shall be upon your own head."

"Yes, Lord," Abiattar said in a meek voice as he bowed and backed away from the dais. "It shall be even as you say."

"Wait," Bilkis commanded, and gestured for Benyahu to intercept the old man. "Remove from him the tokens of the priest's office and bestow them upon their rightful bearer."

Benyahu wrenched the seven-branched golden staff from the former priest's hands and gave it and his stole to one of the guards. The old man yelped as the general swatted off the white turban, then tugged Abiattar's beard and drew the chain of the breastplate over his head. The golden chest piece was studded with gems of various colors. The thirteen settings formed a six-pointed star, one jewel for each of Yisrael's tribes. As Benyahu loosed the scarlet rope that secured the breastplate around Abiattar's waist, Bilkis noticed the center setting was empty.

"There is one missing," she said in a soft voice. The old man blinked at her while Benyahu continued to strip away the rings and robes of the god's servant. "One of the jewels entrusted to you appears to have been lost," Bilkis observed. "Or am I mistaken?"

Abiattar said nothing as Benyahu pulled the tunic over the priest's head, leaving him only his breechcloth.

"You are of the tribe of Levi, yes?" the queen continued. "Then as the gem has been displaced, so shall the people of Levi be. Let them be scattered among their brother tribes, their inheritance entrusted to safer hands."

The stripped priest opened his mouth, but only a mewling whine came out.

"Be assured," Bilkis went on, "you shall be secure on the lands of your fathers. As our guest. And when your bones are gathered unto the earth, we shall dispose of them as the gods direct. Go now." She fought to keep the gloat from her voice, the smile from her lips. "Do not let the sun set before you have reached sanctuary."

Abiattar turned away. All in the chamber watched him leave, their breath stilled. Only the sound of his bare feet slapping the paving stones filled the place. When he disappeared through the doorway, Bilkis clapped her hands once. Several of the attendants jerked, startled by the sound. All heads turned back toward the dais.

"Our king thanks each of you for the honor you do him and his father," Bilkis said. "You may go now, that we might prepare to gather King Tadua to his ancestors."

The people continued to stare at her. Bilkis caught Benyahu's eyes and gestured to him. The warrior nodded and beat the hilt of his sword three times against the heavy timber of the door jamb.

"The queen has spoken," he said in a voice that filled the chamber. "Clear the hall."

Still silent, the assembly shared confused glances then turned and filed to the doorway.

"Except you, Gad," Bilkis said.

The young man looked back, his expression flat as a pond's surface. Bilkis smiled.

"I would speak with you alone."

❉

"What does it take?" Bilkis asked.

She sat upon the king's cushioned chair in the private chamber behind the great hall. The queen poured two cups of wine and gestured Gad to the seat near her, across a low table. The young seer set his shoulders firmly and remained standing.

"What does what take, my lady?" His words were respectful, but his tone was cold as winter rain. Bilkis gave him a pout.

"What does it take to hear the words of the gods?" she said. "More to the point, what does it take to put their words in your ear, their answers in your hand?"

Gad's lips formed a grim line, his eyes flicked away. "I am but the vessel of the gods, moved by them to reveal their wishes."

Bilkis barked out a laugh. "They may be the gods' wishes, but surely the deities are in league with your teacher. Do not mistake me," she added before Gad could object. "Abdi-Havah is as a grandfather to me. I trust his judgment. If not for his wisdom, my son might not wear the crown."

The young man's eyes drifted back to meet Bilkis's gaze, his defiance melting into confusion.

"The priest's wishes have been fulfilled," Bilkis pressed on. "One of his blood sits upon the throne of Urusalim, the seat of *Melchi-tzedek*. Another wears the vestments of the Priest of Yah. He may take comfort that the scepter and the staff are under his sway. All of Yisrael will be the better for it."

The last of Gad's resistance crumbled and he lowered himself into his seat.

"But Abdi-Havah is old. It may not be long before he joins Tadua in Sheol." Bilkis raised her hands in innocence when the seer shot her an angry glance. "Upon the crown of my son, I mean no harm. I speak only the truth. It may be years or it may be days, but Abdi-Havah will go the way of all the earth. When that happens, someone else must whisper in the gods' ears."

Bilkis sipped her wine and set her cup aside. She leaned back in her chair, set her feet upon a stool, and spread her knees beneath her gown.

"So I ask," she continued in languid tones. "What does it take? What can a queen offer one of her most valued councillors to earn his trust and cooperation?"

She ran one hand from her knee along the inside of her thigh, while she drew the other across her bosom. Gad shifted in his chair, cleared his throat and turned his eyes away.

"No?" Bilkis smoothed her gown back into place and leaned her elbows upon her knees. "Perhaps you prefer a figure more masculine. One of Benyahu's guards, perhaps?"

Gad remained silent as a lamb before slaughter, his jaw muscles tight. Bilkis stood and moved behind his chair. She placed her hands on his shoulders and stooped to whisper in his ears.

"Or perhaps you'd prefer … " She moved to his other side and spoke even more softly, less a whisper than a sigh. "Rahab."

The young man's head jerked. A tremor rippled through his shoulders, his breathing became ragged. Still, he said nothing.

"You see?" Bilkis said as she moved back to her chair. "One need not be a prophet to have the gift of sight. But Rahab is most dear to me, as a sister. While Tadua was too weak to make a concubine of her, still she shared the royal bed. There lives power between her legs. Perhaps she would make a bride for my son, hmm? From the old king's bed to that of the new?"

"No," Gad said in a whisper.

"What was that?"

"No," Gad repeated, desperation edging his voice. "Rahab's heart belongs to me, and mine to her. Give her to no other, I beg you. Whatever your will, I shall do. You need only tell me what you wish."

Bilkis sat back in the great chair. She pressed her fingertips together and propped them beneath her lips. Then she smiled.

38

Bilkis

"Say it back to me," Bilkis ordered.

Yahshepat, the court scribe, sat to one side of the dais. The man was past his middle years, with thinning hair and drooping shoulders. He sat amid heaps of clay tablets. Stacks of square-cut, stiff fabric lay beside him, along with small jars filled with thick soups of black and red.

"Writing," Abdi-Havah had told Bilkis, by way of explaining the rows of strange symbols Yahshepat made upon the fabric, "is a means of capturing words so they may be carried to distant places."

Yahshepat cleared his throat, combed ink-stained fingers through his beard, then held the fabric to catch his lamp's light.

"Say to the King of Kemet, my father Djeserkheperure Setepenre, the words of Bilkis bat-Saba, Queen of Yisrael. Says your handmaiden—"

"Handmaiden?" Bilkis said, interrupting. "I am no handmaiden. I am the mother, the wife, the daughter of kings. You would cast the words of a serving girl upon my tongue?"

The scribe flapped his lips helplessly, but Abdi-Havah came to his aid. "My child, it is simply a token of good will. The words are not meant to diminish you, but to exalt Pharaoh. Why, in my day I referred to myself as the shovel-bearer in Pharaoh's stables."

Bilkis eyed the man dubiously but nodded for Yahshepat to continue.

"Says your handmaiden, the dust beneath your feet—"

"Dust?" Bilkis demanded.

"A courtesy, child," Abdi-Havah said.

The queen grunted, and the scribe recited the next lines almost too fast to be understood.

"At the feet of the king, my lord, my sun, seven times and seven times I throw myself to the ground."

Bilkis felt rage contort her features, but Abdi-Havah held up a placating hand and gestured for Yahshepat to carry on.

"I pray to Yah and to Havah, to Hadad and Ashtart, to all of my gods and to all of yours, that all goes well with you, with your houses, your wives, your sons, your horses, your chariots, and all your lands. For me, and for my son, for our houses, our lands—"

"Yes, yes," Bilkis interrupted yet again. "Everyone is well. Go on."

Yahshepat mumbled to himself then continued. "My lord the king surely remembers Tadua, of whom Abdi-Havah of Urusalim, Mutbaal of Sekhem, abi-Milku of Tsur, and many others wrote to my lord. I say to the king, my lord, that Tadua abi-Yishai has followed the sun in its setting. I, Bilkis, widow of Tadua, now hold the throne in trust for your servant Yahtadua, King of Yisrael.

"While many complaints reached my lord of Tadua's use of the sword, I say now that the land of Yisrael is at peace. From Barsaba in the south to Danu in the north, the merchant travels without fear. From the plains of Hashpelah to the vale of Yarden, no bandit preys upon the farmer. The lands of Kenahn stand safe behind the spear of Yahtadua, Retenu beneath his shield."

"Must we say the same thing over and over," Bilkis asked. "Yisrael, Kenahn, Retenu. Cannot we simply choose one name and have done with it?"

"It is diplomacy, my lady." Abdi-Havah smiled wearily. "The art of wooing an adversary with sweet words, of lulling him with many." He turned back to the scribe and nodded. "Please proceed, Yahshepat."

"During forty years," the scribe continued reading, "Tadua spoke not to my lord or to my lord's brothers or to his fathers. No scribe set stylus to clay. No tablet carried words of greeting. Hatti has been our mother. Alassiya and Ugaratu, Tsur and Sidon have been our brothers. Now, as a father welcomes a widowed daughter back into his household, let my lord the king receive the messengers of Yisrael, let the Elect of Ra hear the words of Bilkis.

"In celebration of the renewed amity between us, we send with our messenger five and three-score head of cattle, twenty-score goats, twenty-score sheep ... Shall I recite the full list?" Yahshepat asked, looking up from the document.

Bilkis gave a dismissive wave of her hand. "Go to the end."

The scribe scanned down the lines of neat figures.

"And a pair of brass lamp stands. In return, we ask that you send whatever gifts our words and tokens of friendship may invoke of you. Tadua desired to erect a temple unto the gods in thanksgiving for their gift of peace. With the continued blessings of our gods and the generosity of our friends, we intend to undertake the building of this monument. Therefore, send much gold for the adornment of the house of the gods, that wherever the name of Yah is whispered, wherever the blessing of Havah is sought, there too may the name and the goodness of my lord the king be remembered."

The audience hall fell into silence as Bilkis considered the message. Other than the scribe's innovation about handmaidens and dust, the strange markings seemed, indeed, to have captured her words and wishes.

"I still think we should ask for a royal bride for Yahtadua," she said.

"Umma, no," the young king complained. "What do I want with a bride? Maybe a horse. Oh, and a chariot. We should ask for a chariot."

"My lady," Abdi-Havah said with a shake of his head, "in ten-score generations, Kemet has never given a royal bride to wed a foreigner. It is rumored that the last foreign prince who went to take a Kemeti princess was struck down at the very border of the land. And, my lord," he added for Yahtadua's benefit, "in all my years I could not even obtain the loan of Kemeti archers to defend my walls. No, children, let us first see how this humble request is received, then determine what more we may gain."

Yahtadua began to complain, but Bilkis laid a hand upon his arm.

"Very well," she told the scribe. "The letter is acceptable. Now, take these words."

Yahshepat took a clean strip of linen, dipped his sharpened reed into the pot of black ink, and looked expectantly at his queen.

"To Lady Remeg of Tsur, friend of Tadua of Urusalim, say the words of Bilkis, Queen of Yisrael ... "

❖

When all the words had been read back and agreed upon, Bilkis directed Yahshepat to set them to clay. Cloth was, the scribe told her, too meager an instrument for so grand a communication, and too susceptible to forgery. An inscribed clay tablet could be baked to secure its message, then be safely delivered to a Kemeti scribe who would relay the words to his king.

Yahshepat began pressing his bird tracks into the soft clay. Yahtadua hopped down from his throne and squatted beside the scribe to inspect his work.

"My lamb," Bilkis said, "a king has no need to learn such humble things."

"Let him be," Abdi-Havah said gently. "It may not profit him, but it will do no harm. Come. I would speak with you privately."

The old priest gestured toward the private audience chamber. "What is your intention regarding the temple?" he asked after he'd closed the door and taken his seat opposite Bilkis. When the queen was slow to answer, he continued. "Do you use the thought of it simply to extract gifts from our neighbors, or is it truly in your heart to build it?"

Bilkis leaned back in her chair, crossed one leg over the other, then laced her fingers together around her knee.

"I am only the Queen of Yisrael," she demurred. "I couldn't possibly decide such a thing for myself. Perhaps we should inquire of the gods to determine our course."

Abdi-Havah gave a small sigh. "It is true," he admitted, "I have been wont to whisper the gods' words into Gad's ear. But I never insisted the seer stones be consulted. I never forced anyone to request the prophecy or to adhere to the answers given." He clasped his gnarled fingers together and leaned upon his knees. "And I never lied to you."

Bilkis laughed loudly.

"But you did," she insisted. "You told me you were no longer *Melchi-tzedek*, that after Tadua took your city you were relegated to the role of priest. The truth is you have been king all this time, in fact if not in name."

The old man studied his hands for a long moment. When he looked up, his good eye bore a sheen of tears. "When I was a boy," he said, "I watched my grandfather prophesy with the stones. For hundreds of years wanderers have come to this city to inquire of the gods. At first it was only Havah, the mother of us all, who spoke. 'Which crops should I plant?' 'Should I purchase this land or that?' 'What bride price shall I pay?'

"Then Yah began to make his voice known among men, and the questions fell more into his particular realm. 'In what season shall I attack my enemy?' 'Shall I flee or fight?' Whether the answer was favorable or not, the supplicant left his tribute and went his way."

Abdi-Havah sat back in his chair and scratched under his beard. "I was only a young man when I realized the gods' answers were invariably in line with the best result for Urusalim. When the time came for me to take the throne, my father gave me the secret of the seer stones. When Tadua took the city, I in turn passed the stones to the Habiru holy man, Shemval. In exchange, he allowed me to live."

"And to decide the gods' answers?" Bilkis asked, her tone bitter.

"By Havah's womb, no," the priest said with a harsh laugh. "Shemval was a vicious old fool who cared only for Yah's vengeance. His only mercy was to take my one eye rather than both, and to hobble me rather than breaking my back."

"He did this to you?"

"Of course not." Abdi-Havah laughed. "Far be it from a man of the gods to raise a hand in violence. 'Twas Ayub made me lame and blind, by order of Tadua and the hand of the gods."

Bilkis sat quietly for a time. With an effort, she raised her eyes to meet Abdi-Havah's.

"You won't tell me, will you?"

The old man sighed.

"I cannot, child," he said. "After Shemval, I swore before Havah I would reveal the secret of the stones to none but a worthy successor."

"Yet you told Gad."

"He is a good man. He truly seeks to discern the gods' intent for the people."

"And I do not?"

"You are strong," Abdi-Havah allowed. "Perhaps as strong as any king of Urusalim. Certainly, the strongest among the Habiru. But, as with the legs of a footstool, it takes three pillars to hold a throne upright. Strength, yes, but it must be balanced by compassion and by wisdom to determine which is appropriate, and in what measure."

A cold needle pierced Bilkis's heart at the priest's words. "You say I lack compassion?"

"Unless it suits you." Abdi-Havah leaned forward to rest his hands upon hers. "You can care fiercely for those around you, but your sympathies extend only so far as is expedient to your will."

Bilkis pulled her hands from the priest's cold grip. She took the pillow from her backrest and hugged it close.

"I do not say these things in judgment or to cause harm. The days of a ruler are fraught with hard choices. You may yet become a great queen over these people, but only when you've learned to put the needs of others ahead of your own desire."

The queen rose, pillow still clutched to her chest, and paced about the little chamber. Abdi-Havah leaned back in his chair, thumb and forefinger of one hand pinching the bridge of his nose.

"But you don't need me to tell you the stones' secrets, do you?" His gaze followed her around the room. "You've already extorted their use from Gad. It shouldn't take much more—"

Abdi-Havah's words were lost as Bilkis pressed the cushion to his face and pulled him against the back of his chair. The old man struggled against her, raking his nails across her hands and clawing at her hair.

What madness is this? a voice screamed in Bilkis's heart. The queen looked at her hands, as at those of a stranger. She almost released the pillow, but she'd already attacked the old man. She could not bear to look him in the eye after this. She pulled the pillow tighter. "You have been a great help to me." She spoke the words softly, her lips close to the dying priest's ear. "I would not be where I am were it not for you. But it's clear you're no longer with me, and you're right—my compassion and tolerance extend only so far."

The man's hands fell away. He convulsed a few times then went still. Bilkis kept the pillow fully in place as she kissed his cheek and whispered in his ear.

"Carry my blessing to Sheol. Greet my husbands and my sons and pray for me before the goddess."

The queen removed the cushion and carefully studied the old man. His features were oddly peaceful, as if at his midmorning nap. Bilkis pried a wrinkled eyelid open and snapped her fingers. The man did not react.

"That really was unnecessary," Bilkis told the warm corpse. "Why keep secret what I would eventually learn?"

She set the cushion back on her chair, careful to turn away the side dampened by the old fool's saliva.

"And why say such cruel things to me?" She faced the body, hands on her hips, posture much as when she scolded Yahtadua. "I have great compassion for those who are worthy of it. And look at what you've done to my hands."

Thin red streaks laced the backs of her hands. She inspected Abdi-Havah's fingers, scraped her flesh from beneath his nails, and retrieved a clump of her hair he'd pulled loose. Bilkis shook her head and made an angry noise. She spoke again as she traced her own nails along the scratches the old man had made.

"And, yes. I do intend to build the temple. And your prophet and your little priest will help me."

After a final survey to see that all was in place, Bilkis loosed a mourning wail. Within moments, Benyahu burst open the heavy cedar door, closely followed by Yahtadua and the others.

"It's Abdi-Havah," Bilkis cried, clutching at her hair and pointing to the still priest. "The servant of the goddess is dead."

39

Yetzer

The trade port of Tsur perched upon its twin rocks off the Kenahni coast. Having claimed his father's remains and possessions from Horemheb's House of Eternity, and after securing passage on a ship of Tsur, Yetzer now climbed the road from the harbor to the city's center. He flipped a small clay tablet in the air as he walked. Inscribed with a stylized sword on one side and a paired hand and camel on the other, the token represented his ownership of the items he'd left in a warehouse.

He'd been reluctant to leave his possessions. His father's sarcophagus and ornate toolbox were all he owned in the world. But Tsur made its living on trade. The city's very existence depended upon the safe transport and storage of goods. Yetzer could be sure his treasure was as secure here as it would be in one of Pharaoh's own storehouses.

Whereas Kemet's center of power resided in Pharaoh's palace, the heart of Tsur lay in the great trading house in the center of the city. A humble thing by the standards of Kemet, the building's cedar timbers sat atop a sandstone foundation and reached to perhaps ten cubits, about the height of three men.

"The son of Yishai was our friend," a woman's voice declared as Yetzer entered the trading hall.

The speaker occupied a simple cedar chair set upon a small dais in the center of the room. Her gown of deepest purple and a silver circlet about her brow suggested her position of power, but the authority in her voice needed no adornment.

"Tadua was indeed a great friend to us," she said. "Where much loyalty is given, much generosity is due."

A group of men stood about the foot of the dais, draped in the brightly patterned robes and caps of Tsurian merchants. They muttered reluctant agreement with the woman.

"I thank you, Lady Remeg." A young man, more simply dressed than the others, knelt before the dais, a fired clay tablet in his hands. "The ancient friendship between Tsur and Yisrael is—"

"But what need has Tadua of our generosity in the grave?" the Queen of Tsur interrupted him. "How can our aid reach him in Sheol? What can we offer that his gods and his fathers cannot provide?"

"My lady," the young man said, his voice rich with the accent of Kenahn's Habiru tribes, "King Yahtadua—"

"Never fought my father's enemies," Remeg cut him off again, her voice sharp and crisp. "He never gave me a city. He probably still pukes up his nurse's milk, so it will be some years before he is of any use to his gods, to his people, or to me."

The queen fixed the young man with a long, cold stare as though daring him to dispute her. When he'd stayed his tongue through a long, uncomfortable silence, Lady Remeg spoke again.

"Yet for the love we bore Tadua," she said, her tone now soft and warm, "for the duty we owe him, we shall consider the request of his widow and of his heir. Leave your message with our Keeper of Accounts. You shall have our decision in time."

The queen gave a dismissive gesture and indicated a man seated at a table to one side of the trading hall. Parchments and clay tablets stood in neat stacks upon the table. The scribe held out a withered hand and snapped his fingers at the messenger from Yisrael.

The young man opened his mouth but then reconsidered. He bowed to the queen, nodded to her councillors, and handed his tablet to the scribe.

"Tadua's widow thinks to make demands of us?" Lady Remeg coolly observed when the messenger had departed. "She speaks of friendship as though she had raised the sword for Tsur, as though her son had defended our gates."

The men about the dais offered muted replies.

"Draft our response," Remeg told the scribe. "Tell this upstart queen that we will consider a gift of half the timber requested, but their return gift of grain and olives must be delivered first. Our foresters cannot work on empty stomachs."

"And the stone?" the scribe asked, looking up from his parchment. "The craftsmen?"

"Are there not rocks in the hills of Yisrael?" Remeg demanded. "Let them scratch the earth for themselves. If any of our artisans wish to work in that wasteland, we will not stop them, nor will we supply them. Let her own gold and grain buy the skill she craves."

"And what of the—"

"You know my will on this." The queen spoke in a tone that brooked no dissent. "Draft our reply then read it to me before you inscribe it. What do you want?"

The question met silence for the span of several heartbeats. Only when Yetzer noticed all eyes in the chamber turned his way did he realize the queen had spoken to him. He pushed himself off the cedar post he'd been leaning against, cleared his throat and approached the dais.

"From Horemheb, Pharaoh of Kemet, I bring greetings."

"Kemet?" Remeg said with a grunt. "Pharaoh sends a bearded man rather than one of his hairless eunuchs?"

Derisive laughter rumbled around the hall. Yetzer still wore the robes of a priest of Amun, but he'd not shaved his scalp or face since leaving the temple of Uaset several weeks before. Though mere stubble, the itchy growth gave him more the appearance of a Tsurian than a Kemeti, and he thanked Djehuti for that bit of forethought.

"I bring Pharaoh's greeting, Lady, but I come upon my own business, as a subject of Tsur. I am Yetzer, son of Huram, son of Tudu-Baal who was brother to my lady's father Abi-Milku."

The laughter stilled and Remeg's face turned sober. The queen slowly rose and descended from the dais. She cautiously studied Yetzer with sharp green eyes.

"Is this the image of my kinsman?" She squinted as she placed her hands on Yetzer's cheeks. "Is this Huram's son?"

"Even so," Yetzer said. "I have returned to lay my father among his ancestors, to see after my mother, and to offer what service I may to my lady."

These last words were muted as the queen kissed Yetzer on both cheeks then pulled him into a tight embrace.

"Rejoice with me, Brothers," Remeg said to the assembled nobles. "For a lost ship of Tsur has returned safely to port."

❖

"It was Ilban-Ay that made Huram a mason instead of a merchant," Queen Remeg told Yetzer later, as they sat on the beach awaiting the tide's retreat.

Following his reception, the queen had joined Yetzer as he claimed his father's body and ferried it to the burial ground on the mainland. Accompanied by a troop of servants and hired mourners, they'd removed the corpse from its cedar box and staked it, along with the clay jars that held Huram's viscera, just above the low tide line. While the tidal flow covered the remains of Yetzer's father, the servants stacked wood for a funeral pyre. Remeg shared with Yetzer a jar of wine and countless stories of her cousin Huram and their youthful adventures, of journeys by land and sea to the edges of the world.

That island of Ilban-Ay lay far to the north of the Pillars of Melkart, which guarded the western gates of the Great Green Sea. The sailors of Tsur braved dangerous, years-long voyages to fetch from those distant shores the tin that made bronze of copper, along with ivory and waterproof pelts.

"The priests there built a great stone circle," Remeg continued. "Granite, mind you, not mere limestone or sandstone. As tall as four men and five times that across. As old as Kemet's pyramids, and as perfect in its construction. If they could do that with tools of bone and flint and rock, your father decided there was no limit to what a real craftsman might be able to achieve."

The queen's stories, more jars of wine, and platters of food sustained them through the long hours as the waters of the sea crept up the shoreline then retreated once more. When the tide dropped, Remeg and Yetzer recovered the water-logged body, the viscera having been lost to the sea.

The lacquer used by Kemet's mortuary priests proved mostly impervious to the water's assault, but a few crabs managed to cut through the linen bands to the desiccated flesh beneath. Queen and craftsman gently shook off the creatures, which scuttled back to the lunging waves.

Remeg commanded her servants to place the body upon the pyre, then she and Yetzer set torches to the pitch-soaked timbers. The fire quickly spread up and around the pyre, held back only by the moisture retained in the funeral bindings. Within a short time, the heat overcame even that, and the body traded its shroud of linen for one of flame.

Fire leapt and danced and lapped at the swollen moon. Drums pounded, sistrums hissed, harps sang their lyrical melodies while servants swayed and spun before the pyre. The mourners sat on the border of firelight and darkness and scratched bloody trails across cheeks and breasts. The mournful song of their ululations joined the more festive music.

When the flames had finished their feast, when only embers and sparks flew toward the heavens, Queen Remeg rose upon tottering legs and raised her bowl to the sky.

"Hear me, Yam," she called with a slurring tongue, "Inhabiter of the Deep. Hear me, Lord Hadad, Rider on the Clouds. We have entrusted to you the body of our friend and kinsman, Huram, son of Tudu-Baal, that wherever the sea meets the shore, wherever the wind blows, there the name of Huram shall be remembered."

The queen splashed wine toward the fire then drained her bowl. Yetzer staggered to his feet and copied the gesture. The beach shifted beneath him as he raised the bottom of his bowl toward the heavens. He fell to the sand on his backside, amid a chorus of cheers and laughter. His eye went unfocused and his eyelid fluttered.

By the time Yetzer pried his eye back open, daylight shone upon the beach and a canopy fluttered above him. The cloth held out the sun's assault, but the brilliant sky and flashes of light upon the waves sent lances of pain through his eye to the base of his neck. The tide crashed upon the shore as gulls screeched overhead.

A churning in his belly overcame the ache in his head. Yetzer rolled over and pushed himself onto his knees. A spasm squeezed his stomach and several bowls' worth of wine spilled onto the sand. The nausea left with the wine, but the pounding in his skull kept time with the crashing of the waves.

"Drink this."

Yetzer squinted against the daylight to see Queen Remeg offering a small gourd bowl.

"No more," Yetzer said, waving a sand-encrusted hand in front of him.

"Drink," the queen insisted. "It's only water."

Yetzer nodded and accepted the bowl. He raised it to his lips with unsteady hands. The cool water soothed his lips and tongue as he swirled it around his mouth. He spat and rinsed again before allowing a sip to carve out a path to his stomach. When he was sure his body would not rebel, he drank again and drained the bowl.

Now able to look around without his head threatening to rupture, his eye settled on the smoking pile of scorched timbers that popped and hissed in the high tide. Men clad in thick leather aprons and gloves picked through the rubble. Occasionally, one of them would pull a slender, blackened object from the debris, rinse it in the surf, then place it in a tall, wide-mouthed jar set in the sand just above the tide line.

"Come," Lady Remeg said as she stood over Yetzer and offered him her hand. "Let us see your father to his rest."

She helped Yetzer to his feet. Another workman dashed from the waves, deposited his find in the jar, then resumed his search among the ashes. Yetzer followed Remeg toward the jar, but retreated a couple of steps. Resting in the sand was a skull, set atop a pelvic bone. Empty eye sockets stared toward the city across the channel, teeth set in a grim smile.

The queen tugged Yetzer's hand and he stepped closer to the jar. It had been nearly ten years since his father's death, but a fresh wave of grief surged through him. Huram, so tall, so strong, so commanding in life, was reduced to a jumble of bone that weighed little more than the great stone maul he'd once used to ply his trade.

Yetzer peered into the jar. The long arm and leg bones stood within the container, surrounded by jutting ribs and a collection of smaller bones. Recalling his studies in the Hall of the Body at Amun's temple, Yetzer identified plate-like shoulder blades and knobby vertebrae among the bones of fingers and toes.

Another worker dropped a few more scraps into the jar, and Yetzer looked up to see the rest of the men standing in a row.

"Is it complete?" Remeg asked him.

Yetzer looked more closely, estimated the number and types of bones, then nodded. The queen reached into a pocket of her robe, pulled out a handful of copper rings, and placed one into the outstretched hand of each of the workers. The men smiled and nodded their thanks, then hurried along the beach in the direction of the mainland village.

"Let us give him rest," Remeg said solemnly. She pointed to a steep mound higher up the beach where the tool chest Yetzer had brought from Pharaoh's tomb rested beside a bucket of pitch and a short wooden shovel. Yetzer stooped down to retrieve the pelvis and skull.

Blood rushed to his head. Stars flashed around the edges of his vision and a high-pitched whine flooded his ears. He fell to the sand upon hands and knees and found himself nose to nose socket with his father's skull.

Yetzer squeezed his eye closed to clear his vision. Behind his eyelid and through his empty left eye the skull transformed. Muscle, sinew, and flesh blossomed upon the soot-stained bone. Grinning teeth disappeared behind stern lips, and the empty sockets filled with penetrating green orbs.

The enlivened head retreated enough for Yetzer to see his father completely restored, his lambskin apron about his waist, tools in his hands. Two figures stood beside him, shadowed and hazy as in a fog.

Huram raised the maul in his right hand and pointed the chisel at Yetzer with his left. His lips parted in speech, but the ringing in Yetzer's ears masked the words. A muscled arm swung the maul and struck the head of the chisel a mighty blow. The sound of the impact rang clear and bright and louder than a thousand trumpet blasts.

Yetzer jerked back. His eye opened, vision and hearing instantly cleared. The charred skull sat before him, stark and lifeless. The queen again pulled Yetzer to his feet, making a small sound of reprimand. She left him wobbling, picked up the remaining bones and shoved them toward him. Still unsteady, Yetzer took them, nestled the pelvis among the bones in the jar, then crowned them with the skull.

He picked up the jar and followed Remeg to the dune. She pointed at a wooden plug and the bucket of pitch. Yetzer understood she meant for him to seal the jar. He nodded and set the urn in the sand. Before closing the jar, he opened the tool chest and retrieved his father's apron. Yetzer kissed the *Udjat* of Haru upon the lambskin, then rolled up the apron. He tucked it among Huram's remains and sealed them away.

The earth readily gave way to the shovel's blade. Yetzer hadn't dug far before he found another burial urn. He cleared a space beside it and settled his father's remains next to the stranger who would be his last companion.

Words fled Yetzer's lips. It seemed he should say something, offer a blessing to send his father to his rest. In the place of benediction, his heart echoed with silence as the sands of this foreign homeland swallowed the vestiges of his past.

40

Yetzer

Clouds filled the sky, low and rumbling. While the members of the caravan scrambled to set up their tents, Yetzer knelt alone atop a hill, sheltered from the pelting rain by the branches of an ancient walnut tree. A few of the caravanners, whom Yetzer had joined at Tsur, shouted and beckoned him to them, but he paid no heed. Instead, he laid his hands atop the lid of his father's tool chest and raised his face to the sky.

"I am Yetzer abi-Huram," he shouted, "Beloved of Djehuti, Friend of Pharaoh, Adept of Amun. But I was born of the soil of Kenahn, and I have returned to the land of my fathers."

The sky flashed and thundered in response. His father had often spoken of the Kenahni gods' sky dance. In Kemet, Yetzer had known only earthbound water, drawn from wells or the ever-flowing Iteru. He sometimes wondered if his father's tales of water falling from the skies were meant to ensnare a boy's imaginings. As the sky fell and the earth trembled with the gods' power, it seemed Huram had been sparing in his stories.

Yetzer grasped the lid of the chest more tightly. The box was made in the Kemeti fashion, inscribed with magical spells to guard the tools inside. Gold-leafed wooden statues of the vulture form of the goddess Mut and the falcon-god Khonsu spread their protecting wings over the lid. Between them, the gold inlay of the dot-and-circle symbol of the great god Amun shone with splendor. Yetzer invoked the gods' aegis upon himself as well. Even as he whispered the silent prayer, Amun's sign seemed to grow brighter. The hair on Yetzer's arms and neck bristled as power filled the air. His heart went still, and even the muddy puddles were frozen with concentric ripples. Raindrops hung as from invisible threads. A cold rippling sensation rose up Yetzer's spine and crawled over his scalp before the sky, the horizon, the world flashed white.

What might have been a moment or a day later, Yetzer opened his eye to find himself upon the sodden ground beneath the tree's smoldering branches. Half of the gnarled trunk hung drunkenly from raw, woody tendrils. Cold fire, liquid light danced across Mut's and Khonsu's wings and over Yetzer's hands, a white nimbus that slowly faded from sight.

Strong hands grasped him by the shoulders and helped him to sit up. Yetzer was slow to recognize Eliam, a Habiru merchant who had befriended him. The ringing in his ears blocked out the man's speech, but Yetzer thought he recognized the word *fool* on the older man's lips.

When the storm passed and folk ventured out from their tents, many shared Eliam's opinion. Marked by the gods, others claimed. Perhaps both. Yetzer knew only that he had stood before Baal Hadad, Rider on the Clouds. He had been rinsed of the taint of Kemet and the River Iteru, purified by water and fire to rise a son of Kenahn. He cut a length of wood from the lightning-split trunk to make a staff, a reminder of the god's blessing.

A few days later, staff in hand, dressed in the striped woolen robe of Kenahn rather than the priestly linen of Kemet, he stood before the hill of Danu. In this northernmost town of Yisrael, Yetzer hoped to find his mother.

At the heart of her tribe's lands, the city stood in the shadows of Kenahn's snow-tipped mountains where spring waters, snowmelt and frequent rains gathered to make the lands green. Here, too, met the trade routes of the Great Green Sea Road and the King's Highway, which carried goods, armies, and wanderers among the world's empires.

"Safe journey," Yetzer said as he clasped the merchant's arm.

"Havah smile upon you," Eliam replied.

Eliam, his son Abram, and a handful of travelers would be taking the southern road toward their homes in Yisrael, while others would take the eastern road to distant Subartu. Still others might venture to lands even farther removed, though Yetzer doubted the tales of golden temples set on mountains so high they pierced the sky.

He took the reins of his donkey, laden with his tool chest, and led it up the winding road of Danu's hill.

"State your merchandise and your trade," a man ordered him from behind a low table.

"I am no trader. I am Yetzer abi-Huram, son of the widow Dvora of the tribe Naftali, clan of Yetzer."

The man's rodent-like eyes narrowed to slits. "Dvora has no son. He died with his father in Kemet."

"True enough," Yetzer said with a smile, then planted his hands on the table and leaned close to the man. "I got better. Where is my mother?"

"I don't know Dvora," the man stammered.

"You know of her dead husband and once-dead son, but you don't know of her?" Yetzer brought his nose to within a finger's breadth of the other man's. "Where is she?"

"Y-you must speak with Governor Rakem."

"Where?" Yetzer demanded.

With a trembling hand, the man pointed through the gateway. "Beyond the courtyard, before the high place."

Yetzer pushed himself upright, shoving the table against the man's chest. He took the reins of his donkey and led it into the city.

"You must pay the gate toll," the man squeaked.

Yetzer ignored him. He passed through the gate tower, the air thick with rotting fruit and incense, offerings to Yisrael's gods, and followed the narrow, winding street past mudbrick hovels and stone-built houses, past alleys that rang with children's laughter and reeked of night soil. Finally, the street opened into a courtyard centered about a stone-capped cistern. Goats roamed the yard, picking at the sparse grass. Children raced one another to collect the droppings which they delivered to a group of ragged old women who mixed the dung with straw to make bricks.

Beyond the cistern, next to a smaller gate, sat a low platform beneath an awning on which a fat man of middle years sat on a cushion surrounded by a group of men. By his over-loud voice and imperious air, Yetzer reckoned he'd found Governor Rakem.

"And I told him," the fat man said, choking on his laughter, "that's no she-goat."

He looked expectantly at the other men who shared pained looks before bursting into forced laughter. The loudest laughter came from the governor himself, who reared his head back and slapped his knees, tears rolling down vein-splotched cheeks.

"Hear this," he said when he regained his composure. "Hear this. A priest, an oracle, and a scribe enter a tavern."

Yetzer stood before the platform and cleared his throat. The gathered men looked up in curiosity. Rakem seemed not to notice.

"Said the priest to the tavern-keeper—"

"'That is for naught'," Yetzer said, interrupting the joke. "'You should have seen the burnt offering.'"

Five pairs of eyes turned toward Yetzer. Four sets shifted from surprise to barely disguised humor. The other pair flashed with indignation.

"Who is this who dares interrupt—"

"I seek Dvora abi-Shimon," Yetzer said, and the chieftain's face grew red. "I seek the widow of Huram of Tsur."

"What business could you have with her?" The governor's words were clipped.

"My business is my own," Yetzer said. "Only tell me where to find her, and I'll trouble you no more."

Some of the men glanced beyond Yetzer's shoulder, but the governor's gaze never wavered.

"You come before this council, in our city, at the gateway to our holy place, and presume to make demands?"

The odor of dung wafted beneath Yetzer's nose. He struggled to keep his expression fixed.

"Give me the information I seek, and I'll be on my way. I wish only—"

A light grip tugged at Yetzer's elbow. He looked down to see a wrinkled, age-spotted hand, fingers stained with filth. The stench choked the breath from his throat.

"Woman, I beg you—"

His voice trailed off when he saw the looks on the men's faces. Rakem's matched those of the others, blanched and wide-eyed. Yetzer looked back down. His eye searched an old woman's features. Wispy grey hair. Dull, listless eyes. Sallow skin. None of these matched his memory. Only when the eyes narrowed and the wrinkled lips pursed into a disapproving frown did recognition awaken.

"Mother?"

He turned toward her, and she pressed dung-encrusted hands to his face, her eyes bright with tears. Yetzer fought against revulsion and his own rising emotion.

"My son," Dvora said, her voice rough as cedar bark.

Yetzer stooped to embrace her, careful lest he shatter her frail bones. Skinny arms squeezed his neck and tears dampened his cheek. A soft, ghostly moan escaped her lips. After a time, Yetzer released her and stepped back. He wiped her tears away then took a deep breath. The air fueled his rage as bellows stoke a furnace. He turned slowly toward the elders then smote the ground with the butt of his staff.

"What is the meaning of this?" he demanded. "Is this how you care for a widow in Yisrael? She is a daughter of Naftali, of the house of Yetzer, and you treat her as one unclean? As a slave?"

The four elders, faces ashen, sank against the wall, creating distance between them and the governor.

"There was," the fat man stammered. "There was the matter of a debt."

"Debt?" Yetzer spat the word, and the governor recoiled as though he'd been struck. "She married more than twenty years past. She lived among the household of the Pharaoh of Kemet until only a short time ago. What debt could she have amassed that would reduce her to this?"

The governor pressed his hands together as sweat trickled down his jowls. "It was not her debt, so much as that of her kinsmen. Not everyone fared so well while she sojourned in Kemet." Rakem sneered. "Her family's lands were given in surety. It required most of Pharaoh's silver to redeem them."

"Then why," Yetzer said, his voice a low growl, "is she not on her lands?"

"Taxes," the governor pleaded. "The contribution for Yah's new temple. The land had to be sold to pay what was owed."

Yetzer's ears rang as fury wrapped him in its fiery grip. "She redeemed her family's lands only to have them stolen away?" he shouted. "Where are her kinsmen? Where are those who would take her kindness then sell her to shape dung in the streets?"

Yetzer glared at the governor, at the elders. The men avoided his look, except for one. The youngest, a man dressed in a simple robe, met Yetzer's gaze then slowly inclined his head and rolled his eyes toward Rakem.

The ringing turned to a drone. Fire edged Yetzer's vision as he towered over the governor.

"You," he rasped, and dropped his staff as he reached for the man. Rakem shrank away from him and it took much of Yetzer's strength to catch the man by his robes and haul him to his feet.

"Who are you to her?" Yetzer demanded. "What have you done?"

"I am Rakem abi-Zebed," the governor wheezed. "I am the son of your mother's brother. We—we are cousins, you and I."

Yetzer threw Rakem to the ground, then stooped to retrieve his staff. The shaved walnut made a low whirring sound as he spun it through a few circles. Yetzer turned toward the governor, who crawled away from him on ungainly limbs.

"Where is goodness?" Yetzer said as he stalked after Rakem. "Where is justice?"

He rammed his staff upon the ground in front of the slithering wretch. Rakem stopped and Yetzer kicked him in the side. The man's fat absorbed most of the blow but he rolled onto his back. Yetzer raised the staff over his head, ready to administer his own justice, when another of the old women threw herself atop the governor.

"Mercy," she cried. "In Yah's name, for the sake of Havah, have mercy."

Yetzer's arms shook, his breathing became ragged. He raised a foot to push the woman—Rakem's own mother, he assumed—out of the way, so he could begin the beating without interference.

"Yetzer." The voice behind him was soft but strong, accompanied by a light touch upon his back. "Yetzer," his mother said again, even more softly. "Do not shame yourself. Do not soil your hands on one who is unworthy to lick the dust from your sandals."

The red faded from Yetzer's vision and his breathing steadied. He lowered the staff until its butt rested beneath Rakem's quavering chins.

"You will return her silver," Yetzer said in a low, menacing voice. "You will restore her to her lands."

233

"I can't," Rakem said in a mewling voice.

Yetzer applied pressure to the staff, and the man choked as tears streamed from his eyes.

"They've gone for taxes," the governor wheezed. "The land to the priests, the silver to the king."

"Get them back," Yetzer said, and added more pressure.

Rakem's cheeks turned crimson, his eyes wide as he shook his head. "Can't," he rasped.

"Why not?" Yetzer shouted, and leaned hard on the staff.

The governor's eyes bulged. His cheeks flashed purple as he struggled and slapped at the staff. Rakem's mother tugged on Yetzer's right arm while Dvora pulled on the other. Yetzer relented and pulled back his staff.

"Why not?" he repeated, the anger seeping from his voice.

Rakem's hands surrounded his throat and he gulped at the air. His fear-filled eyes flitted from his mother to Dvora to the elders, who remained beneath their canopy. At last his gaze settled on Yetzer.

"I am only the governor," Rakem said, his tone like that of a child seeking to escape blame for a broken pot. "All unredeemed lands and all taxes have been claimed by King Yahtadua. Only he can restore them."

"And where is this king of yours?" Yetzer demanded.

"In the royal city, of course. In Urusalim."

Yetzer swallowed the bitterness rising in his throat. He leaned upon his staff and laid a gentle hand on his mother's shoulder. "Make yourself clean and prepare for a journey. We will go to find justice. We will go to Urusalim."

❧

"Do you think it's true?" Dvora asked Yetzer.

The pair had rejoined the southbound caravan after leaving Danu, and the merchant Eliam had greeted them warmly. After two weeks of travel beside the River Yarden, they had reached the village of Tzeretan, its furnaces and bronze works casting a smoky pall over the town. While Eliam and his son Abram forged a trade for their supply of tin ingots, Yetzer and his mother helped set up the camp.

"Do you think Eliam can help us?" Dvora pressed. She looked up from stirring a porridge of lentils. The quivering air above the campfire lent an ethereal air to her hopeful expression.

The merchant had been effusive in his optimism when he learned of Yetzer's intent to petition King Yahtadua for return of his mother's lands. Yetzer put on what he hoped was an encouraging look.

"He seems to believe it," he offered. "He may well have access to the king, but what we see as just and what a ruler deems expedient are rarely the same thing."

"But you are Pharaoh's friend," Dvora insisted, "the kinsman of Queen Remeg. Surely you can win the favor of Yahtadua and his mother."

"Perhaps," Yetzer said with a shrug.

"Praise be to Yah for all his blessings," Eliam's voice boomed behind them.

Yetzer turned to see the merchant and his son entering the camp. Abram struggled with a wooden box about a third the size of Yetzer's tool chest. The younger man grinned despite his burden, while his father's face beamed with joy.

"It's just like days past," Eliam exulted, "when the gods smiled on all we did. Ah, Leah, you should have seen it."

The merchant strode straight toward Dvora, caught her up in a sweeping embrace, and kissed her lips.

"Father!" Abram shouted. He set his burden down, then rushed to Eliam and tugged on the elder man's shoulder.

Yetzer had barely risen to his feet, laughter caught up in his throat, when Eliam broke his embrace and staggered back.

"Forgive us," Abram pleaded as he fell to his knees before Yetzer. "No disrespect was meant, no harm intended."

"And none given, I think," Yetzer replied.

Dvora stood rigid, arms straight by her sides. Her eyes stared far into the distance. Her breath came deeply and, though she neared her fortieth year, the color in her cheeks was that of a maiden's.

"No," Yetzer decided, placing a steadying arm about his mother's shoulders. "No harm done. Leah?"

"My mother," Abram said. "Gone these nine years."

"Ah. My father was taken not long before then."

Dvora stirred, blinked several times then breathed a deep sigh. Yetzer looked from her to Eliam, and a smile tugged at the corner of his mouth.

"Come," he said to Abram. "Let me help you with your crate."

"It's fine," Abram replied, "it doesn't—"

"Let me help you," Yetzer repeated with more insistence.

Abram glanced at the two elders then gave a nod of understanding. He grasped one handle of the chest while Yetzer took the other. The pair left their parents alone and carried the crate to the great canopy Eliam's porters had set up.

"How did your father die?" Abram asked.

"Quarry explosion. Your mother?"

"Nabati raiders."

Yetzer grunted sympathetically. They reached the canopy and stored the chest among Eliam's other belongings, then settled onto cushions while a servant poured goat's milk for them.

"Is that it?" Yetzer asked, gesturing toward the small chest behind Abram. "Seems a small prize for a score of donkeys laden with tin. Unless it's filled with gold."

"Better," Abram declared, then leaned back to flip open the chest's lid.

The merchant's son drew out a clay tablet and handed it to Yetzer. He took the small tablet and rotated it until he could make sense of the Kenahni script.

To the bearer, one part in five thousand, Elat's Bower, *embarked from Tsur, Year Five of Baalat Remeg.*

Yetzer flipped the tablet over, but there was no more script, only the scribe's mark set in the hardened clay. He handed it back to Abram.

"A shipping manifest?"

Abram laughed as he tucked the piece of clay back into the chest. "Trade shares," he said with a triumphant laugh.

When Yetzer failed to match his enthusiasm, Abram laced his fingers together, rested his hands on his knees, and spoke in the manner of a patient tutor.

"Most of Tsur's fortune comes from sea trade," he said. "To put a ship to sea requires a fortune all its own. Beyond the ship itself, sufficient stores must be put in to feed a score of men on a voyage of two years, three, maybe more. Add to that the goods they must trade for the tin or ivory or amber at the other end of the journey."

Yetzer considered that. He well knew the allotment of bread and beer to feed a gang of quarrymen for a month. Multiply that by a duration thirty times as long, then fit all those goods in a ship, and the cost was staggering. Abram smiled.

"You see my meaning. Now consider the risk that the ship might never return, and the cost to one man, even to a small group, would be disastrous." He gestured toward the crate. "But spread the cost among hundreds, thousands of people, and allow them to spread their risk among several ships trading to different lands—"

"And most everyone will have a successful venture," Yetzer finished the thought.

"Each one of those tablets may be worth its weight in gold," Abram said, his voice now hushed. "Perhaps ten or twenty times its weight."

"Or they might be worthless," Yetzer suggested.

"Or they might be worthless," Abram allowed. "But if even one of ten ships come in, that chest could buy a kingdom."

"A temple, at the very least," Eliam's jovial voice rang out.

Yetzer looked to where the merchant approached, hands behind his back, a respectful distance between himself and a beaming Dvora.

"You'll have your audience with the queen, boy," Eliam said, conviction in his voice. "Your mother will have her lands back, and the queen will have her great work."

The older man helped Dvora onto her cushion, then moved to his place across from her. When he'd settled, he leaned to Yetzer and clapped him firmly on the shoulder. "Now, tell me," he said, his eyes aglow. "What do you know about temple-building?"

41

Bilkis

B ilkis considered her reflection upon the polished silver and adjusted the gold circlet about her head. Much as she loathed what was to come, she knew it was necessary to her position as queen, so she must look perfect. And she did.

Rahab had painted Bilkis's face exquisitely. The queen's hair was strewn with pearls and bound up to display her slender neck. Her gown had been expertly crafted to invite men's looks while maintaining an air of inaccessibility. Satisfied, Bilkis smoothed the silk fabric along her hips and across her flat belly, then opened the door to the audience hall.

As soon as her foot crossed the threshold, Benyahu rapped the butt of his spear upon the floor. The assembly dropped to their knees, eyes downcast, heads bowed. Only Yahtadua and Benyahu remained standing. The king, by his throne, awaited his mother, while the general stood his post at the foot of the dais.

Benyahu offered the queen his hand as she approached, and Bilkis allowed him to help her up the steps. The man's fingers were warm, his gaze intense. It had been some time since Bilkis had shared her couch with Benyahu, and she reasoned she should do so again soon. Not for any desire of her own, of course. It would simply be wise to reaffirm the general's loyalty.

She squeezed Benyahu's hand before releasing it, and the warrior's smoldering eyes came ablaze. Bilkis smiled inwardly as she climbed the last step and moved toward her throne. She allowed the smile to surface as Yahtadua took her hand, kissed it, and ushered her to her seat.

"You look pretty, Umma," the boy-king whispered, and Bilkis patted his cheek.

"In the name of Yah and Havah," Benyahu pronounced in his commanding voice, "all who come in peace may stand before Yahtadua, King of Yisrael, and Queen Bilkis."

The general smote the floor once more with his spear, and the people rose to their feet. Bilkis drew a deep breath to gather her patience for what was certain to be a trying morning. She nodded to Gad who stood by with his pouch of magic rocks, then looked out upon the crowd.

"Since the Days of Wandering," she began, her voice clear and strong, "the people have left their flocks and fields upon the turning of the seasons, upon the birth of the new year. At the high places of Danu, Beit-El, Sekhem, and here by the most holy mountain Morhavah, they gathered in celebration of the gods, to seek justice from elder and priest. Now do I invite all who would to lay your grievances before the throne and before the gods."

42

Yetzer

"You're late," a young woman said as Eliam led Yetzer and Dvora through the palace gate. The caravan had arrived in Urusalim the night before, and Eliam insisted the mother and son be his guests.

"It's good to see you, too, Daughter," Eliam said warmly. He wrapped the girl in a sweeping embrace before making introductions.

"Bilkis has already begun hearing petitions," Rahab explained as she led them to the great cedar doors of the palace. "There may not be time for you to be heard today."

"Surely she will make time for our friends," Eliam suggested, and gave Yetzer a broad, reassuring grin.

"The queen cannot be seen to be partial," Rahab replied. "She must be neutral and fair in all things."

"But we're practically family," Eliam insisted.

"It's all right," Yetzer said. "We can bide our time. The festival lasts the week?" Rahab nodded.

"Then if we are not heard today, we will return tomorrow or the next day or the one after that. In the meantime, it will do no harm to witness how justice is dispensed in Yisrael."

They followed Rahab to a doorway along the side of the palace. The guard—dressed in armor of bronze scales and bearing a thick-shafted spear—nodded to Rahab and pulled open the wooden door. Eliam's daughter guided them along a narrow corridor to the rear of the great audience hall itself.

Dozens of people filled the space, their robes and complexions, beards and hairstyles testimony to the varied nature of Yisrael's people. All stood silently attentive, save for the pair of men who stood before the dais, reciting their complaints before the throne, which was hidden from Yetzer's sight by a canopy of blue and white.

The hall was less grand than Remeg's throne room in Tsur but built in the same style. The cedar floor spanned between walls of dressed stones, which supported heavy timber rafters. Metal grilles covered openings, high and low in the walls, allowing fresh air to carry away the smoke of lamps and the stink of the occupants. Movement caught Yetzer's attention. The supplicants had apparently finished making their appeals and a slight figure of a man, robed in sackcloth, stepped to the edge of the dais. A warm, melodious voice rose from beneath the canopy to fill the chamber.

"You have each presented your claims with conviction and eloquence," a woman said. "I fear mortal wisdom ill-suited to judge the matter."

Through no effort of his own, Yetzer found himself pushing through the crowd until he had a clear view of the speaker. Bilkis, Queen of Yisrael, sat upon her throne, regal as any queen—any pharaoh, for that matter—of Kemet. She might have been the sculpted image of a goddess, so lovely and perfectly proportioned were her features. Eyes sharp and intelligent, lips full and inviting, fingers graceful and slender as they absently tapped …

Yetzer shook the mantle of desire from the shoulders of reason. The queen had been asking questions of the dark-robed man, who then reached into a pouch to withdraw a stone of white or black. Yetzer hadn't heard the questions, but as he focused now on the proceedings, a pattern arose. What had seemed to be the queen's idle tapping of her fingers upon the throne's armrest now resolved into a signal.

"Shall the payment be seven head of sheep?" Bilkis asked the seer as her thumb twitched.

The man reached into his pouch, withdrew his gloved hand and produced a black stone.

"Shall it be ten head?"

The queen's fingers lightly strummed upon her armrest, and her oracle produced a white stone.

"And what share shall be the crown's? Shall it be one?"

Twitch. Black.

"Shall it be three?"

Twitch. Black.

"Shall it be five?"

Strum. White.

Yetzer's stomach soured. His fingers cramped as he squeezed them into fists. Throughout the settled world, a nation's ruler was chosen by the gods. Such election might be by bloodline or by sword, but a people could be certain that, by whatever measure their gods valued, the sovereign was divinely chosen. Yetzer had brought his mother to Urusalim to invoke the gods' justice before the throne. What justice might they find where the gods' will was shaped to suit the crown's desire?

The queen heard four more challenges. Three she decided on her own, not unjustly. The fourth she submitted to the gods' judgment, with a profitable verdict for the crown. Yetzer restrained his anger, then slid behind a thick cedar post when the royal warden rapped his spear and ordered all to kneel.

"Those who have not been heard are invited to return on the morrow," the warden declared after the queen and her child-king left the hall. "Those who would propose to build the temple unto the gods shall be present on the following day."

Yetzer remained in the shadow of the post while the petitioners filed from the hall. Only when he felt a cool touch on his hand and looked down to see his mother did he unfurl his fists and allow his wrath to drain away.

"I'm sorry you couldn't be heard today," Rahab said. "Perhaps if you are earlier tomorrow."

"Perhaps," Yetzer allowed, and offered a polite smile.

He followed along as Eliam led Dvora and Rahab out of the palace grounds and back to his home. Only after they had gathered in the courtyard beneath the shade of a tamarisk tree, after servants had set flatbreads and date cakes and cold, spiced lamb before them—only after Eliam invoked the blessing of Havah and broke the bread—only then did Yetzer speak.

"Tell me more about the temple and about this prophet."

❀

The evening sun rested upon the crest of Urusalim's western hill. By its stark light Yetzer picked his way along the well-worn path toward the high place on Mount Morhavah. For hundreds, perhaps thousands of years, pilgrims had come to seek their gods' blessings and make sacrifice before them. One, an ancestor of the Habiru had very nearly become one of those sacrifices, by command of the blood-thirsty Yah. The goddess Havah, however, had interceded and produced a ram as substitute.

Following Eliam's directions, Yetzer passed a walled estate on the broad terrace of the hill. Farther along, the smell of sweet incense and the giggles of young women heralded the shrine of Ashtart. As Yetzer neared the summit of the hill, the screech of carrion birds and the growling of dogs proclaimed the Holy Place.

Patched woolen curtains formed a large enclosure. Yetzer entered the holy precinct and was assaulted by the stench of rot. Animal carcasses lay heaped in one corner, picked over by scavengers. Bloody tracks led from the refuse pile to a dry stone altar. Yetzer walked around the gore, its stink fading as he neared the Sanctuary.

Braziers surrounded the tent, sending incense-laden smoke to the heavens. A red-robed priest snored as he dozed against a tent post, between a pair of flaps held back by frayed cords of faded blue and purple and scarlet. Careful not to disturb the man, Yetzer ducked under the lintel. He kicked off his sandals and traced a pentacle across his forehead, chest and shoulders.

He was standing on holy ground.

For a moment, Yetzer questioned his plan. He had excused himself after dinner in order to visit the high place, to see if the gods might inspire him as to the nature of the temple to be built here. His true intent was to seek out just how the queen and her prophet manipulated the will of the gods.

As he stood within the holy enclosure, its threadbare curtains somehow holding out the reek and noise of the charnel grounds, he wondered if he was mistaken. Yetzer could feel the power of this Sanctuary, as sacred as any temple of Kemet. How, then, could the gods allow their seer stones—housed here when not about the prophet's neck—to be corrupted?

As Yetzer approached the Most Holy Place, an unseen miasma filled the tent and slowed his movements. The foul stillness grew thicker as he stepped through the rear partition of the tent.

A small lamp hung in the middle of the space, suspended from the tent posts by golden chains. Its wick burned brightly, though its light failed to reach to the corners of the small chamber. When Yetzer's eye adjusted to the gloom, he found himself standing in more of a storeroom than a holy shrine.

There were the graven effigies of the gods—Yah with his long beard and tall crown, and Havah, serene of face and swollen of breasts and belly. These stood about as high as Yetzer's shoulder, tucked in a corner. About them lay all manner of clutter. A pair of wooden staves, one of which was carved with sprouting almond buds, leaned against the figures of the gods. A rectangular stone, not a cubit in its longest dimension, sat in a sling along the far wall. Boxes that looked like ossuaries lay haphazardly stacked.

Dozens of other pieces littered the space, but it was the table beneath the lamp that drew Yetzer's attention. Set upon three legs of alabaster, the top was of marble inlaid with the signs of the night sky, star pictures of bull and ram, scorpion and fishes, lion and scales of Mayat and a half-dozen others that represented the course of the year. Upon the center of the table lay a pair of gloves and a soft leather pouch, the object of Yetzer's search.

He lifted the pouch and shook it to hear the rattle of stone upon stone. He glanced at the gods in their corner, reaffirmed to them his good intent, then reached into the bag.

The paired stones were cool to the touch, smooth and faceted, and each sized to fit comfortably in the hollow of Yetzer's hand. And that was all. One was not perceptibly heavier than the other, nor larger nor thicker nor different in any way that his touch could perceive. He withdrew the stones and studied them under the light. Other than their colors, there was nothing to distinguish them.

"You should try using gloves," a voice said from behind, and Yetzer's heart leapt into his throat. "Gad always wears gloves."

43
Yetzer

Yetzer spun into a crouch, eye focused on the darkness beyond the lamp's throw. The susurrus of feet on carpet shuffled toward him. A child stepped into the small ring of light. The coarse robes and sandals, the unkempt hair and wide eyes bespoke a wild thing, likely abandoned in the temple grounds at birth.

"I have no food," Yetzer said, using the tone he might employ with a feral dog. The creature cocked his head and ran his eyes over Yetzer, as though gauging whether to target his hands or neck. Yetzer had little fear of an attack—he'd fling the waif aside like an empty sack—but the noise of a scuffle was certain to wake the guard.

Yetzer gestured toward the outer sanctuary. "There is bread in the Holy Place."

"That's the Bread of Havah's Presence," the child replied in a scolding tone, "sacred to the goddess. If you're hungry, I can find other food for you."

Yetzer started to offer something else, then stopped himself. Instead, he asked, "Who are you?"

"I am Natan, high priest of Yah and Havah," the child replied boldly. "Who are you?"

"I—" Yetzer began, but could find no other words.

This ragged child served as high priest? Yetzer tumbled forward onto his knees. The young priest sat cross-legged before him, large eyes shining in the lamplight. He rested his chin upon his fists and stared at Yetzer.

"How did you hurt your eye?" the boy asked. "I burned my hand once on the brazier. But Gad always wears gloves when he consults the stones, so you probably should, too."

Only half understanding the string of words, Yetzer glanced down at the pouch and stones still in his hands. "Do you know about these?" Yetzer asked.

"The seer stones?" the boy said. "Of course. When questions are quite difficult or very important, or if the queen wants something but doesn't want people angry with her, Gad picks the black or the white one to give the answer."

"And do you know how he does it?" Yetzer continued.

The boy's lips pursed and his brows knitted. "He reaches into the pouch," he said, his words slow and distinct. "He picks a stone and draws it out."

"But how does he choose?" Yetzer pressed. "How does he know which stone to take?"

Natan's eyes flicked away and he rubbed the back of his hand against his nose. "The gods tell him, of course."

Yetzer smiled for the first time since arriving in Urusalim. The boy couldn't have seen ten years, yet he bore the weight of his responsibility with more care than some men four or five times his age.

"How did you come to be priest?" Yetzer asked as he took the gloves from the table and inspected them.

"I was born a child of Havah," the boy said, "raised by her priest and trained in the holy arts from the days of my youth."

Yetzer bit his lower lip to keep from laughing. It was comical, and not a little sad, to hear a boy scarcely past infancy speak so.

"When the old priest of Yah left," Natan continued, "the god chose me to take up his mantle. And when my master died, I was chosen to bear the mantle of Havah as well."

"Did the gods use the stones to choose you?" Yetzer asked.

The boy's downcast eyes gave him the answer.

Yetzer tugged a glove onto his right hand. He dropped the stones back into the pouch, rattled them around, then reached in with his gloved fingertips. The first stone felt the same as before. The second stone, however, now caught upon the threads of the glove.

Yetzer pulled out the white stone and examined it in the thin lamplight. What had first seemed the glitter of quartz now proved to be tiny nodes, too fine for Yetzer's callused fingers to sense, but coarse enough to snag lightly upon the glove.

"Ask me a question," Yetzer told the boy. "Anything you want answered with a yes."

The young priest fixed Yetzer with a dubious expression but gave in with a forbearing sigh.

"Is my name Natan?"

White.

"Am I priest of Yah?"

White.

"Am I also priest of Havah?"

White.

A light sheen rose upon the boy's eyes, and his voice fell low. "Am I all alone in the world?"

Black.

"Hah!" the boy scoffed. "You can't make them work. Only the oracle of the gods can rightly draw the stones."

"I told you to ask questions that would only be answered 'yes'," Yetzer chided him, then cleared his throat. "Is my name Yetzer abi-Huram?"

White.

"Am I a rightful priest of Amun?"

White.

"Is not Amun a brother to Yah and Havah?"

White.

"So am I not a brother to the priest of Yah and Havah?"

White.

Natan's eyes brightened. A smile stretched across his mouth and grew even wider with Yetzer's next question.

"And shall we together build a temple to the gods of Yisrael?"

❁

After leaving the Sanctuary, Yetzer sat in the star-canopied courtyard of Eliam's house, his father's trestleboard in his lap. Line by line, he scratched the image of a temple into the soft clay. The proportions were like any proper shrine of Kemet, with its porch, sanctuary, and inner chamber. Unlike the temples of that desert land, Havah and Yah's house must be roofed over to protect against the rains that nourished Yisrael.

By morning, he had worked out the elevations. He broke his fast with his mother, then stuffed the trestle board into a satchel, along with his stylus, measuring line and a few other tools.

"We're not petitioning the queen today, then?" Dvora said when Yetzer started toward the gate.

"Tomorrow," he assured her, and his mother made the sad, proud expression she'd so often given his father when he started a new commission for Pharaoh.

The sun had just cleared the horizon as Natan led Yetzer across the hilltop.

"It is our most sacred place," the boy said in hushed tones as he pointed toward a rocky scarp edged with scrub brush.

"Then why is it not enclosed by your Sanctuary?"

Natan stopped and looked up at Yetzer with a dismal expression.

"It is our most sacred place," he repeated slowly. "Sacred before King Tadua took Urusalim. Sacred before the Habiru carried the tent of the gods about the wilderness. Sacred even before the fathers of Yisrael stood their altars upon these hills."

Yetzer followed the boy up a narrow path to the mountain's peak. The scarp towered over the hilltop, nearly to the height of two men. Yetzer followed Natan's example and kicked off his sandals before climbing atop the rock. The sun had yet to strike this part of the mountain, but warmth radiated from the ground and sent ripples of energy through the soles of Yetzer's feet.

The priests stretched for handholds as they scrabbled up the last cubit to the summit. The very air seemed to shimmer as the sun's power lanced along the opposite hillside, across the steep Valley of Kederon, to the summit of Morhavah. This was no place of man's choosing, Yetzer decided as he sat facing the sunrise.

A man, be he king or holy fool, would have chosen his sacred place atop one of the neighboring peaks, which rose fifty cubits or more above Havah's humble crest. There was nothing here to impress the profane, nothing to proclaim to the world a ruler's greatness. There was only the subtle power of the divine expressed through this knuckle of rock upon the humblest of hills.

"And your queen would have her temple here?" Yetzer said.

Natan nodded and sat beside him. "The Sanctuary has much power in the memories of the people, from the time of our fathers' wanderings. The stone of Yaakob, the flowering staff—these are easily carried from one place to another."

"But Bilkis is not a Queen of Wanderers."

"The old priests and prophets would go out among the people," Natan said, "to where the need was. The queen would have the people come to her."

Yetzer pulled his knees to his chest, rested his chin on them and looked out across the hilltop. Crows hopped across the piles of waste, while an occasional pilgrim made his way up from the city with a bit of grain and oil for the priests and a bird or goat to burn upon the altar and add to the charnel heaps.

Most stopped at the Tent of Sanctuary, some went to the neighboring shrine of Ashtart, but a few found the path to the goddess's rock, making obeisance to Yetzer and Natan before leaving their offerings. The scene was little different than in Kemet, though there the priests had ample slaves to carry the filthy remains away from the gods' dwelling.

"Help me with my line," Yetzer said to the young priest. He pulled the rope—knotted at precise half-cubit intervals—from his satchel and handed one end to the boy. "If Bilkis would enclose this place of the gods, let us do our part to make it worthy of them."

"And then we see to the stones?" Natan asked as he took his end of the line.

Yetzer gave him a smile.

"And then we see to the stones."

44

Bilkis

The sun caressed Bilkis's face. The queen had ordered her servants to carry the thrones to the palace gate for the day's event, so the people might see her as judge and benefactor. Half a dozen craftsmen had come to claim the privilege of building her temple, two from within Yisrael and the others from neighboring lands. That Bilkis had already sold the honor mattered little. She would be proclaimed the people's judge, the voice of the gods.

Elhoreb, a priest from the northern town of Sekhem, had built no temple. Having presided at the high place there, however, he was able to provide the queen with offerings of silk and gold. The other contenders might be better qualified, but the priest of Sekhem had paid well to become the builder of Yah and Havah's temple.

"The gods must surely smile upon our endeavors," Bilkis told the craftsmen and the gathered crowd, "for any one of these men would build a magnificent home for them. As it was my husband's desire to honor the gods in this manner, it is fitting they should choose the builder. I call upon the prophet Gad to inquire of the ancient ones."

Cheers rose from the people. All would have heard of the seer stones. For most, though, this would be their first time to witness the miracle, and it was Bilkis who gave them the privilege.

Gad approached the throne and the crowd's excitement grew. The prophet carried the Staff of Havah with its coiled bronze serpent, the bearer of holy wisdom. Gad bowed to the queen and king, closed his eyes then loudly intoned a few nonsensical words.

Yahtadua had seen this many times before, but still quivered with delight when the prophet opened his eyes to reveal only empty white. Those toward the front of the crowd gasped in awe, and Bilkis waited for the wonder to spread among all the people before she spoke.

"Let those who would serve the gods present themselves and inquire of the oracle." She gestured toward the nearest man, a squat foreigner dressed in a striped robe. The man bowed low before the thrones then turned toward Gad.

"I am Kalhba of Ugaratu, priest of Kothar and initiate of the sacred arts. Shall I build the temple of Yah?"

Gad slowly raised his pouch and shook it for all to hear the rattle of the stones. He reached into the pouch with his gloved hand—

And hesitated.

Lines creased his forehead. His eyes twitched toward Bilkis before rolling back once more. His throat bobbed, then he drew out his hand and revealed the black stone.

The priest from Ugaratu offered the royal pair a disappointed bow, then stepped back to his place.

"I am Magon of Tsur, servant of Melkart," the next man said. "Shall I raise the temple of Yah?"

The scene repeated itself, with the same negative result. Elhoreb stepped forward, patting Magon's shoulder as he passed. The priest made his obeisance and loudly proclaimed, "I am Elhoreb, servant of Yah at the holy place of Sekhem. Shall I set my hand to build the god's temple at Urusalim?"

Gad's hand trembled as he reached into the pouch. His hesitation stretched out longer, and Bilkis smiled inwardly at her prophet's sense for the dramatic. When he withdrew the stone, Bilkis didn't even bother to look before she clapped her hands together.

"The gods have spoken," she said, "and so—"

"Umma." Yahtadua tugged on her sleeve. "Umma, no."

The queen gave her son an angry glare, but he pointed toward Gad. Bilkis turned her head and her anger redoubled when she saw the black stone in the prophet's hand.

"Inquire again, Prophet," she said, trying and failing to keep her voice even. "Shall Elhoreb of Sekhem build the temple unto Yah and Havah?"

A trickle of sweat ran down Gad's cheek, but he replaced the stone, shook the pouch and drew again.

"No," Yahtadua said when the black stone was again revealed. "It is not to be Elhoreb."

The young king made a gesture of dismissal toward the fuming priest and waved the next candidate forward. This priest, from Dibon in Moab, had shown the audacity to rebuff Bilkis's suggestion that a goodwill offering to the queen might incline the gods in his favor. When the black stone was revealed for him and the fifth man, Bilkis wondered if the fool Gad had forgotten the white stone.

Her thoughts raced as she tried to fabricate a justification to petition the gods again on behalf of Elhoreb—perhaps with a change in the moon or after an offering before the Tent of Sanctuary. The schemes fled her heart as the final candidate stepped forward.

The man was younger than any of the others—perhaps of an age with the queen herself—and might have been thrown on the very pottery wheel of the gods. For stature and beauty, he rivaled even Auriyah. His frame was thicker, more of the laborer's bulk than the warrior's slender lines, but he moved with the grace of a lion. About his head he wore a blue scarf, his natural left eye covered by an embroidered one. A tear of golden thread streamed from one corner and met a scar that ran halfway down his cheek.

"I am Yetzer abi-Huram," he said in a deep voice that thrummed in the queen's breast, "a widow's son of Danu, adept of the mysteries of Amun. Shall I be the one to build a house unto Havah and Yah?"

Bilkis almost regretted that she would have to turn away the young builder. She mightn't mind taking him to her couch. Benyahu was adequate as a lover but was more useful to her in keeping Yisrael's mercenaries and fighting men loyal to the House of Tadua.

This widow's son might serve to fill a deeper need. Perhaps, once she'd brought Gad back in line and showed the gods' approval of Elhoreb as their temple-builder, she might find a way to have Yetzer—

A great intake of breath from the assembly interrupted her musings. The queen blinked and silently chastised herself for allowing her attention to wander.

"It's him," Yahtadua said excitedly. "Yetzer abi-Huram shall build the temple!"

Bilkis put a hand on the boy's arm to stop his clapping, then her eyes drifted to where Gad stood, white stone in the palm of his hand. Rage surged up from her belly, and it took all her strength to hold back a scream. She cared little about who might build the temple, but that this little worm, this false prophet should dare to challenge her will sent fury through her veins.

The stares of the crowd bore heavily upon her, their anticipation a palpable force. As Gad's eyes returned to normal, albeit downcast, Bilkis put on a pleasant expression, then looked upon the handsome young builder.

"Yah and Havah smile upon you, Yetzer of Danu. You will attend us this evening, that we may further discuss the erection of the gods' house."

The young man's expression was inscrutable, even to the queen who prized her ability to read a man's heart. Yetzer offered a curt nod then stepped back with the other would-be builders.

"People of Urusalim, all you Children of Yisrael," Bilkis said, turning her attention to the crowd, "rejoice, for this day the gods have raised a builder in Tsion. Give thanks, for the dwelling of Yah and Havah shall be among their chosen ones forever."

❧

"Do you wish me to give Rahab to another?" Bilkis demanded from her seat in the private audience chamber. "Or have you grown so weary of life that you place your neck beneath my sword?"

Gad knelt before Bilkis, blood and tears mingling in his beard. Benyahu's fists had been first messenger of the queen's displeaure.

"My lady—"

"I have given you gold. I have given you food and wine. I would give you the desire of your heart, and you repay my kindness with this betrayal? Speak!"

"My lady, I don't know what happened." Gad's lies came out mangled by his swollen lips. "You must believe I would never defy you. Something happened to the stones. I couldn't tell one from the other."

"Nonsense," Bilkis spat. "If there were no difference, in six draws there should have been three black and three white. Instead, you draw black five times in a row, and white only on the final one. Who is this Yetzer of Danu? What is he to you?"

"My lady, upon my beard, by Yah and by Havah, I don't know him. I tried to draw for Elhoreb, but I could not tell between the stones."

"Then how do you explain this? How does chance favor this one man?"

Gad opened his mouth, then closed it again, his eyes downcast. He picked dried blood from his beard. When he at last raised his eyes to meet the queen's, they held a look of woeful conviction.

"Perhaps the gods have indeed chosen him."

Bilkis reached behind her for the cushion. She thought to do unto Gad as she'd done to Abdi-Havah. Certainly the man's betrayal merited no less. Instead, she hurled the pillow at the prophet, hitting him squarely in his battered face.

"Get out," she screamed. "Take your lying, faithless stones and go. And next time you stand before me, you'd best have found a way to bend them once more to my will."

The door opened before the startled Gad could rise.

"Is everything well, Lady?" Benyahu asked from the doorway, drawn sword in his hand.

"Take him from my sight," Bilkis ordered her general. "Do him no more harm but send him away."

Benyahu stepped forward and jerked the seer up by his arm.

"As you say, my lady." The warrior pulled Gad toward the door, then looked briefly back. "Eliam, Natan, and the builder have come to speak with you."

"Fine," Bilkis snapped. "Is the king with them?"

"Yes, Lady," Benyahu said.

"Very well. Rid the palace of this rubbish, then return. Order food and wine for our guests."

"Yes, Lady."

"And close the door."

The general made no reply, but pulled the door shut after he chivvied the prophet from the room.

Bilkis pressed the heels of her hands to her eyes and took several deep breaths. Pain spread from the back of her neck throughout her skull, but with effort she managed to clear her thoughts. She practiced her welcoming smile a few times before she rose and moved to the door.

"Will there be a ladder to reach the gods?" Yahtadua said as Bilkis entered the audience hall.

"No," came the rich-toned reply. "We approach the gods with our hearts. The temple serves to free us of earthly burdens so that our hearts may ascend to the heavens."

The boy frowned and propped his cheeks upon his fists. "I wanted to climb there."

"A king doesn't climb," Bilkis said in a mock-scolding tone. "He has chosen warriors to climb for him."

"Ah, my child," Eliam said, and bowed low before the queen.

Natan went to his knees, while the builder bowed his head but remained standing.

"My father," Bilkis said as she took the merchant by the hand and bade him stand. "Your travels take you too long from us."

She embraced Eliam then turned to Natan.

"And you, young priest, must not become so distracted that you fail to attend us at the palace."

Bilkis kissed the boy on the cheek.

"Yes, my lady," the child said.

Bilkis turned to the final visitor and, with effort, kept a stutter from her breathing. The man's one eye was the color of the first buds of spring, his expression at once open and guarded. She offered her hand and the man took it with his callused fingers, his grip firm, gentle, as one comfortable with his strength. He touched his forehead to the back of her hand, then looked Bilkis in the eye with a gaze that seemed to penetrate to her very core.

"Allow me to present Yetzer abi-Huram," Eliam said after clearing his throat.

Bilkis pulled her hand back, and only then recognized the long moment of silence just passed.

"You are welcome," Bilkis said when she found her tongue. "I congratulate you on your selection."

"It was the will of the gods," Yetzer said. "I am humbled to have been chosen, and only hope to prove worthy of the honor."

Bilkis narrowed her eyes at that. Such pious responses belonged only to charlatans or fools. She gave the builder a neutral nod, then turned and stepped to the dais.

"And when do you expect to begin this great work?" she asked as she took her seat beside Yahtadua.

"I have only just begun planning," Yetzer said as he patted a leather satchel hung from his shoulder. "There is still the final size to be agreed upon, then workmen to be selected, provisions and shelter made for them, the site leveled, roads built. It may be a year before the first stone is laid."

"A year?" Yahtadua demanded.

"How many slaves do you require?" Bilkis asked. The coldness of Yetzer's expression sent a shudder along her spine.

"I will have no slaves." The builder's voice rumbled like distant thunder. "The gods' house will be established by free hands, bound to the work only by oath."

"How many men will you need?" Bilkis corrected herself, too abashed to respond with anger.

"That depends on many things." The threat eased from Yetzer's voice. "In principle, two men could do the work, but it would take many lifetimes to complete. Permit me to think upon the work another day or two, and I will have a counting of men, animals, material, and all else that will be needful."

Eliam stepped forward, a broad smile upon his face and a small box in his hands. "In the meantime, child," he said, "allow me to aid the funding of this grand labor."

A SONG OF
JOINING TOGETHER

45

Yetzer

For six months Yetzer refined his design while workmen gathered to clear the temple site. Following the harvest, while the fields rested, the laborers scraped and leveled the ground around Havah's rock. They dug the trench that would hold the temple's foundation, then smoothed the earth with tools of granite as Yetzer had smoothed the seer stone.

Eliam purchased land upon the hillside west of the city. Yetzer set up his work camp there, a tiny nation within the borders of Yisrael itself, a nation sworn to the work of the temple.

The queen had forbidden the use of any metal tools upon the temple mount, lest their noise disturb her in the palace. Yetzer tried to reason with her, but to no avail. When his workers returned to their fields, the builder and a handful of skilled masons from Tsur and Hatti and Kemet set their picks to the limestone beneath the northern edge of Havah's mountain.

And it came to pass, after the fields had again been sown, on the twelfth day of Ziv, in the fourth year of Yahtadua's reign, Yetzer donned his finest robe and put over it the apron his mother had fashioned for him. Made of lambskin and trimmed with blue silk, the apron bore in its center an embroidered triangle set around the *Udjat*, the eye of Haru. In its pupil was the Kenahni letter *yod*, the first letter of Yetzer's name, but also that of Yah-Havah, and of *yetzirah*, formation.

Yetzer's men wore similar aprons. Along with their families, they followed the Master of Masons up the long path from the quarry to the temple site. They filled the skies with their songs of praise and thanksgiving to the newly risen sun, to Havah, to Yah, and to the divine craftsman Kothar.

Priests and elders, nobles and peasants lined the way and waved palm branches in celebration. Yetzer received the adulation with cool detachment until he crested the hill and saw his mother with her new husband, Eliam.

This was the sort of reception, the recognition she'd always wanted for Huram, Yetzer's father. But in Kemet, where one would be hard pressed to swing a sacred cat without hitting some temple or shrine, even the greatest builder's work might easily go without notice. Yetzer's vision misted at Dvora's gleam of joy. This was the honor Huram had earned several times over. Now it fell to his son to restore to this people their gods and their dwelling place.

Yetzer smiled at his mother, then led the masons to what would become the great court of the temple, east of the grand portico that would daily receive the rising sun. Upon a wooden platform the queen and her young king awaited Yetzer.

Bilkis had not been idle during the period of Yetzer's labors. While he had set his skill to preparing the temple, the queen's energy had been spent in diplomacy. A dozen brides had been chosen for Yahtadua, taken from each of the land-holding tribes of Yisrael. Three more had recently been added from the neighboring lands of Edom, Moab, and Ammon, and all of Yahtadua's consorts now gathered behind their husband.

The men's song came to an end as Yetzer reached the dais. He offered his customary bow to king and queen. Bilkis returned a cool greeting, while Yahtadua's smile outshone the midday sun. The six-score workmen formed an arc about the court, their families behind them. A pair of Yetzer's overseers left the group and climbed into a great oaken treadwheel. Two more led a team of oxen to the northeast corner of the foundation. Their sledge, burdened with Yetzer's tool chest and the heavy cornerstone, grated upon the rocky surface of the mount. While the men fastened hoisting clamps to the stone, Yetzer turned to face the assembly.

"From time past remembering," he said, using the tone of voice that could fill a quarry, "since the first builder fashioned a tool and thought to reshape the world about him, man has been a co-creator with the gods, tasked to finish the work they began. Across the nations, beyond the rising and falling of kingdoms, the builder's art strives to emulate the perfection of nature, and to raise before the eyes of men temples that echo the dwellings of the ancient ones.

"We gather here on ground made holy," he continued, with a broad gesture that encompassed the hilltop. "Holy, not because man has made it so, but because the gods have willed it. In such places where the veil between the mortal and the eternal wears thin, we raise our altars and shrines and temples as markers to tell the wanderer that here the gods have spoken, and here they might again be heard."

Yetzer invited the king and high priest to accompany him, then stepped into the trench. The day before, he'd dug a small cist beneath the place of the foundation stone, lined it with cedar boards and sealed it with pitch. As the boys clambered down beside him, he opened the lid of his tool chest.

"It is fitting," he told the crowd, "that we place beneath this stone the words and the tools that brought it into being, that the temple's foundation should rest upon those principles that guide us."

Yetzer held up a fired clay tablet, inscribed front and back with the rules of conduct drawn up for his workers.

"The words of the law," he said, "inscribed upon the heart, but written here to remind us how we ought to act toward others, toward ourselves, and toward the gods."

He offered the tablet to Yahtadua, who gently laid it in the earth. Yetzer then took from the box a pair of small clay jars.

"Grain and wine," he continued, "to remind us that from the earth we take the flesh and the blood of the gods to nourish and refresh us."

He gave these to Natan, and the young priest set them beside the tablet. Yetzer finally produced a set of builder's tools, cast in gold.

"The setting square, by which we true our actions before the gods." He gave this to Yahtadua. "The compasses, with which we circumscribe our passions, that we transgress not against our fellow man." Yetzer offered it to Natan. "And the plumb, by which we live uprightly, that our prayers may ascend to the heavens."

Yetzer knelt beside the boys and arranged the tools within the cist. He then signaled his men. The pair in the treadwheel raised the foundation stone from its sledge while the other overseers positioned it over the cist. At another signal, the men in the wheel reversed their climb, and Yetzer guided the stone in its descent. When it neared the floor of the trench, he instructed king and priest to lay their hands atop the stone while he used a prybar to ease it into place.

"Let this stone represent the fulfillment of King Tadua's vow unto the gods," Bilkis proclaimed from the dais.

Yetzer lifted the boys out of the trench, then climbed out and turned his attention to the queen as she continued.

"Let it demonstrate our commitment to Tadua's vision and to the well-being of our people." Bilkis raised her hands and turned her face toward the heavens. "Rejoice, O Children of Yisrael, for your gods will soon have their dwelling among you."

The cheers of the people came like the roar of divine Kothar's furnace. Yetzer turned to look at the cornerstone, alone in the long, broad foundation trench.

One stone set, he told himself. *Only ten thousand more to follow.*

46

Bilkis

"It must have more gold," Bilkis insisted. "More gold and more jewels, more—everything."

"Gold is not suited for tools," Yetzer repeated his tired argument. "It is too soft, too easily damaged."

The pair sat, along with Eliam, around a low table in the small audience chamber. "I do not speak of forks and shovels," Bilkis said, "but of adornment and splendor. If my temple is to draw offerings from foreign lands, it must be the most magnificent edifice among all the nations."

"The plans call for carved cedar finishing," her builder stubbornly insisted, "not gold plate. If I am to change the design at this point—"

"I'm not asking you to change anything," Bilkis said in her best soothing voice, and laid a hand upon Yetzer's. He hesitated before pulling away, which Bilkis took as a small victory. "I simply suggest you add a bit of the gods' glory to your work. Gold leaf upon the engravings, jewels to accent the designs."

"Ivory inlays upon the doors," Eliam suggested.

"Lovely, yes. The gods have heaped kindness upon us," Bilkis added with a gracious nod to the merchant. "It is only fitting we should return to them a share of that abundance."

Yetzer pushed back from the table and heaved a deep sigh. "The foundation is nearly complete," he said, his tone one of surrender. "It will be some years yet before the finishes must be decided upon. If you wish to contribute treasure to the work, I will find a way to incorporate it."

Bilkis offered him a conciliatory smile. "Thank you, Master Yetzer. I'll not keep you from your labors any longer."

Yetzer rose with a fluid grace, nodded to Bilkis and the merchant, then left the chamber.

"You can acquire all these things?" Bilkis asked Eliam when they were alone.

The merchant held a piece of ink-stained linen at arm's length and studied the rows of characters.

"Gold, silver, gems, ivory. Copper and bronze, of course. And incense."

"No olibanum," Bilkis told him. "I'll not pollute my temple with that stench. Spices and herbs will suffice."

Eliam gave her a quizzical look but said nothing. He dipped a quill into a jar of ink and struck through a row of characters.

"As you wish, my lady. Yes, I can get all of these."

The merchant scratched his face thoughtfully and left a smear of ink upon his cheek.

"There is something more?" Bilkis prompted him.

"All these things can be had through the regular trade routes, through Kemet and Tsur, Hatti and Subartu. But I wonder … "

Bilkis waited silently, drumming her fingers upon the table while the merchant chased his thoughts.

"By the normal routes, these goods must all pass through many hands. Their cost increases with each merchant who touches them, every border crossed. But if they could all be had from one place, on one journey— " Eliam's eyes flitted about, as though to catch sight of whatever idea eluded him.

"Go on," Bilkis said, her patience wearing thin.

"Yes, of course. There is a land called Opiru, far out upon the Southern Sea. If we were to charter a ship, everything you desire for your temple could be had in a single voyage."

"The Southern Sea is a year's journey from here," Bilkis objected. "And you must cross wretched Saba to get there. Would you carry your ship upon the backs of donkeys?"

"No, my child, no. Now that your son is allied with Edom, we can reach the sea from their lands. The journey to Elath, on the coast, is a matter of weeks. Another few weeks to reach the Southern Sea, then a year or two to Opiru."

"Two years?" Bilkis asked in disbelief.

"Perhaps," Eliam said. "No more than three. As I understand it, the winds of the Southern Sea blow one way for half the year and the opposite direction for the other half. Travel is only possible when the winds are favorable."

"Why not simply row when the winds are contrary?"

Eliam thought about that for a moment. "It might be possible, but it would require a larger ship with more men and provisions. If such a ship is even available in Edom."

Bilkis considered that for a time. She'd never heard of Opiru, but she trusted the merchant's judgment. If she could directly obtain the treasures she desired— better, if she were to have sole control over such a trade route—she might rival the wealth of Tsur and Sidon, perhaps even Kemet itself.

"Go," she said finally. "Collect whatever trade goods you may need. I will send word to King Gabri of Edom to provide the ships and men you require. Return within five years for the dedication of the temple. And if you chance to meet anyone from Saba, you say naught of me. Understand?"

"It shall be even as you say, my lady." Eliam leaned forward. "There is, however, just one thing more."

❀

"Since the days before our wanderings," Natan said, "from the time Yah first breathed life into Kadmon's nostrils and Havah stirred his heart, man has yearned for woman to be his helpmate, to soothe the passions in his breast, and to ease the burden upon his back."

The young priest stood upon the newly completed foundation of the temple, before a blue-and-white canopy. He wore the formal vestments of the high priest, the white turban and jeweled breastplate. He was slender but had begun to grow tall. Though Bilkis had closed her heart to him in favor of Yahtadua, she couldn't deny a sliver of pride for the young servant of the gods.

"Gad abi-Sheg," the lad continued, "you have declared your intention to take to wife Rahab ab-Eliam. Is it still your desire to do so?"

The prophet, dressed in a new black robe, looked down at his bride, her face hidden behind layers of veils.

"It is," he said in an almost-whisper.

"Eliam abi-Terah, you present your daughter for marriage. Are you satisfied with the bride-price and with this man's character?"

"I am," the merchant said, then snuffled loudly.

Bilkis's mood soured at that. The merchant had been satisfied with Auriyah's character upon a time. But, as she had learned, flaws of character could easily be gilded over—the more the gold, the greater the flaws they covered. She resented that the shrewd merchant had bargained her temple's treasure for Rahab's marriage, removing the queen's greatest power over Gad.

"The two parties having agreed," Natan pronounced, then leaned toward Rahab and whispered, "is it all right with you?"

"Yes," Rahab said with a laugh.

"Then before Yah and Havah, upon their temple—"

The pounding of horses' hooves rumbled across the hilltop. Bilkis turned to see Prince Baaliyah and a troop of a dozen riders racing toward them. The prince's black mount was flanked with sweat and whinnied its protest as Baaliyah reined it in and, sword drawn, leapt from its back to the platform.

Benyahu shouted as he lowered his spear and rushed toward the son of Tadua. Baaliyah batted away the strike with his blade. He stepped inside the arc of Benyahu's weapon, grabbed the shaft and used the momentum of the general's charge to toss him off the stone wall. The prince's men disarmed the stunned warrior and held him captive below.

"I claim the daughter of Eliam," the prince shouted. "I claim Rahab, concubine of my father Tadua."

"She was never a concubine," Gad spat back, pushing Rahab behind him.

Baaliyah stalked toward the prophet and, with his bronze-stripped glove, delivered a backhanded blow that dropped Gad to his knees. The prince grasped Rahab by the wrist and pulled her to him. She struggled futilely as he tore away the veils to reveal her face, then kissed her long and hard on the mouth.

"Stop this," Yahtadua shouted. "Release her, I command you."

The warrior-prince broke his embrace and swung Rahab to the side but did not release her. He faced the king, swept a low, mocking bow and sneered at the boy.

"Ah, little brother. Or is it *nephew*? It gets terribly confusing, what with fathers and sons trading wives. Now be a good boy and still your tongue, or I'll help myself to some of your bed-warmers as well."

All the brides Bilkis had chosen for Yahtadua were lovely. The eldest two—Marah of the tribe Yehuda, and Wisal, a princess of Edom—had reached womanhood. To take any of Yahtadua's wives would be an insult and a humiliation of the king. To take one or both of these two would strengthen Baaliyah's position within Yisrael and without.

"Take her," Bilkis said. "Take Rahab with my blessing and leave us in peace."

"Umma, no," Yahtadua cried, his objection supported by a half-dozen other voices.

"Listen to your mother, boy," Baaliyah said, a sneer twisting his lips, "and you might just make it to manhood."

Then his expression faltered. Bilkis caught the movement of a shadow from the corner of her eye. Baaliyah held his sword before him as Yetzer stepped forward.

"Stay back, mason. This is not your concern."

"This is my temple," Yetzer said in a low tone, "my domain. All that happens here is my concern. Rahab, do you wish to go with this man?"

"No," she cried, and renewed her futile struggles.

"She does not wish to go with you." Yetzer strode forward. "Release her."

The prince screamed a curse and swung his blade toward Yetzer's neck. With startling speed, the builder stepped inside the sword's path, trapped Baaliyah's arm beneath his own, then stabbed his thumb into the hollow at the base of the man's neck. Baaliyah released Rahab and clutched at his throat.

Yetzer pulled the prince's arm back until, with a loud pop and a strangled scream from Baaliyah, Yetzer separated arm and shoulder. The sword fell to the foundation stones, followed a moment later by the prince.

A pair of Baaliyah's men leapt onto the platform. Natan yelled a warning to Yetzer. The craftsman spun away in time to turn what might have been a fatal stab into a glancing strike along his arm. With a cry of rage, he clouted the man on the back of the head and sent him to the ground, then ducked below the second man's blade. From his crouch he rammed his fist into the warrior's side and the sound of snapping ribs joined the din.

"Call them off," Yetzer demanded as he hauled a gagging Baaliyah to his feet.

The prince smiled drunkenly and spat in Yetzer's face.

47

Yetzer

Pain lanced through Yetzer's left arm where the sword had taken him. Blood ran warm and was already soaking his sleeve. He glowered at the prince. The pair of dazed warriors were recovering themselves, and more of their comrades scrambled atop the platform. Two or three remained below to keep watch over Benyahu. With the better part of a dozen armed warriors to face, and amid the collection of women and children, too much could go wrong.

"Don't make me do this," Yetzer told Baaliyah in a soft voice.

The prince looked as though he might spit again. Resolved, Yetzer tugged the dislocated arm and spun the man around. Baaliyah's scream was cut short as Yetzer wrapped his arms around the royal neck.

"Leave this place now, and he'll live," Yetzer told the men who moved into a half-circle around him. He backed up to an edge of the platform where none could attack him from behind. "Come closer, and you'll need a new patron."

The men hesitated and looked to one another. Most heads turned toward the warrior with the broken ribs. Yetzer watched him, saw his eyes change from uncertainty to hatred. The warrior took a step forward.

Yetzer silently begged Havah's forgiveness for what he must do. Yah, he supposed, would understand. He tightened his grip—one hand on Baaliyah's chin, the other about the back of his head—and pulled.

The crack made the earlier injuries seem a mere snapping of twigs. Baaliyah slumped in Yetzer's arms. The builder picked up the prince and threw him at the rib-cracked one. The man fell to the ground under the weight of the corpse, along with the fighters on either side of him.

Yetzer clenched his fists, turned his face to the sky and loosed a roar. A roar of victory, a roar of pain, a roar of anguish for having desecrated the place of the goddess with death. Lest more death pollute the holy precinct, he turned his eye back to the approaching warriors.

"Take your lord and bury him or join him in Sheol."

The men who remained upright looked to one another. In silent agreement they sheathed their swords, collected the fallen prince, and vacated the temple platform.

"Keep riding," Benyahu shouted after the men had bound their leader to his horse and reined their mounts away from the temple. "If tomorrow finds you still among the tribes of Yisrael, I'll wash my blade with your blood."

Dvora rushed to Yetzer and embraced him while Rahab and Gad found one another.

"I thought I raised you with more sense," Dvora scolded her son, then kissed his cheek and fussed over his arm.

Eliam came up and clapped a hand on Yetzer's good shoulder. "I see my family will be in safe keeping while I'm away."

The other members of the wedding party all looked at Yetzer, their eyes full of wonder. The queen nodded her gratitude, though her eyes held something more. Yetzer dropped his gaze and looked to Natan.

"Well, priest, will you finish what you began, or must these two wait even longer for their wedding couch?"

48

Makeda

Season followed season. Flood after flood, harvest after harvest, the years flowed by. The Wadi Dhanah filled and quenched the fields. Maryaba fed the people of Saba, who in turn harvested the myrrh and olibanum trees and brought the resin to Maryaba's storehouses. And Saba prospered.

From Uwene across the Western Sea, merchants brought ivory and gems, furs and feathers and countless other treasures in trade for the precious incense. Nobles bore pledges of peace and amity, even a few proposals of marriage. I was already wed to the god Athtar, however, but in exchange for the exotic gifts all were pleased to leave Saba with even a few bags of hardened sap.

By the twelfth year of my reign, I ruled over a kingdom more peaceful, more prosperous than any of my ancestors had known. From the Southern and Western Seas, to the edge of the endless eastern desert, and as far north as Nahran, all the people of Saba thrived. Strife between cities ended. Conflict between Bedou and townsfolk was no more.

Disputes still arose—over property claims or marriage contracts or grazing rights—but these were settled by the local chieftain. If the matter could not be resolved, or if the lord was involved in the dispute, the Council of Elders would hear the case. Failing this, I as Mukarrib—at once queen, high priestess, and judge—settled the issue. Four times each year, at the sun's festivals, I took the Seat of Wisdom to dispense justice to my people.

"The mukarrib has spoken," Yanuf declared in a gruff voice after I announced my ruling in one such case involving a lord's meddling in his city's pottery trade.

"So shall it be done." The assembly of the court intoned the words together. "So shall it be remembered."

I glanced at the remembrancer, still unaccustomed to his voice. Son had succeeded father after the previous harvest, when the elder had been stricken with tremors and lost his power of speech. The old man still sat in assembly, though his eyes were unfocused as he moved his silent lips. His son seemed to share the father's facility for memory, but I mused, not for the first time, that there should be a more certain means of preserving our laws and history.

Startled cries and shouts of protest rose from the people gathered before the steps of the tower house. Yanuf stepped to my side and flexed his fingers about the shaft of his spear. A low growl rumbled in his throat when Dhamar of Timnah pushed through the crowd to stand before the council. I glanced at Watar, whose cheeks blanched as his son made a low, sweeping bow.

"Peace be unto the Mukarrib of all Saba." Dhamar's tone did not match his blessing. "I bring tribute to the Wife of the God and to the Council of Elders."

"I welcome the son of Watar," I said in an even voice, "but Timnah's tribute is in the protection of Saba's borders, in the safekeeping of her roads."

"It is from our border that I bring this tribute," Dhamar replied. He snapped his fingers and a pair of men climbed the steps behind him, a bound and hooded figure between them. "Behold your gift, your slave if you will have him, taken from the Gate of Tears near Adaneh upon the Southern Sea."

The heir of Watar snatched off the hood to reveal an older man with gaunt face and sunken eyes. His beard had been crudely shorn, his face an uneven field of stubble and scrapes. The man blinked as he shifted bleary eyes from one councillor to another. His gaze settled upon me and he began to speak, but Dhamar kicked at his legs and dropped the man to his knees.

"You will kneel before the Mukarrib and the Council of Saba," he said.

"Enough," I snapped. "I accept the tribute of Dhamar abi-Watar, but you well know I will have no slaves. You will untie him and explain why he has been so ill-used." Dhamar's jaw clenched, but he motioned to one of his men to cut the ropes from the prisoner's arms. The older man crawled to me and kissed my feet.

"Yah and Havah's blessings be upon you, Lady," he began, but Dhamar shoved him away with a boot to the backside.

"Silence, dog. Do not foul this air with the names of your foreign gods."

I rose and stared down at the young lord of Timnah.

"You will not foul this place with your bile," I said. "You have brought this man to me as tribute, and I have accepted him."

"He is a foreigner and a spy—"

I cut off Dhamar's protest. "Whatever he was, he is now a guest under my roof. You would do well to remember the law of hospitality if you wish to remain so yourself."

Dhamar glowered at me but held his tongue. From the corner of my eye, I caught Watar's sharp gesture of dismissal. His son curtly bowed his head, then led his men from the council chamber.

I stooped down to the foreigner and took his hand. "Rise," I said, "and be welcome. Bring water," I commanded a servant. "Bring bread and oil that our guest may be comforted."

The man nodded his thanks and greedily accepted the tokens of hospitality. When he had devoured a loaf of bread drenched in olive oil and washed it down with a pitcher of water, he again knelt before me and beamed up at me.

"The gods' blessings upon you, my lady," he said, his words thick with a northern accent. "I am pleased to bring you greetings from King Yahtadua of Yisrael, and to be his humble servant, Eliam abi-Terah."

❖

"A temple of stone?" I doubted the words even as I spoke them.

"Yes, Lady," Eliam assured me. "Stone, cedar, bronze. And gold, had the gods not frowned upon my journey."

After I dismissed the council, I'd invited Eliam to accompany me on a tour of Maryaba. Followed closely by the vigilant Yanuf, we crossed the dam that spanned the Wadi Dhanah. The flood's first harvest had been taken in, and the waters yet rose halfway up the earthen wall. Eliam paused at the midpoint of the dam, slowly turning as he took in the verdant fields that surrounded the city.

"Frown they may upon me," he said, awe in his voice, "but surely they smile for you. In all my years, I never dreamed I'd see a green Saba."

"It was my mother's doing," I said. "But, yes, the gods have indeed been kind to us. I regret their hard treatment of you."

Eliam had told of how he'd long before traded with Saba, how he'd lost his first wife on one such trading journey, how he'd hoped to return to Yisrael with a treasure from Opiru, far out upon the Southern Sea. Indeed, the merchant had claimed just such a treasure. He had crossed and returned upon the waters. He was only a fortnight away from his home country, his ship's belly filled with gold and gems and spices for his gods, when Saba's storm god swallowed ship and treasure in the wild waters where Southern and Western Seas met.

"What Havah gave," he said with a rueful smile, "Elmakah has taken away. Yisrael's gods grow weak this far from their home. Perhaps when their temple is completed their power will reach farther."

"Their temple of stone," I prompted him again, "not brick?"

"Oh, no, Lady," the merchant assured me. "Only of stone and wood, fit together so perfectly not even a feather can slip between the joints. My son—my wife's son, that is—even now builds the finest home any god ever had. Grand enough to house Yah and Havah and all the hosts of heaven. Commands the very demons of the Pit, does Yetzer, along with the beasts of the field and birds of the air."

I wasn't certain whether Eliam spoke in earnestness or jest, but the pride on his face suggested the truth of his words, however marvelous. I looked down at the dam, at the mud bricks cracked from more than a dozen years under Shams's harsh rays. I looked at the waters held back by the dam, and my heart ached with the secret hidden beneath the muddy surface.

Known only to me, Yanuf, and a handful of trusted others, the dam would likely stand only a few more floods. Each year, when the Wadi Dhanah had given the last drink of water to the fields, dredgers removed the silt and debris that collected at the foot of the dam. With each passing year the very surface of the dam receded, so that scarcely half its original thickness remained. It only stood to reason that, having been fashioned of mud, to mud it must return. That reason brought little comfort, for when the dam at last failed, so would the peace and prosperity of Saba.

I swatted away the gloomy thoughts as at a fly. I looped my arm through Eliam's and guided the merchant back toward Maryaba's walls.

"Tell me more of this temple of yours."

49
Bilkis

Bilkis waited in the courtyard of Abdi-Havah's old estate. Set upon the brow of Morhavah, the retreat was visited by the cooling summertime breezes that somehow avoided Tsion and the palace. She sipped sweetened goat's milk, chilled with snow brought by fast riders from the northern mountains.

Not for the first time this afternoon, the queen shifted the skirts of her gown, adjusted her breasts beneath the gauzy silk and felt her hair to be sure all was in place. She missed Rahab's trusted hand with her cosmetics, but her erstwhile sister and handmaid was confined to the birthing chamber.

Bilkis had offered a place in the palace and the ministrations of the royal midwife. Rahab declined her queen's generosity, preferring Eliam's little house and none but Dvora to help with her labor.

"The builder Yetzer abi-Huram," Benyahu announced from the gate, dispelling her thoughts.

"Show him in."

Bilkis filled her lungs in an effort to still her fluttering stomach. These monthly appointments with Yetzer, to discuss the temple's progress, had become her only opportunities to spend time with the builder.

"Welcome, Master Yetzer," she said as the builder ducked under the gate arbor.

With the summer's heat, Yetzer had cropped his beard, and the solid line of his jaw showed clearly beneath the stubble. He'd replaced his robe with a sleeveless tunic and kilt that bared his muscled arms and calves. Bilkis took in the builder's form, then realized no one had spoken for several long moments.

"Come, sit," she told Yetzer. "Refresh yourself."

Yetzer bowed his head and silently obeyed.

"Benyahu," Bilkis said in the silky tone that most easily won his assent, "do go down to the city and attend Rahab. Bring me word as soon as she is delivered of her child, that I may rejoice with her."

"Of course, Lady," Benyahu replied. "I'll send one of my men straight away."

"No, no," Bilkis insisted, "it must be you. I'll not have some unwashed Pelesti befoul Eliam's house. Go now and return with glad tidings."

The grey warrior glared at Yetzer, who seemed oblivious as he plucked grapes from a small cluster on the table. Benyahu's knuckles turned white as he gripped the hilt of his sword, but he bowed to his queen and left.

50

Yetzer

"How comes the work?" Bilkis asked when they were alone.

"Well, Lady," Yetzer answered tersely. The queen kept her eyes on him as he chewed a grape. He swallowed before adding, "The wall is nearly to the floor of the Most Holy Place, almost five cubits."

"And it will be how high?"

"Thirty cubits."

Yetzer plucked another grape as Bilkis leaned back on her couch. The queen's gown drew tight across her breasts, capturing Yetzer's gaze. He'd seen the darkness in her soul, but his base desire was ignorant of good or ill and knew only the shapely beauty before him.

"So it is another five years before it is complete?" Bilkis asked, her disappointment like a hot brand upon Yetzer's heart.

"No, Lady," he hastened to reply. "The walls above the level of the Most Holy Place will rise much faster."

"Good," the queen said, her full crimson lips quirked into a smile. "And the finish work? The furnishings?"

"My carpenters have begun carving the wall panels. By the time Eliam returns, we will be ready for the gilders."

Bilkis's eyes fixed on Yetzer as she traced her fingers along her jawline and down her neck, then toyed with the braided gold necklace that disappeared beneath the neckline of her gown.

"The—ah—the castings," Yetzer stammered, "the molds, rather, will be started after harvest. We will need only Abram's tin to make sufficient bronze for the statues and tools."

The queen tilted her head to one side. The smooth skin of her neck stretched taut so that Yetzer could see the throbbing of her heartbeat. Its rhythm matched his. Bilkis's breasts rose and fell. She slowly blinked her eyes and when she opened them again, Yetzer had to fight the sensation of falling into them.

"And is there aught else you need?" Bilkis asked him, her voice low. "Anything I can do to ease your burden?"

"We have all we need to complete the work on time," Yetzer managed to say without tripping upon his words.

Bilkis rose and slowly moved toward Yetzer. She sat upon the low, stone table, her knees nearly touching his. "I do not speak of the work or of your men," she said, and laid a hand atop his where it rested in his lap. "What need has Yetzer abi-Huram that I can fulfill?"

She leaned toward Yetzer as she spoke, until the world about him was reduced to her penetrating eyes, her honeyed breath, her inviting mouth. What part of Yetzer's reason that remained sent a warning shudder along his spine, but the rest of him leaned forward to taste the sweetness of her lips. Gentle, tentative at first, the hunger of their kisses rapidly mounted until they all but consumed one another.

Yetzer tugged at the silk of her gown until it gave way to him and fell off her shoulders. Her bare flesh was hot and soft beneath his hands. His lips moved to her neck as he pulled her closer.

"Yes," Bilkis whispered in his ear.

She pushed up his kilt, raised the skirts of her ruined gown and slid onto Yetzer's knees. Her breasts pressed against his chest, but the gateway to her pleasures remained just beyond the reach of his aching need. Yetzer grasped her hips to pull her closer, but the queen pushed back, bit his earlobe and made a hungry sound.

"Only," she said in a deep, breathy voice, "you must first vow to share with Yahtadua the secrets of your craft."

Yetzer barely heard the words over the pounding rhythm of desire in his ears. "I sha— I—" he stammered before the meaning of the queen's words reached the reasoning chamber of his heart.

Bilkis's lips and teeth and tongue had resumed their play upon Yetzer's ear and neck. Yetzer pushed her back by the shoulders and there was the pause of a heart's beating before her eyes met his and resumed their sultry, inviting gaze. In that instant, Yetzer saw the calculation, the stagecraft, before the mask of desire fell back into place.

"Come, now," Bilkis purred. "Such a small thing to ask for what I would give you."

She stretched her hips forward, arching her back deliciously, but reason now won the battle with lust. Yetzer grasped her again by the hips, but this time cast her away from him. The queen landed roughly upon the table, sprawling among the tangled remnants of her gown.

"Foul temptress of the Pit," Yetzer snarled. He stood and put the chair between himself and the queen. "My honor will not be so cheaply bought."

"How dare you—" Bilkis started to speak but Yetzer cut her off.

"If your son would learn the mysteries of the builders, let him first come out from the harem to labor in the quarry."

The king had gotten a child on one of his brides and, if rumor met truth, spent most of his time trying to recreate the feat with the others.

"You will speak of your king with respect," Bilkis hissed as she fumbled with the torn silk to cover her nakedness.

"He's no king of mine," Yetzer retorted. "And king or no, he gets the respect from me that his actions merit. Gods have mercy on this people, ruled by a king of rutters and a queen of whores."

Yetzer dodged the golden cup Bilkis threw at his head.

"Get out," she screamed. "Go back to your dirt heap and your pile of rocks."

"Gladly," Yetzer said, but did not move quickly enough to avoid the hurled cluster of grapes.

He turned toward the gate, and the queen's shouted curses nipped his heels as he stalked away. A pair of guards approached from the outer wall of the estate, drawn by the queen's shouts. Yetzer pushed past them, stormed through the outer gate and found the path that led up to the high place. He fumbled with his pouch as he walked, stabbed his hand into the leather mouth and brought out a few pieces of silver.

Enough.

Where the uphill path split, Yetzer took the right-hand branch toward the shrine of Ashtart, where his silver could buy the companionship of one of the goddess's priestesses.

Or, this night, perhaps two.

�֍

"Yetzer, come forth."

The call came from somewhere beyond the thick curtain that shrouded Yetzer's head.

"Yetzer of Danu, show yourself."

A delicate hand shook Yetzer by the shoulder. He grumbled and shrugged it off, then rolled over and draped his arm across a slender, naked belly.

"Yetzer abi-Huram, I summon you."

Light glowed from somewhere beyond Yetzer's closed eyelid.

"You'd best be bringing wine or a pisspot," Yetzer slurred.

"You, out," a stern, matronly voice ordered.

The woman beneath Yetzer's arm extricated herself and the one behind him rose from the other side of the cot. Yetzer rolled onto his back, head and stomach protesting at the movement. He cracked open his sleep-clotted eyelid, and the protest turned to open revolt. He managed to swallow back the bile that rose in his throat, loosing only a belch and a groan in its stead.

Ashtart's high priestess stood at the foot of the bed. One hand held the glaring lamp while the other, curled into a tight fist, was planted against an ample hip.

"Why do you torture me, my sweet?" Yetzer asked the older woman. "If I tell your goddess's parents' priest how you treat her devotees, you'll have Sheol to pay." He waggled a scolding finger at her and a grin staggered across his lips. The priestess was unimpressed.

"The queen's general is at the gate to the shrine," she told him with the same tone in which she might discuss the weather.

"Then take his offering or send him away," Yetzer suggested, and draped his arm across his face.

"He's here for you."

Yetzer grimaced at that and peeked out from beneath his arm. "Haven't you boys for that? I don't serve the goddess that way."

"He carries a different sort of sword than most of our supplicants," the high priestess observed. "I'd let him come in for you, but I'd rather spare the sheets your blood."

Before Yetzer could frame a reply, his wine-stained tunic and kilt landed upon his chest.

"I'll inform the general you'll be along soon," the priestess said. "Do not make a truth-slayer of me."

The woman left the room, leaving Yetzer in the grey gloom of twilight. The faintest glow shone beneath the curtain that provided but little privacy from the others who came to celebrate the goddess of love and conquest. Grunts and oaths and squeals sounded from the small chambers surrounding his.

He thought to close his eye once more, but a shouted curse from outside the shrine made him rouse himself. He cared little if he provoked the general's wrath, but he had no desire to unsettle Ashtart's servants. With great effort, Yetzer sat up, then worked the tunic over his head and arms. His stomach coiled and slithered, but his head remained intact. He lurched to a standing position, belched again, then leaned his back against the wall while he wrapped the kilt about his waist. The stink of sweat and stale wine clogged his nostrils as he made his way toward the shrine's entrance where sweet jasmine welcomed him into the cool evening air.

"You dare show yourself?" Benyahu growled as Yetzer staggered along the flower-lined path to the outer gate.

"Isn't that what you want—"

The question hadn't left Yetzer's lips before the pommel of a sword slammed into his belly. Yetzer doubled over and heaved, splashing his stomachful of wine onto the warrior's sandals. He might have laughed, but an elbow to the back of his head dropped him to the vomit-stained earth.

With a howl of rage, Benyahu kicked Yetzer in the ribs. The mason rolled away from the assault. He took a blow to a kidney before the wine's expulsion and the warrior's attack combined to restore his wits. A bronze-clad foot flew toward his head, but Yetzer caught it in his quarry-hardened hands. He twisted it toe-to-heel and Benyahu staggered, hopped, then fell to the ground.

"What's the meaning of this?" Yetzer demanded, the general's foot still in his grasp.

In reply, Benyahu swung his sword at him. The stroke flew awkwardly from his supine position, but it bore enough menace that Yetzer released his hold and scuttled away. He rolled into a crouch even as the battle-bled warrior regained his feet.

"I deny the queen and this is the cost?" Yetzer said. He looked for some path of escape, but Benyahu stalked him like a lion.

"You violated her honor, and you'll pay with your life."

The general lunged the sword toward Yetzer's middle, catching the fine woven tunic when Yetzer failed to dodge quickly enough. Benyahu checked his attack and swung the sword in a great backhanded arc. Yetzer had more time to avoid this stroke. He ducked under the scything blade and rolled out of reach.

"Perhaps I allowed things to get too friendly," Yetzer admitted, "but I showed her no more dishonor than she deserved."

With a terrible roar Benyahu bore down on Yetzer, his blade whistling as it sundered the air between them. Yetzer backed away but slipped in the puddle of his vomit. Again, he fell. Again, he rolled away from a sword stroke that would surely have cleaved him from crown to navel. With speed born of desperation he circled to the general's left, keeping the warrior's body between himself and the mighty sword arm.

Yetzer noted a hitch in Benyahu's step and dropped to the earth even as the general reversed his turn and swung at Yetzer's right side. The younger man sprang up behind the spinning general, snaked his arms beneath Benyahu's then clasped his hands behind the warrior's neck. Benyahu wriggled and flailed and twisted his sword, but his attempts to break free were useless.

"I'm sorry," Yetzer said through teeth gritted against the warrior's struggles. "I know you've claimed Bilkis, yet I nearly allowed myself to take her."

Benyahu raged and struggled still. He raked a metal-clad sandal along Yetzer's shin. The builder cursed, then kicked out the warrior's legs. He managed to keep the pair of them upright as they fell to their knees, and used his height advantage to maintain his hold.

"You took her," Benyahu declared, his voice somewhere between a growl and a moan. "You attacked her and you took her."

Yetzer's grip faltered at that. He fell upon his backside, but when Benyahu whipped his blade around yet again, Yetzer grasped the general by the wrist. He squeezed, his gaze fixed on Benyahu's rage-clouded eyes.

"You know her better than I," Yetzer said, grunting as he struggled with the warrior. "You know no one forces her to do anything."

Benyahu hammered his free hand against Yetzer's neck. The temple-builder grasped this wrist too, then rose to his feet. When he stood before the general, Yetzer rammed his forehead against the bridge of Benyahu's nose. The warrior's gaze went distant as blood streamed into his beard.

"You know her," Yetzer repeated. "I'm curious. Did she take you to her couch before her husband died, or did she wait until his body was cold?"

The general's eyes focused at that, his look more shamed than angry. Yetzer pushed him away and took a step back. Benyahu made no advance.

"I'm done with her," Yetzer said. "I'll complete the temple, then leave this accursed land."

"She means to stop your food," Benyahu said, so softly Yetzer almost missed it. "If she can't get what she wants from you, she'll starve out your workers."

Yetzer simply looked at the general without reply. Benyahu grunted and shook his head. He cursed as he wiped at his nose with the back of his hand, then spat a bloody gob upon the ground.

"Ashtart's cunny," the warrior said. "If Bilkis wants the king to play the mason, just give the boy your secrets. He's so busy with his queens and the new toy he's found between his legs, he'll not have time to get in your way."

Yetzer stooped to retrieve the fallen sword. A splash of blood marked the edge, and he put his fingers to his side where the blade had pierced his tunic. He winced when he discovered the wound and came away with red-stained fingers. Benyahu gave a half-apologetic shrug.

"And when she has it in her heart to make Yahtadua play the warrior?" Yetzer said as he wiped the blade with his kilt. "What then?"

He offered the sword to Benyahu, hilt first. The general nodded and accepted the truce token.

"I'd hope he's as good a fighter as his Master of Masons." Benyahu rested the sword in its scabbard and cuffed at his nose again. "Is the honor of your order truly worth this? The queen will not soon forgive the insult."

The warning gave Yetzer pause. He thought of his men, of the scores of masons and quarriers, carpenters and carters and a dozen other trades. Add to these their wives and children, the oxen and asses, and Yetzer had more than a thousand mouths to feed. His honor would not fill their bellies, nor his pride their cups. But he also thought of what he'd created, what his father had so often spoken of.

The souls under his care were a new nation, formed not by blood-ties or accidents of landscape, but by free will and a commitment to a common goal. His overseers were not the wealthiest men, but those best able to turn that common vision into reality. Advancement came not from force of arms, but from the best ability to work and best to serve.

Were Yetzer to accede to the queen's demand, were he to undermine the very principles he'd established, his brotherhood of builders would perish by betrayal as surely as by starvation.

"The quarry is open to the king as it is to all men," Yetzer said.

Benyahu grunted and gave a humorless smile. "So be it. And may the gods be merciful, for the queen will not."

51

Makeda

"Athtar speed your way," I told Eliam as he climbed upon his donkey. "You and your gods have been most generous to me already, my lady," the merchant replied. "I pray I might prove worthy of the kindness."

"Only remember me to your king," I said, "that our countries may become friends."

A shadow flitted across Eliam's expression but was just as quickly replaced by his usual good humor. "Of course, my lady, I shall lay your greetings before the throne."

The promise fell short of what I'd hoped for but it would have to do. As wise and able a merchant as Eliam had proved to be during his short stay in Maryaba, even his influence would be limited before so great a ruler as Yisrael must have.

I patted the donkey, smiled up at the man, then turned back toward the city gates. Eliam gave a command, and the patter of hooves upon sand filled the morning air.

Four-score donkeys and their handlers followed Eliam's lead and set out along the northbound caravan route. The trail had been little used these last dozen years or more, but I hoped the gift of donkeys and olibanum might reopen trade. More so, I prayed the road might carry to our country the means for my people's lasting prosperity. If a temple could be built all of stone, would not a dam be even simpler?

"Lord Watar awaits you, my lady," Yanuf said when I reached the gates.

"Watar?" I said. "Why has he come?" The council would not meet for another six weeks.

Yanuf shrugged, but the mischievous glint in his eye suggested I needn't worry. The old warrior fell in beside me and accompanied me to the tower house, where I found the Lord of Timnah, a pair of camels kneeling nearby. Watar fell to his knees when he saw me, and sprinkled dust upon his head.

"May the mukarrib forgive my house," he implored as I approached. "May the Wife of the God have mercy on Timnah."

Despite Yanuf's silent assurance, a cold hand squeezed my belly.

"Rise, Lord Watar," I said, and shot a questioning glance at Yanuf. "Your house has proven a worthy brother to Maryaba, and a faithful servant to Athtar."

The Lord of Timnah stood and brushed the dirt from his robe. The man must be nearing fifty years, yet his features remained strong and proud, with only a hint of grey beginning to show in his neat beard.

"Thank you, Lady," Watar said, his eyes still downcast.

"What word do you bring me?" I asked, my words clipped. "What news so troubles you?"

"The mukarrib knows the nature of my son," Watar began, and the nervous grip squeezed tighter. "He may yet become a good man, if he can learn to see beyond his own nose."

I folded my arms, as much to hide my shaking hands as to express my impatience.

"When I learned what he had done," Watar continued, "I put an end to his scheme and immediately came to lay the matter before you."

"Which is … ?" Yanuf prompted the man.

Watar at last looked up. A sheepish expression replaced the shame that had colored his features. "My son returned to the Gate of Tears," he explained, "where the merchant Eliam had been cast ashore. With the help of the fishermen of Adaneh, he found where the ship from Yisrael sank. He hired men to dive into the sea to recover that which was lost."

The Lord of Timnah removed the woven lids from the panniers hung on each side of the camels. My heart raced as I peered in to see gems, spice boxes, pelt-shaped gold ingots larger than Yanuf's hand.

"The treasure from Opiru," I breathed, scarcely believing the gods' mercy.

"A portion of it," Watar said, and I tore my gaze away from the riches to look at him.

"There's more?"

"Yes, Lady. This is but a hundredth part of the ship's cargo. I've sent trusted men to secure the remainder until you determine how to proceed."

I barely heard these last words as the world went silent and dim, lit only by Shams's light reflecting off the precious metal. A familiar whisper spoke to my heart and a smile stretched my lips as the living world came back into focus.

"Athtar's spoken to you again, has he?" Yanuf said.

I nodded and told the men what the god had suggested to me. Watar's expression twisted into disbelief, but Yanuf, more accustomed to my divine revelations, simply nodded. He looked from me to the treasure baskets, then back again.

"We're going to need more camels."

❦

All was in order. Preparations had taken a year, and their planning might have overwhelmed me were it not for Yanuf and Watar's help.

Following the harvest, while the fields lay fallow and resting, the might of Saba turned from farming to ferrying. Trains of donkeys crossed the mountains between Maryaba and the sea to bring the treasure of Opiru to the city. The smaller beasts could carry only a quarter of the load of a camel but were more sure-footed on the rough mountain trails. And I had other plans for the larger beasts.

By the time all the treasure was recovered, an army of workers had fashioned panniers and saddles for some three hundred camels. Before the next appearance of the floodwaters, the goods and people to fill them were also ready.

"You should let me go with you," Yanuf said. He stood at my side, atop the dam, as I made my parting survey of the source of Saba's wealth.

"You are the Guardian of the Gates of Maryaba, not of the mukarrib." I looked up at the man—guardian, teacher, friend—who had shaped my life more than any other. His empty sleeve waved on the light breeze, and the low morning sun danced off the grey that now dominated his hair and beard. Not handsome of face nor eloquent of speech nor graceful of movement, yet he embodied the best of manhood—wit, humor, loyalty, compassion.

"None knows my heart so well as you," I told him, my voice low. "Watar will lead the council well in my absence, but I trust only you to speak and act in my stead. Even when it goes against your better judgment," I added with a smile.

The old warrior grunted and sniffed. I stretched up to kiss his bristly cheek, then turned toward the crowd gathered below the dam.

"People of Saba." The rocky walls of the upper wadi amplified my voice, and the crowd hushed and focused on me. I tried to capture each face in my memory. "Favored among the nations. Give thanks, for the gods have once more blessed us with a full harvest, and with a great treasure cast upon our shores. But what are gems, compared with bread in our children's mouths? What is gold, compared with clothes upon their backs? What value have spices without the sweet flavor of peace?"

I paused and met the eyes of each elder, several of whom had fiercely opposed my plan.

"I go to restore this treasure to its rightful place, into the house of foreign gods. In return, those gods and ours will secure the peace and prosperity of Saba for countless generations to come.

"With our own hands did we build this dam, to turn ruin into blessing, destruction into life. But as from mud it has risen, so to mud it must surely return. The gods of the northern nations, however, have taught their people to build mountains, immovable by man or flood. We shall win this knowledge, and we shall raise a mountain in the Wadi Dhanah to stand through the ages."

The voices of the people rose in shouts of joy and thanksgiving. A handful of elders seemed unmoved by my words, mired in their desire for foreign riches, unable to see beyond the lump of gold in their hands to the mound of gold on the horizon. Most, however, led by Watar, smiled and nodded their approval. I waited for the cheering to crest before continuing.

"It will be some time before my return—two years, perhaps more. My authority I invest in the Council of Elders, but my heart I leave with you, my people." I raised my hands above my head. "May Shams rise to greet you and warm you from night's chill. May Elmakah send his rains to refresh and nourish you, his clouds to cool your brow. And may Athtar, the most high, whisper good counsel and sustain you all your days."

"So may it be," the people responded as one.

I lowered my hands, my breath tight in my chest, and walked to the waiting caravan at the north end of the dam.

"Ready, my lady," Hazar, hand-picked by Yanuf as captain of my guard, said.

I nodded, then turned to Yanuf who had followed me across the wadi. I pulled the old warrior's forehead to mine, kissed him on each cheek, then released him.

"Tend to my people."

Yanuf nodded, grunted, then helped me into the high saddle on my kneeling camel's back.

"*Kehn*, Dhahbas," I commanded, and clicked my tongue.

The camel gave a snort, and I rocked with the motion as the beast reeled onto her hind legs, then pitched back to stand on all fours.

Along the length of the wadi, drovers shouted and coaxed the herd to their feet. The voices of men, the groans of camels, and the pounding of hooves sounded like the very flooding of the Wadi Dhanah itself.

I drew a deep breath and cast a final smile and nod to Yanuf. I tugged the reins and tapped my feet to guide Dhahbas away from Maryaba and onto the ancient caravan trail toward Yisrael.

Toward Urusalim.

Toward hope.

52

Yetzer

Bilkis made good on her threatened embargo. For three years the small nation of builders survived on the gifts of friends, the charity of Natan's priesthood, and the occasional caravan that passed Yetzer's settlement before reaching Urusalim's gates. A meager harvest had reduced the contributions, however. Yetzer's gold and silver were gone, leaving a store that, even with careful rationing, would last only a few weeks more.

Still, the work continued. Yetzer daily led his men to Morhavah. With each new moon, refusing to see Bilkis himself, he sent his scribe, the priest Elhoreb, to report on progress.

Nearly four years had passed since Eliam left on his three-year trade mission. With him still away, Yetzer had moved his mother from the merchant's house to the builders' town upon the western hill. Rahab and Gad had also moved up the hill, in part for love of Dvora and in part because they feared for their child in a city where Queen Bilkis was no longer a friend.

With each passing day Dvora slid deeper into the darkness of her second widowhood. Rahab kept Dvora company, while Gad instructed the workers' children—both boys and girls—in letters and numbers.

And then Rahab, breathless, ran toward Yetzer and Gad. "It's him!"

Yetzer looked up from the trestle board where he worked the final details for the two columns that would flank the temple's entrance.

Rahab fell into her husband's arms, grasped the front of his tunic and looked up at him with tear-filled eyes.

"Gad, it's him. It's Abba."

"Where?" the seer asked.

"Upon the Ebiren Road, just passing up from Beit-Lahmi with a train of donkeys that must be hundreds long."

Yetzer and Gad shared a look. Beit-Lahmi lay some twenty cable-lengths from Urusalim, about what a man could walk in two summer hours.

"At that distance," Yetzer said, "you'd have trouble telling a donkey from a hyrax. How can you be sure it's him?"

Rahab said nothing but fixed him with a reproachful look disturbingly like his mother's.

"It'll be dark by the time we reach him." Yetzer's objection fell limp as the woman chivvied them toward the town gate.

"And darker still when you return," she countered. "Best hasten on your way."

Both men's mouths fell open, then just as quickly closed as, by unspoken consent, they agreed on the futility of arguing.

"And no stopping by a tavern on your way," Rahab ordered as they passed through the gate. "I'll expect you back with my father by the night's second watch."

"Yes, my flower," Gad dutifully replied.

Yetzer stifled a laugh and received a backhanded smack to the chest from the prophet.

The late summer sun fell toward the horizon, but the two men reached the southern tip of Urusalim by the time the last sliver of fire sank from sight. A full moon lit the rugged terrain, and it was only a short time before the scattered glows of campfires dotted the distant landscape.

"Smells like a caravan," Gad observed as a southern breeze carried the earthy odors to them.

Yetzer grunted agreement, then cocked his head as though a different angle might give the advantage to his nose. Beneath the dung and fodder, sweat and smoke, a subtler, richer scent lay nearly hidden. A memory niggled at the fringes of Yetzer's heart, and it took several more paces before the recollection sprang up before him. The images upon the walls of the Hall of Postulants. The cold, hard flagstones beneath him. And the gentle, other-worldly smell.

"Olibanum," Yetzer said, more to himself than to Gad.

The seer sniffed and, after a few paces more, nodded.

A shouted challenge rang out from the edge of the camp. Yetzer and Gad held out their hands to show them empty as a short, dark-skinned man appeared with a slender spear in his hands.

"We seek the master of your caravan," Yetzer told him.

The small man studied the pair for a few moments, then called back over his shoulder to some unseen companion, his eyes never leaving the two men. After several more moments, a voice called back and the spearman shook his head.

"Come back in the morning," he told Yetzer and Gad, his words thickly accented. "Collect tolls then."

"We're not here for tolls," Gad said. "We seek the merchant Eliam abi-Terah. We're his sons."

The man eyed them warily but called again over his shoulder. A shout of surprise echoed from the camp, followed by the sight of a tall, slender figure hurrying toward them. Yetzer doubted the thin profile could belong to his kinsman, but there was no questioning the booming voice.

"My boys," Eliam cried.

He sped across the dusty ground and threw his arms around the younger men's necks, drawing them into a choking embrace.

"All thanks to Havah," he said, his voice muffled amid the crush. "I feared my eyes might never again behold these faces."

Eliam held the embrace for a moment longer. He loosened his grip but never lost hold of the other men, his hands clamped about their necks as he studied them.

"But where is Dvora?" he asked. "Where are Rahab and Abram?"

"Rahab and my mother even now prepare to celebrate your return," Yetzer said.

The older man's eyes glistened in the torchlight with that news but flitted from one man to the other as the remainder of his question went unanswered. A pained silence masked the noise of locusts and other night sounds until Gad softly cleared his throat.

"Abram has not yet returned," the seer muttered.

"Not returned?" Eliam lowered his trembling hands. "He should have returned a year before me."

"And you are a year late." Yetzer made an effort to keep his voice light. "Perhaps he tarries to make a more exciting return than his father."

"Of course," Eliam agreed, a pained smile stretching his lips. "He is his father's son, after all."

"Come." Gad clasped the older man's hand and took him by the elbow. "If your servants can be trusted, let them watch your goods this night. Your wife and your daughter will give us no rest until they may fuss over you."

Eliam's smile softened.

"Yes, yes," he said, then his brow furrowed. "But I don't suppose we might find a tavern along the way?"

53

Bilkis

Sunlight spilled across the threshold of the audience chamber, a golden carpet spread by the gods to welcome their servant home. Bilkis stood as Eliam entered. She stepped down from the dais, took the merchant's hands, and kissed his cheek.

"All thanks to the gods for returning you to us," she said as she stepped back. "When no word came from Edom for so long, we began to fear the worst. But come, sit. Tell me of your journey."

The queen led Eliam to the palace garden where cushions surrounded a low table laden with fruit, bread, and wine. She gestured the merchant to a seat then filled a cup for him. With a wave of her hand, Bilkis dismissed the guard who stood nearby, then sat opposite Eliam.

"It is good to be back, child," the merchant said, then tasted the wine. "Yah help me, I wish never to be away so long again."

"But your journey was a success?"

Bilkis had sent Benyahu to escort the caravan at first light, as soon as the guards at the city's southern watchtowers reported the trader's camp. The general would ensure the proper share made its way into the palace's storerooms. Already the queen could see the glittering gems, feel the supple silk, and taste the heady spices. The taste turned bitter at the merchant's expression, rancid with his words.

"Every journey is successful that brings the traveler home," he said, "but, sadly, the gods were not so generous as we might have hoped."

The queen's heart thrummed as Eliam told her of the voyage to Opiru and the cargo he'd taken on there—gold and gems, ivory and precious woods, pelts and spices. Bilkis took a deep quaff of wine to settle her stomach and steady her hands when the merchant described the shipwreck at the entrance to the Sea of Reeds, the Western Sea of her youth.

"So great a loss," she said, her voice wavering.

"Thirty men," Eliam intoned somberly. "Plus the ship's master."

"Yes," Bilkis said. "Of course, the men. But could nothing be saved?"

The merchant's eyes flitted to one side before he hid his face behind his cup.

"You return with a great train of donkeys," Bilkis pressed. "Surely the gods must have granted you some favor to return with hands not empty."

Eliam set down his wine and folded his hands upon the table. "I passed through Saba," he said after a moment's pause.

A nearly forgotten, instantly familiar coldness formed in Bilkis's stomach at the mention of her native country. "Why would you return there?" Her voice seemed that of a stranger. "You vowed you need not pass it on your travels."

"When the gods direct a thing, there is little man can do to change it. I did not betray your trust," Eliam hastened to add. "I mentioned only King Yahtadua. So far as Saba is concerned, the Shara Bilkis died these eighteen years past."

The coldness loosened its grip. Bilkis was mistress of her adopted country, ruler of the inland stretches of Kenahn. But before she was the King's Mother, before Auriyah had made her his bride, before Eliam had carried her from Saba, she'd been betrothed to a prince of Timnah, bound before the gods to become his wife. Should Bilkis's survival become known, Lord Watar might enforce his son's claim over her and take Yisrael's crown. Worse, she might be forced to return to those dust-clotted barrens at the edge of the world.

"You're certain you mentioned me to no one?"

"Upon Hadad's phallus," Eliam swore, "your name never passed my lips."

Bilkis gazed into his eyes for a long moment until she was satisfied with the truth in them.

"Very well," she said. "What are these donkeys of yours, then? Does my father send baskets of sand for the bronze works?"

"No, Lady," Eliam replied, a woeful expression in his eyes. "Your father rests with his blessed ancestors."

Nearly twenty years had passed since Bilkis had seen her father, and almost as many since she'd paid him more than a fleeting thought. Still, sorrow squeezed her heart.

"Who, then?" she wondered aloud. "Watar?" With Bilkis gone and none of Karibil's line to succeed him, the Council of Elders would have chosen a new ruler from among their number.

"No, Lady," Eliam said. "Your sister serves as Mukarrib of all Saba."

"Half-sister." The reply was born of some latent habit, and it took a moment for the meaning of Eliam's words to settle in. "Makeda is Mukarrib?"

"Even so," the merchant replied. "She rules her people wisely and well and is much beloved."

"The gods must have dealt harshly with them if they are happy to have a slave as their queen."

One of the palace guards approached and bowed before Bilkis.

"Pardon, Lady, but the scribe Elhoreb begs audience."

"Send him away," Bilkis commanded. "I'm busy."

"Apologies, Lady, but he claims his news is urgent."

"How urgent can a construction report be?" the queen asked no one in particular. "Very well, show him to my audience chamber. I'll be along shortly."

"Yes, Lady."

The guard bowed again and departed.

"I won't keep you, my dear," Eliam said as he rose from his cushions. "I'll send along your share of the trade when the caravan reaches the city."

"The crown's share of dirt?" Bilkis mused aloud.

"No, Lady. Olibanum. Not so great as the trade we'd hoped for, but it should cover ..."

The merchant's words trailed off. Whether because he'd stopped speaking or because fury plugged Bilkis's ears, she wasn't sure. She knew only that this merchant, one of the last few she could rely on, one she'd so long trusted, had failed her. Rage rose from her bowels and warped her words.

"I send you for gold, and you return with sap?"

"My lady—"

"I'll have none of it," Bilkis railed. "My entire childhood was tainted by its stink. The very thought now pollutes my nostrils."

"My child, please."

"I am not your child," Bilkis snarled as she stood to face the old fool. "I've shown favor to you and your family because you rescued me from that miserable country. Now you would befoul my palace and my temple with its stench? Get out."

Eliam began to protest again, but a guard's grip on the back of his neck silenced him.

"Take him from my sight," the queen ordered. "He is never to enter the palace again."

The guard led the simpering merchant away. Bilkis stormed toward her rooms, then remembered the waiting Elhoreb. She deemed the priest a better target for her fury than her vases and bowls, so stalked instead toward her audience chamber.

"This had best be important," she said as she burst into the small room.

Elhoreb jerked his head toward the queen then froze, as a rabbit caught by sudden torchlight. The scribe sat in Bilkis's chair, feet stretched out before him. He lurched from the chair, fell to the floor, then crawled to Bilkis and kissed her sandals.

"Enough," the queen said, and kicked him away. "Deliver your report, then be gone."

The man rubbed his reddening cheek—a delighted smile on his lips as he waited for Bilkis to sit—then sat across from her.

"I have little news about the temple, my lady," he said. "Stones are stacked a bit higher than when last we met."

"Then why do you bother me?"

"For this."

The scribe held up a scroll, his countenance beaming with pride.

"You bring me a message from your master?" Bilkis asked. Her tone was cold, but a part of her hoped it was so, longed for even a scribbled word from Yetzer.

"Not from him, Lady," Elhoreb said. "To him. Or, more exactly, about him."

"I haven't the patience for riddles," Bilkis warned him.

"Your pardon, my lady," the scribe begged without a scrap of sincerity. "But did not the queen command that I seek out some means of turning the builder's secrets to her advantage?"

Bilkis drew a stuttering breath. She had, indeed, given him that command. The master masons she'd summoned had all been as stubborn as Yetzer. Every one of them refused to impart to Yahtadua the secret word by which master builders throughout the nations recognized one another. Might this scroll bear the secret that eluded her?

"Not the word, Lady," Elhoreb said, and Bilkis snapped her head toward him, not realizing she'd asked the question aloud. "But perhaps something even more valuable." The scribe made a show of unrolling the scroll and angled it for the queen to see. Neat rows of figures in black and red ink filled the sheet with birds and feathers and other shapes.

"You bring me a child's picture-scroll?" she said.

"No, my lady," Elhoreb replied in a hushed, reverent tone. "This is the sacred writing of Kemet."

Unimpressed, Bilkis peered at the stick figures and scribbled forms.

"And you can give them voice?"

"Alas, Lady, I cannot. Knowledge of the glyphs is limited to the holy priests of Kemet." The scribe's face resembled that of a cat's after it dropped a mauled rat at its master's feet.

"Shall I have my guards throw you from the wall or will you provide worthy information?"

A bit of bluster drained away with the color from Elhoreb's cheeks.

"Your pardon, my lady."

He unrolled the scroll further to reveal another set of neatly spaced figures, different from the upper picture-writing.

"This is the common script of Kemet, used by merchants and generals."

Bilkis's cold stare somehow wilted the scribe's smug expression. He cleared his throat, held the scroll to the light, and began to read.

"He who bears this is the friend of Pharaoh Horemheb Djeserkheperure, Chosen of Ra. Into his hands shall be given whatsoever he desires, even should he ask for half my kingdom. The blessings of Amun be upon all who come to his aid, for such a one shall have aided Pharaoh himself."

The queen's first hint that she was staring at the wretched scribe was the dryness in her eyes. She blinked a few times, then covered her mouth with a trembling hand as she licked her lips.

"Half the kingdom."

"A courtesy, my lady," Elhoreb hastened to explain. "It is the habit of—"

Bilkis didn't hear the rest of his prattle as she stormed to the door of the audience chamber and flung it open. "Summon Yahshepat," she ordered the nearest guard. "We have a message to send."

54

Yetzer

Yetzer stood atop the southwest corner of the Most Holy Place. The limestone blocks enclosed a perfect cube, twenty cubits in each dimension. Five cubits more must be added around the sanctuary, and yet again five to the portico, but the *Debir*, the place of divine communion, lay ready for its roof of cedar timbers.

A smudge on the horizon drew Yetzer's attention from the stones, from the men, from the ropes and pulleys and wheels that raised his imagination into the realm of being. The low rays of morning's sun slashed along the sky to cast a yellow-brown haze along the southern approaches to Urusalim.

Not since Eliam had returned, since his donkeys laden with incense had ferried the wealth to feed Yetzer's men and their families, not in six months had a caravan of more than a half-dozen spavined beasts come up the road from Edom. No mere handful of underfed asses raised this cloud of dust.

Yetzer chided himself. The winds would soon disperse the sands that rose above the horizon. Time would draw the travelers near. But with only a year remaining to deliver Yah and Havah's temple, Queen Bilkis would bide no dalliance. The first of a new course of blocks edged its way above the top of the wall.

"Set to her, lads," he called.

The words were needless, as his well-practiced men looped ropes about the ashlar, suspended from its timber frame, to haul the shaped limestone into place.

Yetzer cast a final, curious glance toward the south, then drew the stone maul from his belt to bless the start of the temple's thirtieth course.

55
Bilkis

"**A** caravan, my lady," Benyahu announced to the court.
Bilkis looked up from where Marah, Yahtadua's bride from Yehuda, nursed her newborn son.

"The roads of Yisrael see many caravans," the queen told her general. "Unless it comes from the west—"

"The south, my lady," Benyahu clarified.

"Then what is it to me? Does Edom produce more than dust? Does Elath breed aught but salt?"

"My lady," the warrior pressed.

"Disturb not my grandson," Bilkis snapped, and the audience hall filled with the wails of Yahtadua's heir. "Look what you have done. Send a rider if you must. Collect what tolls may be had, if they be of any value. Only leave us in peace."

"As you say, my lady," Benyahu grumbled. The general bowed low, his burnished scalp shining brightly beneath thinning grey hair. Benyahu turned and stalked from the hall. His obedience had seemed more grudging during the last few months, but Bilkis cared little. Yahtadua, her heart's delight, had produced an heir from his father's tribe. The greatest of Yisrael's clans was staunchly behind the throne, and the rest would soon follow.

"I think I'll take the sun, my lamb," Bilkis told the king.

Yahtadua—at sixteen, his manhood secured—scarcely glanced up from where the infant greedily suckled his mother's teat. "As you wish," he said, and just managed to tilt his head to receive the queen's kiss on his cheek.

Bilkis left the hall, with its slupping infant and simpering consorts. Silence held vigil in the palace's cedar-lined corridors, a welcome respite from what had become a noisy, unruly throne room. When the doors of her chamber closed behind her, the queen leaned against them briefly and pressed a hand to her warm cheek.

A cup of cool water soothed her throat and calmed her breast, washing away the irritations of court. Bilkis considered dropping her gown, but her roof was easily seen from the city and from Havah's hill. Though she longed to feel the sun's warmth upon her skin, that pleasure was not worth the cost. She had no more need to invite men's desires, and she would not debase herself before mere peasants.

The queen climbed the steps to the roof, moved to the parapet and leaned her elbows upon it. The city spread away to the south, a desert of ocher-colored buildings speckled with awnings of red and blue and yellow. Upon the fortress tower flew Yahtadua's banner with its rearing lion that pawed at a six-pointed star.

A rider descended from the Tower Gate and, before long, the flawless blue sky became sullied with the dust of the earth as it dared rise to the heavens.

Bilkis turned away, her throat made ragged by the mere sight of so much dust. Once her temple was complete, once her fame and glory spread among the nations, she would welcome the caravans with their offerings and tributes. Until then, she craved only the arrival of Kemeti gold, perhaps more. The queen sat beneath her awning, poured a cup of wine, and freed her thoughts of the dirty caravan from the south.

56

Makeda

I grimaced as my camel lurched upon a patch of uneven ground. My craftsmen had fashioned a magnificent saddle for me, shaped and supported and padded to provide comfort on my travels. No amount of skill, however, could ease the burden of sitting atop a camel for the better part of every daylight hour over a span of six months.

The camel brayed, and I reached forward to pat the beast's neck. "Yes, Dhahbas, yes," I said in a placating tone. "You're a wonderful companion, much better than some donkey."

The camel twitched her ears and jangled her harness as she plodded along the northward trail. I shifted my weight to find a less painful position. I knew not how women had managed on earlier caravans, carried by donkeys that took twice as long to cover great distances. The gods had blessed me with beasts ideally suited to this journey, but I longed to give my bones rest.

"My lady." A gruff voice spoke and raised my thoughts above my aching backside. I turned to see Hazar, captain of my guard, as he brought his mount even with mine. "A rider," the warrior said, and pointed toward the horizon.

I squinted in the indicated direction. I could just make out something that might be a dust cloud but that could just as well be a shimmering of air. "Very well," I told him.

The sun was halfway to her zenith before the cloud drew close enough for me to pick out the shape of a rider amid the dust. Hazar signaled to his nearest men to form a protective screen around me.

As had happened several times during our journey, the approaching horse shied as it neared the camels, and the shout of its rider echoed across the plain. Camels were not uncommon in the lands about the great eastern desert, but mostly traveled in wild herds, or occasionally driven by Bedou herdsmen.

Before this journey, I'd never imagined a caravan of laden camels, let alone mounted by riders. From the reactions we received along the way, it seemed a safe guess that no one else had either.

After a short discussion with Hazar, the rider turned his horse back along the northern track, and the captain returned.

"He was from the court of Yahtadua," Hazar said as he drew his camel alongside mine.

"Are we that close?" I peered into the distance.

"We should see the walls of Urusalim before noon."

My heart—along with my rump—gave thanks that the journey might soon end.

"Did he not want tribute?"

Hazar gave a wry grin. "He did. I told him to take his pick of camels. He said it could wait until we reach the city."

We continued northward. Workers in the fields paused in their labors to gape at our passing caravan. I found myself gaping as well, not at the people but at the surrounding countryside. The hills and valleys glowed a brilliant green under the gentle touch of the springtime sun.

The scene reminded me of the fields and gardens about Maryaba, but these needed no dam, no network of irrigation canals to carry the life-giving water. Moisture seemed to spring from the very earth, as attested by the droplets that clung to grass blades not yet touched by the sun.

A shout sounded before us, and Hazar urged his camel ahead to where a rider jounced upon his donkey, trotting toward the caravan. The rider called and waved, and recognition dawned as he neared.

"Let him pass," I ordered, then smiled as the rider drew near.

"Welcome, my lady!" he greeted me, his broad smile as warm as summer.

"Well met, Eliam," I said. "I'm happy to see you returned home safely."

"Safe and well," the merchant said, and patted his belly, grown fat since I'd last seen him. "Thanks to you, my lady. When I heard the rumors of a train of camels coming from the south, I scarcely believed it would be you, though I prayed it might."

"After your tales of the temple, how could I not come see for myself?" I gestured toward the line of camels behind me. "I have brought gifts for your King Yahtadua, as a token of goodwill and a hope for his friendship. When might I meet him?"

The merchant's bright expression dimmed with the question. "I saw the king's general—I believe you met him along the road? I passed him on his way back to the city and asked that he arrange an audience. In the meantime, I have a plot of land below the city, where you are welcome to stay during your visit."

"Will it hold us all?" When encamped, our caravan filled enough land that might otherwise feed twenty families for a year.

"Yes, Lady, not to worry. Porters should even now be carrying up water and fodder, and wood for fires."

"Wood?" I said, surprised. Such extravagance.

"Of course, my lady. Dung fires are prohibited about the royal city."

"Athtar smile upon you, my friend," I said, suddenly aware of how tired I felt, and how ragged I must look.

I longed to be still, to bathe, to look forward to a morrow when I needn't take to the saddle. But I also remembered the reason for my journey.

"Now, when may I meet your family and see this temple of yours?"

❀

A red-faced Eliam huffed alongside Dhahbas as he escorted my smaller caravan up the winding road to Tsion, Urusalim's royal hill. I'd offered, almost begged to walk with the merchant, but he insisted I ride.

"All of Yisrael will want to see the marvel of the queen who tamed the wild beast," he'd said.

So I rode at the head of a shortened camel train. Dhahbas, perfumed and draped with silk trappings, led five other beasts, each laden with a sampling of the great treasure recovered from the Strait of Tears. Hazar and another guard rode with me while the rest of the travelers, beast and man, remained in the camp near the city's spring.

I strained my neck as I looked up from the bottom of the hillside to the stone wall about the city. A banner of blue and white beat at the wind from its post atop the fortress that dominated the narrow valley.

Less impressive was the sewage that flowed from openings in the wall and cascaded to a cesspit at the foot of the mount. Mercifully, the wind carried the stench away and the air soon filled with the shouted greetings of people along the road.

Children, everywhere the same, gawped at the passing camels. My eyes were just as wide as I took in the hundreds, thousands of people who lined the way. They seemed to rival the entire population of Maryaba for number, and that was only the portion who had turned out. Among the fields and pastures were many more. Yisrael must be a great and blessed country, indeed, to be able to feed and clothe so many.

Or, perhaps, not so many.

As we neared the gate, my heart ached at the sight of the hungry and naked beggars that lined the wall, hands outstretched for mercy. The camels carried no food. Even if they had, the press of well-wishers would have made it impossible to reach the needy. Eliam urged a boy out of the road as he led us around the final bend.

I glanced back along the wall, the height of three men and longer than the widest stretch of the Wadi Dhanah. Even if not all prospered, a people capable of such a work could surely build a dam to last through the ages.

As we reached the city's entrance, I bent low in my saddle, hugging Dhahbas's neck to avoid striking the gate's lintel. Candle smoke and the smell of decayed offerings filled the passage. It took several of the camel's long strides before Eliam ushered us back into daylight.

Another wall, this one made from rows of smoothed stones and wooden beams stretched along one side of the broad road, its other side fronted by massive mudbrick buildings. Flowers climbed lattices along the walls, while the leaves of small trees joined the occupants in peeking over the parapets. The buzz of voices, laughter of children, and barking of dogs stirred the air.

A second, smaller gate passed through the inner wall, perhaps high enough for a mounted horseman to pass, but too low for the camels. Eliam led me to a wooden platform before the gate. Upon it stood a tall, well-fed young man surrounded by a dozen or more girls. All wore silk, brightly dyed and finely woven, and all wore looks of wonder.

I drew on the camel's reins. *"Khara,"* I commanded Dhahbas.

Excited murmurs rose from the crowd as the camel settled onto her knees and haunches, followed by the others in the train. Eliam offered his hand to help me down from the saddle, then guided me up the steps of the platform. The merchant bowed low before the young man.

"Rise, Eliam," the lad said in a voice much younger than befitted so noble an appearance. "You have kept yourself too long from our gates."

"My humblest apologies, Lord," the merchant said. "I did not wish to disturb your young and growing family."

The boy made a gesture that conveyed both acceptance and impatience, then stared pointedly at me.

"My lord Yahtadua abi-Tadua, King of Yisrael," Eliam said in a tone rich with formality, "I beg to present Makeda umm-Ayana, Mukarrib of all Saba."

"Mukarrib?" Yahtadua said and looked as though the word tickled his lips.

"Queen of my people," I explained, "and high priestess of our gods."

"And your king permits you to leave the harem, to leave your country?" The question seemed to hold both curiosity and distaste.

"We have no harem in Saba," I said, making an effort to keep my voice even. "And we have no king at present. My father was Mukarrib, and my mother after him. Now I am honored to serve my people."

"Surely you have a husband," Yahtadua said, his distaste now bordering on offense, "for how can a woman hold a country?"

I swallowed back my indignation. After so long a journey, I had thought to be welcomed, not to have my traditions questioned.

"I am wife to no man," I said in a firm, level tone, "but bride to the high god Athtar. My husband has blessed our land, and I have brought the fruits of that bounty, as a token of the friendship I hope will grow between our two great nations."

"What have you brought me?" Yahtadua asked, the tone of a quarrelsome king replaced by that of an overindulged child. "Can I have the camels, too?"

Eliam gave me a smile and a wink as I joined Yahtadua at the edge of the platform.

"Of course, you may," I said, warmth restored to my voice. "The two bulls and three cows should make an excellent breeding herd."

"These are even better than a chariot," Yahtadua said. Casting off his dignity, and much to the delight of the onlookers, the King of Yisrael hopped down from the platform and rushed toward one of the kneeling camels. The young bull flattened its ears, bellowed and reared back its head. Yahtadua held out a hand and spoke gently to the startled beast, who returned the kindness by gnashing at the royal fingers. The lad snatched back his hand, tripped and fell on his backside in the dust of the high road.

A deathly hush fell over the crowd at their king's humiliation. When he began laughing, however, the people heartily joined in with him.

"These are not pets, my lamb," said a hauntingly familiar voice from behind me. "They must be treated with gentleness and caution."

The assembly again fell silent. I turned as a chill snaked up my spine and raised goose flesh on my arms. A woman stood at the rear of the platform, dressed in a fine blue gown and veil. Eliam and the girls fell to their knees, the motion copied by all the people. Yahtadua dashed up the steps and stood beside the veiled figure.

"Umma, this is Makeda of Saba. She's brought us gifts. Makeda, this is my mother."

The woman stood motionless for some time, seeming to examine me with her hidden eyes. For an age, I heard nothing, felt nothing, saw nothing more than the featureless blue veil, endless as the sea. When it seemed enough time had passed to turn the mountains of Saba into sand, the woman reached up and drew back her veil.

My stomach clenched, my heart swelled, and tears spilled from my eyes. I stepped forward, haltingly at first, then with greater speed. The woman drew back, but I would not let her escape. I threw my arms about the woman's neck and held her close.

"My sister," I cried.

57

Bilkis

Bilkis struggled to breathe, so tightly did the half-breed cling to her. With effort, she lifted her arms and gently patted Makeda's back. "There, there," she said. "All is well."

"Is it truly you?" Makeda released her hold and gazed at Bilkis, studied her face, pulled her close again. "We thought the gods had taken you from us." Her words were muffled by her sobs and Bilkis's hair.

"Indeed they did," Bilkis replied when she could grasp breath to speak. She freed herself from Makeda's clutch and held her half-sister's hands, almost hot to the touch. When had her own gone so cold?

Bilkis studied the younger woman, so different from the child she'd left behind those many years before. The round-faced brat had grown into a tall, slender woman. With the high cheekbones and full lips, Bilkis might have been looking at her own reflection upon polished jet, but for the piss-colored eyes.

"The gods delivered me from the flood," she explained, "then again from the desert. Our friend Eliam found me and took me into his care. He brought me with his family to Urusalim, where the gods of Yisrael have truly blessed me. Now rise, Eliam," she told the merchant, her tone warm and generous. "Rise, all my people, and rejoice with me, for the holy ones have restored to me my sister." She barely managed to choke back *half.*

Cheers of jubilation and wonder dutifully rose from the assembly. Bilkis gestured for Yahtadua to stand with her. "But we are being ungracious hosts," she told the lad. "Come, let us see what your aunt has brought you."

58

Makeda

I floated, drifted, fell. And I cared not. Bilkis had insisted I stay in the palace, rather than camp with my people outside the walls.

"I have been kept too long from your company," she'd said. "I will not so easily again be parted from you."

At first, I refused the offer. Now, as I soaked in a copper tub filled with hot, rose-scented water, behind walls that did not move with every breath of wind, I thanked Athtar for Bilkis's craft of persuasion.

Fazia, my handmaid, brought up my things and promptly turned a set of rooms into a second Saba. Goat hair mats adorned floors and walls. Brass censers filled with myrrh, olibanum, and spices smoked in every corner. With the scents and textures of home about me, I let the water steep the aches from my muscles, while Fazia combed the sand from my hair and scrubbed the grit from my skin.

That evening, Bilkis laid a great feast of roasted kid and lamb, fruits of every variety, and rich wine the color of blood. I tried to be a polite guest, but the sun had only just disappeared behind the western hill when I begged leave of Bilkis and Yahtadua and retired to my bed.

Daylight again peered through the shuttered windows when I opened my eyes. After a bath and a repast of cold lamb and figs, I dressed simply in a dun-colored woolen robe and soft boots.

"The demons did not carry you away in the night, after all," Bilkis said when I found her in the audience chamber.

I smiled, took my sister's outstretched hands, and kissed her on the cheek. "I've not slept so well since leaving Maryaba." I accepted a cup of goat's milk from Bilkis and was about to drink when I saw a pair of crystalline lumps floating in the cup. "What is this?"

Bilkis laughed. "Ice, my sister. Water that has grown so cold it becomes as stone."

I poked one of the lumps, and it bobbed away from my touch. "I've never seen a stone float. Can you build with it? Could you make a ship of it?"

"I am told that far to the north, beyond even Mount Lebanon where my ice is mined, there are tribes of men who make their homes of ice. Unfortunately, it melts too quickly in water to make it useful for shipbuilding. But even as it again becomes water it leaves a most wondrous gift."

Bilkis gestured for me to drink. I sniffed at the milk then took a tentative sip. My eyes widened as the sweet liquid caressed my tongue, colder than floodwater or darkest night. The cold milk stirred my spirit and brightened my mood. What a land of marvels Bilkis had found, with entire buildings made of stout timbers, great walls of solid rock, and magical water that turned to stone.

"Might I see your temple today?" I asked after I drained my cup. "Eliam has told me it's magnificent."

Bilkis's countenance darkened as under a passing cloud, then just as quickly brightened again. "Of course," she said cheerily. "I've not been there in some months. It would be good to see what progress has been made."

A short time later I rode with Bilkis, Yahtadua, and a pair of his young wives upon a canopied wooden platform carried by servants. The litter rocked gently upon the men's shoulders as they snaked along the hillside road north of the palace. People knelt as the king and queen-mother passed by, and it took only a short time to reach the hill's summit. With scarcely a jostle, the servants lowered their burden to the ground. Yahtadua pulled back the curtain and leapt from the carriage.

"That child," Bilkis said in a low tone as the young queens quickly followed their husband. "Abi-Huram slights him, but still Yahtadua can't wait to visit him."

"Abi-Huram?" I said. I yearned to follow my nephew, to dash out and explore the wonder I'd so long dreamed of but didn't wish to be rude.

"My temple-builder," Bilkis said, in a tone with which she might refer to a wart. "How the gods ever chose to breathe life into such a disagreeable man, I know not."

I frowned. "Eliam claims he is aided by the birds of the air, the beasts of the field, even the demons of the Pit."

Bilkis scoffed and gestured as though she were waving away a bothersome fly.

"Then why did you choose him?" I asked.

"I assure you, I did not," Bilkis said, then swung her legs out of the litter. "The gods of this land have greatly blessed me, but the price of their goodness is that I must endure this mason. But no matter. Come, see my little tribute."

I stepped out after her and felt a wonder greater even than when I'd stood before the ruins of lost Eram.

Blocks of polished stone sprang from the hilltop, straining, it seemed, to reach the very heavens. The neatly stacked walls surpassed the height of the tower house in Maryaba, and stretched so far and wide they might have enclosed my entire city. Scores of men sang in harmony as they moved around and upon the structure, hauling ropes or carrying burdens in a grand, chaotic dance.

Twin rails of heavy timber ran along the sides and front of the temple. Upon these rested great wooden creatures. Their long, spindly legs resembled those of a heron or some other water bird, and their necks reached even higher than the walls. Where the body would have been, there sat a spoked wheel, within which a pair of men animated the beast.

"Welcome, my lady," said a gentle voice that rose above the singing.

I turned to see a young man dressed in a crisp white robe and turban. He bowed to Bilkis then turned to me.

"My sister," Bilkis offered by way of introduction.

"Ah," the lad said, and offered a polite bow. "You're the one who has sparked so much wonder. I am Natan umm-Havah, priest of Yah and Havah. On behalf of our gods and our people, I thank you for your gifts."

"The gods have more than repaid me by restoring my sister to me," I said. "Though my gift seems a small thing compared to such a marvel as this."

Natan glanced over his shoulder toward the nascent temple and gave a smile, an expression that seemed to come easily to him. The young priest began to speak, but was interrupted by a sharp crack that rang across the building site. Song turned to shouts as men dropped their burdens and scrambled away. I looked toward the commotion, to where workers shouted for one of their comrades to move. Heedless of their warnings, the man tugged on his rope, which was spooled about the base of one of the wooden birds. The machine reluctantly turned on its pivot and swung away from the temple wall.

Another crack drew my attention to the ropes that ran from the wheel, up the bird's neck, then down to a large stone block. A pair of the braided cables had snapped, and the stone swayed drunkenly in its cradle.

A thunderous voice bellowed an order, and the men within the wheel began moving in the opposite direction, as though climbing down a ladder. A large man, stoutly built and bearing a wooden staff, shouted another order as he sprinted toward the worker who held the rope. He'd almost reached the other man when the last cable failed.

The stone plunged toward the earth with terrible speed. The worker beneath it finally released his line but fell as he tried to move away. Man and stone met the ground in the same instant. The man with the staff raced onward, then disappeared in the cloud of white dust that bloomed from the horror.

As if the man were one of my own people and without thought to the shouts behind me, I ran into the cloud. I coughed and stumbled my way through the blinding dust that clogged my nostrils, caked my throat, and stung my eyes. Following the deep voice that spoke now in softer tones, I moved farther into the cloud until I saw the man's spectral outline. He must have noticed me as well as he pointed to one side.

"Be ready to pull him clear when I say."

Without a word, I felt my way to the fallen man's shoulders and rolled the fabric of his tunic into my fists. I settled my weight as I heard a sharp intake of breath and the groan of wood.

"Now," a strained voice said.

I leaned back and pushed with my legs. The earth was reluctant to loosen its hold on the man, but at last relented. A finger's breadth he moved, then three, then five more. I lost my balance and landed on my backside, dragging the man atop me.

The ground shuddered as the stone fell clear of the man's legs. I slipped out from under him as gently as I could. His eyes were closed and the dust had painted his face with a deathly pallor, but his chest rose and fell with shallow breaths. I ran my eyes along the rest of his body.

My stomach twisted when I reached the mangled remains of his leg.

"Come away, my lady," I heard through the drumming of my heartbeat in my ears. Gentle hands raised me by my shoulders, while men moved in to tend their comrade. I tore my eyes from the carnage and looked down to see it was Yahtadua's young wives who guided me away.

"Oh, my sister," Bilkis said when we reached her, "what were you thinking? You might have been hurt. And you look a mess."

"I'm fine," I said.

"Just like that fool to endanger his men, giving them cheap ropes while he puts gold in his purse. Come," Bilkis said, and led the way to the litter. "I'll not stand here to watch more men die."

"He lives still," I said as the girls helped me into the carrying platform behind Bilkis, "but one leg was shattered."

"All the more shame." Bilkis leaned back upon her cushions and stifled a yawn. "The gods would have been more merciful to carry him to Sheol. As it is, he'll most likely land among the beggars at the gate."

I glanced back toward the temple where the man with the staff—the temple-builder himself, I reasoned—joined three other men in raising the newly made cripple upon a litter. Anger welled within me at the thought of a poor man brought to ruin by his master's greed.

Yahtadua pulled the curtain closed, and the litter lurched as the servants raised it to their shoulders. I silently denounced abi-Huram to my gods, this man who would, for a few scraps of gold, sell the well-being of those entrusted to him. I begged Athtar to rain dust and ruin upon abi-Huram's head, as the builder had brought them upon the heads of I knew not how many others.

I shivered as a coldness I'd never known settled over me. As waters turned to ice in the distant northlands, so my heart became as stone. I had hoped to find a builder for my dam, to secure the future of my people. I could not, however, entrust that future to one who so little regarded those in his care. The gods, I decided, would have to show me another way.

59

Yetzer

"Whose mark was on the rope?" Yetzer demanded of Elhoreb, trying and failing to keep his voice level.

"I don't know, Master," the priest-turned-scribe said.

"Who attested to the ropes having been replaced?"

"I don't know, Master."

"Then find out," Yetzer barked. "One of my men, a life entrusted to me, almost lost that life. As the gods live, he will surely lose his leg. If the rope was new, I would know who wove it. If it was old, I would know why it was still in use."

"As you say," Elhoreb replied, "but it will take some time to find the records."

"Then start looking." The words grated against Yetzer's throat. He made an effort to quell the rage that boiled within him. "And draw up a transfer for some of my lands in Naftali. If Pelti cannot work, I shall at least see that he and his family can eat. Three yokes should do. No, make it six."

"So much?" Elhoreb asked. "He has but three children—"

The scribe ended his protest when Yetzer glowered at him.

"It shall be even as you say, Master."

Yetzer gave a curt nod then ducked beneath the lintel of his scribe's house. He absently accepted words of comfort and good will as he passed his men and their families on the way to Pelti's little cottage. He'd left the man unconscious with a wailing wife, sobbing children, and a butcher he'd promised a purse of silver if he could cleanly remove the leg.

When Yetzer reached the house, wails no longer filled the air, rather the reek of hot pitch and scorched flesh. He knocked on the doorpost and stooped to enter.

Pelti lay on his mat, eyes closed, face drawn and wan. His blanket seemed misshapen as it covered one leg whole, the other foreshortened. Still, the man breathed steadily. His children huddled about him, the youngest in the lap of their mother who sang a song of the ancestors.

"It went well?" Yetzer asked the bloody-aproned butcher.

The man grunted and finished wiping down his grisly tools. "Well as can be. The bone was whole just below the knee, so I was able to take it at the joint." He nodded toward a bucket covered by a scarlet-stained cloth.

"I'll take you at your word," Yetzer said. He little doubted the leg would find its way into a pigsty that evening and made a silent vow to refrain from pork for a time. Yetzer offered a pouch to the butcher.

"For your good care."

The man weighed the purse in his meaty hand and smiled. He threw it in with his tools and gathered them up along with the bucket.

"Why me?" he asked Yetzer before he left. "Why not call for a priest of Havah or of Hadad?"

"If I want someone to tend a man's shade or read entrails, I'll call a priest. If I want someone to tend to the body, I'd sooner have one who knows how a body is put together."

The man shook his head as he left. Yetzer spoke briefly with Pelti's wife, a plain creature with eyes and nose like a hawk's. He gave her another purse, this one filled with gold, and assured her they could stay in the workers' town as long as they wished. Their land would be waiting. Yetzer accepted a hug from the woman, intoned a blessing upon Pelti and the children, then left the little family in peace.

The sun had begun to creep behind the hills, and the streets grew quiet as people gathered in their homes for the evening meal. Yetzer started toward Elhoreb's house to help his scribe search the records, when a lone figure caught his glance.

A woman, lean of figure and dark of complexion, wandered among the houses, a woven basket balanced atop her head.

"Are you lost?" Yetzer asked as he found himself standing before her.

The woman looked up, and Yetzer's heartbeat trebled. Eyes like liquid gold bored into him. A long nose and proud cheekbones sat above slightly parted lips that revealed straight, white teeth. Recognition dawned in those remarkable eyes, and the lips pursed together.

"You," the woman hissed at him. Freckles stood out on her dark skin as blood coursed into her cheeks. The basket shifted on her head, and Yetzer reached out to help her steady it and lower it to the ground. The woman jerked her hand back from where Yetzer's touched hers on the handle.

"You would do well to see to the care of those in your trust, rather than lining your purse with their sweat and blood." She poked a slender finger against his chest before continuing. "To be raised over a people, to hold their fortunes in your hands is a sacred trust, not a means to enrich yourself."

Warm, dry air rolled over Yetzer's lips as his mouth fell open in silent reply. The woman glared at him and he had a feeling, if the stories of *mashitim* shooting fire from their eyes were true, she would have burned him down where he stood. The angry, beautiful, avenging angel stooped to take up her basket, then disappeared through Pelti's doorway.

Yetzer stood there, silent as a lamb before its shearer. Few people ever spoke to him in such a manner. The only women to do so were his mother and the queen. For this stranger to lash out at him with such righteous fury was as startling as it was undeserved. He needed no lessons, yet this woman would teach him the proper treatment of his own people? Outrageous.

The temple-builder turned away—and a smile crept along his lips.

60

Makeda

I wandered slowly down the hillside. I was lost, confused, and not by the foreign landscape. The workman's wife had accepted my token of olibanum, the trade of which should feed the little family for two years or more.

"What merciful gods," the woman had said, "to heap such blessings atop sorrow."

She'd gone on to describe how the Master Builder had bestowed enough gold and lands to tend to her great-grandchildren.

It was a poor miser who would enrich himself at his people's expense only to give away his wealth to ease the pain he'd caused. Either this Yetzer abi-Huram was a king of fools, or Bilkis had told me wrong. I saw no reason for my sister to mislead me, but the accounting she'd given of her temple-builder now seemed unjust.

The half moon lit my way to the bottom of Urusalim's western hill. The sound of a rolling pebble made me turn and look back, but I saw nothing more than the stark landscape cloaked in night's embrace. I followed the cart path across a narrow valley, then began the short climb up to the royal city.

The smell of beggars grew stronger as I neared the gate. I chided myself for not bringing food, but Bilkis must surely provide for them.

"What do you want, little sister?" asked a gruff voice in a thickly accented slur. The guardsman at the gate swayed a little and leaned upon his spear as he might a walking staff. His companion stood against the wall and lowered a wineskin from his lips as I approached.

"Gates are closed," the second man said after wiping his mouth with the back of his hand. "Come back tomorrow to ply your trade."

"I'm not—" I began, but the first guard spoke over me.

"Of course, for a sampling of your wares we could let you in." He stood up straight—straighter, in any case—and lumbered toward me. "But you'd have to open your gates to us first."

"I have no wares," I said, and backed away a few steps. "I wish only to go to the palace."

"The palace, is it?" the other guard said as he moved to flank me. "And what business would a little duck like you have at the palace?"

"I'm the queen's sister," I said, making an effort to put authority in my voice even as I backed away a few more steps.

The guards followed my retreat, and I found myself moving deeper into a shadowed corner of the gatehouse.

"Her sister, eh?" the first guard retorted. "Why, I'm brother to the Prince of Subartu. That makes us royal relations. Come, sweet one, and give your cousin a kiss."

The guards closed in on me. I tried to cry out, but one of them covered my mouth with his. The men pinned my arms against the wall. One roughly fondled my breasts, while the other tried to raise my skirts.

A whistling sound sliced through the air, followed by a sickening crack. One of the attackers released me and slid to the ground. A hand emerged from the sleeve of a black cloak, then clamped beneath the remaining guard's chin and jerked him away from me.

The guard alternately tore at the hands and beat at the arms of this cloaked savior. His assault became more frantic as the figure lifted him from the ground by his throat.

"Shall I kill him?" a man asked in a deep, incongruously soft tone.

I adjusted my robe and wiped the guard's saliva from my mouth.

"No," I said, my voice tight. "There's no real harm done."

"As you wish," the man replied.

He threw his captive to the ground. The guard called out in strangled tones, and his cry turned to a scream as the tall figure raised his staff and brought it down between the man's legs.

"Perhaps that will teach you to treat women with respect."

Another voice shouted a challenge from atop the wall. An arrow sprouted from the ground with a hiss. My rescuer took me firmly but gently by the wrist.

"Let us away," he said. "They'll more likely kill us than bother to learn what's happened."

I nodded and pulled close to the man as another arrow whistled past. His body was firm, his cloak smelled of olibanum. He wrapped a stout arm about my shoulders and guided me through the press of curious beggars.

Keeping to the moon-cast shadows, we followed a track to the edge of the city wall, crossed a shallow ditch, then started up the slope of the northern hill. When the brush and trees hid us from view of the palace, my guide led me beneath the boughs of a thick-trunked tree and released his hold.

I sank to my knees as the fear that had filled my veins drained away. The night air fell cold across my shoulders where the man's arm had been, and I fought the urge to draw nearer to him as he knelt before me.

"Are you hurt?" he asked as he pulled back the hood of his cloak.

"No. I'm—"

The words dashed against my teeth as moonlight revealed the face of Yetzer abi-Huram. A scarf covered the left side of his face, and wan light bounced off the embroidered eye there. His natural one shone with concern.

"I'm all right," I stammered. "Thank you."

"I should thank you," he said with a smile that drove away the shadows. "Your kindness to Pelti and his family was— " He seemed to struggle to find the word. "Unexpected. My name is Yetzer abi-Huram."

Of course, it was, I thought before it dawned on me I hadn't given him the chance to introduce himself earlier.

"I'm Makeda umm-Ayana," I said, then frowned as the light flickered out in Yetzer's eye.

61

Yetzer

"Makeda?" Yetzer said. "Queen of Saba?"

Bitterness squeezed his heart. He'd thought this woman a *mashit*, an angel of mercy and righteousness. She was just another lady of high birth—the very sister of Bilkis, if Natan's gossip was true. As he studied her features, the moonlight gave truth to the rumor. What he'd mistaken for generosity had clearly been some means for Bilkis to gain advantage.

"Yes," Makeda replied, "but—"

"My apologies, Lady," Yetzer interrupted. "I'll see you back to the palace."

"What about the guards?" Makeda asked, her tone that of a child denied a treat.

Yetzer considered that. He'd happily face the Pelesti arrows to rid himself of this royal nuisance. Fear, however, seemed to creep in with the petulance in the queen's eyes. He silently cursed himself as the weaker part of his nature, that part he feared would ever put a woman's pleas above his better judgment, did just that.

"Very well," he said, rising. "I'll take you to the Sanctuary. The priest of Havah will see to your safety."

"No," Makeda said. She stood and squared her shoulders, and Yetzer failed to keep his eyes from her moon-limned figure. "My people are encamped below the city. I will go to them."

"As you say."

Without another word, he started back down the track toward the Spring Gate and the Kederon Valley. The Queen of Saba easily matched his stride and kept up a steady banter as they walked. Yetzer replied with his most polite grunts, unwilling to be ensnared in her conversation.

Fires burned in the Sabaean camp as they drew near. The sentries eyed Yetzer warily but warmly greeted their queen.

"I've not eaten yet," Makeda told Yetzer. "Will you join me for a meal?"

"No," Yetzer said, loudly enough to cover the rumbling of his stomach. "I have much to prepare for the morrow."

The queen showed him a smile despite the disappointment in her eyes.

"Well, then, thank you for your help. I fear what might have happened if you hadn't intervened."

Yetzer dipped his head and turned to go, not trusting himself any longer to look into those soft, golden eyes.

"And, please," Makeda called after him, "if there is anything more I can offer your men and their families, do let me know."

The builder paused and chanced a look back. Torchlight showed the woman's face, clear and free of guile. This Queen of Saba was either sincere or a better liar than her sister. Too many thoughts and questions and worries tumbled about Yetzer's heart for him to make order of them. He gave a curt nod, then hastened back up the hill.

A plate of cold lamb and leeks waited upon his table. Yetzer picked at the food but found no pleasure in his mother's best dish or in the cup of wine he drained to wash it down. He lay upon his cot, striving in vain to rid his thoughts of worn ropes and shattered legs and dark-skinned goddesses.

Sleep never visited him. When his brass water clock showed only two hours before dawn, Yetzer abandoned the effort. He rose, splashed some water on his face, then pulled on his tunic and kilt.

He moved through a world as silent as the Pit. Even the crickets slumbered, and the birds had yet to awaken. Stars flooded the sky and spilled enough light on the earth to guide Yetzer to Morhavah.

Once upon the sacred hill, Yetzer mounted the scaffolding that surrounded the aborning temple. To the highest point he climbed, to the top of the wall between the portico and the Holy Place. Here he could just see over the top of the eastern hill with its olive groves that nestled in shade throughout the mornings.

A hazy dawn glowed far beyond that hill, and it seemed to Yetzer he could see to the very edge of the world, where Shapash daily burst from the endless sea upon her chariot of flame to race across the sky. The glory of the heavens spread above him, the glories of earth about him. He stood upon the very pinnacle of man's creation in a place made holy by the gods.

And it was all meaningless.

Yes, men might look upon his work in wonder. Word of his skill might spread. Kings might ask him to build great temples in their lands, where he might feed and shelter other crews and other families.

But to what end?

There was nothing new under the sun. Kings and queens would still rule by the sword, by cunning and guile. Priests would still extort their tithes by false promises of the gods' blessings and threats of the Pit. Armies would wage war to feed a prince's pride. Thousands upon thousands would hunger and thirst, would sweat and bleed and die to bring a soft chair and a full table to the few.

And what was Yetzer's part? He stacked stones and filled his men's heads with dreams of honor and righteousness. Their work would be complete in less than a year's time. Gold would fill Bilkis's coffers, while his men went back to field or forest or mine. Their lives would be unchanged, save for the occasional missing limb.

And Yetzer would go to find other work, having accomplished nothing.

"It's not *nothing.*"

Yetzer flinched at the unexpected sound of the youthful voice. He spread his feet to keep balanced as the temple's porch yawned hungrily at him from thirty-five cubits below. He turned to see Natan standing beside him and wondered how much he'd said aloud.

"Sorry," the young priest said, "but it isn't *nothing.*"

"What isn't?" Yetzer said as he settled onto the stone wall, his legs dangling over the side.

"What you've done here," Natan said, and sat beside him. "What you're doing here. You can't change kings and queens, and priests will be what they will be. Some are wise and good, like Abdi-Havah was, and some are ... not."

The young man glanced south, toward the palace, but elaborated no further. A wise priest, indeed.

"The gods are just," Natan continued. "They expect us to serve well in those areas we can. What is beyond our ability to change is also beyond our responsibility."

"I can't change a kingdom," Yetzer said, his voice tight. "I can't change its rulers, so what good does a temple do?" It seemed odd to seek advice from a boy not half his age but talking to himself had brought Yetzer no clarity.

"You've changed the lives of every man on your crews. And the lives of their families, too."

"And when the work is finished, their lives will be just as they were before," Yetzer countered.

"Their lots in life may be the same," Natan allowed, "but no one who has been a part of this wonder will go away unchanged. You've created a brotherhood, a family based on a shared dream, not simply blood or tribe. You've shown them a world where skill and effort count for more than wealth or a sword."

Yetzer gave a short, humorless laugh as the young priest echoed his own lofty words. "And what merit have such noble ideals in a world ruled by gold and violence?"

"Perhaps little," Natan allowed as he plucked at the new fuzz on his chin. "Perhaps much. Good wine does not come from a seed just planted. Years pass before fruit is borne, decades before it gladdens a king's heart. Your men will tell their sons of the time when merit meant more than heritage. Women will teach their daughters that they have value beyond hearth or bedchamber."

Yetzer grinned at that. Natan's words brightened his spirit even as the sun brightened the horizon. The hillside began to awaken as men arrived to change out the ropes on their wheels, or to drive their cattle teams to the quarry.

"This is your namesake," Natan said, gesturing toward the workers. "These men are your true temple. They come here not for fear of being beaten or turned out of their homes. They come to take part in a new creation. It will take generations—maybe ten, maybe a hundred—but the seeds you've planted among this people, and the seeds they engender will one day bear fruit, and the gods will surely smile and call it good."

62

Makeda

I slapped at a fly on my donkey's neck. My hand came away gory and left a trickle of blood behind, but the animal seemed not to notice. I'd wanted to bring Dhahbas on this journey, but Eliam convinced me a donkey was far better suited to the terrain than a camel, so I sat atop the little grey creature in the small caravan that wended its way down from Urusalim.

The donkey stumbled over a cobble and I clutched its mane to keep from sliding off the blanket across the animal's back. Eliam had spoken true about the terrain. Rocks littered the steep, winding road that led from the city to a deep river valley called Yarden.

Word of the return of Abram, Eliam's son, had reached the merchant two days earlier. The younger man, I learned, was years late in his arrival, but had apparently brought a great treasure in copper and tin. Yetzer needed these for the furnishings of the temple, so he'd chosen a pair of artisans for the trip to Tzeretan and the bronze foundry there.

I was eager to see the metal works, and though Bilkis had tried to talk me out of traveling to the bleak wilderness, I'd won her leave. Yetzer had been reluctant to allow me to join them, but Eliam and Dvora and Rahab prevailed in changing his heart.

We camped that night on a narrow plain beside the road. A pair of my men stood watch with four guards hired by Eliam. Fazia and I, along with Yetzer and his artisans, joined Eliam and his family about the fire. Even though the builder spoke little, he listened intently as I told stories of my gods and lands and people.

At the second night's encampment, Yetzer engaged in the conversation. What roles did each god play? How did the people feed themselves if it never rained? How did I manage land and water rights? We talked well into the night, and on the third day of the journey, he approached me as we paused to water the donkeys.

"Would you care to walk with me, Lady?"

My cheeks grew warm. I smiled and nodded. The rest of the party and the unburdened donkeys went ahead while my guards walked a few paces behind us.

"I owe you an apology," Yetzer said when enough distance separated us from the others that we could speak privately.

"Oh?" I replied, unsure what wrong he'd done.

"I fear I've ill-judged you." He turned his face so I could see only his unblinking embroidered eye. "You showed kindness to my man and his family. I was happy to give you thanks when I thought you a servant, then mistrusted you when I learned you are a queen."

"Is it such a bad thing to be a queen?" I asked, a teasing note in my voice.

Yetzer turned to look at me and offered a wry smile. "In my experience, royal women show generosity only when it benefits them."

"And have you known many royal women?"

"Enough." Yetzer looked away and cleared his throat. "But now I know that not all are shaped from the same quarry. I instruct my men to judge others by their actions and their merits, not by title or blood. I should have given you that same courtesy."

I smiled and drew a deep breath of sun-blasted air. An unseen burden fell away as though I'd cast off a water-logged cloak. "Thank you. In my experience, men find it difficult to admit a wrong."

"And have you been misjudged by many fools?" It was Yetzer's turn to tease, but the question stung.

"Enough. But when you're bastard-born to a slave, it is to be expected." I fixed my eyes upon the ground.

"A slave?"

He took a step closer to my side and we walked on while I told him of my mother, how she'd been stolen from her homeland across the Western Sea and sold to the Mukarrib of Saba. I told of the flood that had swept Bilkis away, how my mother became Mukarrib, and how I took up that mantle upon her death.

"Such a land," Yetzer said in a hushed tone, "where a woman can rise from slave to Wife of the God."

Talk of Saba and my people stirred a longing in my heart. The barrenness and heat of the land about us brought some comfort, but I remained homesick.

"And what of you?" I asked Yetzer in turn. "How did you become a temple-builder?"

My heart ached as he spoke of his father's death, of his own failure, and enslavement.

"How did you learn the secret word?" I asked after Yetzer described his return to freedom.

He shrugged. "I watched. I listened. The truth of the mysteries is written upon the world around us, available to all who have eyes to see and ears to hear."

"Then why guard those secrets so zealously?" I asked. "If the knowledge is free to all, why not simply proclaim it?"

"The knowledge is free," Yetzer said, "but its proper use requires training and discipline. A child can learn to make fire, but if he is not first taught to handle it safely he puts himself and his house in danger."

"And his kingdom?" I ventured to add.

Yetzer looked at me, his eye narrowed.

"Bilkis told me you refused to tell Yahtadua the builders' secrets," I said.

"And she asked you to change my heart?"

I lowered my eyes and nodded.

"She'll be angry when you tell her you've failed," Yetzer said, humor in his voice.

"She's been angry with me before."

Yetzer laughed at that, a deep rumble that made my heart sing. We walked on, heedless of the growing heat as we descended deeper into the valley. Steep, rocky steps lay in the path where the road turned back on itself. Yetzer offered his hand to steady me, and my blood raced, my breathing quick and shallow, as the warmth of his touch suffused me.

We caught up with the others as evening approached. The simple meal of bread and hummus and olives seemed a feast as Yetzer sat beside me. Stories and laughter filled the rapidly cooling night air, and I felt no longer a stranger but a part of this extended family.

With the new day's light, we set out once more. By midmorning, plumes of smoke rose above the horizon. Before long, we came to a ford in the River Yarden, a wondrous stream that ran with water all throughout the year.

"My son," Eliam cried as a middle-aged man waded through the water to meet us. The merchant clasped his son in a tight embrace, and after Rahab had her turn to weep and fuss over her brother, Eliam introduced Abram to me. We all crossed the river to the town Tzeretan. While Eliam and family became reacquainted, Fazia and my men set up our camp, and Yetzer showed me around.

Enough wood to fill a forest lay chopped and stacked into neat piles around several forges that bellowed black smoke into the air. Soot and ash seemed as thick upon the ground and buildings as sand after a windstorm. I minded none of it. Yetzer led me into a storehouse where a dozen figures of various shapes sat beneath oiled linen sheets. He began pulling down the sailcloth covers, and I gaped at each statue he revealed.

"They're beautiful," I whispered.

I drew near to one of the marvels, a lion ready to pounce. The polished wood gleamed in the scant light that filtered through gaps in wall and roof. The light shifted as I moved around the statue, and it seemed the creature's muscles rippled beneath its oiled flesh.

"Do you recognize them?" Yetzer asked as he moved beside me.

I looked at the other carvings. A bull and a ram stood on either side of the lion. These in turn were flanked by a scorpion and a spiny lobster. A pair of fishes, a goat and several human figures rounded out the assembly.

Memories of old Shayma's stories flooded over me. The great twins who tore apart Mother Earth and Father Sky in the days of creation. The Bull of Heaven that pulled the plow to carve out the wadis. The Maiden who lent her fertility to fields and vineyards. These and their companions marked the seasons as they made their yearly night-walk across the sky.

My voice was full of wonder. "The Star Dwellers."

Yetzer smiled at my recognition. He explained how he intended for the statues to stand before his temple in the place of their stars, to mark upon the earth the course of the heavens and the turning of the seasons.

"My lady?"

I turned at the sound of Fazia's familiar voice. The interruption annoyed me, and my face must have betrayed the emotion. The younger woman took a step back and lowered her head.

"My apologies, Lady. I only wished to let you know your tent and dinner are ready."

"Of course," I said, "thank you." I turned to Yetzer and gave a rueful grin. "And thank you." I gestured toward the statues. "For this."

Yetzer smiled, took my hand, and pressed his forehead to the back of it. "Rest well, my lady."

I followed my handmaid back to the camp. I hardly tasted my dinner, hardly heard the songs and stories my people told around the fire. When I went to my cot, even as I closed my eyes, I saw only the images of the Star Dwellers. And my builder.

63

Makeda

The morning sun burned clear and bright, and drove away the smoke from all the furnaces, save one. Fire raged within that foundry, pouring its heat into a great cauldron.

I stood with Eliam and his family, awaiting commencement of the great work. Around them stood the Star Dwellers, each one resplendent in freshly cast bronze.

In the center of the circle, beside the furnace, rose a stout wooden frame. Nearly twice the height of a man, and twice again that length on each side, the mold stood ready to receive its charge of molten metal.

Yetzer stood upon the frame, wrapped in boots and gloves and apron of heavy leather. Sunlight caught the strands of red in his hair and short beard. He seemed the very craftsman of the gods.

"In the beginning," he said, his voice a whisper yet as clear as if he stood at my side, "the gods placed the great lights in the heavens to separate night from day, to stand as guideposts for the seasons, and to shape the natures of men and of the ages. As we drift in the great Celestial Sea, so shall we bring that sea to earth. Though clouds may come, let this Molten Sea stand to mark the seasons."

A breath of wind caressed my cheek. I smoothed back a strand of hair, and my fingers brushed the comb at the back of my head. With a delicate flutter of wings, the silver dragonfly left its perch. It flitted twice around me, then flew up to where Yetzer stood.

I blinked and found myself beside him. The builder held me in his green-eyed gaze and smiled. Warmth flooded over me like the waters of Wadi Dhanah crashing down from the mountains. At a nod from Yetzer, I picked up the end of a rope, its other end attached to the furnace's gate. Yetzer did the same on his side, and we pulled the ropes to raise the gate.

Molten bronze spilled down a sluice in the casting's sand to a shaped funnel, the liquid fire outshining even the sun. The assembled people clapped their hands, while the statues in their circle bowed in admiration. Another movement caught my attention, but when I looked I saw nothing more than a fleeting shadow. I turned back to Yetzer, tall and strong, the craftsman's pride bright upon his countenance.

Pride turned to something else as the earth began to shiver. Yetzer looked toward the mold and I followed his gaze. Bronze still flowed from the furnace, but now climbed the sides of the sand-crafted funnel, rather than entering the cast.

More quickly than a blink, a jet of steam burst from the funnel. Droplets of fire trailed in its wake and showered down upon the frame, the people, the statues. Amid bellows and wails of pain, the Star Dwellers melted into a ring of fiery bronze that crept inward like a snare. Blossoms of flame sprouted up where the molten ring met stands of grass or scraps of wood.

The people fared little better. Cloaks of fire replaced those of wool, and burning crowns flared upon their heads under the rain of destruction. The wooden frame, the platform, the roof and walls of the foundry burst alight. I reached for Yetzer, tried to run to him, but my legs seemed mired as in the muck at the foot of my dam.

Yetzer pulled me to him, held me close and kissed my lips. Despite the horror around us, despite the panic in my breast, I kissed him back. If my final moments were upon me, I would take solace in them.

"Yetzer," a deep voice called out.

We broke our embrace and turned toward the sound. Three men stood opposite us on the remains of the wooden frame.

A clean-shaven, middle-aged man stood bare-chested, a starched linen kilt about his waist, copper bands upon his arms. Beside him was an old man, his long white beard spilling down the front of a striped woolen robe. To the other side stood a handsome youth dressed in leather kilt and apron.

Between the furnace and the men, the casting's funnel sank into a yawning chasm that belched smoke and flame and globules of molten bronze.

"Father?" Yetzer said.

"What destruction have you wrought?" said the bald man in the center of the trio.

"I did not cause this," Yetzer protested.

"Is this not your mold, the work of your hands? See what you have done." The man spread his arms in a gesture that encompassed the ruined foundry, the scorched earth, the charred and shrunken bodies that had moments earlier joined in celebration.

"The secrets of foundry and forge are not for the simple of heart," Huram continued. "He who would chase the art with folly forfeits his life, the lives of innocents."

"No," Yetzer shouted as tears streamed down his cheek. "The casting was true and well vented."

"Still you have murdered those who loved you, trusted you."

"No!" Yetzer raised his staff like a war club. He seemed ready to leap across the fiery gap, but the eldest man raised his hands.

"Peace, my sons," he chided them. "Be still."

"Father Tubaal," Yetzer pleaded, "you know the care of my work."

"Indeed," the man acknowledged. "And for all that care, those you esteemed have perished."

Yetzer's shoulders drooped, his head bowed in defeat.

"However true your hand," the old man said, "you must be ever wary of the children of Yubaal. While we seek to bring order to the world, my brother's sons would cast it back into the ancient chaos. A lifetime of careful work may be undone by a moment of perfidy."

Yetzer looked up at that. "By whose hand was this done?" The menace in his voice made me take a step back. "Tell me," Yetzer snarled, "and I will deliver him to the Pit this very morning."

"You care more for vengeance than for life?" His father's voice dripped with scorn.

"I care for these lives above all," Yetzer protested, "but can flesh become unburned? Can life be redeemed from death?"

Laughter rumbled across the plain, so rich it invited me to join in despite the carnage about me.

"All things are possible, if sufficient price be paid." No mouth opened, yet I knew the voice to be the third man's. His eyes shone brightly, his expression placid, and I felt the same peace as when Athtar whispered to me.

"Tell me." Yetzer fell to his knees and thrice touched his head to the scorched wood of the platform. "Name the price. What would you have me do?"

"Child, it is not a question of what I would take, but of what you would give."

"Then take me," Yetzer declared. "Exchange my life for theirs."

"No," I heard myself say. I hadn't intended to speak, hadn't even suspected I might. For the first time in my life—certainly since becoming Mukarrib—my heart spoke out against will and duty.

It was right and just, of course, that Yetzer offer his life in exchange for his loved ones. I would make the same trade. But to lose this man who had become the harmony to my heart's song was a cost past bearing.

The stares of seven eyes weighed upon me. I looked from one stranger to the next, then finally to Yetzer. Flames reflected upon the vibrant green eye that pierced to my core.

"I must do this," Yetzer said.

He touched my cheek, his fingers coarse but light upon my skin, then smoothed an errant lock of hair behind my ear. The unseen hand that squeezed my heart also squeezed the breath from my throat. I could not beg him to stay, could not speak my approval of his sacrifice. I could only twist my lips into a sickly smile and offer an encouraging nod.

Yetzer returned the smile with a heart-rending one of his own. He gathered my hands in his, kissed the inside of my wrist, then turned away. He stepped to the edge of the platform's remains, before the flaming pit. Huram crossed his arms and scowled at his son, but Tubaal offered a beneficent smile. The third man seemed unmoved, an enigmatic expression on his face.

Yetzer touched his staff to the swirling, fiery vortex. Flames leapt up the lightning-tempered walnut, but the wood was not consumed. Tension played across the muscles of Yetzer's back as he squared his shoulders, stood upright, stepped off the edge.

And was gone.

64

Yetzer

Yetzer plunged into the void. Makeda's kiss still burned his lips, even as heat engulfed him and flames erupted upon his hair and clothing. Leather turned to fire, his nostrils filled with the infernal stench, but his flesh remained untouched.

Still he fell, sliding down a slope of molten bronze as smooth as obsidian. Flames twice his size danced about him, replaced by giant spheres of steam as darkness conquered light and he crossed the boundary from liquid metal to watery abyss.

Pressure folded about him like the fist of the sea god Yam, relentless and unforgiving. Deeper he sank, his naked body flayed as he scraped along walls now jagged. The unseen hand squeezed tighter. Yetzer wanted to cry out, to give voice to his agony, but his lungs defied him. The only sound was that of the terror that surged with each beat of his heart.

The rocky wall gave way to a floor just as coarse and cruel. The drag of skin over stone brought him to a stop, and he lay facedown, surrounded by blackness and crushed by the weight of the sea.

"Yetzer."

The word echoed around him, rolling out of the dark from every direction and none.

The builder pushed himself up. Rock cut into his hands and knees, but the pain was as nothing, shut out by the cloak of oblivion that hung tightly about him.

"He doesn't understand." His father's voice came from behind him, hot with scorn that striped Yetzer's heart as the stones did his flesh.

"You are too demanding, Huram," spoke another on Yetzer's right. "As I recall, your own awakening took quite some time."

Yetzer recognized the speaker as his ancestor Tubaal, his voice abraded with age.

"The secrets are intended to be challenging," said a youthful voice before him, the voice of the one who had lured Yetzer into this fiery grave. "There are truths meant for only the blind to see."

Yetzer's friends were dead, his work destroyed, and he'd thrown himself into the Pit just as he'd discovered a woman every bit his match. His world was consumed in fire, and these three offered him derision and riddles as recompense.

He sat back on his heels in frustration and ran his hands over his scalp, fire-shorn and bald as a priest of Kemet. His cheeks bore not even a trace of stubble. Without the protection of his headscarf, his fingers easily found the hollow of his vacant left …

Yetzer closed his right eye to shut out the impenetrable darkness. He settled into the crushing embrace, content to be at one with his *ka*, his indestructible nature.

Pressure built behind his forehead, like a finger trying to push through from the inside. Sparks flitted before Yetzer's left eye. Remembering his long-ago instruction in the Temple of Amun, he did his best to ignore them, lest by his attention he chase them away.

The sparks stretched into strands of color that danced before him, deep green and blue, mingled and intertwined. These gave birth to yellow and magenta, then again to orange and red and all the hues of nature. Color resolved into shape and form, then the scene about him snapped into focus.

Yetzer rose before the young man who radiated warmth and welcome. A barren landscape stretched around them, dun-colored and sown with shards of quartz and granite, the quarrier's banes. Before and behind, the land swept up into darkness, while to left and right it seemed to go on forever.

"You see?" Tubaal said behind Yetzer, a chiding tone in his voice. "His eye opens as well as yours or mine."

Huram grunted. "Perhaps, but I doubt he knows where he stands."

Yetzer spun toward his father. "*He* stands before a stubborn fool," he growled. "If you have aught to say to me, speak it as a man, not as a bitter old crone."

Tubaal chuckled in his rich baritone, but Huram glared at his son.

"You mightn't care to hear what I would say."

A ball of fiery wrath formed in Yetzer's very core and threatened to burst out of him. He clenched his teeth, cheek quivering and nostrils flaring.

"And what would that be?" he demanded. "That I should have warned you sooner? That it's my fault you and your men died? That this," he pointed to his empty left eye, "was cheap redemption for so great a loss?"

Huram folded his arms and looked down his nose at his son.

Crimson rage surged from Yetzer in a howl equal parts fury and pain. He rushed his father, grasped him by his copper armbands and glared into those implacable green eyes.

"It wasn't," he screamed, but Huram didn't even flinch at the spittle that flew to his cheek. "I was only a boy, not yet entered as an apprentice, but I saw it. I knew what the rock would do. I warned you, but you didn't listen." Tears blurred Yetzer's vision as the scene from the Kemeti quarry played before him. The steam vents bursting from the earth. The explosion of rock. Red life spurting from Huram's throat.

"I tried." Yetzer shook his father by the arms, his strength sapped by grief. "You didn't listen. It wasn't my fault." Huram's eyes held no emotion, his expression fixed in grim disapproval. "It wasn't my fault," Yetzer insisted. A tear spilled down his cheek. Sorrow squeezed his throat, but he managed to make his tremulous voice heard. "It was yours." He blinked his vision clear and met his father's cold, unfeeling glare. "It was your fault," he whispered.

Disdain and tension drained from Huram's expression. His eyes softened and a smile tilted the corners of his mouth.

"That's right, my son," he said. He unfolded his arms and clasped a hand gently behind Yetzer's neck. "It was my fault, not yours." He touched his forehead to Yetzer's. "You did what you could. Naught that happened that day was your fault."

A sob escaped Yetzer's throat and he fell into the embrace of his forgiving father.

"You've a sound reason." Huram's words were a balm upon Yetzer's heart. "Fear not. Have a care for the people in your trust, but don't be afraid of your heart or your passions. The true master finds his greatness in their balance."

Yetzer nodded and clung to his father a bit longer, until a rough, phlegmy rattle broke the silence.

"Touching," Tubaal said. "Truly. But shall we do something for those poor scorched folk out there? And for Kothar's sake," he added as Yetzer and Huram parted, "put this on."

He produced Yetzer's apron, embroidered with the triangle and eye of Haru.

"What is this place?" Yetzer asked as he tied the apron about his waist.

"You don't recognize it?" His father gazed at him. "You had a hand in creating it."

Yetzer gave Huram a quizzical look then turned his attention to his surroundings. The place was every bit as featureless as before, save for the high sloping wall behind Kothar, where a pattern came into focus. A series of lines, about the thickness of Yetzer's leg, stood out in bold relief upon the wall in a wavelike pattern. Yetzer envisioned the lines inverted, and recognized the motif he'd designed for his Molten Sea.

"The casting," he said, not quite trusting his answer. "We're inside the mold?"

"If we are to undo what has been done," Kothar said, "we must begin at the source of the error."

"The mold is true," Yetzer insisted. "I'm sure of it."

"And yet the vents were fouled," Tubaal added.

Yetzer had shaped his Molten Sea, the centerpiece for the temple's forecourt, in sand. The great mound reflected the interior surface of the basin. Over this he'd spread a layer of pitch followed by a coating of wax as thick as his thumb. When the wax had set, Yetzer and his artisans etched into its surface the final design for the basin's exterior, the outlines of the world's great islands long visited by Kenahni seafarers. They fixed waxen brackets to match those that would mount the Sea upon the backs and shoulders of the brazen Star Dwellers, then added a spidery network of sprues and encased the entire piece in pitch and fine sand.

Without the sprue vents, there would be no pathway for the molten bronze to fill the mold or—just as importantly—for trapped air and moisture to be vented. If those vents were plugged, if any wax remained within the mold, the heat of the liquid bronze could have flashed the wax to vapor with devastating results.

"There, you see?"

Yetzer had been lost in thoughts of the mold's construction. He scarcely realized he'd been walking until he stopped as Tubaal pointed out an area where floor sloped into wall.

An ugly grey pock, almost the width of Yetzer's stride, marred the sand's mottled surface. Yetzer knelt to study it, a circle of dull, murky liquid. He dipped the end of his staff into the pool, probing less than a hand's breadth before the wood met a solid floor. He removed the staff, its tip coated with liquid that dried into a metallic sheath.

"Lead," he murmured, then realization struck him. "Someone plugged the vents with lead."

His three guides offered no objection as they stared at him expectantly.

"Who would do this?" Yetzer rubbed a hand over his face.

"Who would want to see the casting fail?" Huram asked him.

"Or the temple?" Tubaal chimed in.

"Or its builder?"

Yetzer looked at Kothar, who spoke this last, and shook his head. "Not even Bilkis could do such a thing."

"The temple is nearly complete," the divine craftsman replied. "It is a simple matter to finish the work, so you are now more nuisance than help to her."

"But to endanger my mother? Eliam and Rahab? Her own sister?"

"Perhaps an acceptable accident," Tubaal suggested. "Or perhaps a desire to be rid of those close to her."

"Those who knew her as something other than a queen," Huram added.

Yetzer shook his head again, though in truth such a possibility surprised him no more than seeing water run downhill.

"What do I do? You said it would be possible to restore what was lost."

"You possess the very tool within your hands," Kothar answered.

Yetzer looked at his staff, now with its leaded tip. The walnut had been hardened by lightning cast by the hand of Hadad, whose celestial palace Kothar himself had built. Tubaal nodded and smiled at Yetzer as Huram stepped forward. The Overseer of Pharaoh's Works wrapped his thick arms about Yetzer.

"Your mother is well?"

"If this works," Yetzer replied.

Huram laughed at that and pounded his son on the back. He stepped away, still clasping Yetzer by the shoulders.

"Go," he said. "Complete your work but know that a task greater still lies before you."

"What—" Yetzer began, but his father stepped back, gently silencing him with a raised hand.

Tubaal and Kothar took up position behind and to either side of Yetzer, then all three stretched out their arms, enclosing him in a triangle of blessing.

You are about to quit this sacred place, to mix again with the world, the three men intoned, their lips still even as their voices filled Yetzer's heart.

Yetzer lifted his staff then drove it down between his feet. The thick liquid resisted the assault.

Amidst the concerns and distractions of the profane, forget not that which has been instilled in you here.

Yetzer repeated the motion, this time striking the plug below.

Be ever vigilant and wise, modest and discreet.

Once more he raised the staff and drove it down. The tip stuck in the semi-solid mass and molten lead leeched up the stout walnut. Yetzer tried to release his grip, to cast the staff away, but his hands held fast. He looked to Huram, who smiled at his son as he continued the priestly injunction.

Act unto your fellows as you would have them act unto you, and do good unto all.

The lead reached Yetzer's hands and coated his arms and legs, sheathing him in its molten embrace. It climbed his chest, spanned his shoulders, covered his mouth before he could scream.

Be as one with those of like heart, live in peace.

Yetzer cast a final glance at his father before darkness entombed him.

And may the god of peace and love delight to dwell with and bless you.

65

Yetzer

Yetzer bolted upright on his pallet as a sharp, ragged breath filled his lungs. He flexed his fingers and raised his hands to his face. His breathing came more easily when he found flesh instead of lead. His heart still raced, but he calmed himself and took in the familiar surroundings of his tent. The sweat on his skin rapidly cooled him as he rose, wrapped his kilt about his waist and laced on his sandals.

His dreams seldom remained more than a few moments after waking, but the visitation of his father and the others continued to haunt him. He took up his lamp and set out to the foundry. The new-moon sky blazed with stars that illumined his way to the great furnace and his casting.

A shadow moved against the wooden framework as Yetzer approached. Without a thought, Yetzer dashed forward and caught hold of the cloaked figure's arm. A feminine voice cried out in alarm, and Yetzer spun the woman around to peer into a set of amber eyes. Recognition dawned there and Makeda threw her free arm about Yetzer's neck.

"Bless Athtar," she whispered in his ear. "You're safe."

Yetzer released his grip and wrapped his arms about Makeda, savoring the pressure of her body against his.

"What are you doing here?" he asked, his voice soft.

"I had a terrible dream," Makeda replied. "The casting failed and everyone was killed." She pulled back and placed her hands on Yetzer's cheeks. "And you— "

"Leapt into the flames," Yetzer finished for her.

Makeda cocked her head, a puzzled look in her eyes.

"Yes," she said, "but how could you know that?"

A smile quirked Yetzer's lips. "Because I had the same dream. My father and the founders of my craft gave me the means to right this."

"I don't understand," Makeda said. "How is it possible?"

"Let us see if our dream is true," Yetzer suggested, "then we can explore how we both shared the same vision and what it means."

Her hand fit perfectly in his as their fingers intertwined seemingly of their own volition. Yetzer guided her to the ladder that reached up to the furnace's platform, then out onto the mold itself. The rammed sand was solid underfoot as he led the way across the sluice, then knelt beside the funnel. The sprue vents formed a pattern of dots upon the surface. Black pocks marked the voids left behind when the casting had been heated and the wax melted to leave behind the empty mold.

Yetzer scraped the sand away from one of the vents, a hole no larger than his little finger. He hadn't dug far before his nails scratched against something solid. He brushed away more sand to reveal a plug of metal that filled the vent.

"Lead," he muttered. "It's just as they showed me."

"What does it mean?" Makeda asked, kneeling beside him.

"It means someone has betrayed me," Yetzer growled, anger grating against his throat. Someone had plotted against him, conspired with Bilkis to destroy his work and sully his name. Worse, they had put lives in danger to do so. Fury rose in Yetzer's breast, but Makeda leaned closer to him and laid her hand atop his, her long slender fingers hot upon his skin.

"But what does it mean?"

His rage was quenched by Makeda's gaze, smothered by her touch. He looked at the stoppered vent and knew it could be easily fixed, that however many vents had been plugged could be unplugged, and that he could prevent the saboteur from destroying his work and murdering the people he loved. He looked back at Makeda and held her gaze as the world fell away like sand from a finished casting.

What does it mean? Gone were the trappings of power, the folly of pride, the perfidy of ambition, and all that remained was the woman beside him and the pounding of his heart beating in time with the pulse in her fingers. They had shared this night's vision. What other dreams might they share?

What does it mean? He didn't know, and his heart left no space for curiosity or reason as he leaned into Makeda and kissed her.

66

Bilkis

"A widow?" Bilkis demanded from her throne. "I send to Kemet for a bride of royal blood, and they offer up a widow?"

She punctuated the question with a goblet of wine she hurled at Yahshepat. The scribe blocked his head with the fired-clay tablet that bore the scurrilous message. The heavy silver chalice took a bite from the tablet and spilled its golden wine over his tunic and scrolls.

"My lady," the scribe sputtered, "she is not just any widow, but the bride of the old pharaoh himself."

"And will this old woman be able to bear a son?" Bilkis demanded. "Alliances are made not beneath the wedding canopy, but upon the bridal sheets. Without an heir of shared blood, it makes little difference whether the bride be princess or commoner or slave. This Pharaoh Menmayatre makes of us a mockery, and I'll not forget it."

"My lady," Elhoreb joined in, "it is no insult to be given a royal bride of Kemet. While he yet lives, the Kemeti king is seen as the very god Haru. His children are not simply of royal blood, but divine. Upon Pharaoh's death, he rises to the throne of Osaure, their chief god. His widow becomes Auset, the mother goddess. Crone or not, whether her womb be fertile or fallow, your son will have the Wife of the God as his bride."

Wife of the God. Bilkis mouthed the words, sweet as summer wine and with a familiar tang. Should her son marry this Wife of the God, what would that make him? What would it make Bilkis herself?

"Very well," she told the scribes. "We will accept Pharaoh's offer. Reply that he may send two-score archers as escort, and that we would consider taking into our governance one of his coastal vassal cities. Ghazzat, perhaps? Or possibly Asqanu."

The court scribe scratched a ragged line across his linen sheet as his stylus slipped, while the builders' scribe stood slack-jawed.

"A city, Lady?" Elhoreb was first to recover his wits.

Bilkis raised a painted brow. "Surely my son's wife will desire comforts from her native land from time to time. With a port city in our realm, we may more readily see to her wishes than if we were forced to rely upon caravans."

Elhoreb grinned, crooked teeth showing behind his unkempt beard. "My lady is ever wise," he said, and bowed.

"Yahshepat, draft our reply," Bilkis said, rising. "Come, Elhoreb. I would hear of progress upon the mount."

"Yes, Lady," the builders' scribe said in a tremulous voice, his eagerness evident beneath the skirt of his tunic.

Benyahu, ever the faithful guardian, had stood silently by the dais throughout, and now offered his hand to help Bilkis down the steps. His fingers were cold but stolid, a marked contrast from the passion they'd conveyed in years past—a passion repulsively bespoken by Elhoreb's hot, moist grip on her other hand. Bilkis resisted the compulsion to wipe her hand on her gown. She'd be soiled with worse before long.

"What news from Tzeretan?" Bilkis asked the scribe when they were behind the closed door of her private audience chamber. She'd learned Elhoreb was rendered incoherent after he took his pleasure with her, so it was best to resolve all business dealings before giving him his reward.

"None, my lady," the scribe replied, his words clipped.

"But you are certain the casting was fouled?" Bilkis sat and crossed one leg over the other.

"Yes, Lady." Elhoreb licked his lips as he sat across from her, his gaze fixed on the queen's bosom. Only when several long moments passed in silence did he raise his eyes to meet Bilkis's glare.

"My man assured me he plugged every vent and wetted the mold. When Yetzer attempts to cast, it will be utterly ruined."

"Then why does he tarry?" Bilkis demanded, her stomach becoming sour. "Why no word yet? Might he have discovered something amiss?"

"No, my lady," Elhoreb answered quickly, with a glib laugh. His expression melted to one more sober under the queen's hot gaze. "That is, the plugs were set deeply so they could not be discovered unless someone was looking for them."

"And would abi-Huram be so diligent as that?" Bilkis asked, having found it easier to refer to the builder by his surname.

"No, no, my lady." The scribe again answered too quickly, then roughly cleared his throat. "Not very likely."

Bilkis crossed her arms and cocked an eyebrow.

"It's possible, yes," the fool at last admitted with a palsied nod.

"Out," Bilkis said in a low, menacing tone.

"But, my lady—"

"Out," she demanded. "When—if I receive word of abi-Huram's failure, then you may claim your reward, but not before."

"B-but what of the Queen of Kemet?" Elhoreb's desperation sickened Bilkis. "Did I not help to secure your son's bride?"

"When she arrives with her archers," Bilkis said as she rose and moved past the scribe, "and when Yahtadua has his port city and his son of Kemeti blood, then you may receive my thanks." She pushed the door open and leaned against the jamb. "Deliver my temple. Deliver the word of the Masters to my son, and perhaps our gratitude will be sooner in coming. Benyahu?"

The old warrior stood by her side in mere moments.

"The scribe Elhoreb has completed his service to us. See him to the gate. We will call for him if he might again be of use."

"Yes, my lady," Benyahu replied.

Elhoreb started to protest, but the general quietly rested his hand on the hilt of his great iron sword. The scribe swallowed then rose, hiding his discomfiture as best he could. Bilkis backed away from him as he sidled through the doorway, where Benyahu took him by the scruff of his robe and helped him toward the gates of the great hall.

"I've delivered to your son the Wife of the God, my lady," Elhoreb called in strangled tones as Benyahu hustled him to the door. "I will deliver to you the builders' word."

The smack of Benyahu's hand against the scribe's head echoed from limestone and cedar, but only one thing resounded in Bilkis's ears.

Wife of the God.

67

Makeda

The western hills cast the land in shadow, but my heart bathed in warmth and light. Yetzer's bronzes had been successfully cast. While the oxen pulling the great Molten Sea lagged behind, my builder and I brought the train of wagons laden with the Star Dwellers and columns up the mountain trails to Urusalim.

My builder?

Yes, I admitted to myself even as my cheeks grew warm and my heart raced. At the very least, he would be. I'd shared with Yetzer my concerns about the earthwork dam across the Wadi Dhanah. He readily offered to travel with me and lend his hands to a more permanent solution, once the temple was complete.

But there was more.

I was Athtar's wife, I reminded myself, placed upon the high seat of Maryaba by his will rather than my parents' blood. I could give myself to no man while my husband lived, and the gods possessed exceptional longevity.

Still, I'd never known a man like Yetzer. Something deep within me stirred as I watched him among his men. Stripped down to his breechcloth, he led them as they grunted and cursed and hauled on ropes to move the heavy bronze statues into place before the broad steps of the temple. Even from a distance, I could see the angry red scars of his slavery, see the muscles of his arms and legs and chest glistening with sweat.

It was more than his physical bearing that drew me to him. He had an easy way with his men, leading from among them, as he did now, rather than guiding them with the flail. He revered the gods but sought to understand their roles in man's advancement instead of simply appeasing their priests. He treated women with courtesy and deference, not as mere objects of property or pleasure. He'd even begun to teach me his sound-pictures, those figures whereby speech could be communicated silently and across great distances. I couldn't love Yetzer abi-Huram, for such affection belonged solely to my husband-god. What else I might call the regard I had for this man, though, I did not know.

The blare of a ram's horn shattered my reverie. I looked up to the summit of the temple's portico, high above the holy mountain.

Natan held the horn to his lips, drew out the long blast, and followed it with a series of short trills. The young priest repeated the signal twice more, and the grunts of men and the creak of ropes gradually ceased. Workers filed from the temple and gathered around the bronze statues in admiration.

"Why so early, priest?" Yetzer asked with mock sternness as Natan joined us.

"Orders of the Master Builder," he replied without hesitation, and pointed toward the west. "When the sun drops behind the mountains, the men shall be called from labor to rest."

"The true craftsman needs only the light within him," Yetzer gruffly chided the younger man, then grinned and tousled the priest's curly hair.

Natan ducked away and joined the men by the statues.

"She's beautiful," he breathlessly observed as he stood before the Kemeti goddess Mayat with her balanced scales.

My cheeks grew warm, for the bronze goddess had been cast in my image. Mine was not the only likeness Yetzer had borrowed for his work. The Twins were fashioned after Natan and King Yahtadua who, I had to admit, did share a striking resemblance. General Benyahu found expression in the Archer. The Water-Bearer, too, had been crafted in the image of Yetzer's father Huram.

"Will not Bilkis feel slighted?" I'd asked Yetzer when he finished breaking open all the molds. "You've dedicated none of the Star Dwellers to her."

"I wouldn't say that," he replied as he scraped away a casting's sand to reveal the Scorpion, its tail poised to strike. "I think this one captures her perfectly."

I smiled now at the memory, but the expression soon faded.

Natan now stood before the Maiden. Her lower body was covered by a sheaf of wheat, while she balanced a jar of wine on her hip. So unique were the woman's features, so perfect her lithe figure, I knew the sculpture was more the child of Yetzer's memory than his imaginings.

The young priest stared open-mouthed at the brazen beauty. I followed his gaze not, as I expected, to the naked twin breasts, but to the lovely face with wide-set, almond shaped eyes.

"That's her," Natan said in hushed awe. "That's Yahtadua's new bride."

68

Yetzer

Yetzer led Makeda toward the darkening temple, his ears still buzzing with Natan's words.

Yahtadua's new bride.

Makeda's hand was warm upon his arm as they silently climbed the fifteen steps to the open-air portico of the temple. On either side sat the bases for the twin columns that would support the roof of the porch, the polished bronze gleaming faintly in the waning light.

Makeda followed Yetzer's example in unlacing her sandals before the temple's doorway. She caught his eye as they stood together, and Yetzer smiled.

His heart told him this was his match, the echo of his desire. But another set of eyes seemed to gaze back at him, eyes belonging to another royal woman, beneath the canopy of a temple to other gods in a distant land. He blinked to clear his vision, until his Queen of Saba again stood before him.

He knelt before the golden band in the floor that marked the threshold to the Sanctuary. Makeda came to her knees beside him and followed his motions.

"I honor you, Yah and Havah," Yetzer intoned softly as he touched his forehead to the floor, "father and mother of the world." He sat upright then bowed again. "I honor you, Hadad my protector, and Kothar my patron." Again he sat up, then bowed a third time. "All you gods above and below, I humble myself before you."

They rose and stepped through the doorway. Though the temple had yet to be consecrated, a familiar, welcome chill washed over Yetzer as he crossed the boundary between profane and divine. Makeda grasped his arm, her sharp intake of breath suggesting she too felt the change.

Yetzer struck a light and took Makeda's hand, then led her toward the rear of the temple. The lamplight failed to reach the cedar rafters, but Makeda inhaled in awe as it revealed animals and plants and geometric shapes, all precisely detailed and overlaid with gold.

"That's olibanum," Makeda said as they neared the end of the Sanctuary.

"It is. Your country offers the gods their favorite incense, better favored even than my cedar."

She laughed at that, and Yetzer guided her up the curved steps to the sacred enclosure of the *Debir*, the Most Holy Place. He paused outside the cedar doors, beneath their stone arch, and silently spoke the word of his craft.

The word itself was common enough, spoken daily by multitudes without import. When given with reverence and intent, however, as Yetzer said it now, the word opened the heart to all the wonders and possibilities of Creation. Though the room beyond was empty, Yetzer knocked thrice upon the door then pulled it open and stepped inside.

Unlike the Sanctuary with its wood-paneled walls and floor, the Most Holy Place was all stone, save for the doors and ceiling. Tiles of black and white marble lined the floor, concealing all but the very peak of Havah's holy rock, that natural altar where the Ram, upon a time, had taken the place of sacrifice for Father Abram's son.

Yetzer now led Makeda to that holy rock, sat cross-legged upon it, and rested his hands upon his knees. Makeda mimicked his movements. Eye closed, Yetzer drew several slow, deep breaths then began to hum. Low at first, he raised the pitch until his tone matched the sacred note. Makeda added her voice to his, and Yetzer's heart thrilled. The very walls and floor joined in the music, magnifying the simple hum into a great choir. Power filled the space and resonated within his breast. A tingling sensation rippled upon his skin, reached to his very core, and faded only after he paused to take another breath. Six times more they joined their song with the Holy Ones until, light-headed, Yetzer resumed his slow, steady breathing and silenced his heart that he might hear the gods speak.

The Ancients whispered not, but Makeda's hand upon his was worth more than all the gods' wisdom or all the gold that lined the holy walls. She leaned toward him, her eyes gleaming in the low light. He bent his head to meet her, their lips touching in a kiss as divine and perfect as the union of Yah and Havah.

A pounding upon the cedar doors dispelled the moment. Yetzer drew away from Makeda with a shuddering breath. He offered a smile. Heart racing, he stood and moved to the door. He raised the latch and drew open the panel to reveal Benyahu, his face distorted in the flickering light.

"Forgive me," he said in a husky voice, then cleared his throat. "The queen commanded me to escort her sister back to the palace."

"Of course," Makeda said as she joined Yetzer at the doorway. "It was thoughtless of me not to go to her when we returned."

She looked up at Yetzer and placed a hand on his cheek.

"May I revisit the temple in the daylight?" she asked, her eyes suggesting more than architectural curiosity.

"Tomorrow," Yetzer said, and kissed the inside of her wrist. *And all the days after*, he didn't add.

He gave Makeda the lamp, then leaned against the doorpost as she and Benyahu faded into the darkness of the Holy Place. Only when the light disappeared through the outer doors did he draw a deep breath and start after them.

Before his foot reached the first step, rough hands grasped him by his tunic and threw him to the floor below. His head struck hard upon timber, dazing him. Yetzer was barely aware of the rough hands that pinned his arms and legs, but he came fully alert at the press of cold, sharp metal against his breast.

"Give me the word of the Masters."

The command was no less threatening for having been whispered. The speaker wore a scarf about his head and Yetzer recognized neither voice nor face.

"I can reveal it only to the worthy," Yetzer replied in as calm a tone as he could manage.

The blade cut across his chest. A hand clamped over his mouth to stifle his cry. Warm blood pooled above his breastbone and spilled along his ribs. Yetzer struggled vainly against his captors, succeeding only in dashing his own head upon the wooden floor a few times more.

"Give me the word," the one with the knife repeated.

Yetzer's heavy breathing came in snorts as he sucked air through his nose and noisily expelled it. When he'd managed to calm himself, his questioner removed his hand from Yetzer's mouth.

"I made my vow before the gods," Yetzer croaked, his voice thick with pain. "I'll not break it."

Fire lanced across his belly as the blade again tore through his flesh. Yetzer's back arched with the pain as the assailant's hand once more clamped over his mouth. The knife pierced the tender flesh beneath his jaw.

"The word!"

In his wrath, the man failed to disguise his voice. Yetzer now recognized Elhoreb's narrow eyes behind the scarf, his ink-stained fingers about the dagger's hilt. His own scribe had become Bilkis's creature, a venomous spider within his camp. If the queen had made him promises even half so enticing as those with which she'd tried to ensnare Yetzer, there was no boundary Elhoreb wouldn't cross to win her favor. Resistance or reason were folly in the face of such ambition.

Yetzer met the man's gaze and nodded. Lines creased about Elhoreb's eyes, and Yetzer could envision the victorious smile behind the cloth. The man released his hold and brought his ear close to Yetzer's mouth. The builder clamped his teeth about the man's ear.

A howl of rage filled the Holy Place. The traitorous scribe tore himself away, blood streaming dark along his neck. He stood, blade raised high above his head, hatred burning in his expression. Yetzer spat out a bit of flesh and stared up at him, calmly awaiting the stroke that would deliver him to Death's embrace. When it fell, pain filled him for but the briefest moment before oblivion closed mercifully about him.

69

Bilkis

"What do you mean they will not work?" Bilkis demanded. The scribe Elhoreb stood before her in the great hall, a bandage wrapped around his head, his rat face twitching as though to scent out a kitchen midden.

"My lady," he answered, "the builders demand a time of mourning before resuming their labors."

"Have they not observed it during this past week?" the queen asked. "Since abi-Huram left them, not a scrap of work has been done."

"Tradition requires a month of mourning, my lady."

"A month?" Bilkis shouted. "Why not a year? Why not three years?"

None dared to reply. Elhoreb for once seemed speechless. Yahtadua, fresh from a week in his bridal chamber, sat upon his throne but his gaze seemed still fixed on the marital couch. Makeda was in her place of honor beside the dais, her weeping at last silenced, though her eyes were shot through with red and her sniffling was as a sickly child's. Benyahu and Yahshepat stoically manned their posts, while the balance of the court studied their fingers or toes or the tassels on their robes.

"A month may be appropriate to mark the death of a beloved master," Bilkis allowed, "but abi-Huram has been missing for a week and no body has been found. Might he not simply have abandoned his men, his family?"

Makeda made a whimpering noise, as though she might protest, but she covered her mouth with a handkerchief and kept silent.

"There is the matter of the pool of blood, Lady," Elhoreb needlessly reminded her.

"Yes," Bilkis replied, lancing the fool with her eyes. "There is that. But it might as easily have been lamb's blood as a man's, no?"

"No," Elhoreb said, but the shake of his head promptly turned to a nod. "Yes," he amended. "Yes, my lady, it easily could be."

Bilkis drew a deep, steadying breath. How she had allowed herself to put trust in this venal fool was beyond her.

"Who presides over the builders now?"

"Magon abi-Abda, my lady," Elhoreb answered.

"Very well. Relay to the Master that I will grant his men another two days to collect themselves, then the work must start again. If abi-Huram's body is found, if it happens that he has not simply abandoned his work, then they may have their customary time of mourning."

"It shall be done, my lady," the simpering scribe replied, and gave a low bow. "And may I say—"

"That will be all," Bilkis interrupted with a wave of her hand. "Benyahu, clear the court. We will resume tomorrow. For now, I have matters to discuss with the king and with my sister."

Benyahu bowed his head, then rapped the butt of his spear three times upon the cedar-planked floor.

"All kneel before Yahtadua, King of Yisrael, and Bilkis the Queen," he commanded. "May Yah and Havah uplift and keep them."

The rustle of wool and silk and the creaking of old bones resounded throughout the hall. Bilkis stood and motioned for Yahtadua and Makeda to accompany her. They complied, though it was clear Yahtadua's heart was still in the bedchamber, while Makeda's was in the tomb with her dear builder. She must have been a bigger fool than Bilkis had imagined, to have opened her heart to abi-Huram. So long as she hadn't yet opened her legs to him …

Bilkis led the pair to Yahtadua's chambers. She'd ordered the place aired out after the week of connubial excess, the linens changed, braziers charged with fresh spices, and every other little matter prepared. Neither Makeda nor Yahtadua seemed to have noticed where she'd brought them until Bilkis closed the doors behind them with a resounding thud.

"Why are we here, Umma?" Yahtadua asked.

His curiosity seemed not over-great as he picked a bunch of grapes from the table and carried them to his bed. A good start.

"How was your week, my lamb?" Bilkis asked. "How did you find your new bride? Not too old, I trust."

Yahtadua's cheeks reddened as he absently twiddled a grape between thumb and forefinger.

"Ameniye is not so old, Umma. She's but a few years younger than you. And she knows things ... " His voice trailed off and his eyes grew distant.

"I'm glad you find her pleasing."

Bilkis struggled to keep her voice even. If Yahtadua was already so enamored of his Kemeti widow, she'd best set this plan into motion.

"Since her age is not objectionable, I would propose another match for you. One between your father's house and mine, between Yisrael and my own home of Saba."

The mention of that desert flea's nest finally brought Makeda out of her stupor.

"Of whom do you speak, Sister?" she asked. "Our father had no other rightful children."

Bilkis took Makeda's hand and tugged her toward the bed. She bade Yahtadua to put aside his grapes, then took his hand in her other.

"This is the union I propose." She placed their hands together. "A union between the King of Yisrael and the Queen of Saba."

70
Makeda

I snatched my hand back, as from a flame. I'd been in a stupor of worry and grief since I learned of Yetzer's disappearance and the discovery of a pool of blood in the temple. The miasma of self-pity now vanished as quickly as morning mist upon sunrise.

My eyes narrowed, and I looked hard at Bilkis. "What are you saying? I cannot marry."

"Umma, no," Yahtadua complained. "She's your sister."

"Half-sister," Bilkis snapped before her expression again turned placid. "That is to say, we share only our father's blood. It is good, strong blood that will give you a fine son and heir."

"I can marry no man," I said. "I am already wed to the god Athtar."

"As Ameniye is wed to Osaure," Bilkis calmly observed. The promptness of her answer suggested she'd considered this well. "The Kemeti god has not opposed my son's marriage, nor, I think, will Saba's."

"Your son is a fine husband to his many wives," I said, trying another tactic. "Surely I have nothing to offer that his brides cannot. Yisrael has an able queen and a noble king, while Saba must be content with only me as Mukarrib. I cannot be a queen both here and there."

"Oh, make no mistake," Bilkis said as she settled into a chair. "You will not be queen here. Once you give Yahtadua a son, you may go back to that sand pit you love so much. The boy will remain here, and when he comes of age he shall rule over Yisrael and Saba and all the lands between. Ours shall be an empire to rival Kemet, Hatti, and Subartu." Bilkis offered a beatific smile that turned to a pout when I—unable even to form another rebuttal—said nothing.

"Do not frown so," Bilkis chided me. "I do this for you, Sister. A woman cannot long rule in her own name. Soon the chieftains will tire of Athtar's rule. They will clamor for a man of flesh and blood to govern them." She rose and circled me as a crow about carrion. "When they do, you will have three choices: give the throne to another, marry some lord and let him rule, or present your heir and rule in his stead. Only until he comes of age, of course," she added, and patted Yahtadua's cheek.

"But mark me," she continued. "A king may have several sisters, he will take many wives, but he will only ever have one mother." She kissed Yahtadua's crimson cheek. "Far better to be a mother, no?"

I wanted to flee. I wanted to scream, to wake up in Tzeretan, or even back in Saba, and find this madness only a dream. I managed a step toward the door, a second and a third, but stopped with a jolt at the smack of wood upon wood. Slowly, I turned back to face a triumphant Bilkis, who stood by the table that now held a staff.

Yetzer's staff.

"I offer you a future, dear Sister, a legacy," Bilkis said. "But if you'll not do it for me, for Yahtadua, or even for yourself, you will do it for your builder."

"What cruelty is this?" I demanded as rage and grief fueled my blood.

"No cruelty, sweet one," Bilkis said, and drew her fingers along the lightning-tempered wood. "'Tis a mercy."

"Yetzer is dead! How dare you mock my sorrow?" I could scarcely breathe, scarcely believe my ears.

"Not dead," Bilkis said. "Injured, yes. Grievously even, but most assuredly alive. And if you would keep him that way, if you would spare him, his family, your own people— "

A red veil descended over my vision. My head spun. I might have collapsed if Yahtadua hadn't caught me and borne me up. The young king helped me to a seat on the edge of the bed and—once I proved able to stay upright—fetched me a cup of water.

"Take abi-Huram with you when you go," Bilkis offered as she leaned against the table. "Let him build for you a temple of stone or straw or dirt. I care not. But if you would have him survive to accompany you, you will do this."

"He will despise me," I muttered, my voice so soft I could barely hear it through the drumbeat in my ears.

"For having lain with a king?" Bilkis retorted. "He should be honored to take Yahtadua's castoffs. But then abi-Huram has never shown a proper understanding of such things." She came to me, took my hands and knelt before me. "Even so, better he should despise you upon the earth than cherish you from the Pit, yes?"

"Umma, I can't do this," Yahtadua said in a child's voice. "Yetzer has been a friend to me."

Bilkis rose and put her hands on my shoulders. "If you would help save your friend, my lamb, then you must do this."

I sat, numb, as Bilkis prepared my dishonor. She took the silver comb from my hair, inspected it briefly, then tossed it aside. With deft fingers she undid the lacing along the back of my gown, then gave a sharp tug of the fabric. The green silk fell about my waist, and Bilkis fanned my hair about my naked shoulders.

"Is she not lovely, my lamb?" she said as she stood back to inspect her work. "Her mother was from the darkest heart of Uwene. It is said the women there know such secrets of lovemaking as to make a man lose his reasoning."

Yahtadua stood motionless. His breathing changed to a shallow, ragged pattern. His eyes took on a bestial sharpness as they ranged up and down my body.

"Yes, my son," Bilkis said. She stepped behind him and ran her hands along his shoulders. "Do you not wish to take her? To sheathe yourself in her? Her arms reach for your embrace," she continued as she untied the scarlet sash about his waist. "Her womanhood burns to receive you. The garden of delight lies between her thighs."

As a mother prepares a child to bathe, so Bilkis gently undressed her son, cajoling him all the while with whispered promises of the ecstasy that awaited him. By the time she stripped away his breechcloth, Yahtadua's desire was fully mounted, his manhood tumescent and throbbing with hunger.

He took a lurching step forward and something within me split. I seemed to stand outside myself, a spectator rather than an actor in the sordid scene. Yet my bodily self came awake as Yahtadua approached. Slowly, as though mired in a dream, I crawled back from my nephew, emerging from my loosened gown as from a cocoon. The headboard arrested my retreat as he reached the foot of the bed and climbed upon it.

My sensing, thinking self circled about the bed. Yahtadua stalked toward my body, his head twitching as he scented my fear. The young king forced his hips between my knees, his eyes black and hungry as they fixed on mine.

He lanced into me, and the pain knit my two halves back together. Sense and reason betrayed me. I was no longer outside myself, but fully aware of the violation, fully aware of Yahtadua's musk in my nostrils, fully aware of his weight pressed against me, fully aware of his slick sweat smeared on my skin as his lust filled the void between my legs, the Holy of Holies devoted to my god.

I turned my head away from the passion-distorted face of my sister's son. My sight fell upon the comb, the jeweled silver dragonfly I'd liberated from Bilkis's neglect so long ago. Its wings seemed to beat in time with Yahtadua's rough thrusts. I longed to shrink away, small enough to escape upon the insect's back, or to become the very dragonfly itself and flit to freedom.

Yahtadua drew a deep breath and pressed himself so deeply inside me it seemed he would surely cleave through my belly. He loosed a throaty moan, and I felt the pulse of his seed as it filled me. The full weight of his body settled onto me, his ragged breath hot upon the crook of my neck.

My jaw ached from clenching my teeth to hold back my cries. I loosened cramped fingers from their grip upon the bed linens, all the while praying for the dragonfly to carry me away.

Bilkis settled into view at the edge of the bed, just beyond the comb.

"Well done, my lamb," she said in a soft voice. "That was not so bad, was it? Truly, Sister, I think you should come to enjoy it by the time he puts a son in you."

71

Yetzer

Yetzer lay in darkness, suspended between awareness and oblivion. He knew not how much time had passed since his murder, since he'd been cast into Sheol. It might have been a day, it could have been an age. He knew only that his *ka* remained trapped, unable to ascend to the abode of the gods.

The manacle he imagined about his ankle, and the chain that seemed to secure it to the rocky earth were not of bronze, he knew. They were forged by his pride, link by stubborn link. Oh, he'd thought himself exalted, flattered himself that he'd seen into the heart of Creation and unlocked its secrets. But it had been folly, so much hubris. Had he attained half so much Light as he'd fancied, his *ka* should have sprung from his body like a dove from its cote.

As it was, his eternal self remained trapped in Darkness, a slave to ignorance as surely as his physical being had been enslaved in Kemet so long ago.

Voices echoed in the darkness. Yetzer curled in on himself, cursing his weakness even as he did so. The demons came frequently to taunt and test him.

Sometimes they brought the semblance of food, the thinnest of gruels to test how tightly he clung to the physical. Occasionally he managed to resist, but more often than not he gave in to the temptation, his heart succumbing to the imagined pangs of hunger. The sense of starvation would abate for a time, but the fetid water and rancid fat ran through him as swiftly as the River Yarden. His bowels ached while his *ka* sat mired in filth.

Other times the tormentors brought scourges. They rained blows of fire and agony upon him, cursed him and taunted him into denying his vows, his sacred obligations. In these tests he fared better.

The torture of his soul was beyond any pain or privation he'd known in life. The demons promised him release if he simply acquiesced, but he knew if he broke his solemn oath, if he revealed to them the secret word of his craft, his agony would be everlasting.

Light broke upon the darkness as the echoes drew nearer. Flames danced upon the walls of his grave, which his pride had fashioned in the image of the quarry beneath Havah's mountain. The footfalls seemed more urgent and more numerous than in previous visitations, and demons' voices swam about him in the tongues of both Kenahn and Kemet. Yetzer called upon his resolve, uncertain what this change portended.

"Sweet Auset," said a feminine voice in the Kemeti language. "What have you done to him? Release him."

Another voice, brittle as ancient papyrus, repeated the command in Kenahni. Yetzer loosed a cry and kicked at the hands that reached for his legs.

"Be still," the aged voice said as a cold, dry hand touched Yetzer's fevered brow. With a rattle and the scrape of metal against metal, the bite upon Yetzer's ankle loosened then fell away. He felt himself uplifted, and shadows danced on the walls as the guardians of the Pit ferried his soul to some new way station. A light came into view, brighter than a thousand torches. Yetzer's eye watered at the brilliance. He stretched forth his hand, as though he might catch hold of the saving light and drag himself from the mouth of the grave.

"Put him here," the old one said.

Yetzer settled to the ground just inside the opening, his outstretched hand barely able to reach the warm light. Slender fingers fell gently upon his cheeks and turned his head away from the opening.

"Do you know me?" a woman's voice asked. The eternity in darkness left Yetzer's sight unfocused. A glowing nimbus floated before him, the ethereal outline of a lotus that shifted into the visage of whatever goddess had come to rescue his soul. Cool water rained upon his forehead, washed his eye and fell sweetly across his lips. A second and a third time the blessed shower came, and when his eye was wiped clean, the haze fell away like a veil.

"Ameniye," Yetzer croaked.

The woman smiled. Her expression was not of the carefree openness he remembered, but that of one who has tasted fully of life and appreciates its occasional sweetness.

"And surely you remember your old friend Sinuhe?"

Yetzer turned his head slowly, painfully to the other side. A cadaverous skull peered at him through sunken eyes. Wispy strands of hair sprouted from desiccated flesh, and sere lips cracked into a skeletal grin.

"I truly am dead," Yetzer groaned, for the man had been ancient when he'd first tended Yetzer all those years before.

"Then I shall have to call upon all my powers of resurrection," the old physician laughed.

"Begging my lady's pardon," another voice said, and by its sibilant tone Yetzer recognized Elhoreb. "I have led you to him as agreed. There was a promise of reward …"

Sinuhe translated the man's request and Ameniye's reply.

"Of course. Your actions have proven your worth." Ameniye rose as she spoke and walked toward him. To her guards, the men who had carried Yetzer, she said, "Hold him."

"My lady," Elhoreb stammered as the men gripped him by his arms, "I have done as you commanded."

"And I do as justice commands," Ameniye assured him. She accepted a spear from one of the guards and, without hesitation, thrust it into the scribe's stomach. The squelch of metal upon flesh and bone was accompanied by a shrill scream. The cry was cut short as one of the guards drew a dagger and slid it skillfully across the traitor's throat. Elhoreb's eyes danced frantically about as he jerked against the guards' firm grips and as his life spilled down his chest and belly.

"Put him with the others," Ameniye ordered, and the men dragged the still-twitching corpse away.

Pharaoh's daughter watched them go, then turned back to Yetzer and again knelt beside him.

"Can you tend him here?" she asked Sinuhe.

"That is a twofold question, my lady," the old man said. "Can I tend him? Yes. There is corruption in his wounds and he's been poorly fed these last weeks.

His is a great stubbornness, however. These—how did they call themselves, *Yubaalim?*—these sons of Yubaal would have done better to have killed him outright. So, yes, I can tend him. Can I do so here?" He shrugged his bony shoulders.

"I cannot ensure his safety in the palace," Ameniye said. "There are too many secret ways, too many prying eyes and loose tongues. Here, there is but one entrance, which my men can easily protect."

"Take me back to my camp," Yetzer said, surprised by the effort needed to arrange his thoughts. "I'll be safe among my men, my family."

Ameniye shook her head. "We do not know how far the corruption spreads. This queen of yours weaves a broad web. You would be no safer in your camp than in Bilkis's own throne room."

"Then take me to the camp of the Sabaeans. Bilkis has no spies among her sister's people."

This suggestion was met by a quick exchange of glances between Ameniye and Sinuhe.

"The people of Saba are dead," Ameniye said, "butchered by the queen's command."

The words were delivered gently, but they fell upon Yetzer as a thousand blades, piercing his very heart. A low moan rose in his throat and he longed for his cold grave, for the demons' torments that were but gentle play compared to this new torture.

"Be still, my brother, my cherished one," Ameniye said, and kissed his cheek.

Yetzer wanted to pull away from the touch of her lips, but his will failed him. He might have welcomed the Pit in that moment, but his traitorous heart continued to beat, his lungs to draw breath.

"I will tend him here, my lady," Sinuhe said in an assuring voice.

"And when you are well enough to travel," Ameniye told Yetzer, "I will find a place of safekeeping for you." She laid a hand upon the crusted wounds above his heart. "I took your life from you once. Let me now give it back."

72

Makeda

Even the sky wept.

Cold, bitter tears—snow, one of Yahtadua's wives called it—drifted from the heavens, collected in the corners of the terrace, or danced on eddies of wind. It might have been beautiful, I thought, had any beauty been left in the world.

For three months I'd been held in Yahtadua's harem, a prisoner to the king's lust and Bilkis's madness. My one display of resistance had prompted Bilkis to bring my handmaid Fazia before me, where General Benyahu cut the girl's throat.

"How many more would you sacrifice to your pride?" Bilkis had scolded.

And so, three or four times each week, the young king visited and cast his seed within me. My only respites had been during the times of my monthly flow, when I was confined to a special quarter of the harem and Yahtadua's attentions were shared among his wives. They were times of mixed feelings. For seven days I was free from violation, free of the indignity and base enslavement. But each renewal of my womb meant my captivity must continue, as must Yetzer's.

Yetzer.

My builder.

My heart ached at the very thought of his name. Yetzer, who had filled my imaginings with fresh wonder. Yetzer, who would hate me for what I'd become.

Most days I could set aside the thoughts of my builder with a prayer for his safety and a focus on the indignities I must suffer. But in these long, solitary days of my confinement my thoughts flew to him as bees to nectar.

There was no distraction, for Bilkis forbade me any writing or diversion or even the menial task of spinning wool. There was no companionship, for Yahtadua's wives shunned me. No, in those long days when my womb ached along with my heart, I had only my loneliness and my fears and my thoughts of Yetzer.

This day was even lonelier than most, as the palace, the city, the very world, it seemed, was deserted. For the eighteenth celebration of Yahtadua's birth Bilkis had called a great festival, coinciding with the dedication of her temple. The entire country, every tribe and kindred, had been invited to join in. Even those of Yahtadua's wives whose flows had begun were permitted to attend. Only I remained, with the two guards outside the harem for company.

Those guards now rapped on the heavy timbers and swung the door open.

"The queen," one of them announced.

I turned away from the terrace, rubbing my arms against a sudden chill as a woman, heavily cloaked against the cold, crossed the threshold. The guards pulled the door closed and the woman stood motionless for a time. Her deep hood concealed her features as she stared at me.

"You do not celebrate?" I said coldly, for how could Bilkis forgo this day of glory?

Elegant fingers emerged from the woolen sleeves and pulled back the hood to reveal Yahtadua's latest bride.

"I celebrate in my own manner," Ameniye replied with her heavy accent. "And I may give you cause to celebrate."

The princess from Kemet—*Queen*, I supposed—stepped closer and clasped my hands.

"You will leave this city," Ameniye proclaimed.

"Leave?" I said.

"Go back to your lands. Return to your country." Ameniye stared quizzically at me. "Unless you wish to stay?"

"No," I exclaimed, and pulled my hands back. I again wrapped my arms about myself and in a softer voice added, "But I cannot."

Ameniye frowned. "Why can you not? You are not happy to be here. I am not happy for you to be here. If you go, we can both be happy."

I gave a bitter laugh at that simple solution. But was it so simple?

"As unhappy as I am," I said, "if I leave I should bring even more unhappiness."

"It would grieve you to leave your sister?" Ameniye asked. "Or her son?"

I tightened my jaw and squared my shoulders at that. "I would gladly be rid of them both," I said. "But there are others who would suffer should I go without Bilkis's leave."

Ameniye's dark, painted eyes grew distant and she looked away. "You speak of Yetzer." It was not a question.

"Yes," I said breathlessly, my heart seeming to beat anew. "What do you know of him?"

"He was raised in my father's household," Ameniye said slowly, as though measuring each word. "He was as a brother to me."

I pursed my lips. I had seen Yetzer's sculpting of the young Kemeti princess. The care he'd taken with each feature, his attention to every detail bespoke more than sibling affection. Whatever thoughts my face betrayed I wasn't sure, but Ameniye's sympathetic expression deepened. Yahtadua's bride again took my hand and led me to a couch.

"I tell you this," she said as she sat and pulled me down beside her, "so you will know my sorrow, too. Yetzer is gone."

My heart squeezed to a painful halt. I swallowed against a throat gone suddenly dry.

"Where has he gone?" I asked, my voice like that of a stranger.

"He was betrayed to your sister by his own men," Ameniye explained. "Attacked." She dragged her hands in a cutting motion along her breast and stomach. "Beaten. Starved. By the time I found him, his wounds were sour. Very bad."

I wanted to scream, but I had no voice. I wanted to drag the bitter words from this queen, but I had no strength. I could only sit, unblinking, as Ameniye relayed her tale.

"Yetzer told you of Kemet? Of the Temple of Amun? Of ... of his enslavement?"

"Yes," I managed to say.

"And did he tell you it was I who betrayed him?"

I was taken aback at that and could only shake my head.

"I trusted someone," Ameniye went on, "a priest of our highest god. He told me I was Yetzer's reward, but I was his trap. What has your sister told you?"

The question surprised me. I thought to evade it, but Ameniye had opened her past to me. This seemed the time for sharing secrets.

"She said that I may leave after I have given Yahtadua a son." I looked into the other woman's eyes. "And that I may take Yetzer with me."

Ameniye offered a sad smile and said, "He was to be your reward?"

"But he is my trap," I finished the thought.

"He was."

A knife twisted deep into my core. I searched Ameniye's eyes, desperate for some sign of hope, but there was none.

"My personal physician, a man wise in all the healing arts, tended Yetzer but ... "Ameniye looked away. She blinked her eyes several times, dabbed at one with her thumb and left a grey-green smudge upon her cheek. "I once stole Yetzer's liberty," she said after a time. "It was not my intent, but the fault was mine. I have dealt justice to those who harmed him, and he was among friends when he went to his final freedom." The woman hooked a finger beneath my chin. "Now I give you yours."

War waged within my breast. I wanted to cry, to lash out at this woman who had once harmed Yetzer, to embrace her as a sister. When the battle ended, reason bore up my heart's banner. I raised my chin, harvested my calm and became once more Mukarrib of all Saba.

"Yetzer's family?" I said.

"They will accompany you," Ameniye said. "Eliam knows the trade route and will guide you safely home."

"But my people," I said. "It will take days to prepare for the journey. How can we make ready without drawing Bilkis's attention?"

Emotion stormed in Ameniye's eyes. "Your people have gone to the West."

"West?" I said. "Why would they...?" Realization scored my heart, and I cursed Bilkis for robbing me of the tears to mourn my people.

"They began asking after you," Ameniye explained. "Yahtadua's mother feared they might raise a rebellion."The woman sat beside me and once more took my hands. "My husband is now of age to reign in his own name. I shall see he governs wisely and well. Those needing justice shall have it."

My shoulders relaxed, despite the aching void where my heart had once been. I nodded and rose.

Ameniye stood and embraced me warmly, holding me for a long moment. When she released me, she unclasped her cloak and held it out.

"Take this. My guards will escort you to Eliam, but it is best if you are not seen to leave the palace."

I accepted the cloak and swung it over my shoulders.

"Sela in Edom is along your route," Ameniye added. "I will send ahead and have provisions prepared for you. It is a long road you travel, yes?"

"Yes," I said. "Thank you."

"You belong with your people," Ameniye said with a shrug. "It is *mayat* that you should go to them."

"It's what?" I asked as the foreign word rang in my ears.

"*Mayat*," Ameniye repeated, and tilted her hand from side to side. "It is balance. It is just so, yes?"

"Just so," I agreed as a thought burst forth fully formed. I hurried to my table and found the silver comb among my things. I had no writing materials, so I pulled the linen from a cushion, borrowed a bit of charcoal from a brazier, and carefully scratched out a message. I gave the comb and linen to Ameniye.

"Please see that Bilkis gets these."

Ameniye gave me a curious look but bowed her head. "It shall be as you say. Go now. My men await you at the gate."

I pulled the hood over my head, tucked my hands into the sleeves and moved to the door. The harem guards nodded as I opened the door and moved past. I walked quickly but stately through the empty corridors until I reached the gate. As promised, a pair of Kemeti archers waited there with a donkey to carry me from the city.

Great clouds of smoke rose from the temple's mount, from the altars of sacrifice and dedication. Songs and cheers rode with the snows upon the light breeze. I closed my eyes and ears and heart to these, to all that Urusalim had given and taken from me. I set my attention solely upon the road before me.

The road home.

The road to freedom.

73

Bilkis

Bilkis pushed open the door to her rooms. The dedication had been a great success. Despite the foul weather, the people of Yisrael and the foreign guests had been duly awed by the marvel of her temple and had lauded her and Yahtadua. But she was sick of people, sick of smoke and the stench of burning meat, sick of the mud churned up beneath the frozen rain. She wanted nothing so much as a fire, a bath, and a cup of wine. She called for her handmaid, called again when the girl was slow to respond.

"Yes, my lady?" the imbecile said as she emerged from her chamber.

"Draw me a bath and see to the fire," Bilkis commanded.

"Yes, my lady," the girl replied. "Wine is on your table."

Perhaps the fool wasn't entirely worthless. Bilkis moved to the table and took a sip from her chalice. The heady wine, a rich red from Galil, warmed her stomach and eased her foul humor.

An unfamiliar glint caught her eye, there beside the wine jar. A silver dragonfly, jeweled with gold and lapis, sat upon her table, a linen cloth wrapped about the tines of its comb. A comb much like the one Makeda—

"What is this?" she asked the maid who was, as usual, slow about her tasks.

"From my lady's sister," the girl answered in a quavering voice.

Bilkis unfolded the linen and found a set of ragged characters in uneven rows. She recognized the scribbles as writing, but she could not read them. A tightness grew about her throat as a chill displaced the wine's warmth.

"Have my bath ready," she ordered as she left the room.

She stalked down corridors lined with simpering servants, passed the guards outside the harem, and burst through the doors.

"What is this?" she demanded, comb and linen upraised as her eyes scanned the room.

Yahtadua's wives sat in a circle, hands suspended midair where Bilkis had interrupted their silly clapping game.

"Where is she?" she demanded.

"Who?" one of the impudent cows asked.

"The Queen of Saba," Bilkis replied in her most cloying tone. "Where is my sister?"

"She's not here, my lady."

At least one of the bitches showed the proper respect. The courtesy, however, did not prevent a cry of rage. Bilkis spun toward the open doors and strode toward the guards.

"Where is Makeda?" she demanded of them.

The men stared blankly at her, then peeked through the doorway and back to their queen.

"She has not left, Lady," one had the dull wits to reply.

"But she is not here, so what does that mean?"

The dolts looked to one another then back to Bilkis, and shrugged.

A cry of rage echoed along the corridor as fire surged in Bilkis's stomach. She tore along the cedar-lined hallway until she reached the throne room.

"Read this," she ordered Yahshepat as she burst through the doors. She stopped midway to the dais as the weight of dozens of eyes fell upon her.

Yahshepat sat in his place beside the thrones, but that was the only thing in order. One of Benyahu's captains stood in his place at the foot of the dais. Yahtadua sat upon his throne, while he would normally have taken one or more of his brides to bed following so great a celebration. Most out of place, Ameniye sat beside him on Bilkis's throne.

"You're in my seat," Bilkis said in a low, menacing tone.

The Kemeti crone smiled back with false sweetness.

"The queen's place is beside her king," she said, and placed a hand atop Yahtadua's. With the other she gestured to a small chair beside the dais. "The king's mother, however, will always have a place of honor in this court."

"A place of—" Bilkis began before fury choked off her words. She moved toward the dais, her legs seeming to propel her of their own accord. She might have leapt upon the dais to strangle the impertinent whore, but a guard stepped in to block her approach.

"You are, of course, welcome, Mother," Yahtadua said from his high seat, the boy for the first time speaking as a man. "And you have a message you wished to have read? Yahshepat, would you?"

The little scribe rose and Bilkis had no strength to resist as he drew the linen from her fingers. He returned to his seat, unfolded the cloth and angled it to catch the lamplight.

"My sister," he read, "I return to you this comb, the last of your possessions from Saba. I also leave you the word you have so long sought. It is *mayat*, but though you possess it, what it signifies you will never attain."

Bilkis's vision grew hazy around the edges. Her hand trembled as her fingers tightened about the teeth of the comb.

"I, too, have a gift for you," Ameniye said, "to honor the completion of your great work. I've had it sent to your chambers. Senby," she addressed one of her Kemeti archers, "would you escort the king's mother to her rooms? She appears unwell."

The foreigner stepped forward, bowed toward the dais and wrapped a hand about Bilkis's arm. She did not protest, did not attempt to pull away. She simply stared at her throne, occupied by this stranger she herself had brought under her roof.

"You do look tired, Mother," Yahtadua declared. "Go to your rest. I have much to attend to and will call upon you when I am able."

Bilkis peered through a gathering fog as her escort led her from the hall. Of habit, she turned toward the corridor to her chambers, but the Kemeti shook his head and pointed in the opposite direction.

Without complaint, Bilkis followed along as he led her past Yahtadua's chambers, beyond the harem, to a small set of rooms at the rear of the palace. The Kemeti opened the door, drew her inside, and left her alone.

The haze dissipated enough for her to make out a few features. Braziers burned in two corners pouring their foul smoke of olibanum into the space. The chamber wasn't half the size of her rooms and had sparse furnishings that were plain but functional. On the narrow bed rested a basket decked with bright ribbons, no doubt Ameniye's gift to her.

Bilkis drew near to the bed, listening for a hiss of vipers or scorpions. No noise came from within the basket, so she drew back the cover.

Elhoreb's and Benyahu's heads looked up at her, their flesh a ghastly pallor. Dried blood streaked from the corners of their mouths and the jagged edges of their necks. A familiar ringing rose in Bilkis's ears, almost loud enough to block out her scream that echoed from the close, plain, dingy walls.

74

Makeda

The warm desert breeze caressed my cheek. The highlands of Yisrael had given way to the red sands of Edom, and the drier clime was a balm to my spirit. Not that all was made right.

As often as not, in the twilight between sleep and waking, the weight of my blankets seemed that of Yahtadua atop me. I would awaken in the night kicking and thrashing. I could not bear to be touched when Rahab came to comfort me, but her songs would lull me back to sleep.

During the day, as Dhahbas's rocking motion and Eliam's constant banter freed my thoughts, memories of Yetzer came to flog my heart. Tears would not flow. Even had I any left to shed, I would not loose them before Dvora, whose son had been killed for my sake. My grief found expression through my sunken eyes, my hollow cheeks, the unending nightmares, and occasional bouts of nausea.

Still, during the two-week journey from Urusalim, the sun and fresh air combined to revive me. Each long stride away from that accursed city freed my heart by degrees. My appetite returned. Flesh again grew upon my bones until, by the time we reached the borders of Edom, I once more considered myself among the living.

As we descended now into the sandstone canyons that marked the approach to Sela, I couldn't shirk the feeling of entering the depths of the Pit. The road narrowed, in some places scarcely wide enough for the camels to pass single file. At last the trail opened into a clearing sufficient to make camp.

The place was still tightly enclosed by sandstone cliffs, but there was room to raise our tents and picket the camels off the road. A stone-rimmed well promised refreshment for man and animal alike. A half-dozen elders of Sela waited beside the well to meet us.

"In the name of Qos we welcome you," proclaimed the eldest.

He spread his hands in greet'ng, and his withered fingers trembled as I climbed down from Dhahbas and approached the men. Six pairs of dark, sun-creased eyes turned from warm courtesy to cold appraisal, but I was too weary from the journey to think much on it.

"I thank you," I said with a nod.

"I am Korah. King Yahtadua, my son-in-law, requested we extend to you every grace," the old chieftain continued as he boldly studied my appearance. "Such water and food as we have are at your disposal."

The man's intense gaze belied the courteous words, but I forced a smile.

"I welcome your kindness," I said. "We will tarry but a night or two to refresh our animals and replenish our supplies."

A few of the men whispered to one another, and I fought the urge to shrink away from their leers. Eliam must have sensed my unease. He came alongside me, hands outstretched in peaceful greeting as he enquired after the elders' health and introduced his family.

The merchant's diversion had only temporary success, for as soon as the courtesies were made, the Edomites fell back to their whispers and gestures. Heat rose along my neck as my belly grew tight. I could not hear their words, but on their faces I saw their meaning clearly enough.

Foreigner. Slave. Whore.

"I thank you for your hospitality," I said to Korah, "but is it your custom to make a spectacle of your guests? If so, then we will trouble you only for a bit of water and be on our way."

Korah's cheeks reddened beneath his thick, grey beard.

"A thousand pardons, Lady. No offense was intended. It is only ... That is to say ... Would you come with me?"

The old man gestured toward the crease in the rock that, presumably, led into Sela. My back stiffened. What payment might these men require for their provisions?

"Your companions may, of course, accompany you," Korah added, as though he sensed my trepidation. "You are a guest in my house."

The implied promise of protection carried little comfort. Had I not been a guest in Bilkis's house? I saw no guile in the man's eyes, though, only a burning curiosity. I motioned for Eliam and Dvora to join me, then nodded to our host.

Korah smiled and took me by the elbow. He led me toward the city, alongside a sluice cut into the rock and leading from the well. The other elders followed behind Eliam and Dvora. We'd gone only a few paces before Korah stopped and pointed toward the sandstone wall.

"Here, my lady, is the cause of our wonder."

I looked to where he indicated.

A narrow border had been cut into the rock, in the shape of a pair of water jars supporting a vine-entangled trellis. The frame surrounded a low-relief carving.

I knelt to view the image more clearly, and found my own reflection staring back at me, just as my statue had upon Mount Morhavah. I fell to my knees and raised trembling fingers to my mouth.

"What is this?" I said.

"The work of a craftsman," Korah said. "He came to us with a warrant from my son-in-law to serve how best seemed fit. He built this waterway and warded it at intervals with this image. He told us it was Anath the protectress. That is her sign," he added, indicating the water jars of the frame, "but I see now who inspired the very image of the goddess."

"Who is he?" I asked, my throat compressed against the words.

"He calls himself *Lo-Shem*, the Nameless One. Whether man or demon I cannot say ..."

I scarcely heard the man. Of its own volition, my body rose to its feet and carried me farther along the waterway. Twenty paces from the first framed image sat a second identical one, and yet another at twenty paces more. The footfalls between became fewer as I raced along the track into the city.

The gorge opened into the wide crevasse of Sela. A part of me marveled at this city cut into the rock, but my heart forbade me to waste any time. I paused only long enough to listen.

I heard the questioning shouts of Dvora and Eliam behind me, the curious buzz of the people about the street. I cocked my head, attention fully upon my ears until I heard what I sought, the high note of hammer upon chisel.

I followed the sound and passed among the murmuring spectators. The ringing of the tools grew stronger until I stood outside a stone-carved doorway surmounted by a triangle around an eye.

I climbed the short wooden ladder to the entrance. It took a few moments for my eyes to adjust to the ruddy glow within. A broad-shouldered workman dressed only in a rough-spun kilt sat before a wooden table, his lash-scarred back to the door.

"You're making a shadow," came the gruff voice.

My heart swelled and my breathing faltered as joy flooded through me. "The true craftsman needs only the light within him," I managed to say.

The tapping of the hammer stopped. Tools clattered onto the tabletop. The man's back straightened, and he slowly stood and turned toward me.

Fresh, pink scars puckered the skin of his chest and stomach. A plain strip of linen covered the left side of his face, but there was no mistaking my builder. My heart sang as I dashed across the room and fell into Yetzer's embrace.

❖

Two days later, we left the rocky warren of Sela for the open sands of the southern road. Shams blazed within a pale blue sky.

Though the desert track felt familiar, it would be some months before we reached my city, my people. Months of blowing sand, of scorching days and bitterly cold nights. Months of sore backsides and aching muscles as we made our way from well to well.

But I cared not. Twin flutters, like the beating of a dragonfly's wings, rose in my heart and deep within my belly. I looked to Yetzer, riding alongside me. However much farther we must travel, my journey was already complete. For where Yetzer was, there was my home.

My builder looked over to me and reached out his hand. I extended mine and hooked my fingers in his. Dhahbas snapped as Yetzer's camel came too close. The beasts parted and Yetzer gave a hearty laugh.

I smiled, hoping my secret pain did not show through. I drew a deep breath, tamped down my emotions, and set my eyes upon the southern horizon. Whatever might come, for the time I was content. I rode toward my country, my people. My love was safe and by my side.

While within my womb grew the seed of hate.

Selah

Historical Notes

The legend of the Queen of Sheba has captured the imaginations of storytellers and their audiences for nearly three thousand years. The most famous version of the tale (at least in the Western world) consists of a mere 13 verses in the Hebrew Bible and leaves the fabled queen nameless. While this definitive version likely took form around 550 BCE, it reports on events that—assuming they actually happened—would have been some four hundred years in the past.

Other versions and elaborations of the Sheba story can be found in Ethiopian and Arabic sources, as well as Christian legends. Outside the religious milieu, the lore of Freemasonry—whose foundation myth centers on the building of Solomon's Temple—offers its own insights to the legend, and I have shamelessly borrowed from all these sources.

Given the mythic nature and scope of the various stories, I've taken generous liberties with the source material. In particular, my gloss of the familiar Biblical stories surrounding the reigns of Kings David and Solomon (here, Tadua and Yahtadua) merit a bit of discussion.

The obvious sacred cow on the altar is the polytheistic nature of my Kingdom of Yisrael. It must be remembered that the story—indeed, the entire Hebrew canon—was set to parchment only after the return of the Jewish exiles from captivity in Babylon in 538 BCE. Convinced their defeat and return were due, respectively, to the wrath and restored favor of their tutelary, now exclusive, deity, the political and religious elite recast the preceding 1500 years as a time of patriarchal monotheism, only briefly and scandalously interrupted by periods of polytheistic corruption from the surrounding heathen peoples. The archaeological record, however, tells a very different story.

Recent digs near Jerusalem and throughout the Biblical lands of Israel and Judah suggest that polytheism was extensively and consistently practiced right up to the time of the return from exile and the construction of the Second Temple under Nehemiah. The remains of shrines, both public and private, contain figurines presumed to represent Yah, Asherah, Ba'al Hadad, and others. An excellent, approachable treatment of these findings and interpretations is given in William G. Dever's *Did God Have a Wife?: Archaeology and Folk Religion in Ancient Israel* (Eerdmans, 2008).

My identification of the mother goddess, Havah, also deserves some explanation. Havah is an early rendering of the name Eve. Through a feat of linguistic acrobatics, I have identified her with Hepat, or Heba, a mother-goddess worshipped in the northern reaches of the Arabian peninsula. One epithet of this deity was "the mother of all living," a role that certainly fits Havah/Eve. Though northern Mesopotamia would seem to be too far removed from the lands of Israel, we have a record of one Abdi-Heba (literally, servant/slave of Heba) much closer to home. The El Amarna tablets, dated to the reign of the Egyptian Pharaoh Akhenaten, include letters sent by this Adbi-Heba, then ruler of Jerusalem, begging for military aid against the raids of Habiru brigands. This chieftain, of course, was the basis for my Abdi-Havah. The letters (EA 285-290), along with the entire collection of diplomatic correspondence from ancient Akhetaten, can be found in *The Amarna Letters* (Johns Hopkins University Press, 2002), edited and translated by William L. Moran.

As I mention in my *Author's Note*, I have chosen to adopt the New Chronology of Egypt and the Near East for the timeline of this story. The problems with the academically orthodox chronology (and their resolution by the New Chronology) are too extensive to detail here. Suffice it to say, there are many sound reasons why I've removed some 350 years from accepted history to place Pharaoh Horemheb and his successors in the time of Kings David and Solomon. For a complete explanation, I refer the reader to David Rohl's excellent *Pharaohs and Kings: A Biblical Quest* (Crown, 1996).

As to the events in Saba (generally accepted as the Biblical Sheba), I must admit to a high degree of literary license. While some scholars date the foundation of the Sabaean kingdom to at least 1200 BCE, the historical record is generally silent until around 700 BCE. The dam at Ma'rib (Maryaba) is a true wonder of the ancient world, and early archaeological investigations date its earliest remnants as far back as 2000 BCE. Modern archaeological methods might go a long way toward opening the book on this magnificent culture, but the political and religious challenges of the region force us to be patient. With the damage taken by the dam during recent Saudi air strikes, we can only hope there will be something left to investigate in coming years.

Despite the absence of a historical record, Makeda and Bilkis are not simply creations of my imagination. The accounts of the Queen of Sheba in both Arabian and Ethiopian legends provide beautiful embroideries upon the rather plain Biblical fabric. The Ethiopian dynastic legend *Kebra Nagast* (Glory of Kings) provides a charming (if anachronistically monotheist) version of Makeda, mother to the founder of Ethiopia's royal dynasty. The Arabic accounts of Bilkis as the Queen of Sheba are decidedly less sympathetic, but I've tried to weave together the disparate pieces of these tales to give depth and character to both of my queens.

The character of Yetzer abi-Huram is somewhat more speculative. I have liberally drawn him from the legends of Freemasonry, where the builder of Solomon's Temple is identified as Hiram Abiff (loosely derived from the Biblical Adoniram, or Lord Hiram). Yetzer's trials in Egypt are loosely based on my own Masonic initiations, elaborated by the accounts of Egyptian initiation rites described in *The Golden Ass: The Transformations of Lucius* (Farrar, Straus & Giroux, 1998). I'll leave it to the conspiracy theorists to argue over which was which. Suffice it to say, no oaths were broken in the writing of this novel.

The balance of the story is equal parts writerly musing and homage to the original lore, informed and enriched by the archaeological and epigraphic record. I've attempted to reverse-engineer the surviving tales, peering backward through the political lens of patriarchal societies and the religious lens of monotheism. The resulting view is an admittedly distorted glimpse of a world still firmly rooted in adoration of the divine feminine and acceptance of a multitude of deities. While I've drawn heavily on the sources mentioned above and countless others, my interpretations and conclusions are, of course, my own.

This story is now at an ending, but Makeda and Yetzer's tale has only just begun.

Glossary of Principal Names & Places

As much as possible, I've tried to use the names of places, people, and gods as they would have been at the turn of the first millennium BCE, prior to being changed by Hellenic, Roman, and Arab conquerors. This was not done simply to make for more challenging reading, but to provide a more authentic feel to the story.

Many of the names are based on interpretations from the El Amarna [Akhetaten] tablets, which date to within a few decades of the events in this story. Where the popular literature uses a descriptor in lieu of a personal name (e.g., Melchizedek, which literally means king-priest), I've tried to read between the lines to identify the person's true identity. In the end, this is a work of fiction, but I hope this guide will aid the reader's enjoyment of the story.

Abiattar	Alternate name-form of Abiathar, Biblical high priest under Kings David and Solomon.
Abdi-Havah	Alternate name-form of Abdi-Heba, ruler of Jerusalem attested in the Amarna tablets prior to the Habiru capture of the city.
Alassiya	Alternate name-form of Alashiya/Alasiya, a major naval and economic power attested in the Amarna tablets. Believed to be located on the island of Cyprus.
Ameniye	Historical wife of Egyptian Pharaoh Horemheb. died without issue. Fictionalized as Biblical "Daughter of Pharaoh," named for her deceased mother.

Amun	Principal Egyptian deity, considered the creator-god.
Ashtart	Canaanite diety associated with the hunt, love, and war.
Athtar	Alternate name-form of Attar, Sabaean deity.
Auriyah	Alternate name-form of Uriah, "Light of Yah." Speculatively identified with both Uriah the Hittite (or leader of the Hittite mercenaries) and Absalom (arguably, "Father of Solomon"), son of King David who rebelled against his father.
Auset	Early name-form of the Egyptian mother-goddess Isis, wife of Osiris and mother of Horus.
Ayana	Fictionalized Mukarrib of Saba, mother of Makeda. Ethiopian name meaning "flower."
Ayub	Alternate name-form of Yoav/Joab as attested in the Armana tablets. Biblical nephew of King David of Israel, and commander of the army.
Baaliyah	Alternate name-form of Biblical Adoniyah, meaning "Yah is Lord." Son of King David.
Bakhu	Fictionalized Egyptian limestone quarry.
Benyahu	Alternate name-form of Biblical Benaiah. General under Kings David and Solomon.
Bilkis (bat-Saba)	Alternately, Bilqis or Balqis. Name of the Queen of Sheba as identified in the Quran. Speculatively identified as Bathsheba, wife of Uriah (Auriyah) and King David, and mother of Solomon (Jedidiah) and Nathan.
Danu	Alternate name-form of Biblical Dan, the northernmost town of Israel.
Dhamar	Fictionalized Sabaean noble. Common name among the king-lists of Saba.
Ebiren	Alternate name-form of Biblical Hebron, holy place and traditional burial site of Hebrew patriarchs.
Elhoreb	Alternate name-form of Elihoreph, Biblical scribe in Solomon's court.
Eliam	Fictionalized merchant of Jerusalem. Biblical father of Bathsheba.
Elmakah	Alternate name-form of Al-Maqah/Al-muqh. Lunar deity, storm god, and mythical ancestor of the rulers of ancient Saba.

Eram	Alternate name-form of Ulam, a legendary city lost in the south Arabian desert.
Gad	Biblical Israelite prophet during the reigns of Kings David and Solomon.
Habiru	Alternately Hapiru or 'Apiru. Name of a wandering band of Semitic peoples as recorded in the Amarna tablets and other contemporary documents, generally referred to in disparaging terms. Currently debated whether or not this refers to the Biblical Israelites or their Hebrew forebears as they wandered about and settled in occupied Canaanites lands.
Hadad	Formally, Baal Hadad (Lord Hadad), often shortened to Baal. Canaanite storm god.
Haru	Ancient name-form of Horus, Egyptian tutelary deity.
Hattusah/Hatti	Ancient capital of the Hittite Empire, sometimes used to refer to the empire itself.
Havah	Alternate name-form of Heba/Hepat or Khepat, ancient Middle Eastern mother goddess. Speculatively equated with Havah/Eve, mythical mother of humanity.
Horemheb	Last pharaoh of the Egyptian 18ᵗʰ Dynasty. Commander-in-chief of the armies of predecessors Tutanhkamun and Ay. Married to Pharoah Ay's daughter Mutnedjmet.
Huram	Fictionalized Tyrian stonemason. Common name among Tyrian king-lists.
Hut-Uaret	Alternate name-form of Hut-Waret, ancient Egyptian name of the city Avaris.
Huy	Fictionalized high priest of Amun. Name attested in Egyptian tomb engravings.
Ilban-Ay	Alternate name-form of Alban/Albion, the ancient Celtic name for Britain.
Iteru	Ancient Egyptian name for the River Nile, literally "river."
Iunet	Ancient Egyptian name for Dendera in Upper Egypt.
Iunu	Alternate name-form of Iwnw, meaning "the pillars." Egyptian name of Heliopolis.
Karibil	Fictionalized Mukarrib of Saba, father of Bilkis and Makeda. Common name among the king lists of Saba.

Kemet	Alternate name-form of km.t, ancient indigenous name of Egypt, meaning "black land" in reference to the dark soil along the Nile.
Kenahn	Alternate name-form of Canaan, land area associated with ancient Palestine, inhabited by Semitic-speaking peoples. Generally encompassing modern Israel, Palestine, Lebanon, and parts of Egypt, Jordan, and Syria.
Kothar	Divine craftsman of the Canaanite pantheon.
Labaya	King of the Habiru tribes preceding Tadua/Dadua, as attested in the Amarna tablets. Speculatively identified as the Biblical King Saul of Israel.
Makeda	Name of the Queen of Sheba as identified in the Ethiopian *Kebra Negast*.
Maryaba	Alternate name-form of Ma'rib, ancient capital of Saba. Present-day capital of Ma'rib Governate, Yemen.
Melchi-Tzedek	Alternate name-form of Mechizedek, Biblical king of ancient Jerusalem. Fictionalized hereditary title, last held by Abdi-Havah.
Melkart	Patron deity of Tyre and the later Carthagenian/Punic people. Later equated with the Greek hero Hercules.
Men-Nefer	Ancient Egyptian name for Memphis, capital of Lower Egypt.
Meren	Abbreviated form of Merenptah, "Beloved of Ptah." Birth name of Seti I Menmayatre, second pharaoh of the Egyptian 19th Dynasty.
Mika	Fictionalized chief steward of Pharaoh Horemheb, in honor of Mika Waltari, author of *The Egyptian*.
Mikhel	Alternate name-form of Michal, Biblical daughter of King Saul and wife of King David.
Morhavah	Fictionalized early name for Moriah (Moryah), "Ordained by Havah (or Yah)." Mythical site of Abraham's abortive sacrifice of his son Isaac (or Ishmael, in the Arabic tradition), and building site of Solomon's Temple, its successors, and the Dome of the Rock.
Naftali	Alternate name-form of Naphtali, one of the Tribes of Israel.

Napata	Ancient Egyptian name for Sudan.
Natan	Alternate name-form of Nathan, Biblically identified as both a prophet in the court of King David, and a son of David and Bathsheba.
Opiru	Alternate name-form of Ophir, Biblical source of great treasures for the temple of King Solomon. Historical identity unknown.
Osaure	Ancient name-form of Osiris, Egyptian god of the dead. Husband of Isis, father of Horus.
Rahab	Fictionalized, loosely associated with Biblical Abishag. Common Hebrew name.
Ramessu	Ancient name-form of Ramesses (grandfather of Ramesses the Great), vazir to Pharaoh Horemheb and founder of Egypt's 19ᵗʰ Dynasty.
Remeg	Speculatively, Queen of Tyre shortly after the time of Pharaoh Akhenaten, as attested by the Amarna tablets. Under the New Chronology of Near-East history, contemporary of King David.
Retenu	Alternate name-form of Retjenu, Egyptian designation for Canaan and Syria.
Saba	Speculative alternate name-form of Sheba. Ancient South Arabian kingdom, which included parts of modern Yemen, Oman, Arabia, Somalia, Eritrea, and Ethiopia.
Sekhem	Alternate name-form of Shechem, a city in ancient northern Israel, present-day northern Palestine.
Sela	Ancient name of Petra, Jordan, as referenced in the Amarna tablets.
Sena	Ancient Egyptian name of Pelusium, city on the Mediterranean coast.
Shams	Ancient Sabaean sun goddess.
Shapash	Ancient Canaanite sun goddess.
Shemval	Alternate name-form of Samuel, Biblical prophet during the reigns of Kings Saul and David of Israel.
Sinuhe	Fictionalized Egyptian priest. Name attested in Egyptian tomb engravings.
Subartu	Alternate name-form of Assyria, as attested in the Amarna tablets.

Sutah	Alternate name-form of Seti, Egyptian god of chaos. Brother of Osiris and Isis.
Tadua	Alternate name-form of Dadua/Daud, or David. Mentioned in the Amarna tablets, which describe a bandit (Habiru) chieftain who captures Jerusalem.
Timnah	Prominent city of ancient Saba.
Tsion	Alternate name-form of Zion, the royal enclave within ancient Jerusalem.
Tsur	Alternate name-form of Tyre, a prominent Phoenician (Canaanite) trading post in modern-day Lebanon.
Tubaal	Alternate name-form of Tubal/Tubal-Cain, Biblical founder of blacksmithing and other crafts.
Tutankamun	Regnal name of King Tut, famed pharaoh of ancient Egypt.
Uaset	Ancient Egyptian name of Thebes (Luxor) in Upper Egypt.
Ubasti	Alternate name-form of Bast, ancient Egyptian lion- or cat-goddess.
Ugaratu	Alternate name-form of Ugarit, a city in present-day northern Lebanon, as attested in the Amarna tablets.
Urusalim	Alternate name-form of Jerusalem in present-day Israel, as attested in the Amarna tablets.
Uwene	Alternate name-form of Pwene/pa-Uwene, Biblical Land of Punt. Encompasses the lands around the Horn of Africa.
Wadi Dhanah	Alternate name-form of Wadi Adhanah. Seasonal waterway near Ma'rib, Yemen, fed by monsoon rains. Archaeological evidence of dams and canals date back to 2000 BCE.
Watar	Fictionalized ruler of Timnah, a prominent city-state of ancient Saba. Common name among the king-lists of Saba.
Yah	Tutelar deity of the ancient polytheistic Hebrews.
Yahshepat	Alternate name-form of Jehoshaphat, Biblical scribe under Kings David and Solomon of Israel.
Yahtadua	Alternate name-form of Jedidiah ("Beloved of Yah"). Birth name of King Solomon of Israel.

Yarden	Alternate name-form of Jordan (River).
Yehuda	Alternate name-form of Judah, one of the tribes of Israel.
Yetzer abi-Huram	Alternate name-form of Adoniram (Lord Hiram/ Hurum) and Hiram Abiff (abi-Huram). Fictionalized builder of the first Temple of Jerusalem, and mythical founder of Freemasonry.
Yishai	Alternate name-form of Jesse, Biblical leader of Judah and father of King David of Israel.
Yisrael	*Fights with El*. Patriarch, people, and land of the Biblical Israel.
Yubaal	Alternate name-form of Jubal, Biblical founder of the musical arts and half-brother to Tubal-Cain.
Zauty	Alternate name-form of Asyut, Egypt.

Acknowledgments

The crafting of a novel is a deeply isolating endeavor, but bringing it into the world cannot be done alone. I'm indebted to countless helpers, the merest fraction of whom I now mention.

Bernard Cornwell, Margaret George, CW Gortner, and Kamran Pasha are among the most talented and gracious authors I've had the privilege to meet. Their examples of literary excellence and their personal encouragement have been an inspiration to this fledgling novelist, and I'm deeply grateful to each of them.

Tracy Brogan, Sharon Bingham Kendrew, and Jeanette Schneider helped me shape Makeda's story from the clayey lump of an idea into a workable story. They are among the loveliest and most talented storytellers I know, and I'm honored to call them friends. See you at Arno's.

A special thank-you to the members of Highlands Ranch Fiction Writers who had a hand in this project: Lynn Bisesi, Deirdre Byerly, Claire L. Fishback, Nicole Greene, Michael F. Haspil, LS Hawker, Laura Main, Vicki Pierce, and Chris Scena. You make me a better writer. Because magic.

This book would not be in your hands without the thoughtful and professional guidance of Kristy Makansi and Lisa Miller of Amphorae Publishing Group / Blank Slate Press. My amazing support team at JKS Communications includes Marissa DeCuir, Hannah Robertson, Lana Allen, Lauren Ash, Max Lopez, Jerome McLain, and Benjamin Prosser. Amy Bruno with Historical Fiction Virtual Book Tours was instrumental in helping spread the word. Thank you all!

While it's common to call upon the faithful to pray for the peace of Jerusalem, I would call upon people of good will to pray (to whichever deity or deities you choose) for the peace of Yemen. As of this writing, the UN has declared the war in Yemen to be the world's worst humanitarian crisis. Upward of 8 million people (some estimates put the number as high as 22 million) are without food, clean water, or basic medical care. I am by no means an activist, but in honor of Makeda and her deep concern for her people, I've pledged half of my proceeds from the sale of this story to Yemen humanitarian relief. I'm deeply grateful to the Zakat Foundation of America, who have pledged matching funds to provide aid to the modern-day people of Saba.

Finally, I give my deepest thanks and love to my bride, Laura. I could probably tell my stories without you, but it wouldn't be nearly as fun. ILYWATIA.

About the Author

Marc Graham studied mechanical engineering at Rice University in Texas, but has been writing since his first attempt at science fiction penned when he was ten. From there, he graduated to knock-off political thrillers, all safely locked away to protect the public, before settling on historical fiction. His first novel, *Of Ashes and Dust*, was published in March 2017.

He has won numerous writing contests including, the National Writers Assocation Manuscript Contest (*Of Ashes and Dust*), the Paul Gillette Memorial Writing Contest - Historical (*Of Ashes and Dust*, *Song of Songs*), and the Colorado Gold Writing Contest - Mainstream (*Prince of the West*, coming from Blank Slate Press in Fall 2019).

He lives in Colorado on the front range of the Rocky Mountains, and in addition to writing, he is an actor, narrator, speaker, story coach, shamanic practitioner, and whisky afficianado (Macallan 18, one ice cube). When not on stage or studio, in a pub, or bound to his computer, he can be found hiking with his wife and their Greater Swiss Mountain Dog.